The
Girl
in
the
Photograph

OTHER WORKS IN DALKEY ARCHIVE PRESS'S
BRAZILIAN LITERATURE SERIES

Anonymous Celebrity
Ignácio de Loyola Brandão

Avalovara
Osman Lins

The Celebration
Ivan Ângelo

The Good-Bye Angel
Ignácio de Loyola Brandão

P's Three Women
Paulo Emílio Sales Gomes

The Queen of the Prisons of Greece
Osman Lins

Tower of Glass
Ivan Ângelo

Teeth Under the Sun
Ignácio de Loyola Brandão

Zero
Ignácio de Loyola Brandão

Lygia
Fagundes
Telles

The
Girl
in
the
Photograph

**Translated
by
Margaret
A.
Neves
Introduction
by
Earl
E.
Fitz**

DALKEY ARCHIVE PRESS
CHAMPAIGN / DUBLIN / LONDON

Originally published in Portugese as *As Meninas* by José Olympio, Rio de Janeiro, 1973; and in English by Avon Bard, New York, 1982
Copyright © 1973 by Lygia Fagundes Telles
Translation and copyright © 1982 by Margaret A. Neves
Introduction © 2012 by Earl E. Fitz
First Dalkey Archive edition, 2012

Library of Congress Cataloging-in-Publication Data

Telles, Lygia Fagundes.
  [Meninas. English]
  The girl in the photograph / Lygia Fagundes Telles ; translated by Margaret A. Neves ; introduction by Earl E. Fitz. -- 1st Dalkey Archive ed.
      p. cm.
  "Originally published in Portugese as As Meninas by José Olympio, Rio de Janeiro, 1973; and in English by Avon Bard, New York, 1982."
  ISBN 978-1-56478-784-2 (pbk. : alk. paper)
  1. Women--Fiction. I. Neves, Margaret A. II. Title.
  PQ9697.T49M413 2012
  869.3'42--dc23
                        2012020819

Partially funded by a grant from the Illinois Arts Council, a state agency

Obra publicada com o apoio do Ministério da Cultura do Brasil/ Fundação Biblioteca Nacional / Coordenadoria Geral do Livro e da Leitura.

Work published with the support of Brazil's Ministry of Culture / National Library Foundation / Coordinator General of the Book and Reading.

MINISTÉRIO DA CULTURA
Fundação BIBLIOTECA NACIONAL

www.dalkeyarchive.com

Cover: design and composition by Mikhail Iliatov

Printed on permanent/durable acid-free paper and bound in the United States of America

INTRODUCTION

When it first appeared in 1973, during some of the worst years of the brutal dictatorship that lasted from 1964 to 1985, *The Girl in the Photograph* (*As Meninas*) was hailed by the critics and the general public alike. Written by one of Brazil's most respected writers, Lygia Fagundes Telles, it went through eleven editions in Brazil and was translated into a number of languages. Among the many jewels of Brazilian literature, *The Girl in the Photograph* stands out for being that rarest of literary birds, a serious work of art that has also had immense popular appeal. The passage of time has done little to diminish the novel's power and relevance, not just for contemporary Brazil but, as American readers will discover, for those living in the United States of 2012, for our entire American hemisphere, and for our globalized and inter-connected world culture in general.

Not limited to Brazil, the problems the novel takes up—political fanaticism and oppression, the erosion of civil liberties under right-wing governments, the prevalence of torture in cultures that claim, piously, to be above such practices, and the devastating effects of drug abuse, poverty, and alienation—are as alive and as prevalent today as they were in the early 1970s. Perhaps more so, if we are to be honest with ourselves. The intellectual and artistic icons of the 1960s are all here, with references to Marx, Malraux, Mayakovsky, Jimi Hendrix, Ché Guevara, Lacan, Barthes, and Sartre abounding, along with the occasional nod to French Structuralism, American interventionism and cultural imperialism, the socio-political significance of "*bricolage*," racism, underdevelopment, pop culture, abortion, sexual politics, and Liberation Fronts. So while *The Girl in the Photograph* is, in some respects, a brilliant if disturbing period piece, a lacerating study of Brazilian society under the heel of a violent and ruthless dictatorship aided and abetted by the government of the United States of America, it is also a cautionary tale of universal significance, a parable about the need for human solidarity, responsible behavior, equality, and justice for all.

As such, *The Girl in the Photograph* operates on two narrative planes. One, the dominant one, deals with the private lives of three young Brazilian women living together in a boarding house run by Catholic nuns, a residence which, replete with the appropriate tangle of religion and politics circa the late 1960s, can be taken as a metaphor for Brazil itself. The other, less obvious one (but, for the author, much more dangerous, given Brazil's grim political situation at the time of the novel's appearance), functions as a thinly-veiled protest against the crimes committed by the leaders of the dictatorship and the abuse of power they exhibited in doing so. By early April of 1964, after President Goulart had been deposed, the Brazilian Congress, thoroughly purged of its liberal faction by right-wing supporters of the CIA assisted *coup d'état*, elected Humberto de Alencar Castelo Branco as the new President. Shortly afterwards, on April 9, 1964, it then rushed to pass the infamous (for Brazilians) First Institutional Act, which, among other things, declared that a state of siege existed in Brazil, expanded the powers of the President to near dictatorial levels, and suspended Brazilian civil rights for a ten year period. Vowing to "follow the international leadership of Washington," Castelo Branco, a staunch advocate of the "linha dura," or "hard line," as this related to the stifling of liberal thought and political action, created a nightmarish Brazil, a Kafkaesque horror-chamber of violence and repression, one in which a "book-burning mentality predominated—not only figuratively but literally. In Rio Grande do Sul, the commander of the Third Army, General Alves Bastos, ordered burned all the books which he branded as subversive. His capricious list of dangerous literature contained, it is reported, Stendhal's *The Red and the Black*" (Burns 510, 511). And yet, against the very real threats of political imprisonment, torture, and even murder, Brazilian young people, along with many artists, writers, and intellectuals fought back. Protest songs, taking the form of folk music (also popular, and for not entirely dissimilar reasons, in the United States of this same period), became a powerful form of resistance, one especially effective in a land where half the people were still illiterate (Burns 513). All in all, the 1960s and 1970s were a dangerous time to be, as Telles was, a liberal supporter of democracy and democratic process in Brazil.

Although the action of her novel is set in the 1960s, not long after the dictatorship subverted the democratically elected but left-leaning government of João Goulart, its significance far outstrips its time and place. The novel's unrelenting emphasis on the deeply intertwined inner lives of the three young women involved, and the degree to which their lives reflect the turbulent times in when they were coming of age, make *The Girl in the Photograph*, if anything, more powerful and affecting today than at the time of its publication. With the rise of Brazil in our Western hemisphere and on the contemporary world scene, it is clear that its own journey from liberal democracy to dictatorship and, now, its admirable effort to become a model democracy for the twenty-first century, can be taken as a sobering lesson about the absolute need for responsible, socially-conscious conduct, not only in one's private life but in one's public, or civic, life as well. Readers everywhere, but perhaps most especially those in the United States, should take heed of this lesson as they go about trying to save their own society and their own democracy in 2012. As a close and engaged reading of *The Girl in the Photograph* makes chillingly clear, the same issues, forces, and conflicts are very much in play.

Each of the novel's three women, Lorena, Ana Clara, and Lia—rendered far more complexly than they might otherwise be by the story's interlocking interior monologues—embodies, though in a different way, both of these narratives planes. The result is a very complicated narrative web—one that offers, however, a panoramic view of 1960s Brazil, a nation caught up in the throes of change and one which is, in 1964, about to be consumed by the repressive and anti-democratic forces within it. Indeed, the reader interested in inter-American comparisons will find much to ponder here.

The privileged scion of an old and wealthy São Paulo family, Lorena, who is determinedly virginal, also indulges in sexual fantasies concerning a tryst she burns to have with a married man, one Dr. Marcus Nemesio, whose initials, M. N., recur throughout the narrative, and whose perverse presence in Lorena's feverish mind amounts to something very like an obsession.

A child of poverty and despair, Ana Clara has quickly risen on the prevailing social and economic ladder, although for the most meretricious of reasons; born a great beauty in the *favelas*, or slums, she has, upon her discovery by the fashion industry, been transformed into a highly paid model, a young woman whose material fame and fortune cannot mask the despair that eats away at her. Although outwardly the epitome of what it means for many young women—in Brazil and elsewhere—to "make it" in a consumer society, she is vitiated by her drug addition and tormented by her enervating sense of emptiness. Desiring most of all to "wallow in pleasure" (151), she effectively allows herself, commodity-like, to be purchased by a wealthy *fiancé*, even as she ever more desperately carries on a pitiful, and ultimately ruinous, relationship with Max, another drug addict and a dealer as well. Dramatically illustrating as it does the utter waste of two young lives, the ill-starred relationship between Ana Clara and Max constitutes one of the novel's most tragic elements. And it requires no stretch of the imagination to read the pair of them, too, as symbols of Brazil under the dictatorship; as the people who, supposedly benefitting from the "economic miracle" that accompanied the early years of the regime—and that, according to the generals, justified its stringent measures—were, in reality, only suffering from it.

Finally, there is Lia, the young revolutionary whose story differs from those of Lorena and Ana Clara in that it has a very distinct social and political dimension to it. The racially mixed daughter of an apostate Dutch Nazi who, having abandoned Nazism, fled to Brazil, Lia is a convincing and sympathetic character. She is also the key player in what more than one reader will regard as the novel's funniest moment, mordant humor being a quality of Telles's work that her many admirers do not fail to applaud. When the sexually liberated (but not, as in the case of Ana Clara, pathologically promiscuous) Lia encounters a pitiful and sexually uncertain young man, she is so bemused by his multiform innocence that, in a moment of carnal magnanimity, she decides to instruct him in the art of lovemaking—an art which, as the text makes clear, he is far from mastering. But because this key scene takes place in the very office where the resistance is being plotted, and because the specific identity of the young man in question is less important, arguably, than his gender, it reveals itself to be more politically charged than one might expect. An *engagé*, albeit somewhat naïve intellectual, the appealing Lia commands the reader's attention for most of the novel.

Her story also stands out because it was, without doubt, the one that would have been the most perilous for Telles to develop under the dictatorship. Although Lia is clearly a fictional character, her story ties in with one of the most dramatic events of this turbulent period, the 1969 kidnapping by urban guerrillas of the American Ambassador to Brazil, Charles Burke Elbrick. In Telles's novel, Lia's lover and co-revolutionary, Pedro, is released from prison as part of the negotiations by which, in real life, Ambassador Elbrick was freed, unhurt, by the guerrillas after the Brazilian government acceded to their demands. Also connecting the two narrative planes, as well as the three young women involved in them, are a series of recurring motifs, chief among which are

Lia's need to use her friend's car for an act of political protest, Ana Clara's anguished desire to scratch out the pain she feels inside her head, and, for Lorena, the telephone call that never comes from the rich and connected married man, whom she believes, in her feverish fantasy world, would be her ideal lover.

What is perhaps most intriguing in the novel is the extent to which the author uses women as the barometer of Brazil's social, political, and psychological health in the second half of the twentieth-century. In a way that, though focused on Brazil, is also directly applicable to our globalized and interconnected world culture of 2012, *The Girl in the Photograph* emphatically suggests that no society will ever be truly healthy and strong until its women are. This point—more radical, perhaps, in 1973, when Simone de Beauvoir (whose name also turns up in the text) and others were involved in the early Women's Liberation Movement, than in 2012, when more women than ever enjoy the rights and responsibilities so long denied them—turns up time and again in *The Girl in the Photograph*, and in many different forms. Even the outwardly comic scene in which Lia seeks to sexually "liberate" a young man, whose obnoxious post-coital prattle suggests that he is still an unenlightened prisoner of *machismo*, offers the attentive reader a more serious political message: namely, that in sex, as in so many other things (the planning of a more democratic society, for example), men need, and desire, the instruction of women. As Lia puts it, "Women are finding their way. The men will come along in good time" (112).

At the same time, however, the reader of 2012 will likely note something else about the women of Telles's novel; they are all dependent on, and even subordinate to, the men in their lives. This is obviously (and satirically so) true of Lorena, whose monomaniacal preoccupation with a married man who has little or no interest in her borders on the absurd; but it is also true, in more sinister fashion, of Ana Clara, whose dependence on drugs is equaled only by her dependence on Max, her junkie lover. Sadly, the reader watches as Ana Clara's twin addictions, to drugs and to Max, lead inexorably to her destruction. If Ana Clara's is the most poignant of the three stories, Lia's offers the clearest possibility of something different, a new, more progressive kind of liberation. Yet even here, Lia, portrayed throughout as a kind of Brazilian Rosa Luxemburg and otherwise so in command of her own body and mind, cannot, seemingly, escape being at least emotionally subservient to Pedro, her political prisoner lover. Upon his release from prison, moreover, Pedro decamps, alone, for Algeria, where he will renew his revolutionary activities. Once again separated from her lover, and by the same brand of male dominated politics that had segregated them in the first place, Lia will do anything, submit to any humiliation, in order to join him. Lesbianism also emerges in Telles's text, first in a comic mode, as Lorena's fretful mother worries that, if her daughter cannot soon find a man, she may end up preferring women as love objects, but also as a serious topic of discussion, one relating to the important questions of freedom, women's solidarity and female eroticism. And, not surprisingly, some of Telles's female characters suffer from what we might, today, term body image issues.

An attorney, a venerated writer, and a long-time commentator on issues germane to Brazilian and world culture, Telles asks us here to consider the true nature of "liberation"—its political contexts, yes, but its emotional and intellectual ones as well. More presciently, she also asks us to eschew relationships in which one person is subservient to another person, to a particular ideology, or to a single system of thought. True liberation, Telles suggests, is much more complex and far-reaching than commonly thought, and, running the gamut from the workplace to the bedroom and from the kitchen to the political arena, she takes pains to show that it must be germane for women and men alike. For real social and political progress to occur, in Brazil or anywhere else, women must liberate themselves from their status as chattel and as second class citizens while men must, in turn, liberate themselves from the silly, outdated ideas and ways of thinking that have convinced them they are somehow innately superior beings. To move forward, Telles's reader comes to feel, men and women will have to learn to work together for their common good, though the attaining of this admirable goal will require that both genders make drastic changes in the ways they see themselves and each other.

There are, in fact, very few male characters in the novel, and those who do play a role are feckless and destructive in the extreme. Max, Ana Clara's drug-addled lover, epitomizes this tendency. Other men populate the storyline but do so primarily as vague presences, imaginings or impressions held by the women, figments of their hopes, dreams, and desires. The character known as M. N. (Marcus Nemesius) is the prototype of this approach to male characterization for Telles, though most of the novel's other male presences, like Ana Clara's ultra-wealthy but nameless betrothed, or Lia's fellow revolutionary and *paramour*, Pedro, are of this same type. The case of M. N. stands out, however, because of his real name, which evokes the idea of nemesis, and because he is, as becomes clear from his disregard for Lorena, who wastes her time pining away for him, in all respects antithetical to her best interests. The "love" she wants, or needs, to believe she feels for him is imprisoning without being in the least liberating, exhilarating, or fulfilling. One suspects that something similar could be said of Lia's commitment to, or infatuation with, Pedro. Like the broad spectrum of women (and men) she represents, Lorena is a prisoner not merely of the idea of "love," but to a particularly fatuous, materialistic, and superficial kind of love: a "love" not based on true comradeship and solidarity but produced and sustained by a self-serving web of political and cultural lies, a weakness for self-deception, and by a mind-numbing flood of market-generated fantasies. In Telles's characterization of Lorena, in some ways the novel's most important character (given what her story symbolizes and the class she represents), the reader sees how a callow young woman of means can grow from an unthinking and self-centered obsession with shallow notions about "love" that are both debilitating and enslaving to an awareness of others and a commitment to strength and courage that are both healthy and socially valuable.

At the end of the novel, when Ana Clara has returned to the boardinghouse, fatally battered, beaten, and abused after having attended a "party" at the country estate of her wealthy but (one feels) morally and ethically bankrupt "owner," it is Lorena who, growing up quickly, takes charge and makes the hard decisions that will begin to set things right again. While in a strict sense, her conduct, too, at the end, can be read as grotesquely comic, in another way it can be seen as something much more serious and fraught with political import, a moment of personal realization when a hitherto unconcerned and oblivious female character/citizen realizes that things are unacceptably bad and that something has to be done. By shucking off her earlier status as an unthinking child of privilege and her silly infatuations with the kind of "forbidden" love epitomized by her obsession with M. N., and by showing, in a moment of crisis, the kind of courage, character, and leadership that she (and Brazil) needs, Lorena emerges, at novel's end, as a symbol of Brazil's future, its social and political restoration as a democratic republic. Indeed, her status at the end as a female harbinger of a better Brazil seems amplified by the fact that her two brothers, aptly named Romulo and Remo, end up behaving more like Cain and Abel and less like the founders of Rome. For students of Brazilian literature, Lorena's emergence at the conclusion of *The Girl in the Photograph* as a powerful, new force for change will recall the similar emergence of the impoverished *sertaneja*, Vitória, at the conclusion of her novel, Graciliano Ramos's canonical *Vidas Secas* (1938; *Barren Lives*, 1965). If Ana Clara represents the damage done a society by acquiescence to the seductive charms of substance abuse, mindless consumerism, and the ignoring of political tyranny, and if Lia, another admirably-drawn character, represents the need for active civic engagement and responsibility, then Lorena can be said to represent the need for Brazil's middle and upper classes to step up for justice and democracy as well.

The final chapter, then, lends itself to being read as a political allegory, one that shows the dire consequences that result when a society—any society—decides to abandon its most vulnerable, most disadvantaged citizens and to lavish benefits instead on its elites, its most powerful and politically connected figures. No society that wishes to be a democracy can do this and survive—a point that, while obviously applicable to late 1960s and early 1970s Brazil under its military dictatorship, also speaks directly to American readers in 2012, as their own country struggles against a rising tide of reactionary and oligarchic politics, ever-growing corporate power, and the plutocratic rule of the ultra-wealthy that threatens their own democracy. While men, Telles's story suggests (Remo, for example, lives on, after accidently killing his brother), will continue to play important roles in this struggle for social, political, and economic reform (in Brazil and worldwide), that struggle's potency and viability is being conspicuously enhanced by the ever-stronger participation of women like Lorena. As *The Girl in the Photograph* makes clear, the pro-democracy, pro-justice activism of women must be encouraged and supported by all concerned.

In 2012, when, with Dilma Rousseff, Brazil now has its first woman President (something the United States has not yet been able to achieve), and when women occupy many seats of political power in Brazil, this reading of Lorena's characterization seems more prescient that it might have back in 1973, during some of the grimmest years of the flagrantly patriarchal dictatorship. Interestingly, however, this use of strong female characters to embody the future of Brazil does not begin with Fagundes Telles; indeed, it dates back, in Brazilian literature, at least to the nineteenth-century, and writers as diverse as Joaquim Manuel de Macedo, José de Alencar, Domingos Olímpio, Aluízio Azevedo, and Machado de Assis, though it has continued on unabated in the twentieth and twenty-first centuries with such authors as Graciliano Ramos, Clarice Lispector, Nélida Piñon, and Regina Rheda.

Much more than a novel set during the Brazilian dictatorship, *The Girl in the Photograph* is very much a portrait of our times, and the issues it discusses and the questions it explores should resonate deeply with American readers, who, in numerous ways, will see much of themselves and their own culture in it. Telles's novel will speak to women readers especially, though it will also speak to the men who love them, and to everyone who loves democracy and seeks freedom and justice for all, as opposed to the privileged few. Although it can certainly be read as an important Brazilian novel, it can also be read in a broader, hemispheric context, as an American novel with much to say to the United States of America in 2012. Yet *The Girl in the Photograph* will also be read as a work of fiction that does much to strengthen ties between the United States and Brazil, as well as between these two nations and their New World neighbors. Improved inter-American relations are going to play a major role in New World affairs during the twenty-first century, and writers like Lygia Fagundes Telles are making vital contributions to this mutually beneficial experience.

Finally, a word of praise must go out to the novel's translator, Margaret A. Neves, who has given us a translation as fluent and as natural in English as it is in its original Brazilian Portuguese. This is a major accomplishment when one considers how deeply entwined are the interior monologues which characterize the three women, and by which their stories are interwoven. A careful and discerning reader and a skilled writer (as all good translators must be), Neves manages to keep the three monologues separate, distinct, and vital, and to reproduce for the English reader the many shifts in tone, semantic fields, and stylistic twists and turns that characterize the original text.

EARL E. FITZ
VANDERBILT UNIVERSITY

Works Cited

Burns, E. Bradford. A History of Brazil, 2nd edition. New York: Columbia University Press, 1980.

"Ana Clara, don't squint!" said Sister Clotilde, about to snap the photo, "Quick, Lia, tuck in your blouse! And don't make faces, Lorena, you're making faces!" The pyramid.

Chapter 1

I sit down on the bed. It's too early to take a bath. I flop onto my back, hug the pillow and think about M.N., the best thing in the world isn't drinking the milk from a green coconut and then peeing in the ocean, Lião's uncle said it was but he doesn't know, the best thing is to imagine what M.N. will say and do when my last veil is removed. *The last veil!* Lião would write, she becomes sublime when she writes, she began her novel by saying that in December the city smells of peaches. Imagine, peaches. December is peach season, that's true, sometimes one finds peach pits on the streetcorners with the smell of an orchard about them, but to conclude from that that the *entire* city is perfumed is just too sublime. She dedicated the story to Ché Guevara with a very important-looking quote about life and death, all in Latin. Imagine Latin entering into the Guevarian scheme. Or maybe it does? Suppose he liked Latin; don't I? The delicious hours I used to spend lying on the ground, my hands crossed under my head, Latinizing as I watched the clouds. Death combines with Latin, nothing goes together so well as Latin and death. But to accept that this city smells like peaches, that's going too far. *Que ciudad será esa?* he would ask, thoroughly perplexed. *Tercer mundo?* Yes, Third World. *Y huele a durazno?* Yes, in the opinion of Lia de Melo Schultz, it smells like peaches. Then he would close his eyes, or what used to be his eyes, and smile where his mouth used to be. *Estoy bien listo con esas mis discípulas.* Well, that's her problem, mine is M.N., an M.N. naked and hairy, much hairier than I, he's very hairy, kind of like a monkey. But a beautiful monkey, his face so intellectual, so rare, the right eye slightly smaller than the left, and so sad, all one side of his face is infinitely sadder than the other. Infinitely. I could keep repeating infinitely infinitely. A simple word that extends itself through rivers, mountains, valleys infinitely long, like the arms of God. The words. The move-

1

ments renewing themselves like the smooth new skin of the snake breaking through from under the old. It isn't slimy; I touched one once at the farm, it was green and thick but not slimy. And M.N.'s gestures also new, it isn't true that it will be the same as the other times, he will come with a clean skin, inventing or invented down to the last minutiae. If God is in details, the sharpest pleasure, too, is in small things, you hear that, M.N.? Ana Clara told me about a boyfriend she had who would go crazy when she took off her false eyelashes, the bikini scene didn't have the slightest importance but as soon as she started to remove her eyelashes, it was glory. The naked eye. Verily I say unto you, the day will come when the nakedness of the eyes will be more exciting than that of the sex organs. Pure convention, to think sexual organs are obscene. What about the mouth? Unsettling, the mouth biting, chewing, biting. Biting a peach, remember? If I wrote something, it would be a story entitled "The Peach Man." I watched it from a streetcorner as I was drinking a glass of milk: a completely ordinary man with a peach in his hand. As I looked on he rolled and squeezed it with his fingers, closing his eyes a little as if he wanted to memorize its contours. He had hard features and his need of a shave accentuated their lines like charcoal shading, but the hardness dissolved when he sniffed the peach. I was fascinated. He stroked the fuzz of its skin with his lips, and with them, too, he went over the whole surface of the fruit as he had done with his fingertips. Nostrils dilated, eyes narrowed. I wanted him to get it over with, but it seemed he was in no hurry; almost angrily, he rubbed the peach against his chin, rolling it between his fingers as he hunted for the nipple-point with the tip of his tongue. Did he find it? I was perched at the café counter but I could see it as if through a telescope: He found the rosy nipple and began to caress it with his tongue tip in an intense circular movement. I could see that the tip of his tongue was the same pink as the nipple of the peach, and that he was already licking it with an expression near suffering. When he opened his mouth wide and bit down to make the juice squirt sharply out, I almost gagged on my milk. I still go tense all over when I remember it, oh Lorena Vaz Leme, have you no shame?

"No," says the Seducer Angel out loud. Quickly I light an incense tablet, oh perverse mind. I'd like to be a saint. As pure as this perfume of roses that enfolds me and makes me drowsy, As-

2

tronaut used to get sleepy too when I would light the incense. And he would stretch the same way I do; I learned how to stretch from watching him. Worthless cat, what's become of you? Hmm? He used to give daily lessons in lasciviousness and indolence, but he would never repeat his movements, all ballet dancers should have a cat. The cunning. At the same time, the abandon. The scorn for things that were really to be scorned. And that calculated obsession. Made entirely of dangerous delicacies, my cat. Or was he a demon? During the pauses between lessons, he would stare at me, so much more conscious than I in my unconsciousness, how could I know? I didn't even know M.N. yet, I didn't spend hours and hours woolgathering, Lord, how I've wool-gathered lately. Only Jesus understands and pardons, only He who went through everything like us, Jesus, Jesus, how I love You! I'm going to play a record in your honor, I offer music just like Abel offered the lamb, of course, a lamb is much more important, but Jesus knows I have a horror of blood, my offerings will have to be musical ones. Jimi Hendrix? Listen, my beloved, listen to this last little tune he composed before he died, he died of drugs, poor thing, they all die of drugs, but hear it and I know you'll lower Your hand in blessing upon his sweat-stained, dusty Afro hair, dear Jimi! . . .

With an elastic leap, Lorena threw herself onto the gilded iron bed, which was the same color as the wallpaper. She practiced a few dance steps, raising her leg until her bare foot touched the iron bar of the bedstead, and jumped down onto the blue stripe of the jute rug. She straightened up, shook her hair back and, looking straight ahead, moved forward by balancing herself on the stripe until she got to the record player.

"Jimi, Jimi, where are you?" she asked, examining the pile of records on the bookshelf. She was wearing a pair of soft pajamas, white with yellow flowers, and around her neck was a chain with a small gold heart. She held the record by the tips of her fingers. "And you, Romulo? Where are you now?"

Squeezing her damp eyes shut, she placed the record on the turntable. Softly, she raised the needle and guided it as if it were the beak of a blind bird seeking a dish of water. She let it fall.

"Lorena!"
The voice was coming from the garden. Quickly she pulled

her hair together, wound it up at the back of her neck, and stood on tiptoe. Opening her arms, she walked on the spiral stripe of the carpet, tense as an acrobat on a highwire.

"Lorena, come to the window, I want to talk to you!"

She hesitated dangerously, her right foot planted on the stripe, her left suspended in the air. Only when she managed to put the left one down in front of the other without losing her balance did she relax; she had made it across the wire. She bowed deeply to both sides, her arms arched backwards, her hands touching like the tips of half-opened wings. She waved her thanks to the audience as she moved back slightly, smiling modestly downward. But she thrilled to catch a flower in the air, kissed it threw it triumphantly to the grandstand and went whirling toward the window. She waved to the young woman who was waiting, arms crossed, in the middle of the driveway. Bringing her hands to the left side of her chest, she sighed loudly and said:

"My dear, welcome! Look what a lovely day! It's spring, Lião, *primavera*. Vera, truth, prima, first, naturally, the first truth. Hum? On a morning like this I have to hold onto myself, otherwise I fly right off, look at the daisies, they've all opened!" She pointed to the flower box under the window. "How sweet. Good morning, my little daisies!"

"Lorena, do you think you could listen to me for a minute?"

"Speak, Lia de Melo Schultz, speak!"

With a brusque motion, Lia pulled her heavy white socks up to her knees. Her leather tote bag slid to the ground but she kept her eye attentively on the socks, as if she expected to see them slip downwards immediately. She picked up the bag.

"Do you think your mother could lend me the car? After dinner. Let's say about nine, understand."

Lorena leaned out the window and smiled.

"Your socks are falling."

"Either they strangle my knees or they keep slipping. Look at that. When they were new, this elastic was so tight my legs would get purple."

"But what are you thinking, dear, wearing socks in this heat? And mountain-climbing boots, why didn't you put on your sandals? Those brown ones match your bag."

"Today I have to walk all over the place, dammit. And if I don't wear socks, I get blisters."

4

Probably on the soles of her feet. Super-hick. The only thing worse than blisters is bunions, like Sister Bula's. Bunions must come from onions, there was once an old lady with bumps on her feet like onions, and her grandchildren inherited the deformity, bumps, onions, bunions. Oh Lord. Spring, I'm in love, and Lião talking about blisters on her feet.

"I've got some great socks, I haven't even worn them yet, you want them?"

"Only if they're French, see?"

"They're Swiss."

"I don't like Switzerland, it's too clean."

And they won't even fit her, imagine, she must wear size twelve. How can she possibly wear socks that make her ankles even thicker, the poor thing has legs like an elephant's. Even so, she's thinner, political subversiveness is thinning.

"Lião, Lião, I'm in love. If M.N. doesn't phone, I'll kill myself."

I'm much too annoyed to stand here listening to Lorenense sentiments, oh! Miguel, how I need you. I speak softly but I must be breathing fire.

"Lena, listen, I'm not joking."

"Well, am I? What's the hurry? Come on up and listen to Jimi Hendrix's last album. I'll make some tea, I have some marvelous biscuits."

"English?" I ask. "I prefer our biscuits and our music. Enough cultural colonialism."

"But our music doesn't move me, dearest. If your Bahians say that they're desperate, I believe them, I think it's great, but if John Lennon comes along and says the same thing, then I'm turned on, I become mystic. I *am* mystic."

"You're silly."

"Silly, Lião? You said *silly*," she repeats.

She leans farther out the window and, in the middle of a laugh, turns sideways, puts her thumbs in her head, and wiggles her hands like ears, oh! it takes patience to put up with this girl.

"Lorena, it's serious. I need the car tomorrow," I say.

She doesn't hear me. Suddenly she becomes angelic as she waves to somebody inside the big old house, Mother Alix? Mother Alix who opens the window and is exactly the same height, her hand raised in the manner of the Queen of England.

5

But as soon as the nun goes away, she makes a worse face, the one she reserves for last. Oh, Miguel, "stay cool," you said, and that's what I'm trying to do. But at times I go hollow, don't you see? I can't explain it but it's just too hard to go on in the routine, I wish I were in jail, in your place, why couldn't I go in your place? I wish I could die.

"The university is still on strike," groans Lorena, yawning. "What have you got there? A machine gun?"

She straightens up as if she were using one, squinting down the sights, shoulders shaken by the discharge, tat-tat-tat-tat-tat-tat . . . She aims at the house, tat-tat-tat-tat-tat, and fires at Sister Bula who pretends to play with Cat but whose attention is riveted on us. I am grinning because I know that Miguel would react exactly that way.

"Loreninha, don't start in, I don't like this game. Are you going to get the car? I'll give it back the next day, like the last time. No problem."

"You guys should kidnap M.N., Lião. Why don't you kidnap M.N.? He could stay hidden under my bed *per omnia seculum seculorum, Amen.*"

I light a cigarette. What do I care if I sleep beside the drunks, the whores, the live coal against my breast, yes it hurts, but if I knew you were free, sleeping beside the road or under the bridge—! Only free. I can't stand other people's suffering, understand. Your suffering, Miguel. Mine I could stand all right, I'm tough. But if I think about you I get flaky, I feel like crying. Dying. And we are dying. One way or another, aren't we dying? Never have the masses been so far away from us, they don't want anything to do with us. We even make them angry, the masses are afraid, oh, how afraid they are. The bourgeoisie resplendent at the top. Never have the rich been so rich, they can build houses with door handles of gold, not just the cutlery but the door handles too. The faucets in the bathrooms. All pure gold like the Greek gangster had them on his island. Intact. Watching out the windows and thinking it's funny. There's still the mass of urban delinquents left. Urban neurotics. And half a dozen intellectuals; the friendly sympathizers. I can't explain it but the intellectuals make me sicker than the cops do, the cops at least don't wear a mask. Oh, Miguel. I need you so badly today, I feel so much like crying. But I don't cry. I don't even have a handkerchief, Lorena wouldn't think it was nice to blow my nose on my shirttail.

6

"Lorena, lend me a handkerchief, I've got a cold," I say, wanting to wipe my face which is wet with tears. Handkerchief, hell, what I want is the car. "I want the car, Lorena. Can I count on you?"

"I have white, pink, blue and light green. Ah, and turquoise. Look how beautiful this turquoise one is. So, Lia de Melo Schultz, what color does Madame prefer?"

I gaze at the box of handkerchiefs she brings. She keeps everything in little boxes covered with flowered cloth, this one has red and blue poppies on a black background. Plus the silver and leather boxes which sit on her shelf. And bells. Wherever her brother travels he sends her a bell. Other people collect stamps, or ties. Still others get in line to go to the movies. Maurício grinds his teeth until they break. He doesn't want to scream so he grinds his teeth when the electric rod goes deeper into his anus. In the cartoon, the cat takes a walloping that makes its teeth and bones splinter. But in the next scene they glue themselves together and the cat comes back in one piece. It would be nice if it were like in the cartoons. Sylvia Flute-player. Gigi. Jap. And you, Maurício? When the electric rod goes deeper, you faint. Faint quick, die! We ought to die, Miguel. As a sigh of protest, we should all simply die. "We would, if it would do any good," you said, remember? I know, nobody would pay the slightest attention. We could rip our hearts out, look, here's my blood, here's my heart! But some guy shining shoes nearby would say, What color shoe polish does the gentleman prefer?

"Green."

I take the pale green one, which is third down in the pile, from the box. So delicate, the handkerchiefs Remo sent from Istanbul, farewell, my little hanky. Lião is capable of cleaning her big old shoes with you but think about the "IF" for hankies: dust is just as noble as tears. It won't be moon dust, so white and fine, earth dust is heavy, especially that on my friend's shoes. But never mind, BE A HANDKERCHIEF. I drop it into space. It opens lightly like a parachute which Lião grabs impatiently.

"Are you depressed, Lião? Existential anguish?"

"Exactly. Existential."

Oh Lord, she's furious with me. She's changed so much, poor thing. Meaning Miguel is still in prison? And that Japanese guy. And Gigi. And others, they're all going, what madness. Suppose she's next? Ana Clara did see somebody suspicious-looking hanging around the gate; Aninha lies all the time, of course, but that could be true. Yes, Our Lady of Fatima Roominghouse, a name above investigation. But whenever nuns or priests come onto the horizon, everyone's ears perk up.

"I'll give it back tomorrow," she says, folding the handkerchief.

"Not at all, keep it. Would you like another one?"

I throw her the pink handkerchief which doesn't open as the green one did. Why does my heart stay closed too? Romulo in Mama's arms, I looked for a handkerchief and couldn't find one, a handkerchief to wipe up all that blood bubbling out. Bubbling out. "But what happened, Lorena!" A game, Mama, they were playing and then Remo went to get the shotgun, Run or I'll shoot, he said taking aim. All right, I don't want to think about this now, now I want sunshine. I sit in the window frame and stretch my legs toward the sun.

"I get red, and I want to get tan, look at me, Fabrízio told me my nickname in the Department is Fainting Magnolia, can you imagine?"

"And the old guy? Nothing yet?"

I count to ten before answering, grrrr! Why does she call M.N. old? First of all, he is *not* old. Second, she *knows* I'm the complicated type, with me things just can't be resolved so fast. Third—what was the third thing? I am making an effort to seem unshakable.

"He said he'd call me for dinner. Want to come?"

"What I need is a western movie."

Imagine, the movies. A danger zone, there are thousands of danger zones where his wife or his cousin . . . I think the best place for us to meet is in the hospital because if the world is big, that hospital is even bigger. Is Dr. Marcus Nemesius in? I ask and the head nurse speaks to the subordinate nurse who speaks to the subordinate subordinate, who in turn speaks to another one far on down the line, the one who escaped the current, her shoes white, her memory white. "By any chance are you the one who's waiting to see Dr. Melloni?" she comes and asks after two and a half hours. No, not that doctor. By any chance I'm waiting for Dr. Marcus Nemesius, is he in? "He just left," she answers. "Won't another doctor do?"

8

"If he doesn't phone, let's go together, Lião. I've got venom enough for caviar."

"Russian?"

"No, from Iran, dear. The best caviar in the world. My brother Remo sent a can."

"I'm moved. But I'll grab something on the corner."

Here there's the soup, the de-sexed meat the nuns fix, but still it's better than the things she eats in the street. And she doesn't even take baths any more, poor thing. Before, she would fill up my bathtub and soak so happily; one day she even asked for the bath salts.

"You've changed, Lião."

"For the worse?" she asks, unfolding the handkerchief and blowing her nose.

Like an open drainpipe. Animals are so much more decent about these things; I never saw Astronaut blow his nose in public. Too many holes, too many secretions. Oh Lord. Eating pastries at the café, what madness. But if she came with us, she'd end up poisoning our time together, she adores saying ironic things that M.N. pretends not to understand, so solid. So safe. "More wine, Lião?" The wine she accepts. Also the lobster, she pronounces it *loster*. But she pointedly remembers the statistics about the children dying of hunger in the Northeast, she gets carried away on this subject of the Northeast. I don't know how long we'll have to carry these people on our backs; it's horrible to think that way but, as I've thought before and still think, if God isn't there He probably has His reasons.

"Oh, I'm a monster. Monster. I want so much to be different, so much."

And this tendency to be petty. Oh my Saint Francis, my Saint Theresa, *son tan escuras de entender estas cosas interiores.*

"I'll give it back tomorrow," says Lião putting the handkerchief away in her bag.

She won't, of course. And if she did I wouldn't take it, a handkerchief is like a toothbrush, you can't lend them. Exactly like Ana Clara who still hasn't learned this simplest of things: One doesn't lend *personal items.*

"Lia, Lia!" calls Sister Bula from the window of the big house. The voice of a forest gnome coming out from inside a tree trunk. She wants to yell "Telephone for you!" She places one hand beside her ear and pretends to crank the handle; the

9

phones in her day had to be wound up. Or was she born even earlier? She must be two hundred years old.

Lião is afraid. Ana Clara also pretends to be indifferent but if she doesn't take tranquilizers she starts walking around in a delirium again. Without the slightest ceremony she opened my box of tissues and took over half of them, she goes around with great piles of tissues to clean herself after making love. The right thing would be to take a bath afterwards; it's logical, hygienic and poetic to run naked to the shower. Or in the country to duck under a waterfall, *shuaaaaaaaaaa!* But to put yourself back together like a hurried chambermaid—! Certain gestures and words of Ana Clara's, poor thing. The details give her away. It's all in the details: her origins, her faith, her happiness. God. Especially her origins. "I know nothing about mine," she said to me once when she was drunk. "And I don't want to, either." That daisy down there could say the same thing: I know nothing about my roots. And her? Neither father nor mother. Not even a cousin. She has no one. From the looks of it, all of Bahia must be related to Lião but Ana Clara is the opposite in terms of family. Not even an auntie to teach her that everything one does before and after the act of love should be harmonious. Is it unaesthetic to masturbate? Not exactly unaesthetic, but sad. During the time when Lião was doing thousands of surveys, she did one on the university coeds; how many masturbated? Incredible, the results among the virgins. Incredible. "We are coming out of the Middle Ages," she said examining her papers. "The inheritance from our mothers and grandmothers, see. Added up with the adolescent habits, it gives us this alarming percentage. Do you masturbate too?" she asked, pinning the black eye of the Inquisition on me.

Two blond bees, the kind that only make love and honey, landed on my foot, first one and then the other. I shoo them gently away, the gesture must be gentle so they don't feel rejected, you hear, M.N.? If you don't want me, you should treat me like this, run along, my little bee! run along. Before flying off, the larger of the two rubs his two front legs together, as if he were washing his hands, and then strokes himself all the way down to his yellow-striped abdomen. You can't see exactly where his hand stops, but what if Lião were to research the habits of bees, *Tu quoque, bestiola? Bestiola* means insect. And bees? Anyway she asked me and if I didn't answer with absolute

10

clarity it was because I could never exactly describe that afternoon so long ago. Masturbation? That? Thirteen years old, piano lessons. *The Happy Farmer.* I participated so fully in the happiness that the bench wobbled back and forth, the rhythm getting faster and faster. My chest bursting, my genitalia rubbing against the cushion with the same vehemence as my hands hammering the keyboard, without hesitation, without error. I never played as well as I did that afternoon, something which seems completely extraordinary to me today. I dismounted the bench as one would a horse. At dinnertime, Mama kissed me, quite moved: "I heard you practicing the piano while I was stirring the guava jam; you played divinely!" I smiled down at my plate: my first secret. Romulo threw a ball of soft bread at me and Remo put a wasp in my hair, but when we went out on the veranda I felt as luminous as a star. And if Romulo hadn't frightened me with a sheet, I could have walked on air for over two minutes. The second time was on the farm, too, when I was taking a bath. Also accidental. I got into the empty bathtub, lay down in the bottom and opened the faucet. The hot jet pelted onto my chest with such violence that I slipped, exposing my belly. From there, the water passed to my abdomen; when I opened my legs and it hit me right on, I felt, stunned, the old artistic exaltation, stronger this time although I wasn't playing a piano. I closed my eyes when Felipe crossed and recrossed my body with his red motorcycle, Felipe, the one with the black jacket and motorcycle. I hid my face in my hands, wanting to run away and at the same time glued to the bottom of the bathtub with the hot water rising higher, it was already covering me, the bubbles breaking on my chin, why didn't I open the drain? Satiated or unsatiated, my mouth (I?) asked for more. It penetrated me in waterfalls, it filled my nose, there, I'm going to drown! I thought with a jump. I leaped up and fled. Was it love? Was it death? All one single thing, I replied in a verse. I used to write verses then.

Cat came up to the bag that Lia had left in the middle of the driveway. She sniffed the leather, distrustful, sat down somewhat sideways, because of her pregnancy, and stared at Lorena who was perched on the bedroom windowsill. This room and bath—Lorena was certain of this—had belonged to the chauffeur of the family who had owned the big house. Underneath,

11

the garage with a car which was probably antiquated. Above, absolute master, the untidy and sensual chauffeur, lover of the housemaid whose name was Neusa, a name spelled out many times with a shaving brush or white deodorant stick on the blue-tinted wall. Of her, there remained only a few hairpins pointing out from between the cracks in the floor. And the jasmine perfume in a broken bottle on the bathroom floor. "With a few small repairs, your daughter could be very comfortable here," said Sister Priscilla with an optimism that spread to Lorena, who was hanging onto her mother's arm. Her mother, in turn, was hanging onto Mieux's. She turned to him with a perplexed face, at that time she used to consult him even to find out if she should take an aspirin or not. "Give me your opinion, dear. Won't I spend too much? This is awful," she complained, repulsed by the scent of jasmine mingled with that of urine. Mieux winked at Lorena. He became euphoric when he had an opportunity to show off his prestige: "It will be the most darling thing in the world, I already have some ideas. I want this bathroom pink, it's important for her to feel as though she's in a nest when she undresses for her bath," he said throwing his cigarette butt into the cracked toilet bowl. He slammed the door behind him and sniffed his handkerchief. "I visualize this room in pale yellow; I have the wallpaper. A gold bed there in that corner. The bookshelf and table on that wall. Here in this space, a built-in wardrobe. Over there, a mini-refrigerator and a little bar, hm, Lorena?" He picked a playing card up off the floor; it was a queen of spades, which he stuck upright in a crack in the door. And as Mama had gone on ahead and Sister Priscilla was busy closing the window, he seized the opportunity to run his hand over my ass.

"Anything happen?" I ask Lião who has come back at a run.
Panting, she kicked a wad of newspaper which Cat tore up.
"Is the offer of tea still on? I'll take you up on it after all. One more phone call like that one and I'll go completely insane."
I quickly remove my pajamas and put on my black ballet leotard. I hear Lião coming up the stairs, step by step. When she's happy she comes up them in three jumps, poor thing, flunking all her classes because she cut so many. Her lover in prison, her allowance gone, she gives over half of it to her famous group. Oh Lord.

12

"Can I turn that down?" she asks, going straight in the direction of the record player.

She turned it down so far that Jimi Hendrix's voice sounds like that of a little ant under the table. I light the electric ring, do two more exercises to develop the bustline, and spread the cloth on the table. The cups, the plates. I bring my little breadbasket with its red ribbon woven into the straw, going all the way around until the ends meet in a bow. I pause to admire the graceful pattern of the tablecloth with its big leaves in a hot green tone, through which, half-hidden, peers the Asiatic eye of an occasional orange. The pleasure I take in this simple ritual of preparing tea is almost as intense as that I take in hearing music. Or reading poetry. Or taking a bath. Or or or. There are so many tiny things that give me pleasure that I'll die of pleasure when I get to the bigger thing. Is it really bigger, M.N.?

"I'll kill myself if he doesn't call," I say opening my arms and going on tiptoe to the refrigerator. "I have some marvelous grapes and apples, dear."

Lia sits down on the rug and begins to chew on a biscuit. She is as somber as a shipwrecked mariner eating the last biscuit on the island. She brushes the crumbs which have fallen into the pleats in her skirt, but why this skirt today? In spite of her exorbitant Bahian behind, I think she looks better in jeans.

"Problems, Lena, problems. Oh forget it —" she says, trying to placate her kinky hair with her hands. "Don't forget to ask, you hear?"

I throw her an apple.

"I put a new tablecloth on the table in your honor, isn't it beautiful?"

"Say it's you who's going to use it, understand."

"What?"

"The car, Lena, stop dreaming, pay attention, you're going to ask Mama for her car!"

I lie on my back and start pedaling. I can pedal up to two hundred times.

"This is an excellent exercise to fill out your legs, incredible how skinny my legs are. You'd have to pedal backwards to make yours smaller," I say and hold back my laughter.

She bites into the apple with such fury that I feel my knee reflex jump.

"After dinner, Lorena. Don't forget, after dinner, are you listening? Say it's for you."

13

Car, car. The Machine is sweeping away the beauty of the earth, Oh Lord. And we're entering the Age of Aquarius, meaning, technology will dominate, more machines. Air transport, individual balloons and jets, the sky black with people. I want nothing to do with it. I'll read my poets up in a treetop, there might be a tree left over.

"Yesterday I bought a gorgeous edition of Tagore," I say, sitting down on the rug. I clasp my hands in front of my breast: "'I watch through the long night for the one who has robbed me of sleep. I build up the walls of the one who has torn mine down. I spend my life pulling up thorns and scattering flower seeds. I long to kiss the one who no longer recognizes me.'"

She glances at me, chuckles slightly and said with her mouth full, "You don't have to do that much, it's enough not to want to steal your neighbor's husband, understand, Madame Tagore?"

"But he doesn't love her any more, dear. The love is gone, there's nothing between them. They only belong to each other on paper."

"You think that's so little? I go along with that but you need to see if he does too. And what's so original about that poem? All that is in the Bible, Lena. Don't you read the Bible? Go look it up, it's all there."

I begin to pedal again, more energetically.

"I bought Proust, isn't that high-class? M.N. has a passion for Proust. I'll have to read it, but I confess I'm finding it slightly boring."

"Yugghh. High-class novels are bad and high-class old-fashioned novels are worse. I never had the patience for them," she says taking a cigarette out of her bag.

I run to get an ashtray and on the way back take the lid off the teakettle. The water is almost boiling, you should never let tea water come to a full boil, Daddy taught me. I turn off the burner and drop the tea leaves into the water. With my eyes closed I breathe in their perfume as I put the ashtray under Lião who doesn't know what to do with her apple core. Holding an invisible microphone, I approach on my knees. She clamps the cigarette between her teeth.

"If you please, I'd like your opinion on certain problems our community is facing," I say raising the microphone. "First of all, may we have your name?"

"Lia de Melo Schultz."

14

"Profession?"

"University student. Social sciences."

"And . . . may I ask about your present situation at that institution of learning?"

"I goofed off this year. Cut classes. I ended up dropping all my courses, but I'm still registered."

"Fine, fine. And your book? They tell me you have a book almost ready. According to our information it's a novel, is that right?"

"I tore it all up, understand," she says blowing smoke in my face. "The sea of useless books is already overflowing. After all, fiction, who cares about it?"

I abandon the microphone. Tore it up? It isn't really her vocation, poor thing. But she used to enjoy writing her stories so much, in those big notebooks with the greasy covers, wherever she went she'd take along those notebooks. The city smelling like peaches, imagine. I offer her a cluster of grapes but she refuses. I don't know what to say to her. So precise when she talks but so sentimental when she writes, oh, the moon, oh, the lake.

"You know the latest, Lião? A poetess from the Amazon is going to arrive, how about that? She must be an Indian. She's going to be your roommate, dear."

"Why my room? You here in this penthouse and with a bathroom even, dammit. Indians like baths. Ana Clara's room would hold a whole tribe, too."

"No, not there, imagine! The Indian maiden in her natural state, Ana Clara would be too much of a culture shock, poor thing."

"But by January isn't she supposed to be married to the industrialist? Driving a black Jaguar with red seats. A diamond the size of a saucer on her finger."

"And a full-length leopard coat. Stiiiiinking chic!" I roll my eyes upward and imitate Aninha when she adopts her *femme fatale* air. But Lião is still sober.

"Crazy Ana isn't doing so well. She's already doped up in the mornings now. And she piles up debts something awful, there's swarms of bill collectors at the gate. The nuns are in panic. And that boyfriend of hers, the pusher—"

"Max? He's a pusher?"

"Come on, you mean you don't know?" mutters Lião, tearing a piece of fingernail from her thumb. "And it's not just speed

15

and pot, I've seen the needle marks time and again. She should be put into the hospital immediately. Which wouldn't do any good at this point, she's so far gone. A wreck, in short."

I open my hands on the rug and examine my fingernails.

"It would be fantastic if the millionaire fiancé married her. I'll put out the yenom for the plastic surgery in the southern zone, he would only marry a virgin, she has to become a virgin. Oh Lord."

"You think a rich marriage is going to help anything?" Lião asks with a sad smile. "You should be ashamed to think that way, Lorena. And will there even be a wedding? Doesn't the guy know how she gets her kicks? Instead of hoping for a miraculous wedding, you should hope for a true miracle, understand? I don't know why, but you Christians have such a funny mentality."

I go to the teakettle and fill the cups again, then stop halfway back. He sang while on drugs, this half-hoarse voice, isn't it doped? The twisted voice of someone who cries for help but who doesn't want to be helped.

"Yesterday she was so lucid. She says Mother Alix helps, she's going to start in again with her analysis. Who knows, eh, Lião?"

"Do you think at this point an analyst is going to help? It would have to be an analyst of the Saint Sebastian brand, that one with the arrows, beautiful and good. Then she'd fall in love with him and be saved through love, like in the comic books she adores reading. And get her Jaguar and her leopard coat to boot."

Lorena hands me the teacup with its handsome design of birds and flowers. The linen tablecloth matches the cup, a tablecloth with an exuberant tropical pattern. The small light-colored armchairs. The rare objects.

"Everything here is very attractive, very pretty. Are you still rich, Lorena?"

She became serious, relaxing from her exercises.

"Mieux's so-called advertising agency came to nothing. With the interior-decorating store, Mama spent money like crazy. And she keeps on spending, a thirst for novelty. They remind me of those American millionaires in Europe in the twenties, you know?"

16

"I don't know. I asked if you had money."

"I take care of my part. Why? Do you need some, Lião?"

I pour more tea into my cup. Damn good tea. I jump over Lorena who has stopped pedaling and is now doing her respiratory exercises, she has already explained to me that there is solar respiration and lunar respiration.

"I think I'm going to, Lorena. For some operations far different from Crazy Ana's."

"Oh Lord. I feel so sorry for her."

She feels so sorry for everyone. No doubt she felt sorry for me when I told her I tore up the novel. Isn't it just a way of hiding her feeling of superiority? Isn't feeling sorry for others a way of feeling superior over others? I tore up the novel, I said. And she was silent. I drink the warm tea. She's a good girl. Ana Clara is a good girl too. I'm a good girl.

"How's the collection coming?" I ask examining the bells arranged on the shelf.

"My brother Remo promised me one of those Bedouin ones from Tunisia, he's there now, living in a gorgeous house in Carthage, can you imagine? Carthage still exists, Lião. *Delenda, delenda!* But it still exists."

The other day, all excited, she asked to come to one of the group meetings, this same Lorena who stands there ringing her little bells, ting-ting, tang-tang, tong-tong. She imagines our meetings are sort of like debating festivals: She would go with this leotard, boots and a red turtleneck to break the monotony of black. The intellectuals with their little films on the Vietcong. So much hunger, so much blood on the screen made from a sheet. So terrible to see so much death, dammit. How can it be, my God, how can it be? Revolt and nausea. "Sartrean nausea," murmurs an inexperienced guest. Who shuts up when she feels the icy stares fixed on her in the dark. Silence again, only the exasperated buzzing of the projector, the enjoyment is prolonged, there's miles of film waiting in the little cans. The lights come on, but the faces take some time to light up, how awful. Whiskey and paté to relieve the atmosphere. Considerations about the probable names on the next lists. The films go back into their respective cans while little by little the people go back to their respective houses. Those who don't have transportation ask for rides in the available cars going their way. They are good-humored, the intellectuals. There are even a few jokes.

17

But, in all justice, they're watchful. Above all, informed. They should be, going to meetings all the time. They know you were imprisoned and tortured, a courageous boy this Miguel, one needs to have courage, bravo, bravo. They know Sylvia Flute-player was raped with an ear of corn, the cop knew about the episode in the novel, somebody told him and he found it amusing. "Cooked corn or raw?" his helper asked him, and he went into detail. "Dried corn, with those pointed kernels!" The intellectuals are too moved to speak, they only continue shaking their heads and drinking. It's fortunate that the whiskey isn't a national brand. Some of the more fanatic ones get irritated with the tone of the meetings; after all, it wasn't held only for the wine and cheese when the news is the worst possible: Eurico still hasn't been found; he was arrested just as he disembarked and up to now nobody knows anything about him. He disappeared just like a science-fiction character, when the metallic man emits a ray and the guy dissolves, gun and all, and only a grease spot is left in the place. Jap left a briefcase in his brother's house; he said he would come to get it the next day.

"This one's Greek, Lião. Listen what a divine sound."

I told her I tore up my book and I might as well have said I had torn up a newspaper. She doesn't like what I write. Nobody does, it must be absolute shit. But do people know what's good? Or what's bad? Who knows? And is it valid? I shouldn't have torn it up. But I know it by heart, maybe I could use the text in a diary, I'd like to write a diary. Simple, direct style. I'd dedicate it to him.

"Perfect. Perfect," she repeats and picks up the bag. "Don't forget about the car, Lena."

"Lia de Melo Schultz, if you say that one more time, I'll kill myself. Look, keep this little bell, put it around your neck. When we lose track of each other, you go ding-a-ling and I'll know where you are, everybody should wear a bell around, like goats do." Softly, Lia rang the small bronze bell. She smiled at her friend as she tried to untie a black ribbon from around her neck.

"I'll put it here with my good-luck charm that my mother gave me. I need to write a long letter to Mother, and another to my father, they're opposite types. And alike at the same time. When I don't write, each goes off and cries in a corner, hiding from the other."

18

How they longed to see their daughter receiving her diploma. Getting engaged. Engagement party in the parlor, wedding in the church, hoop-skirted bridal dress. Rice as they dash away. The grandchildren multiplying, everybody together in the same house, that enormous house, there were so many bedrooms, weren't there? "The apartment-building curse has reached us here, too," my father wrote in his last letter. "Our neighborhood is being invaded but we will resist. When you get back and find only one last house in the whole city, you can come in, it's ours."

"If my love phones, want to come and have dinner with us?"

Lia watches me. What are you thinking about, Lião? She pats me on the head and goes out with the air of somebody who carries the weight of the world on her shoulders. I turn up the volume of the record player. *Get out of here*, he screams hoarsely. I peer out the window. She gallops down the steps with her three leaps and is now exactly where she was before coming up. Yet she hesitates as though she had forgotten to say something important, doesn't she remember? She opens the bag, looks inside. Indifferently chews the nail of her little finger, and picks up a pebble. She throws it high in the air.

"Is it the car, dear? Don't worry, did you know Mama gave me one? I didn't even go to get the check, imagine. You can keep a key, I hate to drive, eeh, the faces people make when I drive."

Her attention is completely fixed on a point behind me, which moves farther away and loses itself like the pebble she threw into the air. I make faces, I can make great faces, neither Remo nor Romulo knew how to make faces like I did but Lião is only interested in the far-off point, which seems to have returned and fallen down inside her. Her face ripples like the surface of a well when the stone falls in.

"Don't park by the gate, leave it on the corner. If you go out, leave the key on the shelf. In one of your boxes there."

"In the silver one shaped like a clover, dear."

She knows I know she's involved in a tangled plot, but she also knows I respect her secret. The stone reposes in the depths of the compliant waters. *Requiescat in pace.* I motion her to come closer:

"Who was it had a compliant hymen?"

At last she laughs like she used to in the good old times, wrinkling her sunburned face.

19

"Go on, give in, Lena."

"But isn't that what I'm wanting to do?" I ask, and deep inside I answer myself, I don't think I am, really. The joy I feel in the midst of so much promiscuity, both sexes giving themselves without love, desperately, in affliction. And me, *virgo et intacta.* I open my arms. What a marvelous day.

"If Ana Clara turns up, tell her I need the money I loaned her."

"Yenom, Lião, yenom!" I scream and raise my right arm, fist closed in the antifascist salute.

She clamps her cigarette between her teeth, closes her hand and makes an obscene gesture.

"The finger, Lião? Is that the finger?"

She marches off, and from the way she's shaking her head, I imagine she's smiling. She crosses the garden like a soldier on parade, knapsack beside her, socks falling down, let them fall!—one, two, one, two! She opens the gate sharply, heroically, a gesture of one not merely choosing his path, imagine, too prosaic, but rather assuming his very destiny. Long before she reaches the corner her socks have slipped all the way down. Oh Lord. And Mama herself furnishing transportation for the guerrilla operation. She would probably have one of those attacks if she knew.

Chapter 2

"Bunny! Hey, Bunny, are you asleep?" he asked. He shook her by the shoulders. "What's the matter with you that you don't move?"

Ana Clara made an effort to open her eyes wider. Around her left eye was smeared a charcoal-colored ring as if she had been socked. She rubbed her eyes with her knuckles and the eyeliner spread over her other eye also. Sleepily she turned toward the dense cone of smoke projected by the light of the lamp and kissed the young man's shoulder, disguising her yawn in a love-bite.

"I'm almost fainting, love. So good, Max."

"Then why do you go cold that way? Hanh? It's as if I were making it with a penguin, ever see a penguin?"

She twisted and untwisted a lock of hair around her finger.

"It's just that today I'm not too brilliant."

"I wish you'd tell me the day you are brilliant," he muttered sitting up in bed.

"Max, I love you. I love you."

With fingers bent forward clawlike he scratched his head, his sweat-shiny chest, then his head again.

"But you don't like to make love, Bunny. It's important to make love, hanh?"

"I'm kind of hung up. I need to talk to my analyst, this last treatment got me all screwed up again."

"Tell him that when you make love you close up like an oyster when somebody squeezes lemon over it. Wow, would I like to eat some oysters with white wine, nice and cold," he said stretching his arms.

"Oysters make me sick, I can't stand to look at them. Horrible things."

He searched through his pants heaped on the floor beside the armchair. From the pocket he took a pack of cigarettes and shook it until a small tissue-paper packet fell into his hand.

21

"A nice little dose for Bunny and one for me, hanh? You'll get in gear with this."

I pull the sheet up to my neck. What does he mean, get in gear. If only I could. Get in gear get in gear and climb the walls from getting in gear and if only my head would stop scratch scratch thinking those damn things. Shit, why does my head have to be my enemy? I only think thoughts that make me suffer. Why does this goddamn head hate me so much? That's what no analyst ever explained to me this head business. It only leaves me in peace when I'm high the bastard. And that dumb ass waiting for me peeling the crust off his bread with his fingernail until there's nothing left but the soft inside part, just like a rat. It's my head he's peeling scratch scratch. Bastard.

"I can't stay very long today love," I say.

He picks up the empty glasses from the floor, winks his eye and goes to the kitchen taking the glasses and the ice bucket. He opens the refrigerator. I hug the pillow. Sleep sleep. Sleep until I crack in two from sleeping without a single dream because dreams are just another pain in the ass. There are some good ones. Those. Why can't I ever sleep as long as I want to? Why is there always somebody poking at me, let's have a nice little screw, let's have some fun screwing? But what do they mean fun. I love you Max. I love you but I don't feel a thing with you or with anybody else. It's a long time since I've felt anything. Locked up. There was another word he liked to use what was it? This Hachibe. How will I feel anything with that scaly bastard when I don't with this one that I love? He's already sitting there with the bread in his hand, there's always one wanting to screw me and another one waiting for me at some table. I go from bed to table and from table to bed. Blocked now I remember blocked. "Is it only with me you're so cold?" he asked. That scaly son of a bitch. Pretentious dwarf. "It's because I'm a virgin, dear. You must excuse me but I'm a virgin and virgins can't get turned on like—." Then he looked at me in his indecent way and laughed. All dental plates. Shit it isn't just me. Even with money and everything he didn't do too well as far as teeth go. Poor childhood poor shoulders poor hair. I am five feet ten inches tall. A model. A beautiful model. What more do you want? Bastard. Shit if this head would just leave me alone for awhile. I'd like to have a pumpkin instead of a head, a great big orange pumpkin. Happy. Toasted pumpkin seeds with salt are

22

good for belly worms I can still taste them and that pukey medicine too. I don't want the seeds Ma I want the story. And so at midnight the princess turned into a pumpkin. Who told me that? Not you Ma because you didn't recount stories you only re-counted money. The little face so penniless counting and re-counting the money which was never enough for anything. "It's not enough," she would say. It wasn't enough because she was a fool who didn't charge anyone. It's not enough it's not enough she would repeat showing the money that wasn't enough rolled up in her hand. But give out enough, that she did. For my taste she gave out all too much. A whole crowd of lousy bastards asking and her giving out. The most important one was Dr. Cotton.

"Max, you there? You know what my dentist's name was? Dr. Cotton."

Max poured whiskey into his glass. He swished it around and the whitish deposit in the bottom slowly rose.

"Cotton? Dr. Cotton?"

I clutch the glass in my hand. When Lorena shakes her crystal paperweight the snow rises so lightly. It flutters softly around and then settles on the roof, the fence, and the little girl with the red cape. Then she shakes it again. "This way I have snow all year round." But why snow all year round? Where is there any snow here? She thinks snow is the most. She's sickening. I crunch the ice cube between my teeth.

"Sometimes she sleeps with Donald Duck. She's always squeezing his tummy, quack, quack. Sickening."

I push the piece of ice against the roof of my mouth with my tongue. In reality the sky is way up there without any pain. Hell starts immediately below with its roots. So many roots twining around each other. Solidarity.

"He was forever changing the cotton in people's cavities, weeks, months, years went by and there he was with the little bits of cotton in his tweezers, that's why he got to be called Dr. Cotton."

"But you have good teeth, hanh? Don't you, Bunny?"

My beautiful. My innocent love.

"Yes."

"So your Dr. Cotton was good."

Oh yes. Oh he was great. He would change the cotton while the hole got bigger and bigger. I grew up in that chair with my teeth rotting and him waiting for them to rot completely and me

23

to grow some more so he could do the bridge. A bridge for the mother and another for the daughter. Bastard. Prick. The two bridges falling down in the order they appeared on the scene. First Ma's who went to bed with him first and then. *I went walking across the bridge / It shook before my eyes / Sister the water's made of poison / He who drinks it dies.* Who drinks it dies. She used to sing to put me to sleep but in such a hurry that I would pretend I was asleep so she'd go away faster. In the movies there was always a mother singing romantically to her children who hugged their stuffed animals. Grandmothers used to tell them stories too but where my grandmother might be is something I'd like to know. I wish I had a grandmother like Mother Alix. To have a grandmother like Mother Alix is to have a kingdom.

"Can nuns be grandmothers, love? Answer me, can they?"

His back is turned toward me, he's choosing records. How gorgeous he is naked. Shit he makes me cry from love he's so beautiful. A sun. I think I first fell in love with his teeth, his teeth are perfect, there couldn't be a more perfect mouth. I love you Max. I love you but in January my sweet. In January a new life. Get my feet out of the mud. You were rich once now it's my turn may I? Next year *stop.* He's scaly but filthy rich. So.

"This is my body," he says holding the record up high. He kisses it. "This is my blood."

"I hate God," I say turning my face away.

Do I hate God or this music? This music. I hate this music hate it hate it hate it. Lorena has the same mania. A band of Negroes howling all day long, a hell of a howl. I hate Negroes. But Dr. Cotton was white. Blue eyes the bastard. That was his nickname but his real name? Dr. Hachibe said that we expel everything that was terrible and if that's the case I'll never re-member his goddamn name. But I remember his nickname. What good did it do to erase the name if the scratch scratch of the fat she-rats there in the construction site is still there, day and night scratch scratch in the dark. "But don't those fitches let anybody fleep?" yelled Téo who was toothless and pro-nounced certain letters with an *F* sound. But he would sleep. Ma too. She used to sleep real well that one. But I would lie awake thinking scratch scratch. The waiting room with the black woman, a handkerchief tied around her swollen face. The little basket of artificial flowers covered with dust. The black woman

24

and I were the most assiduous patients with our smell of Dr. Lustosa Wax, when it hurt too much we would take the cotton out and fill up the hole with this wax that spread through our mouths with the smell of heaven. Dona Inês would talk so much about heaven heaven. I only experienced it the instant the nerve quit throbbing and went to sleep, completely waxed over. I went to sleep too. The smell of this wax mixed with the smell of creosote, they're the two smells that pull me back into my childhood, the wax burning in the tooth and the creosote that came from the white can where Dr. Cotton would throw the used pieces of cotton. Another smell that mingles with them is the smell of piss. Real piss and not pee-pee, you hear Lorena? Pee-pee actually smells perfumy when uttered by your buttoned-up, peppermint-scented little mouth. Sen-Sen. "It refreshes one's breath so," she told me with her fresh breath. I chew gum to hide bad breath my gum is stronger easier ah yes I know it's not as refined. Sen-Sen is refined. It's not by accident that you always have one subtly melting in your mouth. So pee-pee ends up smelling like Sen-Sen but the construction site smelled like piss. Somebody who should have used Sen-Sen was Dr. Cotton, he smelled like old beer. To this day I can't even look at beer because he would attend me after supper, the hour reserved for the most miserable patients, and at supper naturally he would swill down his half-bottle. Son of a bitch.

"I'd like to put the drill on his teeth zzzzzzzzzzzz and drill a deep hole zzzzzzzzz and cut through his gum and through his jawbone zzzzzzzzzz."

"Hug me, Bunny, I'm cold, hug me quick because all of a sudden this is the North Pole with bears and all, I don't want him to hug me, I want you to! Bunny, it's great to be like this with you all friendly, I feel like crying it's so good. Listen to this music, listen."

So then he said he'd have to pull out the four front teeth because they were too far gone, what was the point of keeping them if they were so rotten? I started to cry and he consoled me, smoothing the napkin that he had fastened around my neck with a little chain. It was better to put in a bridge nobody would be able to tell because he'd make a perfect bridge like he had for my mother and was going to make for Téo. I dried my eyes on the napkin feeling the cold chain biting into the back of my neck, it wasn't a chain like yours Max. Or Lorena's with the lit-

25

tle golden heart. That one was dark and it held a napkin that had a spot of blood in one corner. Old hardened blood. The clasp hurt my neck, especially after he started smoothing the napkin harder as he repeated about how beautiful the bridge would be. Closer the smell of beer and closer the little eyes blue as beads behind the dirty lenses of his glasses. His icy hand and hot breath faster faster the bridge. The bridge. I closed my mouth but my olfactory memory stayed open. One's memory has a memorable sense of smell. My childhood is all made up of smells. The cold smell of cement at the construction with the warmish funeral smell in the flower shop where I used to work poking wires in the stems of flowers up to their heads because the broken ones had to hold their heads high in the baskets and wreaths. The vomit from those men's drinking sprees and the sweat and the toilets along with the smell of Dr. Cotton. Shit, all added up. I learned thousands of things from those smells, and from the anger, so much anger, everything was hard only she was easy. Her head was just for decoration. With me it's going to be different. Dif-fe-rent, I would repeat with the rats that scratch scratch chewed up my sleep in that roach-filled construction site, dif-fe-rent, dif-fe-rent, I repeated as the hand pulled the button off my blouse. Where did my button get to I said and suddenly it became so important, that button that popped off while the hand searched farther down because my breasts weren't interesting any more. Why weren't they, why? The button I repeated digging my fingernails into the plastic of the chair and closing my eyes so as not to see the cold cylinder of light winking from one corner of the ceiling what about the button? No, no it's not the button I want it's the bridge the bridge. The bridge would take me far away from my mother the men roaches bricks far far away. I'll be able to laugh again and I'll get a job during the day and study at night I'll be a manicurist because all of a sudden some man might fall in love with me while I gave him a manicure. His fingernails ripping the elastic of my panties and ripping the panties off and sticking his roachy-spidery finger into all the holes he could find there were so many there in the construction remember? The thick-shelled cockroaches were black and would stoop down just like people to get through the cracks. They were smart those roaches but I was smarter and as I knew their tricks it was easy to grab their mother by the wings and open the pan and throw her inside.

26

Here, eat your soup with the big cockroach I said crying with fear as he shook Ma by the hair and was about to shake me too, so drunk he couldn't stand up. I'm hungry he would yell breaking the furniture and Ma too because supper wasn't ready and those two tramps mother and daughter were lying around doing nothing. "The place for a whore is in the street!" he would yell. In the street and not in the room the engineer had let him use, just him. The roach opened its wings and started to swim firmly over the pieces of collard green. The soup was boiling hot and to this day I don't know how it managed to swim with such style, an Olympic breaststroke, vupt, vupt, vupt and it was almost climbing out of the pan with its wings dripping grease when I pushed it to the bottom again. It grasped the spoon and got up to the surface and clasped its hands together for the love of God I screamed no no! Why are you screaming that way little girl. Don't scream it can't be hurting that much, just be patient, a little bit more, quiet. Quiet. The soup is ready! I screamed and the drill motor turned on because the black woman with the handkerchief was already knocking on the door I didn't even see her face but I guessed it was her. There. There, I thought crying from happiness now he'll let me go because the Negress knew his wife and he was scared of his wife. He'll let me go because the soup is ready with the swollen cockroach under the collard greens. But he straightened the hair on his forehead and opening the door said very calmly that he really couldn't see her because the girl's treatment was very complicated and painful as well, hadn't she heard a scream? She should come back tomorrow because today he really wouldn't be able to attend her. He understood ah yes indeed he understood how much she was suffering because this infection really did hurt but today was impossible. She should take some of these pills look here you can have this handful free and take two now. If the pain continues, two more and then two more and so on. I heard the clasp of her purse snap to put away the handful of envelopes that he took out of the glass cupboard. Then her steps dying away. The gate opening. I wanted to hear her steps in the street and only heard his steps behind the chair. He wore rubber-soled shoes and the rubber would stick to the linoleum as if they were glued. He lowered the chair. The little chain that held the napkin pinched my neck. The drop of dried blood in one corner of the cloth. Quiet. Quiet, he repeated as he had done during the treatment. You're going to get a bridge. Don't you want a bridge?

"Quick Max, I want a drink," she asked clenching her hands into fists.

"Where's your glass? Hanh? But what's this, you don't need to cry, why are you crying? Don't, love, or I'll start to cry too."

She wiped her face on the sheet. Twined together they rolled as one body among the covers. The glass rolled and fell almost soundlessly onto the rug.

"This depression," she said disentangling herself. She propped herself up on her elbows to drink. "And that Dr. Hachibe? The ass."

It wasn't yenom he wanted, it was really money. Bastard. Group analysis. Just imagine, how could I be open with those lousy pricks? she thought rolling her hair around her finger. Either they complain about their sex life all the time or hash over their doubts, shall I become a queer? Shan't I? What the hell, who cares?

She rolled herself up, closed her hands and hid them against her breasts. Very easy to attribute everything to one's childhood, he had wide shoulders this one here. How shitty, that Dr. Batista went on a trip and that crazy doctor had to take his place, he's worse off than I am. What was he called that fetus? He looked like a fetus. A long name but short legs. Legs and all the rest. A sorry excuse for a man. Shit I got worse with him. A crazy.

"He didn't charge but then how could he?" she asked massaging the back of her neck. "After him I started treatment with an old man, so old he was falling apart and the whole time he talked about his wife who had terminal cancer and was going to die. What did I have to do with that? I went there to relax a little and I had to listen to the old man in love with his wife who was dying of cancer. I felt sorry but at the same time I got mad as hell because even for that he charged. Childhood. In reality everything becomes simpler when you discover way back there some aunt that wanted to poke her fingers in your eyes. With me they wanted to poke other things in other places but didn't I get out all by myself? So. They all stayed there in the cellar. Only me."

She stretched out on her stomach. She was taking things, right. But who could stand anything without some trips and a shrink to talk to?

"Who?" she asked staring fixedly at the pillow. "Even those

flowers with the broken stems. Didn't even they need wire? So. Life is hard to put up with. Bending under from problems. But next year, my sweetie, a new life. Do you hear me love? A new life."

Married to money she wouldn't need any more help, shit, analysis. No more problems in sight. Free. She would go back and open her canceled registration, she would be a brilliant student. The books she would read. The discoveries about herself. About others.

"Even those things that we . . . I grew rich from the experience, didn't I? A bourgeoise intellectual. Very chic. And that terrorist, still so underdeveloped. Worthless talk, my sweetie. Freedom is security. If I feel secure, I am free."

She drank from Max's glass. He was sleeping with an affable expression, his hand raised in the gesture of one who invites some visitor to come closer. With a bag of gold, you could be cured easily. Or could you? Even if she went through one or two crises, what would it matter if they took place inside a Jaguar? The hard thing was to fall apart in a public bus. And Lorena saying that it was some minor French authoress who wrote that. Why minor? Not at all. Shit, you can't be minor if you discover something like that. I agree, it's not very original. But it's like the story of the egg that nobody could make stand on end, very easy very easy, but nobody thought of it until after Galileo. Wasn't it Galileo?

She shook her friend.

"Max, answer me, isn't it better to trip out in a fancy car than in a bus on its way to the outskirts? The hoods pistol-whipping us to death inside?"

So. In December I'll get myself sewed up and in January. Waldo will make the dress. I want white. Medieval style, pearls, a string of white pearls. Enormous ones.

"Max, what time is it? Your watch, where's your watch?"

"I bought a Swiss one that has a little movie theater, I press one button and get my horoscope, press another one and get my bank balance and the day I'm going to be betrayed, neat, hanh? What a watch! The trips, Bunny! The red button is for a five-hour dose, the blue one gives you a day-long trip with transfers included, I get off the train and onto another one. And the black button, eeeh, what a button. What fear! The crazy woman in white comes with a black armband, she comes in mourning, the old bag."

29

"Who did you sell it to, answer me, Max!"

"To my grandpa."

I pound his chest but he bites my neck. Not my neck! I try to say but I'm laughing so much I can't talk all I can do is clap my hand over his mouth, and then he bites my hand. My hand is OK, but you can't bite my neck because the scaly one will see it right away what's that mark? He asks about everything, wants to know everything while he keeps eating the crust of the bread, sickening peeled that way. "I'll have dinner at Nona's house and then we can go out to Zuza's afterward." As if I would get really excited about the idea. Taking his fiancée to a joint like that. Why didn't he invite me to have dinner at Nona's house, why? Bastard. Always flaunting his family in my face.

"I don't have any family," I said. "They all died in an airplane crash. An international flight. They were coming back from Scotland where they had gone to spend Christmas with my uncles." Ah, your uncles live in Scotland? They used to. They all died when one night that lake monster rose up and swallowed my uncles and cousins and their house and all. A Scottish monster, Lorena knows its name, she knows all about these monsters. Rotten chic, to be swallowed by a monster in a Scottish lake. "There was no one left no one, no one, no one," I repeat and drink out of the glass Max hands me. I drink it all down. To the bitter end, wasn't that a movie? Where did I run across that title?

"I want to buy an island, Bunny. You know it isn't hard to buy an island? There's gobs of islands around."

And he has enough family to fill up a ship. The hell with them. The hell with them because the corset is melting there was a bitch of a corset closing off my lungs. Now I can breathe, live. Shit it's good to live. Who said that. I'm beautiful brilliant I'm going to be on ten magazine covers. Super-important magazines. Success. Leave the lousy others behind howling with envy. Miss nha-nha is right one needs to breathe deeply all the time and then you feel fine. He could have invited me the bastard. That Nona with her little leather house slippers. All the grandchildren dying to show off how rich they are and her. She could have invited me. Aren't I his fiancée? It doesn't matter next year stop. It's close.

"Dragon-fly wings in green sauce, hanh? Fabulous that restaurant. Lightning-bug sauce blinking off and on, flick, flick! Hanh?"

30

I turn into a Roman matron. Respect I want respect. That's what Mother Alix doesn't understand. A saint. I'll do everything you say my saint. A sainted grandmother. Lots of milk very good lots of milk and that medicine and I beat my breast never again, never again! We'll see about it tomorrow. If you love me.

"The saints are transparent just like water. There used to be lots of tubes of water, all different colors. At that chemical lab where I worked. I used to clean and the little old Jew who liked me would come up and give me an apron to put on and let me play with the tubes. He would explain to me about the colors blue red green. The water would change colors. The smell. I still remember the smell but this was a smell I liked because it had nothing to do with people. The little glass tubes changing color just like us. Look, love, I drink them and I turn into a rainbow, blue, yellow, ay! Don't touch me or I'll spill. I used to know a song, how did it go?"

"She taught me to dance. Madame Lamas. Mama wanted us to learn to dance because of this or because of that, Madame Lamas, that's it, my little sister and I learned everything. Fun, hanh? All day long there were little parties, a crowd of little girls and parties. We used to dance like crazy, Madame Lamas taught me, La Madame Lamas. Good manners, oh, what a nice boy, you should have seen it."

"I love you, love." I can howl with pleasure but no. Never mind.

"*I saw in a crystal window . . . upon a proud pedestal . . .* how does that go? I have a passion for that song, I get hysterical, here, come on, sing, *in a crystal window, a charming doll . . .*"

She doesn't understand because she is a saint. In reality I grow clean here with him. Cleansed from all those things, cleansed. Don't you see how happy I am? Not even when I had analysis with that Turkish guy, what was his name? It doesn't matter. I lied about everything. Good for me. Good night and we'll tell the truth. We don't at all. Dirty stories about rotten teeth I don't want I don't want.

"You're handsome, love. The handsomest man I ever saw."

"I am beautiful," he said hanging onto the bureau. He hesitated: "That music, do you hear? An angel playing. I can't listen to it because I start to cry like a fool, my eyes are already watering . . ."

31

"You're just like Michelangelo's *David*."

"Where did you see Michelangelo's *David*, where?" he asked, laughing. He grabbed the bottle from the floor. "Where, where?"

"My friend, you dummy. Loreninha has a huge poster of him. She's been all over Europe, you're not the only one, see? Dummy. She's very rich. You used to be. You're not any more, but never mind. It doesn't matter. I think it was Milan. Her brother, the diplomat. I think it was there."

He swirled the glass of whiskey with ice. He took a large gulp and dried his sparse beard with his hand.

"We're going to travel, hanh? Oh, Bunny, we're going to get all kinds of money, okay? Mama used to love to travel, so many ships. Even in hotels we used to read those books, you know the ones with maps? Hanh? Lots of maps. My little sister was there in that school so we used to travel all the time, the visiting bit." He sat down on the bed and smiled. "I used to collect post-cards."

"Lorena collects bells. Ding-a-ling-a-ling. Little bells."

"But my wee-wee is bigger than his."

"Than whose? Bigger than whose wee-wee?"

"David's isn't that the statue you were? Hanh?"

Next year my love. You were rich, you've seen everything. And me. That's just the thing. Shit, I'll become a virgin. I'll marry the scaly one, open my registration and do my course. Brilliant. At vacation time I'll travel to buy things, he said once he adores traveling. Ah what a coincidence so do I. The operation is easy Lorena will lend it to me. She's generous Lena. So. She always gets me out of the tight spots. And if I am. It would be an absolute disaster *eeeh* I said the word Lena says if you say things backwards it's good luck. Wait calm down. There's the r. Then the e. What's the next letter? The next one. Oh never mind that, enough. I am not pregnant. What I am is sober scratch scratch. My head rotten sober.

"I drink and nothing happens. Nothing. That music is crummy."

He stretched his hand toward the pile of records which leaned dangerously sideways, some of them sliding gently to the floor.

"A string quartet. True angels, hanh? You want this one, Bunny? I'm going to put it on, fabulous, *A Certain Sympathy for the Devil*, hanh?"

32

Miserable howling. God, aggressive music. I'm sick of aggression I've seen more of it than I want. Now I want presents, favors. Someday I'll buy a whole truckload of presents all silly things throw money around on silly stuff I want to be silly. She's crazy that one with her demands. And she even—. She must think I'm a whore. So what. I'll bury myself in money take my courses buy a laboratory just like that one. The colored water dripping and me green yellow blue ah I'll dye myself in an ocean. An ocean, love. I'm floating off and the green tongues of the fish are licking my feet. I laugh because the green tongues are licking me my legs no! I cry covering myself because the biggest tongue licks my abdomen and penetrates me so warm ah love. I love you. As happy as.

"We could go live someplace stupid like Ireland. Why Ireland? I don't know either, just Ireland. Hanh? There's money coming."

She opened her eyes and focused them gradually on the young man. He was smoking and smiling vaguely.

"What time is it? What time is it, Max?"

"We didn't come here to get up-tight. Throw everything to the wind, fabulous. An island."

She grabbed the cigarette from his mouth and smoked.

The shorter coat would look great with velvet slacks. She could pay for it in five installments. Ten. Bastard. Queer. He couldn't forgive her because she was beautiful and had breasts. "Flatten down that chest, flatten it!" he yelled at the showing and everybody laughed. Hatred, he was hateful because he wished he had breasts and didn't. It doesn't matter. The scaly one will give me a shipload of coats. Three factories. He'll want a virgin. So what? I'll stuff myself full of baby oil and he'll find one when we go to bed. I could model for Marcil too and he'd give me the little black suit or—. Brando will go crazy but I'll tell him give me the coat then.

"Quick, Bunny! Give me your mouth!"

I give him my mouth give him everything. But tense scratch scratch. And if I am. Lena will pay for plastic surgery but she doesn't have a bag of gold does she? I need yenom yenom Mother Alix said she'd pay. Take money from a saint and give it to the Turk, group analysis for godssake. Stupidity. Next year I start over. And I can pay for individual treatment thank you sir. Thinking I wanted to go to bed. Pretentious Turk. "I'm mar-

ried, very happily married. My wife is a geisha." Geisha geisha.
I'll bet she puts horns on him twenty-four hours a day. Well
done. It wouldn't be any good anyway because one loses respect
for them, look what happened with that dumbass. Crazier than
me that one there. Psychiatrist, shit. How could he help me?
Even a baby. You'll see, I am again. That's just it, not to feel
any pleasure and on top of it all, What day is today? The
twenty-sixth? Twenty-six, twenty-seven, twenty-eight, twenty-
nine . . . does this month have thirty-one days?

"Max, does this month have thirty-one days?"

"Come here, Bunny, I want your mouth."

I open my arms. He falls onto my chest. Yes I love you. So.
To get rich. Get rich. You were once and nha-nha was too. I'd
like to try it may I? Lena said she'd loan it to me she's sweet
Lena. Generous. She offered to come with me and hold my
hand. The scaly one wants a virgin. He's had his fun with every
whore in town but when it comes to. Bastard. All right. If you
really insist, I'll become a virgin. What if I asked him to loan me
the yenom? Why not. Doesn't a girl have the right to ask her fiancé for a little loan? I'll tell him it's for an urgent operation
and he'll ask me what operation there's nobody in the world who
can ask more questions. He'll ask me and I'll say I need to have
my tonsils out my tonsils are rotten my appendix is rotten ah
how depressing. And this one here who doesn't resolve anything.

"I'm cold, Max, cover me. Cover me, love," she said. She
shivered beneath the young man's body. "It's freezing."

He found the woolen blanket among the tangled bedclothes
and pulled it up, covering his head. The ends of the fringe
reached Ana Clara's shoulders. He closed the opening of the
tent in up-and-down movements that grew faster and faster,
reaching a sharp rhythmic pitch. He poised himself above her,
then fell downward in a series of convulsions that made the
cover slide off them in shallow folds. From underneath him
came a fragmented sob, almost a wail.

"Bunny, Bunny, I love you."

She pushed back the fringe of the blanket and turned her face
to the wall, rolling her hair around her finger.

"So good, love."

"Let's get married, Bunny? Let's? I want to get married immediately, hanh? What about it? A great idea, right, Bunny?"

"Yeah, yeah, let's."

34

He kissed Ana Clara repeatedly on the mouth, tenderly straightened her disheveled hair, and rolled off her body as if he were rolling off a sand dune. He lay down on his belly, his face buried in the pillow, one arm hanging down. His hand touched the rug, searching as cautiously as a spider, with two blind fingers stretched out like wiggling antennae. They went around the ashtray where the cigarette still burned; then, inspired, they drew back and found the glass. As he took a gulp, whiskey ran down his chin.

"*Eeeh*, Bunny, I'm all wet, quick, wipe me, I'm all wet."

"I'm the one that's wet. What time is it?"

"Have to look. You remind me of Mademoiselle Germaine after us with her little gold watch, time for this, time for that. '*Maximiliano, tu es en retard! Tu es en retard!*'"

"Did you go to bed with her?"

"She was our governess, Bunny."

"So what?"

"She was horrible looking, all bones and freckles with her hair always standing on end, look, like this," he said holding his fingers up perpendicular to his head. "The way she walked was exactly like the watch, tick, tock, tick, tock. Her hair was like this, look!"

Ana Clara was staring fixedly at the ceiling, stroking her abdomen.

"Yeah, I see. Lorena's governess was English. Nha-nha-nha-nha. She said she learned to write better in English because of the governess living on the ranch. She looks like an insect. Besides, it's all gone, isn't it? There you are. Isn't it all gone? There's no more ranch nor governess nor anything. Finished. What's left of the money Mama's boyfriend takes charge of. Good for him."

"Loads of money. I discovered something, it's easy to have either loads of money or nothing, hanh? Isn't that fabulous? *Yiiipeeeee!*"

"When she puts on those glasses she looks like an insect wearing glasses. And she doesn't even need them, it's sickening. Nha-nha-nha. You remember her? That real skinny girl. Both of them envy me because I'm beautiful, elegant. Magazine covers. So. The nha-nha buys thousands of dresses, her mother sends her bagsful of clothes. For what? She doesn't wear any of them, she only wears those slacks and nha-nha blouses. That's

35

how she talks, squeaky, nha-nha-nha. Her brother's a diplomat. He sends her thousands of things too. Does it do any good? Shit, if I only had half that wardrobe. Super-chic."

"The communist?"

"You're getting it all mixed up, the communist is the fat one from the Northeast. This is the skinny one, the intellectual type. Insect-ish."

"Are you sad, Bunny? Cheer up, love, cheer up. I really wish people would be happier, it's so good to be happy. In the street you see everybody so sad, why are people so sad? Hanh? I'd really like to go out and make people happy. 'Look here, hold my hand and come with me and I'll show you the garden of happiness with God and all, come on . . .'"

"I think I'm pregnant, you hear? Pregnant."

"Hanh?"

She put her mouth close to his ear. "Pregnant, pregnant, pregnant."

He raised his innocent eyebrows. Half of the whiskey in his glass ran down his chest. He put the glass on the floor and bent over her, reaching for her hands under the sheet. They were clenched tightly. He opened them slowly and kissed the palm of one hand, then the other.

"Let's have this baby, Bunny. Let's let him be born, let's be very happy and he'll be born happy . . ."

'Maybe it's twins."

"Fabulous, twins! we'll put them in one of those little double strollers, hanh? The two of them strolling along, we'll call the Mademoiselle and she'll come running, tick, tock, tick tock, '*et alors, mon petit choux?*' If it's a girl we'll call it Celestial Mechanics, isn't that a beautiful name? My professor of Celestial Mechanics was—Where did I learn that? I learned a whole hell of a lot of things but now I forget, tick tock, tick, tock, *et alors?*"

Ana Clara sat up on the bed, encircled her legs and rested her chin on her knees. Her green eyes squinted from the middle of the black circles. She turned sharply to Max who was trying to light a cigarette and shook him. The matches from the box spilled over him.

"Why did you have to go broke, why? Now I have to marry somebody else, you dummy. I want yenom, you know what yenom is? Lorena says that if you say things backwards it brings you luck. Now I have to. And still sober. I'm sober as a dog. I think you gave me aspirin. Why don't you give me that little medallion you have around your neck? Our kid will want that medallion, will you give it to him?"

"Mama wouldn't let me take it off, only when I want to sleep, there was a story about a baby that died because it was strangled by its little chain. . . . Ducha had one just like it."

"Your sister? The one who went crazy?"

"Don't talk like that about my little sister, don't . . ."

"But shit, isn't she in the nuthouse? So. You told me yourself."

"My Ducha, my little Duchinha. So sweet, like a little flower."

"But didn't she lose her memory, Max? You said so, Max. You told me. Am I saying anything bad? Lorena's father lost his memory too, he died in the sanatorium without remembering anything, the last time Lorena went to visit him he asked, 'Who's that girl?' Am I saying anything bad?"

He shook his head and turned over onto his belly, his face buried in the pillow, his shoulders shaken by a dry sob. He covered his ears.

"I don't want to hear about it, I don't want to!" he cried and laughed at the same time. Turning to look at the ceiling he chuckled between the tears that started to run down his face.

"One day we went to the zoo, oh! that animal, that animal that has a horn here, hanh?"

"Is she blond like you? Is she? Answer me, Max, I want to know what she's like. Your little sister."

Slowly he extended his arm in the direction of the record player. His hand opened in slow motion, one finger extended to touch something but without conviction, waiting for the something to come toward it.

"The rug."

"What rug? I'm talking about your sister, your sister! So? Is she blond like you?"

"She would only sleep with the light on, she was afraid of having bad dreams. Say your prayers, Duchinha, say your prayers and tonight you'll have good dreams, don't you want to have good dreams? Say your prayers with me, come on, *me voici, Seigneur, tout couvert de confusion et pénétré de doleur . . . douleur . . . ah . . . ah . . . ah . . . ah . . . d'avoir offensé un Dieu si bon, si aimable et si digne d'être aimé . . .*"

"Was it the Mademoiselle who taught you that prayer? Answer me! Answer or I'll throw this water on your head," she threatened grabbing the ice bucket. "Come on, wake up! Answer me!"

He tried to protect himself with his hands, blowing through the water that flooded his face. Laughing, he struggled as two ice cubes slid down from the bucket onto his chest.

"The champion, look, the champion!" he yelled making swimming motions with his arms. "Time me, Shimoto! You damn Japanese, time me right! You're cheating on the time, I can't go any faster, watch him, Mama! I'm almost fainting, I'm dead tired . . . watch him, Mama, I'm almost there!"

Drying his chest and face, she dropped the wet cigarette into the glass and lighted another.

"Did you win, Max?"

He closed his eyes. With a giggle he gestured theatrically, crooning, " '*I saw in a crystal window . . . Upon a proud . . .*' I wanted to be a goddamn singer. '*Then I saw a perfect Venus, in this doll!*' An idol. If you keep swimming like you are, you can within a year. The impressive thing was my wind."

The wavering smoke wound itself tightly about the lamp, isolating the light which fell over the quiet bed. Again, he stretched out his hand, inviting the vague someone to come closer.

"Mama's rug. The last one she made. It was green with some things on it like . . . everything sort of . . . I used to lie on it. Moss."

"Was she pretty? Your mother. Tell me, Max, was she pretty?"

He made an evasive gesture and began to cry softly. Then he blew his nose on the sheet and laughed.

"Bobbi would come running from way far away and splash! jump into the pool. He would hop on top of me barking like crazy, he wanted to save me, all the time he was wanting to save me or Duchinha, nobody's drowning, you dummy! Shimoto, tie up Bobbi because I can't practice, crazy dog!"

Pulling herself laboriously across the bed she leaned over his body and took the bottle from the floor. She shook her glass until the cigarette butt came unstuck from the bottom. On the rug, an ice cube was melting, a solitary island in the middle of a pool of water. She grabbed it, dropped it in the glass and went back to her place, crawling painfully the same way she had come.

"Everything was happy for you. Rich. But shit, when was I ever. I want only the present entering the future-past-perfect, is there such a thing as future-past-perfect? If I could just wash out the inside of my head. With a scrub brush. I'd scrub and scrub until I drew blood."

"They demolished the house, destroyed everything. Ducha said that there was nothing left, only the tree, they built a great big bitch of an apartment building on the lot. And the tree too, they were going to . . ." he murmured and began to sob again, his face in the pillow. "The jabuticaba tree. It never did anybody any harm, it just made jabuticabas, why? It was our friend, it gave us fruit. She ran away from the sanatorium and went straight to our house, everything was already demolished, all those bricks all over the ground, the doors. The doors were leaning up against a wall. I recognized the door to my room. The doors there, still standing with their handles. The locks," he sobbed, twisting his hand as if to open the nearest one. "She grabbed the tree trunk and started screaming, screaming, I wanted to scream too when I saw her hanging onto our tree that was going to be cut down, I didn't scream because if I did they'd put me in the asylum too, they put everybody in, you can't. Don't scream, Ducha, don't scream Duchinha and I wanted to scream too because it was so horrible to see everything among the bricks that way. And my door. Don't scream I said I'll give you all of them, look at this big cluster, take it, it's yours. Take it, Ducha, this bunch is ripe, here!"

He extends to me his empty-full hands, the jabuticabas rolling on top of us, "Look what a lot, hide them, hide them," he cries and we hide them under the sheet. I kiss his mouth shiny with juice which drips sweet.

"Max, give me your childhood!"

He gives me his tongue. I slide down and escape that's not it. I wanted. My head scratch scratch. That way of massaging the back of your neck is so calming, Lorena knows.

"Rub my neck, Max, start here, that massage. Harder, love. I wish I knew what time it was. I'll say I got delayed in the. He'll ask little questions. Pretentious dwarf. That pretentious dwarf. Bastard. Just some guy. Tell me, Max."

"The little Chinaman seated on a cushion he'd nod his head yes, yes. I had to climb up on the bench to get near him, does Isabel like me, Mr. Chinaman? And he'd put his finger to his

39

forehead yes, yes. Always laughing nodding yes yes. Am I going to pass school this year, Mr. Chinaman? Yes, yes, yes. Eeeh, what a sonovabitch, don't lie or I'll beat you up, tell it right! Yes yes yes, he would answer wearing his little black cap. Is Mama going to get well? Yes yes."

"Harder, love. Right here by this bone. Don't be sad because I'll give you a house with doors, a jabuticaba tree, I'll give it to you never mind. I'll have money and I'll divide it all, thousands of jabuticaba trees, nobody can cut them down, okay? There, rub harder there. . . . Shit, I'll say I was run over. Just the shock."

"That sax, Bunny! Hear it? *Uon, Uon, Uon.* Fabulous."

The hell with that saxophone. And what about the family jewels? A whole bagful of jewels, who kept them? Crazy but smart. What about the jewels. Perfect teeth, beautiful teeth. Tradition of good milk. Fruit. Loreninha used to drink goat's milk. "I used to drink milk like a little calf." She grew up to be a dwarf-insect but her teeth. I believe her, she must never have drunk anything else. This one here nursed the goat dry too.

"Tell me, Max. Talk to me, talk."

The bread is already bare. I'll tell him I went with Lorena and that's why I'm late. There to that place. I doesn't matter now go to sleep. In January my darling. Now sleep. He would.

Chapter 3

Like this it's easy to keep my mouth shut, but what if I'm put to the test some day? I hope that doesn't happen because I won't resist; if they squeeze my little finger the slightest bit I'll talk. I am the delicate type. Sensitive. Cousin to that little lizard spread out on the windowpane: Through the flesh you can see the shadow of the butterfly wing it has just swallowed. Lião knows that she can't count on me, of course, but if she invited me I'd go running right after her. Bank of Boston. Too much, to rob a bank with a name like that. I'd wear an American sailor suit with emblems and all, Lião can't even bear to look at these emblems but wouldn't that kind of detail add a special touch to the scenario? The news would come out in *Time*, isn't the bank in Boston? At least I'd love to say, "This is a holdup!" The shooting, that would be the boring part. Death, violent death. Romulo with the hole in his chest spouting blood, such a small hole that if Mama put her finger over it, eh, Mama? He didn't mean it, how could Remo guess that the Devil had hidden the bullet in the chamber of the shotgun. A shotgun almost bigger than he was. To this day I don't know how I managed to run with it, I don't know. Don't cry, little brother, don't cry, it's not anybody's fault, not anybody's. Papa removed the bullets, didn't he? But there was one that the Devil. Remo dear, it's all over. Past. But sometimes, you see, I need to remember. You galloping about on a wild donkey, disheveled, your eyes burning. You catching flies to throw into Romulo's orange juice. Hiding moths in my bed. Remo a diplomat? The eloquent voice, the gestures. The subtle expression, that's the perfect word, there couldn't be a better word to describe Remo's official expression: subtle. At parties for kings and queens, at the right-hand side. Or is it the left? Protocol. How can a person change so much? Romulo and I were the delicate ones, remember? People used to take such care of us. Like that plant, Sleepy-Mary, sleep, Mary,

41

we used to order it, and even before we touched its leaves they would close up like eyes. I was born in such violent times. Orpheus managed to charm the savage beasts with his lyre and I couldn't even charm Astronaut. True, a cat is a cat, but how I'd love to deliver my message of love and equilibrium to the world —without becoming part of it, naturally. Stay on the outside: MAINTAIN SAFE DISTANCE, says the bus belching so much smoke out its rear exhaust that I can't stay behind it. I detest driving, changing gears. Buzzing around, Annie says. Cogs slipping into place. Intrigues. Far better to stay watching the well-lighted living room of an apartment there in the distance, its inhabitants so inoffensive in their routine. They eat and I don't see what they're eating; they speak and I don't hear what they say, total harmony without sound or fury. If one approaches the slightest bit one smells odors. Hears voices. A little closer and one is no longer a spectator, one becomes a witness. Open your mouth to say "Good evening" and you pass from witness to participant. And it's no good making a face like a dissolving cloud as you shove off because by this time they've pulled the cloud inside and quickly slammed the guillotine-window. Loose ties? They become tentacles. Ah, the joy of being here all alone. Alone. Like eating a sweet cluster of grapes in secret. "*And the engine of the world, forced back, minutely re-composing . . .*" Ah, I need to memorize that. Carlos Drummond de Andrade. My poetry. My music. Occasionally (oh Lord, the occasions could be fewer) my friends. The presence-absence of M.N. Of my dead ones. Romulo, my brother. Daddy. The velvet recollection of Astronaut.

Grapes, there must still be a bunch in the refrigerator, see there? Pink ones. I wash my grapes; Mama sent an enormous crate. I distributed nearly all of them. "I abandoned my little girl in a nuns' roominghouse, in a chauffeur's room over the garage, and went to live with a man who stabs me in the back," she said to Aunt Luci on one of her days of chastisement that run from Monday through Sunday. Number one, imagine Mieux wielding a dagger, poor thing. Let me laugh. The most he can handle are those little plastic toothpicks for spearing olives. Number two, this is *no longer* the chauffeur's room. Neusa's name lies buried beneath the rose-colored ceramic tile, the faded walls of the bedroom with the obscenity written in red pencil are permanently hidden beneath the yellow-gold wallpaper; the room has become a shell. Outside things may be black but in here all is rosy-golden. "You need to have an iron constitution to tolerate this city," says Lião, who crosses it regularly in her blue sneakers. But I don't jump in the stream, nor do I want to. Classes, movies, a short time at the sports club (a closed one), a luncheonette or two, some shopping at my very special stores. The yenom comes in an envelope. There's a day for buying books and records, a day for God to visit me, oh, Lorena. At times, fear; not of the city (so remote with its people) but fear that hatches from under my bed. Imagine if I read newspapers like Lião does, she reads thousands of newspapers a day, cuts out articles. But her hair, which is already uncontrollable by nature, stands on end like Astronaut's when he used to see ghosts—there was a time when the block was haunted. Lião's eyes grow big, she stops biting her nails, "I can't explain it," she begins. And she spends two hours explaining that one must treat one's body like a horse that refuses to jump a hurdle: with a whip. Fear resides in the pupils. Astronaut's jet-black pupils invading the green like paint spilling over as far as his eyelids. Ana Clara's pupils are dilated, but for other reasons, poor thing, drugs excite the pupils with the same force as fear. Two black circles. A brilliance. The lies come brilliantly forth, she lies, oh, how she can lie. She clenches her hands and starts to lie with such fervor, she's perfected this manner of lying gratuitously, without the slightest objective. Are the nuns afraid too? Mother Alix is equilibrium in person. But what about the times when she closes the door? The lamplight. Our Lady of Fear Roominghouse. And you? I ask Jimi Hendrix who screams, hoarse already from so much screaming. I remove the record. Lião gets tigerish when she hears this music, she says it destroys all fiber. But who should I listen to? Wagner?

"I don't have Wagner, dear, will milk do?" murmured Lorena going to the small refrigerator built into the wall. Apathetically she eyed the white pitcher beneath the cold light and bit into an apple. The warm froth of the milk in the stable. Warm smell of cowshit and hay. The little apples from the orchard were sour but they had so much juice. Once Remo climbed up onto the highest branch and ripped his jeans at the knee, he would get himself dirty and torn in the same furious way he tore fruit off the trees. Or played sheriff and bandits, he was always the bandit carrying the gun that was too big for him. So big.

43

"Study?" she invited, bringing the pile of books and notes from the bookshelf and spreading them on the table. She put her glasses, her pen and the transparent plastic ruler on top of them. Squinting, she read the underlined passages through the clear plastic. She already knew that part. And the rest. She knew everything. If the strike was over and they were to have exams the next day, it would be glory. "Music absorbs chaos and orders it," she said and grew alert. Mozart. *Musicalia*. Carelessly she examined the book that Lia had returned to her with various pages marked in red, Lião had the habit (awful) of underlining what interested her not only in her own books but in other people's as well. She paused over a passage indicated by an especially vehement cross: "The Nation holds a man with a sacred bond. It is necessary to love it as one loves religion, obey it as one obeys God. It is necessary to give ourselves to it completely, turn everything over, give everything back to it. One must love it whether it is glorious or obscure, prosperous or disgraced."

Obey the nation as one obeys God? wondered Lorena, perplexed. Why had Lia marked this? She didn't believe in God, did she? And wasn't the Nation, for her, synonymous with the people? She opened the bathtub faucets and sat down on the tub's edge, her hand playing in the water. She laughed softly, remembering the day Lia had arrived with her two huge bursting suitcases and *Das Kapital* under her arm, wrapped in brown paper that showed more than it hid. "Her mother is an olive-skinned woman from Bahia married to a Dutchman," Lorena thought as soon as she saw her. It was a woman from Bahia and a German, Herr Paul, ex-Nazi who became Mr. Pô, a peaceful businessman in love with music and with Miss Dionisia, Diu to her intimates, Diu with that long drawn-out uuuu that seemed to go on forever, Diuuuuuuuuuu . . . the result was Lião. What madness, imagine, a Nazi with an eagle on his chest, *understand*, to turn up in Salvador and there, *I can't explain it*, to fall in love with young Miss Diu. The product is Lia de Melo Schultz, who packs up her *necessaire* and comes to finish her courses while living at Our Lady of Fatima Roominghouse. Half Bahia, half Berlin. Conga tennis shoes. "When my father, who is very absentminded, actually saw what Nazism was all about, he ripped off his uniform and came trotting off to Salvador." Difficult, very difficult to understand that kind of deser-

44

tion, if it weren't for the movies. In the movies hadn't Lorena seen all those actors go across the Red Sea which opened before them like two arms? Total madness, this German to flee from that faraway inferno without his uniform. And to demonstrate, moreover, his complete disdain for racial prejudice upon proudly entering an honorable and blessed local family, the Melos, whose youngest daughter Dionisia was available. Ah, Lião! From her father she inherited the Germanic vigor, the adventurous spirit capable of enduring hunger, frostbite and torture in crocodile-choked rivers. But her glorious proportions she inherited from her mother, proportions and hair like a black sun spreading its rays in all directions, what hairpins, what comb could manage to hold it in place? The sugar in her voice when she grows nostalgic also came from Bahia. Jaca-fruit compote. But Herr Karl firmly under her arm, hidden and exposed, camouflaged and exhibited, "nobody must find out this is my Bible!" Did she read it through to the end? Her German half was solidly rational but what about her Brazilian half? "I've read it," said Lorena pointing to the book. "I'm very smart even though I don't look it; if you want I can explain it to you." Then Lia laughed, the teeth of a German fanatic but the laugh itself tropical, as she tried to gather her sunburst hair into an elastic band. Which snapped, they all snap, there is no elastic in the world that could resist such an explosion.

"Afro type. There are hymn women and ballad women," thought Lorena as she took off her pajamas. Perched on the edge of the tub, she dabbled her fingertips in the water and decided, "I'm a medieval ballad." And Ana Clara? And Lia? What kind of music were they? The only way to help them was to offer them things they didn't have, introduce them to things they didn't know. Lia's surprise when she arrived in her open sandals, a straw bag hanging over her shoulder, it was only later that she bought the leather one at the big market. "Great, understand? Great," she repeated examining the bath accessories in the bathroom. She opened the jar of bath salts, sniffed them. And in the midst of her ecstasy tapped her cigarette ashes onto the floor. Pretending to straighten the bathmat, Lorena gathered up the little roll of ashes as one would a butterfly. "Would you like to take a bath? This tub is so restful," she suggested when, upon leaning over, she saw her friend's sandaled feet at close range. "Oh, may I?" asked Lia, throwing the cigarette

45

butt into the commode. I flushed it and prepared a luxurious bath for her. I offered her cologne for a body massage, she was wearing sandals but it was cold. The talcum powder. The impeccable comb. Tea with biscuits. To culminate, poetry; I read poetry well. When I looked up, she was drowsing in the armchair. Later I discovered that she doesn't like poetry or music. Even so, I turned on the record player and put on the music of her fellow Bahians: Bethania, Caetano. And if I didn't turn on the television for her it's because I simply can't bear TV. Although I'm thinking of getting one just for the sake of the old films. And the long-run ones about vampires and monsters. As Lião was leaving, she made her first ironic remark. I didn't even answer it. I may yet put up a sign in my shell: *Excuse the order, excuse the cleanliness, excuse the style and the superfluity but here resides a civilized citizen of the most civilized city in Brazil.* Will they pardon me? Ana Clara gives me an ambiguous answer and asks me to loan her some yenom. Lião doesn't answer but asks me to loan her the car. You may take it, dear. Pardon me, moreover, if I loan you a Corcel and not a jeep, everybody has to contribute what they can, *understand.* I dive into the golden bathtub with its golden salts. How startled Lião was when she got in and the water began spilling over on all sides, oh! Lião. I had calculated a bath with *my* amount of water. She begged my pardon (for the *damage*) while I saved the bathmat from the waterfall. When things settled down, she gazed smiling at the foam: "A bath like this every day would ruin anybody's backbone. I came prepared for a hard life, understand." About the masses themselves she started talking later on. I love these masses too, Lião, you needn't look at me that way. A cerebral love, I recognize, what other kind could it be? If I don't mix with them (they frighten me to death) at least I don't play the snob like Annie does. Which is natural, she must have been dirt poor. If she were already driving her famous Jaguar do you think she'd lend your group so much as a bicycle? Imagine. She'll pass us by like a transatlantic cruiser, her hipbones parting the waves. And her empty magazine-cover face, "Have we by chance met before?" A white satin turban with an emerald to match her green eyes, which are so much more beautiful than emeralds, she has beautiful eyes she's beautiful all over. Oh Lord. I could look a little less insignificant, couldn't I? Toothpick legs. Washed-out skin, look there, I bake

46

myself in the sun and it has no effect whatsoever. Fainting Magnolia. The worst of all are these poor little breasts, oh! Is this envy? No, of course not, it's a simple statement of fact. I want to see her cured, married to the millionaire although I know that when she becomes marvelously successful she'll never pardon me. I saw her through her drinking sprees, held her hand during the abortions, loaned her thousands of things, half of them never came back. And what about the pile of money I'm going to loan (give) her for the sew-up job in the southern zone? Hard to forgive me for that. "Have we by chance met before?" she'll ask, tapping her cigarette ashes on my head, she's very tall. Not personally, Highness. I'm simply a college student in recess. Aside from the Department, I go to very few places and all of them unimportant. I remember that one day there arrived at Our Lady of Fatima Roominghouse a vague student and model loaded with baggage and debts but it wasn't Your Highness, naturally. She was so mixed-up in the head that I panicked; if I let her into my life she'll create problems. She forced her way in. God knows that I tried to avoid it but now it's too late on the planet. "Getting late on the planet!" Daddy would say as he locked the door that opened onto the veranda. She opens my closets, borrows my things, uses my northern-zone sponge in the southern zone, and only doesn't make off with my books because *in reality* what she likes to read are escape-fiction romances. And Little Lulu comics. She denies it, imagine, whenever possible she goes around with a Herman Hesse or a Kafka under her arm, both from my shelf, let it be said in passing. But only to show off. As for the rest, she installed herself in my bathroom and in me. I made myself practice true acts of Christian charity in order to accept her but now I miss her when she disappears. Ana the Depressing. Depressed and depressing. The lovers. The agonies. I taught her to breathe deeply, then to walk. By taking deep breaths and walking miles, the desire to work returns: salvation through work. But did she learn the lesson? Can analysis, affairs and diamond-buckled shoes change anyone? I think everybody continues the same way to the end. Mama used to make guava dessert, take care of the garden, and embroider little hand towels. She was gling-glong. Now she has facelifts, massages, sessions with her analyst and, principally, makes love to another man. The circumstances changed. But her? Just the same. She doesn't relax with Mieux the way she

47

used to with Daddy, of course. She play-acts. But she continues dissatisfied and catastrophic. More afraid than ever of getting old, because she already is old, poor thing. Gling-glong. I want to be different when I get older, the type of old lady with no makeup and a very white blouse, my ear trumpet raised, virgins end up going deaf, Lião has a story, the orifices close up. All of them? I see Lião as a mother, very fat and very happy, smiling rather ironically at her guerrilla past, the follies of youth, the follies of youth! Ana Clara, extremely made-up and affected, lying about her age and all the rest, her hands always clenched, she's the hand-clenching variety of liar. Getting drunk in private. Oh, what I learned from her. I don't drink but I could write a thesis on alcoholism and drugs. I never had a man and yet I know the arts and blunders of making love.

"*Ni ange ni bête,*" Lorena murmured, bending her body and sliding deeper into the bathtub. She lathered her hair until it was enclosed in a thick helmet of soapsuds, then looked at her reflection in the mirror. With her fingertips she smeared the white suds downward until they reached her eyebrows. In a cap and mask like this M.N. performed operations. The yellow surgical gloves breaking the white, "Ah, how sensual!" If he could make love to her right in the operating room. She would go in on a stretcher like Ana Clara. In the background, the Seducer Angel in his immaculate robes, still immaculate. And masked. "Lena, give me your hand," Ana Clara asked. She took her hand, constrained: She knew Ana Clara's hands perspired terribly and she had a horror of sweat. A sweat as cold as the operating room, as cold as the spotlight. The doctor's eyes were cold too in the narrow space between the cap and mask. Ana Clara's white voice seemed to come filtered through layers of cotton: "One, two, three, four, five, six, ss—" The metallic struggle of the instruments tapping against each other. The weight of blood in the gauze. The ether smell dissolving into the air. *Not to be.*

"Oh Lord," groaned Lorena rolling herself up in the towel. She jumped out onto the bathmat and rubbed her feet on it to dry them. She could see her unreal reflection in the steam-covered mirror. Was she loved? No, certainly not. But she would continue loving, loving, loving, until—not until she died, no, until she came to life with love. She went to the phonograph and turned up the volume. The harsh, intractable sound grew

48

stronger. She turned the button farther and the music expanded, pushing back the furniture, the walls. Dizzy with a fit of laughter, she doubled up, ah, the desire to run naked through the door, grab people and dance with them, play at boxing, make love, eat, oh, how hungry she was!

"How hungry I am!" she yelled, pinching the felt duck perched on the bookshelf. "Quack, quack," she said along with the duck. She took a small sip of milk and sighed. It would be nice to be able to like other things, bloody steaks, soups with fish and octopi swimming between ropes of onions at volcano temperature, blop, blop, blop. Setting down her glass she dressed in a white bikini and a too-big shirt with rolled-up sleeves, and after perfuming herself with lavender and dusting her feet with talcum, she gathered onto a plate things that appealed to her appetite: an apple, a raw carrot scrupulously cleaned, some soda crackers and a triangle of cheese. She settled herself on the sun-bathed marble step, opened her napkin on her lap and set the plate to one side. Viewing the garden through the iron grillwork of the stairway she began to chew on the carrot. Would sex afford her as much pleasure as the sun? "I stay here taking the sun because I can't take the man I love," she thought chewing more energetically. And Ana Clara? The things she was taking, were they to substitute the leopard coat? The Jaguar? Suppose it were simply because she didn't know the sun, childhood, God? "Everything I had and still have; it's so sad to go looking outside for what should be within one."

A little red ant passed by about a centimeter from Lorena's foot. It was carrying a piece of leaf cut out with a certain symmetry along its undulating edges, the sail of a sailboat getting its balance during a difficult crossing. She leaned over to see it better. Now the ant had stopped to talk with another one which was coming from the opposite direction. It set its bit of leaf aside, put its hands on its head, gesticulated elaborately, looked for the leaf in panic, couldn't find it again, gave up and went back rather dizzily along the same route it had come. To what animal would Ana Clara correspond? A fox? She calculated things, lied, always wanted to be the smartest but *in reality* she was as unconscious as a grasshopper. Why did she have to go and get pregnant right before her famous marriage, why? If it were at least the fiancé's. And I'm the one who has to arrange the yenom. And go along to hold her hand when the time comes.

49

I've said more than once that intimacy is the enemy of friendship, this intimacy which exaggerates the banalities of the everyday. She heard me, agreed, and immediately afterward asked to borrow my bathing suit. To love my neighbor as I love myself, in this case, Crazy Ana. "I'm not just crazy, I'm insane," she said in one of her rare moments of good humor. "I'm going from gray moods to black." "The black sheep are the most beloved ones," I replied. "Mother Alix has a real passion for you." Then she looked at me in silence. And her eyes, which are usually shifty, met mine straight. Without a trace of irony (quite the contrary, she was very serious) she squeezed her Agnus Dei through her clothes. It should have been pinned to her bra, but as she doesn't wear a bra she pinned it to one of the bikini straps. "Mother Alix gave it to me," she said. "It's a fragment of the vestments of a nun who became a saint." I asked her what nun that was. "I don't know," she muttered as she put on her false eyelashes, an operation which demands total attention because her hands tremble awfully. She was going to a nightclub and came to borrow some perfume from me. She poured it over herself with such abandon that I had to open the window in spite of the cold night. "Cat got into my room and swept her tail over my dresser, she broke my perfume, my mirror and my bottle of eyedrops, can I take yours?" All a lie. The next day I went to see if she wanted to go to the movies. She wasn't in, but there was the bottle of perfume, the mirror and the empty eyedrop bottle. A mountain of dirty clothes rolled up under the bed. Her jewelry, real and fake, scattered everywhere. A long green satin dress hanging on the wardrobe door. The chaos of shoes escaping through the opening of the large bottom drawer. A black wig and a leather jacket on top of the chair. The makeup box dumped out onto the bed, she must have been looking for something she didn't find. On the walls, pictures of herself with a *very important person*. I was moved to see she had tacked up over the head of the bed the Chagall print that I had given her the night before, a green angel blessing a purple sinner who knelt in a patch of blue. Mother Alix's rosary was also displayed but the presence of the Seducer Angel hovered in the room. Vulgarity and beauty were mixed together in the poster shot she had had taken of herself in a skin-tight bikini and black stockings, a pose more aggressive than sensual. I called Sebastiana and gave her the bundle of clothes to wash. While you're here

50

you could give this floor a sweeping, I said, but the woman couldn't take her eyes off the poster. Ana's beauty illuminated her face; her faded countenance was renewed by the impact. "Is she an actress?" she wanted to know. "More or less," I answered and thought, If I were only half that pretty, M.N. would already have come up these stairs a hundred times. Into my shell, like the pearl in the oyster, isn't that poetic? "We need to think of another plan," he answered when I invited him to have some tea with me. Why another plan? Don't my friends always come up, both boys and girls? We study, listen to music, discuss things, what's the problem? He smiled his M.N. smile. "That's different." On account of this distinction I was somewhat consoled.

"Lorena! A letter from overseas for you! The handwriting is your brother's."

With two fingers, Lorena opened the damp curtain of hair that fell to her shoulders. She spied the nun in the garden, busy pulling out the trailing weeds that sprang up in the daisy planter with all the force of springtime. Sitting down on the top step, she leaned her forehead against the iron grillwork and swallowed her biscuit before answering.

"I'm expecting a telephone call, Sister. Didn't anyone call me?"

Sister Bula suspiciously examined the small roots she had just pulled up. She dropped them, cleaned her hands on her apron and raised her sun-creased face. Her eyes were watering abundantly. Removing her handkerchief from her pocket, she wiped them, and took advantage of the opportunity to blow her nose. Pensively she stared at the greenish snot in the handkerchief. She folded it, bent over the planter, and pulled out a larger tuft which came with a ball of dirt.

"She's ruining the planter," breathed Lorena as she folded her napkin as carefully as the nun had folded the handkerchief. On its white cloth were embroidered in red thread the initials of the Roominghouse: O. L. F. R. Cross-stitch. The letter O was the most painstakingly done. But the rather crooked L was too close to the F, which, to compensate for the defect, left the R marooned off on a pinkish aureola where the dye of the thread had run.

"Terrible weed to get out," muttered the nun, bending her

51

body backward. "His Holiness the Pope said that vice increased in the world just like this weed, we pull it out, pull it out, and before you know it it's sprouted up again."

"You do your gardening just like you embroider," I say, fingering the R so much paler than the other letters, bleeding out and vanishing in the middle of the rosy blotch. Like a fatal wound. Ah, Romulo, Romulo. The blood running down from the hole that Mama tried to stop up with the palm of her hand, his red shirt growing paler, shrinking back before the blood which was so much stronger. "What happened, my son!" she gasped and the sound of her voice was white. I answered for him and my voice too seemed to come out of a snow-filled, sunless landscape. I listened to myself as if I were another person: "Remo shot him but he didn't mean to, they were playing sheriff, they were near the tool shed and Romulo was running toward the river, I think he was going to dive in when Remo aimed and yelled stop! Romulo stumbled, grabbing his chest, and came toward us, it was an accident, they were only playing, it was an accident!" She didn't hear me. "What happened, my son!" she repeated in a whisper, sitting on the ground with his head in her lap. She made a rocking movement backwards and forwards, holding him delicately but the hand which covered the wound was tensely energetic. What if I went to get a cork? A cork. Romulo's face was transparent wax. His smile transparent, humid. His teeth paled. He smiled as if he were asking us to excuse him for dying.

I face the sun until it blinds me, no, I don't want to, not now, I was so happy thinking only about letters and suddenly they began to compose into something, so dangerous when they get together. But at bottom they are careless. Childish. A, B, H, M, O, . . . so rare X. The Z, an amnesiac king in decline, his twin brother S with all the cunning of an usurper. I put my finger on the eviscerated F that Sister Bula embroidered, letters too get stabbed in the guts, shot in the chest, socked, punctured, kicked—letters too are thrown in the ocean, in the abysses, in garbage cans and drains; they get falsified and decomposed, tortured and jailed. Some die but it doesn't matter, they come back in another form, like dead people.

"Like the dead," I say out loud and my heart becomes happy again. "Hallelujah!" I yell to Bulie. But she has already left; her hands are dirty and she must wash them at once. Were they good, the plants she was uprooting? Bad? She has taken the risk of judging and now she is afraid. She loves to garden and embroider. Mother Alix would have to be the marvel she is to permit her to take care of the yard and mark all the linen of the Roominghouse with these red initials. I roll around my finger the thread which is coming loose from one of the letters, which one? Our Lady of Fatima Roominghouse. The *of* is missing but it is understood. I bite into the last cracker and gasp, excited. That's what I've been getting at: Thousands of things are *understood*, between the lines. The omitted side. I want the truth— M.N., my love, listen, understand this, I want the truth. And you suggest reticence. Omissions.

"The open-hearted truth," I say as I face the sun. I may have a sunstroke, smoke is coming out of my ears, but I must keep thinking, woolgathering, woolgatherings done under the sun are always more logical, ah, M.N., you don't yet know the horror I have of lies. I wrote six pages on the crime of omission, I got an A in Penal Code and now you. "My wife shouldn't know, of course." Why of course? An evasive smile. Vagueness. Because she is a shrew, he should answer. All wives are shrews who long ago were fairy godmothers: When they spoke, pearls and roses would issue out of their mouths. But as time elapsed the roses became ambiguous miasmas of bad breath and belches, how can M.N. make love with a woman like that? Obese, cross-eyed, false teeth, Oh Lord, it would be glory if she wore false teeth. And ironic, worse than ironic, sarcastic. A grating voice. How does a gra-a-t-ing voice sound? Suspicious connections with owls and rooks, graaak! Aunt Luci talks that way. Mama said she used to be pretty, thousands of boyfriends and flirtations to burn, in short, she isn't pretty any more but she goes on as if she were, poor thing. Someone should tell her, but who? She's had plastic surgery even on her feet, she wears dresses the *jeunesse dorée* of her time used to wear, and makes those silly faces. She even insisted on radiating her charm on Fabrízio, we were at the movies and she began to display through the slit in her Oriental shift (she adores these shifts) a piece of knee. This particular piece had varicose veins. We got so depressed and yet she went right on, she had had plastic surgery to lift her breasts and she had to show off how great they were, ah! a fifteen-year-old. And the wretched doctors adding fuel to the fire, how about doing your earlobes next? But her voice which didn't have plastic surgery has a bitter sound, her voice shows her real age and can't hide a thing. What if M.N.'s wife is like Aunt Luci? Politely unhappy: "If you think I will give you a divorce, you are greatly mistaken, my dear." She might be the kind who says *my dear* with her jaw hardened in a particular way, Mama falls into that category, in the heat of her arguments with Mieux she says *my dear* but means the opposite. Good manners? Yes, good manners, a rich family, she studied in exclusive schools. Which doesn't mean that M.N. married out of financial interest; he used to be poor, he hinted to me he had been poor but unfortunately he did marry out of love. With the passing of time he began to discover the more serious sins of his beloved, vices characteristic of the bourgeoisie, according to Lião: avarice and pride. Greediness is another one; Lião has already proved in her research that bourgeois women in underdeveloped countries are the greediest: by thirty, they have layered waistlines and bottoms the size of the Jaraguá harbor. And so my love gradually closed himself up with his pipe and his Proust, the loneliness of a periwinkle snail, you can knock but I won't open. But he must have opened a few times. Five children. Why so many children M.N.? It's something that I really can't understand, five children. "A difficult case," said Madame Giomar the first time she dealt the cards, as the king of hearts appeared. She pointed to the queen of spades with her favorite finger and advised that he was very involved with another woman: "Look there, his wife." I looked and must have nearly fainted, because she began trying to cheer me up out of pity. She predicted thousands of marvelous men who are supposed to love me until the end of time, all of them arriving in airplanes with black briefcases, James Bond style. Marvelous men, imagine, I could only think about my forbidden king. *He has a god in him, though I do not know which god*, oh, poet, wherever you are protect this poor love of mine. I know I should ask for protection from Ogum and Iemanjá but I'm sorry, Lião, no Afro-Brazilian deities, please. I can only commune with gods and spirits of other forests, so lovely the word forest. Do we have forests? Forest here is jungle. *He has a god in him*. But he's forbidden, I understand, he is the *verboten* which at times stabs me like a stiletto. In Bahian language one might get around it but in German there is no hope, *verboten, verboten*, ah, what an unbending unrelenting language. If his wife were to die of leukemia. "I have children your age, Lorena; would you accept such an old widower for a husband?" I'd have to kneel at Lião's feet, will you be the maid of honor? "Who wants to get married any more, Lorena? Who? Only priests and prostitutes. And one or two queers, understand." I wanted to say, me, me! I would adore marrying M.N., a better idea couldn't exist, I'd love to marry him, I'm fragile, insecure. I need a full-time man. With all the papers in order, I have great faith in papers, I get that from Mama. Now she shows off the old papers but it's too late, the files aren't in the drawers, they're in her head. How she wanted to marry Mieux, how crazy she was about the idea. She went so far as to design the dress, she came to show me the pattern: "Isn't it better to get married, to normalize our situation?" I agreed with my heart sinking, Of course, of course. And I remembered my conversation with Aunt Luci that started with her telling me the origin of Mieux's nickname: At every party he used to tell the anecdote of the fellow who slept with his wife because there was no one better around at the moment, *faute de mieux, on couche avec sa femme.* And always doubling up with laughter as if he had said the funniest thing in the world. He extended the *faute de mieux* to other circumstances: he'd go to a restaurant, ask for French wine. Don't have French? Then bring a Chilean wine, *faute de mieux.* The Chilean is all gone? Then bring a domestic one, *faute de mieux.* "So he got to be Mieux," she finished up, revolted. So what, Aunt? What does it matter if he's silly? If he's what Mama wants, there's no problem. He dresses well, loves parties, he's her type. You can't demand that he be a great thinker on top of everything else. Then my aunt pulled me closer and made the mysterious face that Mama makes when there's no mystery: "That's just it. He's not at all silly, he's very sharp. I have proof that he has been investigating at the banks, he had the nerve to go to our lawyer, all with the air of wanting to protect Sister. He found out about the houses, the real estate, he found out how much the ranch was sold for and where she invested the money, he found out everything. Undisguised fortune-hunting. If your mother isn't careful, she'll end up in St. Vincent of Paula nursing asylum." So I lost my voice when Mama, all radiant smiles, came to show me her design of a full-length dress in pale pink with lace panels on the bodice and sleeves. Mine would be identical, we'd go as twins, she had seen the pictures of some celebrity's wedding and thought it would be glory for mother and daughter to go with bows in their hair and holding hands, *Let's play in the forest before Mr. Wolf comes!* And Mieux waiting at the altar, hiding his devil's tail in the tail of his frock coat. She gave up the idea *only* because she remembered that when they went to sign the papers the true difference in their ages would be known. Mieux pressuring her and Mama inventing thousands of pretexts not to get married after all, she procrastinated and pretended to be cynical, but she confided to me: "They make me sick, those old yellow papers we have to dig up at the notary public's, Brazilians have a mania for documents, such things don't exist in other parts of the world. I was never born!" We never mentioned the subject again, but one day I felt so sorry for her when I found, all folded up inside a Charles Morgan novel, the design for the wedding dresses. She loaned me this book, she wanted so much for me to read her beloved author. "I used to memorize entire passages of Morgan in my first youth," she said. She had a first, a second, and even a fourth youth. Her fury when Mieux told her one day at the top of his lungs that we are only young once. Poor thing. Since nobody ever touches the novel, it guards the letters I write to M.N. And then don't send, oh Lord. I wrote that my whole life converged in him and that from now on I would only radiate outward from him. "I want to tell you, too, that we human creatures live (or stop living) in function of the imaginings generated by our fears. We imagine consequences, censure, sufferings, that perhaps would never occur, and thus run away from what is more vital, more profound, more alive. The truth, my dear, is that life and the world always bow to our decisions. Let us not forget the scars left by death. Our fulfillment, that is what matters. Let us develop within us the forces that will make us fulfilled and true."

"Be careful of the sun, Lorena!" says Sister Priscilla.

Is it Sister Priscilla's voice? I open my eyes. Sister Priscilla coming up the steps. I advance toward her on my knees and reach for the letter she holds out to me. Her porcelain face opens in a rosy smile.

"From my brother," I say.

Her hands shade her eyes which seem to melt in the light.

"The sun is very hot, dear. Did you wash your hair?"

"And it's dry already, look there."

"Such beautiful blue skies and this girl hidden away in her

room. Mother Alix asked if you were all right, she was a little worried."

"I'm fine, Sister. The Department is on strike, I have nothing to do there. If my love telephones, I'm going out to dinner with him. Didn't anyone call?"

Her small teeth are rounded and white, a little separated. The smile of baby teeth.

"Before you go out with your boyfriend, stop by, there are honey caramels."

She has hope. I throw her a kiss. People *are* good, yes, wasn't it beautiful what she said? An unarguable point that he will phone and we will go out together. Positive thinking. I do my solar respiration through my right nostril and go back to my step. I squeeze the letter which isn't a letter, it's a postcard. I put off the moment of reading it like I used to put off eating the first mangos back on the ranch. Dear Remo. The embassy is in Tunis but his house is in Carthage, does Carthage still exist, Remo? Yes, it exists. A gorgeous suburb with gorgeous houses in the middle of the Roman ruins. "In the garden through which Salammbô walked there are jasmine trees just like the ones on the ranch," he wrote, sometimes he gets poetic. There are olive trees planted in the orchards, the olives are picked right off the trees. And the dates come in clusters. "Like the beggars," interrupted Lião when I read her the letter. "The beggars go around in clusters, like in the Northeast." I didn't even answer, what good would it do? You can't talk about anything pleasant or beautiful because Lião has to attack with the Northeast. Remo only associates with diplomats and banker friends of Bourguiba, what would he know about beggars?

"Was that the telephone?" I ask getting up. I grab the banister and lean over it. "The phone?"

The wide windows of the old house, open to the garden, were empty. On the driveways that curved around the planters, the small stones glittered like lumps of salt. Lorena's perplexed gaze searched the windows. Never had the house seemed so empty as at that moment. "But didn't I hear the telephone?" Cat came up tranquilly to Sister Bula's garden basket, touched her apron experimentally with a paw, and lay down on it. She rolled herself up forming a perfect circle. "She's catted around all she wants and now she's resting," thought Lorena, threading her fingers through the warm-damp tangle of her hair. The wind brought a few chance scraps of voices. But behind them, total, dense, was the voice of Jimi Hendrix repeating the same thing over and over on the phonograph, he's soaked in sweat and desperate but he doesn't stop, he has to tell it fast! "Listen, everyone, before I go away, quick!"

"I already know," she said picking up the plate and glass from the floor. She covered them with the napkin. In the screaming darkness of the bedroom she opened her dazzled eyes wider: Blind thus she could hear even better the silent voice repeating itself, like the record, "Why, M.N., why?"

If even Fabrízio would telephone. The four-to-six movie. A hamburger with beer, he loved beer. *Tu quoque, Fabrici?* His bearded face. His hair standing on end, his way of walking a little like a caveman, "Hi, Lorena."

It was night, and rain was pouring down in bucketfuls. He arrived all wet, laughing and shaking himself all over like a big dog who doesn't quite know where to put its paws, his boots heavy with mud, his notes dripping wet. She threatened to carry him so he wouldn't mess up the rug and in the end was carried herself, whirled in his arms about the room. "Who says you can handle me?" "You don't weigh anything, see there?" When she felt the crispness of his beard on her face, she stopped laughing and pretended to be fragile, melting between his muscular arms as she used to in her father's. The certainty that he had taken a bath recently made her tender; wasn't that the smell of lavender soap? She felt again that exciting dizziness and opened her mouth, struggling weakly against him, "Let me go, let me go!" she cried pulling his hair and thinking at the same time that they would become lovers that very night. *Lovers.* Was it that word that caused her to panic? She untangled herself. "Shall we have some tea? I know how to make delicious tea." He held her back by the hand. He had lost his air of a big happy dog; now he was serious, his eyes low. His voice low: "Sit down here, Lorena, sit here." She ran off to fill the teakettle with water, tea wouldn't take any time at all, not five minutes. It took almost an hour. First it was the electric ring that didn't want to work, I called him to help me, he studies electronics as well as law. When the coils of wires started to work, lightning struck somewhere or other and all the lights in the block went out. Thousands of nuns bringing packages of candles, screams through the neighborhood, Sister Priscilla falling down when she went to rescue Cat, who meowed dreadfully in the darkness of the garden, an umbrella—was it Bulie's? that escaped, open, and went flying off in the wind. When the lights came back on, there was a certain peace around us, the peace of things accounted for, of verification. On the roof, a modest drizzle. Peaceful. I felt that tea was really necessary in order to build a certain atmosphere of confidence, love made to conform to the tea ritual. But isn't there a one-legged demon who gets inside the teapot and blows on the water? I threw the tea in before the water boiled, not that I was nervous, imagine, but I've already said that tea isn't so good with water that has boiled. When, finally, we were face to face without tea and without words, guess who arrived. She never looked so big as on that night with her ancient raincoat and tempestuous hair. She carried under her arm the newspapers and a briefcase full of statistics, that was during her statistics phase. She sat down in her favorite place, which is the rug, asked for a whiskey and took off her water-soaked tennis shoes. I gave her a towel to dry her feet after offering her a bath, which she refused. I love to dive into a hot shower after being in the rain, ah, the sensation of well-being that talcum, perfume and dry clothes bring, I get happy to the point of tears. But Lião doesn't take a bath before or after. She was excited about the interview she'd had with two prostitutes. She talked a little about the questions in her discursive tone, and after touching lightly on the bourgeoise decadence, including the decomposition of our generation and the false morality of the older one, she tore a piece of newspaper off to line her shoes with. The sight of her gathering up her belongings that she had scattered over the rug in preparation to leave gave me such happiness that I offered her the bottle of whiskey which was still half full, take it, dear, I have more. She accepted it joyfully because there was going to be a meeting of her group and with the rain at least two must have caught cold. She was clearly in love with Miguel, he was still free, poor thing. "After the meeting I have an interview in private," she said making a suggestive face. As soon as she went down the steps in her three jumps, I went to the record player, Bach, it should be Bach. Fabrízio was smoking, serious, his arm under his head, stretched out on the floor, here only the nuns use the chairs. Then I heard footsteps. "I'll kill myself if it's Ana Clara!" And I had what people call a *wan smile* when

59

she came in in a black suit, very dignified, she spent more than two weeks that way without wearing makeup, talking for hours with Mother Alix, meditating, and drinking milk. She asked for a glassful, refused the cigarette Fabrízio offered her and sat down on the little armchair, I forgot, Annie also prefers chairs. She wanted to borrow some books, she was about to reopen her registration in the Psychology Department, she says she's in her second year but I suspect that she never finished half a semester of her first. We're having exams, I said pointing to the pile of notes that Fabrízio had left to dry near the electric ring. We have to read through all that, can you believe it? She took her glass of milk and went to the chair beside the bookshelf. She turned on the lamp, took her glasses out of her purse, every time she stops drinking she goes back to wearing glasses: "I won't bother you, I'll stay here looking at some books." And without the smallest ceremony she started unwrapping the one I had bought that morning, *God Exists, I Found Him.* Fabrízio looked at me. I turned off the record player. When we turned the last page of the notes, it was four-thirty in the morning. Ana Clara had covered herself with my shawl and was sleeping profoundly, all curled up in the chair. The rain had passed. "I'll come back tomorrow," he said without the slightest enthusiasm as he mounted his motorcycle. I closed the gate. *Tomorrow* I met M.N.

I squeeze Donald Duck, a present from Fabrízio. Quack, quack! I kiss his beak. My poor clumsy big dog, I think as I hug the duck, be faithful and guard me like that dog in the commercial (a police dog?) who guards the safe. Before Astronaut I used to like dogs better but I discovered that if dogs interest me, cats fascinate me. No, my poet, it's not death that is *clean but cruel*, it's the cat. I was coming back from the cinema with Annie (sober) when I saw that miserable little kitten abandoned on the corner. I made a bottle out of an old medicine container that Sister Bula brought; he slept on my cashmere pullover, made pee-pee and etc. in my bidet until he learned to go in the garden, even got in bed with me, but do you think he turned into a sentimental kitty-cat? Let me laugh. He would spend the day on his pillow, either sleeping or looking at me with minimal interest. Neither affections nor concessions, an Egyptian. He came inside my shell, but I didn't get inside his. One day, without word or gesture, he went out through that door and never came back.

But he will, I know he'll turn up someday all dirty and ragged. I'll bathe his wounds, nurse his illnesses and when he becomes once more a lustrous fat tomcat he'll run off again. Free, free. Who can hang onto a tomcat? Not his wife who is old or almost old, isn't the middle son my age? She must be about the age of Mama, who has already had two facelifts and is on her way to the third. Other structures, other spheres. "I am the mother of your children!" she must remind him three hundred and sixty-five hours a day. Blackmail. My love, my love, how can you allow such blackmail.

"I am destined to live alone," I say and begin to laugh. I hear this from Aunt Luci every time she ends a marriage, just before she starts another one. I put on a Maria Bethânia record, ah, how she reminds me of Lião's amenities when Lião drinks and becomes amenable. Before M.N. I thought that I couldn't live without music, but now I know I can't live without him. I'd die listening to music, hours, days, months passing by and the record going around and around for all eternity, la, la, la, la . . . one day they would discover a skeleton more fragile than skeletons generally are, dressed in a shift so tenuous that the breeze would make it fall apart with one puff. And the record player buried under the dust, the music without record or needle rotating in the tiny tummy of a mouse, li, li, li, li . . . The phone! Oh Lord, the phone.

61

Chapter 4

"There was this great big clock in the tower and I wanted to grab onto its hands, hold the hours back, why wouldn't time stop a little? I wanted to hang there, holding back time. Then Mama took me by the hand and led me to the park, everything was so green, was it in London? The musicians were playing and we were sitting in chairs, 'Listen, Max, it's Mozart. Pay attention, dearest, Mozart.' "

I discover a cookie under the pillow. I chew it slowly because it's a sugary one and I don't want to finish it right away I like sweet things so much I can eat all the sugar I want my body is super-elegant I don't gain weight. I can eat tons of sugar and nothing happens. Lião sure can't. She's on her way to obesity, a few more pounds and she can put on her macumba priestess costume. Lorena doesn't count she's an insect. Is there such a thing as an insect with a weight problem? An insect.

"The hell with Mozart, I like Chopin. Chopin and Renoir, I want sweet artists. The mouth where the mouth should be, everything where it belongs, everything happy, I'm sick of squalor. That's what I told Loreninha, she loves to listen to those crummy singers but she'll only eat English jam on her toast. A snob. Let me laugh, she says and bends backward and goes hah, hah, hah."

He releases the hands of the clock and lies down again.

"We didn't come into this world to get up-tight, that's where the problem is."

I look for more cookies but all I find is crumbs. I take the cigarette from his hand and the smoke is sugary. His kiss is cotton candy.

"Max, do you like Renoir? Renoir the painter, you like him?"

He takes the cigarette back and stretches his arm toward the ceiling. "Bosch, Hieronymus Bosch."

"Ah, all monsters, all torment. Shit, a crazy man's work. I hate crazy people."

63

Sitting on the bed, he started turning his arms propeller fashion. He gave a cry of pain when his closed fists hit each other in midair.

"I broke my hand. *Aiiyyyy*, it hurts . . ."

"Bastards. I want beautiful things, things that remind me of money. Abundance, prosperity. I adore the United States, why shouldn't I. Lião is anti-American because she's hard up, she'll never have anything, let her stay with her subversive friends, but me! The best hotel. How many stars does the best hotel in the world have?"

"He invented the spaceship, it's there in those paintings, a whole hell of a lot of spaceships before anybody had even thought of them. The one they put on the moon is a piece of shit compared. They're all flying, vvrroooooooom . . ."

"The scaly one likes to travel. Well he'll travel all right, look here who's going with him. The best hotels. Next year I'll start studying English again, I want conversation classes with that guy, what's his name. That asshole. Oxford accent."

"Winged devils, look what a mean one . . . he's grabbing that woman by the foot, yeah! Let her have it!"

"I could sleep for three days in a row," Ana Clara murmured slipping in between the young man's legs. She crawled upward until she reached his chest. "Where's your glass? I'm sober, Max. Did you give me aspirin? I'm sober, nothing has any effect, I dunno."

"Eeeeh, that real black one! He has a chamber pot, look, look quick! He can really fly, huh? Go away, go away!" he yelled shielding himself behind her. "He wants to put the pisspot on my head! . . ." he giggled.

"I've lived in a pisspot. Nothing but torment and monsters. I've had my fill of it, why should I want more? Now I want things gilded, rich, with cupids. Nice square paintings, that's what I want, I've had enough abstractionism. In reality misery is abstract. At its highest point it's abstract. Ever experience the abstract in the pit of your stomach? I want a square house, square flowers, roses, I hate exotic flowers, those that. Faces in the place. Shit, Van Gogh. Lorena has a passion for Van Gogh and that other nut. Nha-nha-nha-nha. He paints flowers like meat, you know what meat is? They bleed. Live meat rasped with a file, the blood pours out, confess, confess he would say rasping deeper with his paintbrush. Lião told how her friend was filed over that way. If they'd invited me to join their group when I was a little girl you know I would have? I really would have joined, I used to think so much about justice and stuff, I was a *very special* little girl, you hear, Lorena? But now I plan to join a different kind of group."

"Get him out of here, Bunny! Hold me."

She covered his face with a pillow, rolling a piece of hair around her finger.

"Good idea. Hell, wipe out the establishment. But if now's my chance to. Wait a little, it's my turn, okay? Next year darling a new life. I'll finish my courses and then. I want to be first in everything, you hear? With money you can learn quick, with money it's easy. I'm intelligent, right? A woman psychologist. The scaly one will buy me a high-class clinic, beggars' problems don't interest me. I'll choose the clientele. A bag of gold. So."

Max, doubled with laughter, rolled himself up in the sheets.

"There's one trying to peck at my wee-wee, look at his beak," he yelled uncovering himself. Peaceful suddenly, he closed his eyes, hid his genitals with his hands, and smiled. *"Mon chou . . ."*

Next year he'll see who's the *petit chou.* A new life, my gorgeous boy. Farewell, Ana Clara Conceição daughter of Judith Conceição but is that your last name? Cow. She looked alarmed the cow. Women are really enemies. Did any male professor ever snub me on account of that? Who cares about a name. She did. Cow. Jealous because I'm pretty. You have an incredible resistance to languages Ana! If I had a bag of gold would she have noticed any resistance? Cow. The nha-nha made the same face I know so well when she repeated my name, Ana Clara Conceição? Conceição yes ma'am. So what? Who else worries about names in this city? A wonderful city, there's no more of that now, you just have to know who has a bag of gold at home and who doesn't. If you have one, you can have Crapass as your last name and people salivate and hang a medal around your neck. The name business is finished, everything is finished. New times dearie. She likes to joke calling me by my full name, Ana Clara Conceição are you listening to me? Yes, Lorena Vaz Leme. A descendant of the first settlers. Original *bandeirantes,* old frontiersmen. They raped the Indian women and stuck hot branding irons up the Negroes' rear ends to see if they'd hidden any gold there. But they were so fantastic. Their enormous hats and their names even more enormous. Who cares about *bandeirantes* these days? I'll tear up my birth certificate with the father unknown and unregistered and then I want to see. A new birth certificate, I'll buy a new birth certificate with the father known and registered. I'll baptize my father in order to get married shall I? An emperor's name: Caius Caesar Augustus. Caius Caesar Augustus Conceição. A teacher. Or a physicist? Neat to have a physicist father. A scientist, or better yet, a university professor. Aren't there gobs of universities spread all over the place? Why can't my father be. A half-wit. She would even screw the bums in a vacant lot, she knew how to do that, what she didn't know was how to grab one of them by the hair and take him to the registrar, come on, you're her father, give her your name because you're the father. Am I going to be sentimental about her just because she's dead?

"Nothing but happiness!" he said throwing his arms wide. "If we go under they open themselves up so happily. Life is all sweet and perfumed. A fabulous peace. Joy!"

I stare at Max. He's sleeping so contentedly, holding his dick. What better thing to hold? Very handsome my love. So then. Next year you're going to see. I don't get sentimental just because she. That's what you don't understand, Mother Alix. I don't want to blame anyone, I'm not going to spend the rest of my life accusing but. I don't know. The filthy scum she used to go to bed with. Lucky she didn't like Negroes she must have had something against Negroes. I saw everything but. Jorge had that stiff hair he used a cap made out of an old nylon stocking. But he was white all the same. Like the others. "Your type is Italian. Were your ancestors Italians?" asked Lorena. The scaly one asked me the same thing. Italians no, French. Super-chic to have French ancestors. My father was a Frenchman, Jean-Pierre Lariboisière. Lariboisière? Never mind, I'll decide when the times comes, I'll put whatever name I want, I'm paying right? Conceição comes from my mother's side. After they separated I stayed with her. A loyal daughter. So. But then how. I don't know. Enough questions, don't you see my auburn hair? My skin? All authentic, one hundred percent white. Lião is awfully questionable. And even Lorena with her *bandeirantes*. I shake Max.

"You're white too, love! We have nothing to do with the poor and underdeveloped, we're white, you hear?"

66

"Such a happy morning. A sunny morning. Shake hands with the sun!" I give him my hand, which he holds and then lets go. On Jorge's hand there was a tattooed letter, was it an R? A ring with a red stone on his little finger. She called him *Joge*. The nail on his little finger longer than the others why was that? His nylon stocking to straighten his hair falling over his shoulder. He was good at interpretive dancing, he even won a trophy once on an amateur-talent show, *One Step to Glory*. Queer. He probably offered his ass to the M.C.

"Max, I'm sober, I think I must have taken aspirin. Was it aspirin?"

I search the floor for a cigarette and drink out of the bottle, swallowing until I reach the stratosphere but why this barrier of solid rock? I need to get away from things Mother Alix. I want so much to forget and I can't. At times she's right there in front of me, her expression dripping with love, telling the fat woman that Joge could dance any *moozic* to perfection, and had won a huge trophy on the program. Help me Mother Alix help me help me help me. I don't want to remember any more but I do. I know my childhood is over, everything's past and she was a. Next year I'll start over, it will all be OK and I'll be able to live as if I didn't have that background behind me. But sometimes I hear so plainly the beatings he gave her, putting the ring on his little finger to work. The icy room in the half-finished building which never seemed to get built, a good thing too because the day it did. Aldo. It was Aldo. "Aldo's so good to me," she used to say but I believe she was still thinking of Joge. "I want to go back to Recife when this damn job is over and be rid of you and your damned kid." The gray cement and gray rats powdered with lime, the limy shells of the cockroaches and in fingernails hair and mouth lime lime. It would get in the bread, in our eyes and ears, we used to have to blow on our bread and clothes to get it off. Why do you always shake things Lorena asked me. So fine, the powdery lime so white and fine. Subtle, Loreninha would say. One night I looked at Aldo with his nauseous shirt and cap made of newspaper. Lime powder on his face, in the crevices and on his eyelashes. He looked like a statue in the middle of the room. My mother had just been beaten like a dog and was lying down huddled moaning *aiee* my Jesus, *aiee* my Jesus, *aiee* my little Jesus. But little Jesus wanted to get as far away from us as he could. So I grabbed the first cockroach that went

67

past the stove and threw it inside the pot of soup. Then I stopped crying, I had been crying with hatred and that kind of crying is stimulating, my best ideas were hatched from hate. I watched the roach swim breaststroke across the lake of soup, portage the wrinkly collard-leaf island and arrive on the other shore wringing its hands and pleading to get out of the boiling pot. It even climbed up on the edge with its long wings dripping dripping and looked at me sentimentally, the way my mother was looking at me, *aiee* my Jesus, *aieee* my little Jesus. I took a spoon and pushed the roach to the bottom, no Mother Alix I don't want to lie now. Not now. I had no pity when she came to tell me she had to have another abortion because Sergio would have nothing to do with the baby, this was the Sergio era. "I want nothing to do with it," he roared kicking her hard. She howled to high heaven all day long and that night took ant poison. Dead, she was more shrunken than any ant, I never thought she was so small. She turned dark and shriveled up like an ant and the anthill was finished. The back alleys around Rua dos Guaianenses. There wasn't any lime but there were guitars and soccer. Gaúcho used to sing too. A good kicker. Or was it that other one. It doesn't matter. "He killed your little brother," she whined clutching her pregnant belly. When I went back that evening the first thing I saw was the open can on the floor. I stared at it. I didn't even cry, why should I? I didn't feel anything. Her face was against the black-spotted pillow and her body was shrunken and twisted like the ant advertised on the can label. I turned out the light and left, thinking that if I went to work tomorrow at the florists' I could bring the flowers with broken stems. *But I'm not going back to work at that florists' I hate that florists'. I don't want to any more because I hate it. Nobody will ever see me again. I'm all alone now.* A starry night with people from the tenements hanging out their windows and over walls. "Is your mother there? The soap opera's starting, isn't she coming?" asked Mina, who got pregnant every other day. She would have been thrilled with the Pill. My mother too, but at times it fails.

"Max, I'm pregnant. What will I do, what will I do, what will I do."

The little devils fly overhead and tease me and I pinch Max who doesn't even feel it doesn't even feel it. Is it a party? Forget

68

forget. I raise my head and enter the pure blue stratosphere blue I scream and slide blue to the floor velvet-wombed we should always move this way liquefied and blue along the floor, river-arms flowing and no danger whatever of falling. So much stuff on the floor look there. An ember grinds its teeth and is put out in the water but the adult grasshopper comes up and watches me with his round glasses and stretches out both hands to me, standing in front of me with his black laced-up shoes and white socks. I laugh at his shoes but he is serious, he pleads wringing his green hands, "You promised me, Ana Clara!" I kiss his shoes. Next year Mother Alix. Next year. Everything is all settled, this is just the farewell party, I'm sober am I not? We have to experience all things, go down to the bottom of the well and then take off upward like an airplane, vrooom! My fiancé has a little airplane all his own and. I'll give you a beach house I'm wild about the sea, look at it there. There was that friend of mine who was cross-eyed, remember? Adriana. See how sober I am? Adriana. She didn't know where I lived didn't know anything and thought I could be one of her group we met by chance in line for the movies and afterward had ice cream together and I intuited right away she was rich Loreninha says that a lot, I intuited. Shit, me too. I became as subtle as the rats on moonlight nights they knew the moon lit everything up and took their precautions. I invented tons of things and began to be so alert, intuition guiding me not that way! close your mouth quick now laugh. Now cry. Close your mouth Ana! I was keeping my mouth closed because the bridge was ready to come loose. And the old lady wanted to know why I was so quiet. The house was huge, right on the ocean, nobody but us could go swimming on that beach. So the old lady wanted to know. My father died in an airplane crash and my mother has cancer. She crossed herself, Dear God, how awful. How awful, she kept repeating and shaking her head and consoling me because I had started to cry. "Oh, my poor girl my poor girl." I thought it might happen just like in the story of the important lady who adopts the beautiful penniless orphan. And a nephew appears, proud and cruel at first because I'm poorly dressed but right away he falls madly in love and throws himself at me. And Dr. Cotton? I'll say it happened once when I fell down. No, not a fall, a Negro grabbed me one time when I was on a picnic in the country and tore my dress and I fainted. Dr. Hachibe knows all about it, my analyst.

69

The house on top of a cliff and the mother hating me at first because she wanted her son to marry a rich cross-eyed cousin just like Adriana. The truth Mother Alix my beloved my saint? The truth under miserable conditions looks trashy. The nha-nha has the same mania. If one of those disciples had given Pilate a sack of gold, would he have washed his hands? Never. He would have found a horse and Jesus would have escaped through the back and had a cavalry escort as far as the border to boot. "But is all this really true?" wondered the woman as she worked at her tapestry rug, she was making this rug and demanded as much perfection in her needlework as in her interrogation. Before talking I needed to think but she was stitching so fast I got tangled up in her strands of yarn. "It happened when my father was driving an Opel," I began and her needle stopped. "Opel? But didn't you say an airplane?" I started crying again to gain time. First it was the Opel and then. "But did your father have an airplane?" she asked. He was the pilot. The plane belonged to an old man who had dealings in oil. "Oil?" Yes ma'am, oil. "What was this man's name? This boss of your father's." Oh I don't know, I know he was a very important man, he had an airplane he had a yacht. Ah. "Ah," she said going back to her wretched rug. "And then?" Then the plane was smashed to pieces on the rocks, a horrible storm had come up and my father lost control, that was it. Then my mother's cancer got worse and we lost all we had and went to live with my uncle who is a famous doctor. "Doctor? What's his name?" I started to get mad, why did I have to please her? Yes ma'am a great doctor, very important Uncle Clovis. She was about to ask his last name when in came Squinty holding a shell in her hand. Clovis Sheldon, I replied without batting an eye, Clovis Sheldon. Before she could resume cross-stitch or cross-examination I shrieked and wrang my hand, "A wasp! *Eeh*, it hurts, it hurts!" Nobody returned to the subject of my unknown father or my mother either because I decided to sit down in the antechamber of death, nothing better than death to wipe out footprints like the waves erase whatever is written on the sand. The scintillating nights. Scintillating nights. Scintillating people drinking and laughing with the ocean there before them, I don't know why, when I remember that time I think of precious stones and gelatins, blue red green in the nights tinkling with glasses on the veranda. The colors of the dresses, some were as white as

70

meringues, why? Why did those people make me think of things to eat? Puddings and parfaits, as similar as helpings served from the same dish. Turned from the same mold. My mouth would water as if I were looking at a table spread for a feast, may I? No. Not yet. No cousin to fall in love with me? No married man to seduce me? Let me laugh says the nha-nha. The game was between them and the stakes were high. There was only the old woman left over, I would look at her soulfully, who knows but what she might want my company in her castle? I'd go to the ball in my rags but when the prince saw me among the half-witted princesses. In my story there was even the squinting rich friend, already getting standoffish because the comparison was inevitable. "When my sweetheart turns fifteen she's going to England for her eye operation, aren't you sweetheart?" And the Sweetheart squinting harder than ever from pure happiness her big mouth laughing laughing. I was thrilled. I agreed that of course Adriana would be a doll but inside I was somersaulting with joy because not even God operating on her would fix that face. Not one of them will be my friend Mother Alix not one. You love me but you don't count, you're a saint. In reality. How can they pardon me? Not even Loreninha who gives me presents and money and helps me put on my makeup when my hands shake, not even Lorena who washes my combs. Yenom. That superior little air I know so well. As if I were some hireling. Always referring to her family, the famous branch of *bandeirantes* with sweeping hats and boots. The lords of the earth who founded cities. And all the Negroes' asses? It's not that I don't like her, I do. But she wears my patience with her manner of being so *special*, giving advice by insinuation, complicated little hints, everything about her is complicated. Nha-nha. A wardrobe of gorgeous dresses a collection of marvelous perfumes and she wears those little-girl clothes and smells like soap. "I don't like much perfume, only a tiny drop at times." Very refined the little insect with her mini-drop of Miss Dior. In reality she means I use too much perfume, that I'm vulgar because I pour it on myself. Shit, I do pour it, so what? The other one, the leftist, smiles her left-handed smile and turns up her nose too. "I can smell your perfume all the way from my room." Working for the nation. What the hell. Who's asking her to? Sometimes she stares at me, "What's that on your arm? A needle mark?" Yes a needle mark. What about it. I'll stop when I

71

damn well please. I'm going to be on magazine covers. Marry a millionaire. You can shove it because next year. Since I'm nice maybe I'll even help you and your flea-bitten bunch, I'll help everybody. I'll give you a house for your meetings, I'll give Lorena one too, pretty soon she'll have nothing left with Mommy running through the fortune, it doesn't matter no problem. I'll take care of everything. And then I'll become truthful. "I ask God only that I might always be truthful," she said countless times naturally with the intention of. Truthful. Shit, with money I can be too. I'll turn into a regular fountain gushing truth. It's easy to tell the truth when you're rich. It's neat, famous people recalling in interviews how in their childhood they robbed garbage cans along with the rats very charming such authenticity. Courageous, aren't they? Beautiful. But you need to have four cars in the garage, caviar in the fridge and a villa God knows where for true confessions to be interesting. You have to spit dollars for the story of the rich man disguised as a beggar to be amusing, yes you do Madre Alix my saint my saint. Not just yet. When I get my structure built I'll tell everything, I won't hide it. You know what to structure means? Cover yourself with money. First I'll have myself sewed up and choose a trousseau since the scaly one likes to show me off to his beer-drinking friends. I'll find a good psychiatrist I don't want anything more to do with that Turk. Greedy bastard. I asked him if he had married for love and he answered it was a love which had lasted up to and including the present. Hell, marry for love. If I don't feel anything with this one here whom I love to distraction imagine what it'll be like with that scaly prick. I'll stuff myself full of oil and moan a lot. He's there peeling the crust off his bread, why are you so late? I was assaulted, period. The guy took me into the woods and if it hadn't been for Madre Alix's Agnus Dei medal. I'm out of money all that you gave me's gone. Ah Mother Alix Mother Alix tell me nothing bad's going to happen give me your blessing and put your hand here on my head where it's going scratch scratch, touch me and I'll forget, like when the foaming waves would wash over me.

"We're landing! Coming in to land!" yelled Max spreading his arms and falling belly-down on the pillows. "*I saw in a crystal window, upon a proud pedestal!* Eeh, Bunny, this music, I wish I could sing it all, it's a doll he falls in love with, a doll in a shop window, a bitch of a doll prettier than Venus herself, *in the*
72

bazaar of illusions, in the kingdom of Fantasy!" he sang, drowning in laughter.

The red road. I'm happy because the road is red. A dwarf just passed me, I saw him from the corner of my eye but he's disappeared. The road is red with sunshine, I walk in the sun, I'm contented because it's warm and breezy. Far in the distance I see the singer, he's coming toward me with his electric guitar before I see his face I see the guitar shimmering in the sun it's as if he had another sun hanging over his shoulder. A black man, but I like this one. I like all black people, I like everybody everybody's nice to me and I'm happy with the sun and the music he's singing as he comes down the road and the whole world is singing along with him, a crimson joy so warm have a good trip! I call and he waves at me smiling. I like him with his electric guitar that shines so brightly I have to close my eyes he's a sun! Have a good trip he says in the middle of the red light of the road and now it's far off his face his guitar. The guitar.

"Where am I? What time is it?"

My eyes burn. I rub them and sit up on the rug. What is this? Max's foot is hanging over the edge of the bed. I kiss it. My knee is wet. Whiskey? Whiskey, obviously, how could it be spit. Only if I were a crocodile. I stretch joyfully, ah that road. To talk. One needs to talk about everything, keep talking all the time, let the confession run out like one lets out piss. I need to piss, I crawl to the bathroom now I'm a creeping vine. The stool is too high I have to do it in the bathtub, lift up one leg like Lulu. The only decent thing I had the only thing that ever loved me c'mere Lulu I would call. C'mere. And he'd come running and turning himself inside-out from pure joy. Let's go for a walk Lulu! Walk. When I saw the beach I remembered him first thing. Lulu would love to run here on the beach. The ocean. In the ocean I forgot my unforgettable mother Jorge's rancid hair pomade under the stocking pulled down to his ears, was it during the Jorge period? The Dr. Cotton period, the bridge was already wiggling back and forth in my mouth but the foam would come and cover me and I could laugh without a past without pretense one wave after another and the bits of cotton drowning in the froth. In the ocean I was free because I stuck everything in a bag and tied it shut like Mila did with the kittens and threw it far out where the boats pass, my mother, the room where the men slept, the roaches, the clothes. But not Lulu, Lulu I buried

73

in a white-gold coffin nobody's going to throw my dog in the garbage come back Lulu. Come back. I'll give you a golden bone, come back and lick my hands my face ouch that hurts. It's cold I want the rug. Come on Annie come here, up on the rug I call and I obey. Don't cry I'll give you. Don't cry, come on. The bottle floating on the wave has a message inside if I just crawl a little farther. I reach out and drink the message which says. I float and the sun shines coming and going on the sea of green gems, on each wave so many emeralds. Green stones, a huge mine of jewels all green, I tear off a piece of ocean and wrap myself in it, shit I'd like to know who has a dress like mine now. Who. I'm lighted up by a spotlight focused on my womb. I slide away and the wombdoor takes me to the caverns where I penetrate myself and hide. Careful! A voice tells me and I duck my head and row bent-over because the ceiling is very low. I hear the plash plash of water slapping against the walls. The dark cracks. The bubbles of the shady creatures who stick to the leaves, the biggest one peeks at me through the undergrowth of thick live hairs. Fins. I raise the oar and hit him hard but the leeches wrap themselves around my hands and pull me to the deepest bottom let go! I bite through the threads and keep beating at them until the pain becomes unbearable. I wake up, drenched in sweat. I stare at my throbbing abdomen, clean my face on the rug. Did I have to get pregnant? Yes. Fool. Getting pregnant just the same way. But next year I'll take off like a jet there's the difference she turned into an ant but me. I'll shed this skin and grow another without the slightest blemish. I push away the bottle and laugh, all golden inside. After the sea, the milk, and I-don't-know-what-all, it won't matter. I'll say I was late because that Negro on the road who was so friendly all of a sudden turned around and grabbed me tearing my dress, look there at my torn dress. What was there about Dr. Cotton that reminded me of Negroes? His nails? His nails. Lião gets all worked up over blacks, she has a passion for them. Soccer fan. She said it was abominable to talk that way and only didn't quit speaking to me because she was my friend but if I'd kept on. I understand dearest I understand but I wonder if you'd marry one and she got hysterical of course she would and if she didn't it was because she wanted nothing to do with marriage but if someday she fell in love with a black man did I think. I did think. I do. Or I don't know. You and your whole crowd hate blacks. Worse than me. Everybody hates them. But they don't have the courage to say so and pretend to be so nice. Next year. I'll open my registration and have a brilliant academic career I'm very smart. A fashionable house on the beach I'll entertain, invite everyone, they can live there I'm not selfish I'll share it with you all. I want jewels, everything glittering.

"Jewels!" I cry shaking Max, who looks at me but goes back to sleep. "Max, I'm going to marry a scaly man but I'll never abandon you, you hear me Max? I can marry a thousand scaly guys but I'll never abandon you, never, never!"

"Go to sleep," he says and his spittle runs like a thread of honey into his beard. I kiss his hand, his chest. I kiss the little gold medallion all tangled up in its chain, what saint was it? The medallion, his neck. But I won't leave you. Wherever I go I'll take you with me and protect you. Protect you. I'll buy a beautiful house shit you can keep it. We'll do a rehabilitation treatment with milk, we'll take care of ourselves, no problem. When the scaly one gets to be a bore I'll divorce him. Half the factories and free free. I fall down on the rug and cry out in pain what did I hit my back on?

"You gave me aspirin, Max. I think it was aspirin, I'm completely sober, look."

Now he has the hiccups. Maybe his feet are cold I cover his feet he has statues' feet with the toenails cut straight across like statues have. If he were thrown naked in the middle of all my mother's bums he would stand out so sharply. He could pull a stocking over his head and use hair pomade and he wouldn't ever get rancid, ever. But to hide my mark—! The eschatological mark, Lião talks so much about eschatology there was a play we went to see and she was thrilled. She says it's a vision of the end of the world, eschatology, I don't know. Their world, mine's another one. I work so hard to make the mark disappear but do you think it. Only on the stage on the stage it's real neat for the guy to teach the ragpicker girl how to speak like a noblewoman, that guy in the tweed suit what was his name. All lies. As long as you don't have a bag of gold, good pronunciation makes no difference because Loreninha comes along and discovers. Damn her. An insect.

"Next year, Max. Next year we stop, hear? You're going to drink only milk. Enough. Believe in me, Max, never again, you hear? Max say you believe me for God's sake!"

75

"Ow, Bunny, that hurts."

"Say never again, come on, say *never again!*"

"Never again, never — hic!" he said, his whole body twitching with an especially strong spasm.

I press my mouth against his and blow until the hiccups pass. He struggles and then relaxes smiling at me or at someone in back of me I think he's seeing his mother now he makes that face when he sees his mother. I start to cry but I'm not sad what I am is stimulated like that roach that swam across the soup pot bubbling like a volcano and made it to the other side in one piece, it made it, didn't it? I'll make it to the other side too, and I'll even come back to get you. We'll have money my love and you'll give up this dangerous dirty work I'm so scared they'll catch you Max. What if they catch you. Lião said they're really tightening up their security I'm afraid.

"Wake up, Max, I'm scared, I don't want you to take risks any more, and stop selling to little kids. Help me, Mother Alix, I don't want things this way any more, I don't, you hear Max? Let's start over again, we'll practice sports, sports hour, come on, let's go," I order grabbing his ankles. "Move those legs, let's swim a little, look there, the Japanese boy timing you. Let's pedal, quick, one-two, one-two, harder! One-two!"

I kiss his feet and use them to dry my tears that won't stop falling. I started out crying softly and now I'm sobbing at the top of my lungs I hate to cry because it ruins my face which has to be in order, I bet everything on it, right? But now I have to cry, there's a wind but I howl louder, *oooooh!* I roll over in the clouds and swing down on a piece of dental floss that turns into a seesaw, there's a girl made of white porcelain on the other end when I go up she goes down. Dressed like springtime, what garden has she been visiting? She takes flowers from the basket in her lap and they have wire supporting their heads no, not those flowers! Not these, I say and she begins to sing: *I went walking along the bridge / It shook before my eyes / Sister the water's made of poison / He who drinks it dies.* But I won't drink it, not me, I already know, not me! I yell and she goes dancing off to meet her sisters who come down the lawn hand in hand. They're so white and airy in their china dresses, one saying I am Summer. Another in a hood saying. The music is made up of Lorena's bells and speaks of the joys of each season ah, I want these statues in my garden. "We are the four Sisters, the four

76

Seasons of the year!" Now the hooded one is close by me and she takes off her hood. She smiles. Her four front teeth are missing. I hide my face in the sheets but I hear the laughter of the big toothless ant with its slit for a mouth. If I could. It doesn't matter. It doesn't matter at all, says the dwarf who passes by, winking at me. I pull his beard and we roll over and over blissfully happy oh how I love you. I grab the cigarette from his hand and rise like the smoke inside the conical lampshade. Happiness is this it's to prepare yourself, calculating things step by step. And afterwards throw your crutches in the trash can. A good word, to structure.

"We'll play tennis, Max love. I always wanted to learn, remember?"

"I'm hungry," he moaned, eyes closed. "Boy, am I hungry."

She drew up her legs and rested her chin on her knees, flicking ashes on the sheet. "I want to learn to ride, too. Jumpers, I love those red coats, too much. Foxhunting, are there still foxes?" Spectacular, the control over the horse. A control of nerves. She extended a trembling hand. A detoxication treatment in a chic clinic, Lião pronounced it *detoshication*. Ana Clara chuckled. She'd take both of them to the beach house, actually she liked those two dummies a lot. Yes, she did. She held out the other hand with the cigarette. A good treatment and no more problem. In reality, what tremor could stand up to a Porsche in the garage? A Renoir in the drawing room? Eh? Were there still any Renoirs for sale?

"Max, are there any Renoirs for sale?"

She'd put an ad. Wild about ads. She laughed. Half for a joke, half to snub people. "Shock the bastards. '*South American millionairess wishes to buy Renoir painting, preferably of the demoiselles such-and-such with honey-blond hair gathering flowers in the country*.'" Bathers with pink heels, did feet exist with heels like that? Lorena says he painted the French middle class but if middle-class meant those velvets and flowers then that's the class for me.

"We didn't come to get up-tight, hanh?" he said drawing a circle with one finger in the air. "See color on reverse. Where's she going, the nut?"

Ana Clara opened her legs and ran her hands over her naked body. When they reached her abdomen she rolled them into fists and pounded herself furiously, eyes fixed on her pubis.

More expense, more problems. She let her hands fall in a last weak blow. To get pregnant by a guy who's broke. And now he's sleeping like an angel. Well, he won't be asleep for long.

"Max, wake up, I want to talk. I want to talk!"

"Be careful, Duchinha, the green ones are poisonous. She flies on the wind, so wild . . ."

When he was a little boy he used to go pick mushrooms with his sister but where? Where could there be so many mushrooms. Frogs' umbrellas. The building site was so humid they used to sprout from between the piles of lime-covered brick. The vines and weeds. And the white mushrooms remember? It was fun to shred them up in your fingers sink your nails into those velvety domes that let you tear them apart without resistance. And to step on the red ants but not on the roaches. They would crunch under your feet and the silent pasty insides would squirt out as if from a used-up tube. They were broad-chested and could swim well in a brisk crawl vupt vupt. But they shivered with fear when hunted. The white bald heads of the mushrooms would shiver too. Only the big snub-nosed ant was arrogant, its mouth a slit torn from ear to ear. It was leering leering with its big distended mouth the bastard. Thinking she could come back again, so treacherous. Sometimes it was only the size of a marble. And then suddenly in the black glass a face would start to appear, it would grow incredibly fast beneath the black turned-up nostrils.

"Shit I guess I need it. But I have to pay, everybody's already impatient, nothing but problems, who wants to hear mine? Nobody. Only Mother Alix who is a saint. 'I'm listening my child, you can tell me anything you like, it will do you good.'"

Slowly Ana Clara went back to rolling and unrolling a lock of hair around her finger. "It does do me good, it does. She's the only one who listens without thinking of money the only one. Even Kleber. Dying to get his hands on me the dirty prick. How can I respect somebody like that?"

"How can I?" she demanded pounding the mattress. Fools. All of them were dirty pricks and fools. Lighter fluid would be better because any fluid was better than. Super-expensive.

But she needed to talk. At times she was driven almost mad by the desire to talk, to tell someone about her agonies, her nightmares. And paying by check for the privilege. Pure masochism. "Because I keep talking about the things that hurt

78

me most, rubbing salt in the wounds, remembering what I did and didn't do. And paying in gold for the self-torture."

The nightmares. Some kept coming back like that one about the flowers. Enormous blossoms of all colors, opening and closing their petal-portals, come in, come in! She would dive to the bottom of the stem which got narrower like a tunnel, and there a liquorous river flowed. She would drink the river until coming to a red cherry speared on a toothpick, which she would bite and then double over in pain, bleeding red liqueur. Then she'd pull out the piece of wire, it was her heart speared on a piece of wire. "I ate my heart," she would discover in amazement. "There, fine, now it won't hurt any more." But then the whole glass would overflow with red cherries, thousands of them, multiplying, speared on the ends of wires. "My sacred Heart of Jesus. My Heart of Jesus." Wasn't it my mother praying? She used to pray to die. "Take me, dear Heart of Jesus, take me. Or take him." She was taken. Because Jorge lived on in the best of health. Was it Jorge or Bingo? Or it could have been Aldo. Or the old harelip, at the the time I didn't know what a harelip was. He used to sell the lottery tickets printed with animals for numbers. The colored picture was in a frame that had no glass. What glass could contain that dark red heart skewered on the dripping thorns? "She was taken. All the others were left. Or did they die too? Who knows, it doesn't make any difference." The old harelip had a name tattooed on his chest.

"I want something to eat, Bunny."

"Okay, so sleep."

The needle rose quivering and hovered over the record. From the street came a vague wave of sounds, filtered pastily through the closed venetian blinds. When the needle settled once again on the disc, Ana Clara relaxed from her tense position: She hated that music but even so it was better than listening to herself. She turned her listless gaze to the lamp. The cone of light penetrated the thick smoke. Around it, the shadows were lengthened by the light gray curtain hung to cover an entire wall, a satiny metallic canvas stoically defending the privacy of the room. Max fumbled among the sheets.

"You there, Bunny?"

We used to shake everything and the dust would settle to cover it again, we'd shake clothes, hair, broom and food. Ready to move in next September. Ten apartments per floor, details available from the watchman in the basement. Lime and cement and the cold smell. She had nightmares too, little pinhead shaking out the dish towel and saying she had been dreaming so peacefully, "I was walking along and all of a sudden I fell into a barrel of soft cement, and went sinking down and it got into my ears my mouth. And then Ana all of a sudden it wasn't cement any more it was even worse it was a septic tank. A septic tank. I woke up and had to wash myself like crazy to get rid of the stink." Adamastor. That one was Adamastor. His dry hands hammering in the nails. Carrying the boards mixing cement. He would press one brick on top of the other and it would ooze out escaping through the crack.

"I have to go. He's there with his bread all peeled waiting for me."

"Who?"

"That guy. He's already torn up a whole loaf of bread, he loves to sit and peel the crust off the bread. He's a Corinthian fan too. Him and Lião. What are Corinthians? Lorena asked, she doesn't even know what soccer is—let alone the teams. Have you ever tried to explain soccer to the goddess Diana? So. I can't stand it either, nothing but blacks. But I know who the Corinthians are. Their colors are black and white, like Lião, black and white combined. He's waiting for me there at the table. My fiancé."

"You have a fiancé, Bunny?"

"Yeah. He's a pain in the ass but he has yenom."

"Is he as handsome as me?"

"He's a dwarf. His body is all covered with scales, the scales start here on his belly and go upward, and when they get here, under his armpits, see—?" she continued, her hands advancing. "Here, see? here there's lots of scales."

He shook with giggles. Together they rolled over, laughing.

"There was a story about Death that climbed up on an old fisherman's back and never got off again, the fisherman had to be his horse," Max remembered, lightly caressing her nipple.

"And then what?"

"That's it. The cook we used to have knew so many stories. Come on, Bunny, come with me and I'll show you a diamond the color of your hair, I'll show you gardens, temples! I'll show you the sun and my house painted all white, I'll take you to Afghanistan, come on. The prices there are ridiculous. I'll buy you coconut palms, camels. Want a camel, Bunny? I'll give you one, you can go for rides on it, hanh?"

"You said you rode on a swan once, remember? Remember, Max? You said you rode on a swan once, what swan was that? Huh? Answer, tell me what swan. Answer or I'll punch you."

"I rode a pig."

She made a fist and hit him on the chin. A drop of blood ran from his lip and lost itself in his beard. When he touched his chin and saw the blood, he turned over on his chest, shoulders heaving with sobs.

"You broke my tooth! You broke my tooth!"

"I did not, liar!"

"You did too!"

Balanced on her knees, she pulled him by the hair in order to see his face, which he hid in his hands:

"Max, stop it. Open your mouth, come on, open that mouth!"

Leaning on his elbows, he shook his head, jaw clamped, eyes shut. He growled in refusal, unh-unh, but couldn't resist being tickled. She bent over him.

"You dummy. You scared me, you dummy. Next time you scare me that way, I really will break your tooth, you hear?" Using a corner of the sheet she cleaned his lip. "Does it hurt, love? I swear if I really had broken one of your teeth I just don't know. You can hit me, come on, here, right here!" She turned her stomach toward him. Placing his thumbs together he opened his hands like wings and placed them on her body.

"The moon. I land softly on the moon."

"I'm pregnant."

"Pregnant? A baby, Bunny? Ah, I want this baby. Give him to me, for God's sake, give him to me. I want this baby, hanh? He said he wants to be born, I just now heard his little voice, he's so happy, I want to be born, he said. We'll get rich. I'll buy an island, it's really easy to buy an island in Brazil. There's so much land . . ."

"Why don't you join the Mafia? You could give me a yacht. A helicopter. I could go buzzing around . . ."

"Let's sail around the world, Bunny. Fabulous guests . . ."

"Is Jackie coming?" I ask and he stares at me, innocent. "Jackie Onassis, stupid. She coming? Shit, Mrs. Onassis."

He frowned and gave a long sigh.

81

"We were lovers. She's very hairy, she has hair even on her chest," he confided, pulling me closer by the hand to divulge more secrets. "I discovered something impressive, she has six toes on each foot."

I want to laugh but then I remember. What will I say? By this time he's already peeled ten loaves of bread and is breaking the toothpick he used to clean his teeth into a thousand little pieces. His eyes have turned to ice cubes. I'll have to tell him a really good story. My rich old aunt arrived with my big-busted cousins and forbade me to go out from pure caprice. The oldest and horridest one acting snotty, "Mama, Mama, my cousin is prettier than me, *waanh, waanh!*" They covered my head with so much garbage that when the messenger came, the one with the cornet, all he could see on the hearth was a mound of ashes. "Besides your moustached daughters, is there no other damsel in your palace who could be the owner of this slipper?" Then the aunt pushed her daughters forward. "None, good sir. In reality we only have a bastard ragpicker in the kitchen but obviously she could never wear such finery. Come on, my treasures, cut off your toes and the slipper will fit you perfectly!"

"What time is it? The time, I have to know the time."

"My heart is so full of happiness, so-o-o full . . ."

I'll go without any makeup I'll be ready in ten minutes. Fine. He thinks no makeup is great. The natural look. "Unadorned beauty," Lorena says. Everything has to be unadorned and pure with her, she has a mania for purity OK OK, I'll go unadorned. I'll come in and he'll look at his watch. But isn't your watch fast dear? He doesn't even answer me he just keeps tapping the watch face with his fingernail, he has sickening fingernails with cuticle invading them all. Freckles on his fingers. A mess. "My watch is never fast." Soul of a watchmaker he must have been born in Switzerland. He takes advantage and winds it, *rrk, rrk.* "Where were you?" Well, what happened was, I ate some meat pies in the roominghouse and ended up in the emergency ward, a monstrous case of food poisoning, I almost died. He'll want to know which emergency ward. What medicine I took. Who attended me. Details, little details. Come on. All of them.

"A pain in the ass," mumbled Ana, sliding off the bed. She turned on the light in the bathroom and shrank back from the mirror. She blinked dizzily and turned her frenzied eyes away from her reflection, burying her hands in her hair.

Chapter 5

They answered. Nobody at the window to call me? Nobody. "Sorry, wrong number," says the opaque voice, all wrong-number voices become opaque. Just think, if Lião would write in an opaque tone like that. She's far too clear, the experts want obscurity in the language, a certain fog subtly confusing the silhouette of the words. Screens between the lines garnishing (I love that word, *garnishing*) the mystery of the letters. And the unmysterious letters busily coupling with the Devil. Is there orgasm? The Devil comes and goes by crooked routes, braiding the hair of his lovers up in inextricable knots. Who will come braid mine? Oh Lord. She said she tore it all up. It's probably better, poor thing. Nobody will ever read that the *entire* city smelled of peaches. The phone again? Some terrorist asking for her. Some fiancé asking for Crazy Annie, it's impressive the way Annie collects fiancés. Before this one she's already had at least three. Fiancés and debts, she opens accounts in all the boutiques, piles of dresses. Pounds of costume jewelry. An obsession for covering herself with things that look nice in shop windows and magazines. And she doesn't need any of them with that marvelous face. She could dress like the Greek women, a light tunic and nothing more.

"Nothing," murmured Lorena taking a long amber necklace from the bookcase. She put it around her neck; it came down almost as far as her knees. She wound up the music box and looked at the print on the cover: Dante and Beatrice on the bridge. He was moving away a bit to let her pass, his eyes afire, his right hand clutching his heart. "I am Beatrice, blessed and beautiful, trailing my gown of purple." On the bridge, no longer Dante but M.N. wrinkled and rent asunder with love, "Lorena!" She glimpsed in the corner of the mirror the small surprise snapshot that Sister Clotilde had taken of them in front of the gate: She was between Ana Clara and Lia, all three laughing a sunburned laugh. "Don't squint, Ana Clara, and Lorena, stop making faces, you're making a face!" A pyramid. The poet H.H. had described it: *"Inside the prism, the base, the vertex of its three continuous pyramids,"* she recited, lowering her eyes to her own reflected image.

If she were a couple of pounds lighter she would look the same age as the young Beatrice, about nine and a half. And M.N. with his wife whose hips and breasts overflowed his hands. "Shrew. Witch," she whispered closing her eyes. She shook her head, thinking "polluted little mind," and ran to the drawer where she kept the incense, nothing like a little Jaipur Rose to purify the atmosphere. "I'm giddy, silly." But if M.N. would take her more seriously? Incredible, but when others took us seriously we became serious ourselves. She took a deep breath of rose-perfumed smoke. "An ancient perfume. Wakes. Death could be just that, incense and music. Jazz, it's jazz that combines with death in a state of hopelessness and sin. She went to the record player and turned up the volume, which kicked her ears like a wild horse. "I can't explain it," Lião would say if she came in right now. And she would spend twenty minutes explaining why this kind of music destroys character. But what does she want me to listen to? *L'International?* She was probably singing it full blast right now along with some terrorist group, *groupons-nous et demain . . . Demain.* Tomorrow, the weather forecasters had announced, would be 102 degrees in the shade with thunder late in the afternoon. To band together was to conspire and perspire. She had a revulsion for sweat. She might be hollow sometimes, but would politics fill the gap? She really didn't believe in communism or in anything like that, and there was no point in pretending to, as most people did. She hated the game of make-believe. "If I hardly have time and energy to take care of myself, imagine." A tiny garden with three or four plants, closed in by walls on all sides. And then the extra jobs, like dusting the books which Sebastiana hadn't dusted. There's more dust lately, according to Bulie, the dust of the living and the dust of the dead. The color of the cloth changes, yellow for the living and purple for the dead, I saw the driver of a funeral hearse dusting off a coffin with a piece of royal-purple flannel; the coffin must have traveled a long way. The family was waiting, and he dusting and re-dusting the lid of the coffin. The Moon-Eyed Demon probably dresses in black but Death
84

wears royal purple. With a gold-lamé rose tucked in his wig, ah, M.N., when I looked through the glass door and saw you pass by all in white, with gloves and mask, I almost fainted. Too much, that part when he approaches the table, silent and camouflaged. The field of a hysterical battle of lights, machines. The instruments. Thousands of preparations, is everything ready? And Death, smiling, with his gilded rose and his arms crossed.

"You traitor," whispered Lorena examining the little hole in the spine of the book. She opened it and blew at the hole, which undulated inward through the pages. "Now where? Where?" she asked herself and closed her eyes, no, it wasn't Romulo she was thinking about, it was the bookworm. Subtle creatures, bookworms. Labyrinths, galleries.

She turned toward the calendar which hung on the wall, a long silk banner with the months printed on it. This was the Solar Year. "Never has the sun been so close," she thought throwing the window open. A good time for making love, but not for revolution because very hot weather in underdeveloped places made one limp. Took the starch out of the fiber. "Lião understands that perfectly, the hotter the Third World is, the Thirder it gets."

"Nothing?" screamed Lorena, making a pantomime gesture to Sister Priscilla who appeared in the window of the house. The nun opened her arms and returned the code, like a sailor signaling from the bridge of a ship. "Nothing." She concluded the message by clasping her hands to her chest in an expression of regret. With a pallid wave Lorena thanked her and bit on the largest bead of the amber necklace. "If he hasn't called by this time then he isn't going to." Better to think about the day's routine: bath, exercises. The right order would be to do exercises beforehand but she must have low blood pressure, she needed hot water for the initial stimulus, however short-lived. Oh Lord. Lunch with her mother, how would she find her? Terrible, naturally. Mustn't forget to ask for the car keys, every other day Lia wanted to borrow the car, luckily her mother was totally absent-minded, she never remembered she had just loaned it to her. "May God prevent Lião from getting machine-gunned inside it." The university. Fabrízio must be there stirring up the student strike. She might grab him to go to the movies, Greta Garbo festival, eeeh, how she adored that woman. The suffering and pleasure of knowing exactly how to portray the eternal woman, she who was ephemeral. "Lorena, the Brief," she thought frowning. But the neurotic little poetess must be freed from her hang-ups by now. "Ah, my friend, love a prostitute but not a neurotic, because the former may turn into a saint, but the latter—!" To mount behind him on the motorcycle and clutch him around the waist, smelling the leather of his jacket, the man-animal trembling in the wind, "Want to go, Fabrízio? My allowance is untouched, we'll dine like princes, Portuguese codfish and fado music." She would cry buckets, thinking the whole time of M.N., who in turn would be thinking about his oldest son with acute existential doubts, he has five children.

She twisted the necklace around her head, looping it until it became a diadem of beads about her eyebrows. If one of the nuns went to the drugstore, she would send for some hand cream and Modess, Lião had finished off the supply. The two of them used up everything, all the stock of paints and varnishes, and never replaced anything: soap, dental floss, cotton, etc. "and then when I need something I don't have it. And neither do they." Nail-polish remover was a perfect example, Ana borrowed the full bottle and it came back with two drops in the bottom. Ether too? What madness. She'd have to do something. But what? Was to be understanding also to be convenient? A rigorous treatment might help Ana Clara. But did she want to be treated? "She only thinks of her sew-up job and her rich executive. Plastic surgery of the vagina."

"My best angle," she muttered turning her profile. The necklace was slipping down over her eyes. She hooked it over her ears. The social structure. According to Lia, all responsibility lay with the social structure, she had delivered a one-woman seminar on this structure. "I see dear, I see. I agree completely. But what about Ana Clara?" Outside the context of structures was the perplexed piety of Mother Alix. "And this fiancé? Isn't he going to take any measures either?" Lorena wondered. There was Annie duly classified in the kingdom of words and in the Kingdom of God, was that enough? "I'm in control, I'll stop when I want to," she retorted. Imagine. The reins had slipped from her hands ages ago. She had opened them to let go. But was anyone in control of things? Lia herself, who was always climbing stumps to deliver her speeches, was she still holding those reins? "She lost her lover, flunked her courses because she cut so often, messed everything up. "She doesn't even take baths any more. And in this heat, too," Lorena thought, reminding herself to buy a deodorant. She found it depressing to resort to deodorant, what really worked was soap and water. "But if she doesn't have time, see." She lay down on her back on the rug. "I see, Lia de Melo Schultz, I understand, Ana Clara Conceição. I understand everything because I'm overflowing with love, Lord Jesus, save my friends. Save my mother who is so gling-glong. My poor brother with his cars, his women and his guilt, you sit at the right hand of the Father, but do you ever forget? Save my brother and same M.N. in his fouled-up marriage, if it will make him happy, oh Lord. Don't let Fabrízio get mixed up with the poetess, don't let him wreck his motorcycle, save everybody, peaceful and delirious, hangmen and hanged. Save my cat.

Dominus vobiscum. Et cum spiritu tuo. Ite, missa est—I recite, opening my hands palms up. Two salvers empty to receive grace. Which one day is-to-come. Jesus, I love You. Oh and I almost forgot, save Lião's friends, they're in prison or soon will be, save these children so strong and yet so fragile, we're all so very fragile. I go to the Kleenex box and dry my eyes.

"Lorena!"

The girl crawled on all fours to the bed and lay down. Placing her arms along her body, she raised her legs straight up, toes pointed. Then she brought her legs farther forward, hips supported by her hands. When her feet touched her head with its hair spread fanlike on the mattress, she freed her hands and slapped herself on the buttocks.

"They could be bigger. Incredible the way men like women with big asses."

"Lorena, are you there?"

Did she bring a key? No, she didn't. Sister Bula has medicine labels and handkerchiefs in her pockets, not keys. By now she must have put her good ear to the door, wanting to know who I'm talking to, some man? Curiosity and fear. Courage, dear sister, courage! The eyes of an aged rabbit watering into the hanky-bedsheet. I somersault backwards and land on the big cushion which I embrace with all the strength I don't have. Then she decides to knock. The little raps seem to be part of a code, in an old movie I once saw a lustrous gangster knock that way on the don's door, the fingernails (in all probability varnished) scratching with utmost subtlety.

"Come in!" I yell. She comes in apologetically, she always enters a room with this air of asking pardon for merely occupying space. She announces that she can't stay but installs herself and stays five hours. Sniffing the roses in the mug, she makes a rapturous face, ah, delightful! Then stops in front of the Chagall print.

"You know I'm starting to like this picture of yours? It's strange," she says hiding her hands in the sleeves of her habit. "A horse with a veil and a garland. Hmmm . . . "

It's the hundredth time she's made this comment and naturally she will add that the blue is pretty.

"It's a wedding, sister."

"I know, but that mermaid . . . isn't that a mermaid?"

"At a wedding you have to have one of everything."

"The blue is pretty."

I lift my legs toward the ceiling until my feet touch the light fixture.

"Look, Sister Bula, candle position. The wind blows and the flame bends backward, farther backward, see? I can do it better on the floor."

"All the blood will rush to your head, child. It could cause a hemorrhage."

"It's great for the circulation."

"It must be good for hemorrhoids," she murmured nostalgically, sighing. "Old age is a disease, child. Everything aches. Some parts worse than others. God knows what He does, praise be to God."

"Amen."

"From my room I could see that you got up so early. I thought you might need something."

"I need to be alone."

"Hmm?"

"And some more meat right here, a smaller bottom couldn't exist. In sport clothes it doesn't matter so much, but in a long dress, just picture it!"

She doesn't hear me. Her eyes are membranous, the eyes of those fish in the still life that used to hang in our living room at the ranch house. Cooking pots, fish and rabbits, all dead. A braided rope of onions hung from the table and only the golden braid had a certain shine to it. "Juliet's braid," Daddy used to say.

"Such insomnia, child. I don't like the night, only the daytime. I like the sun so much. I wish I could live in a place where there was only sun. A place without night, without pain."

With the tip of my toe I make the lantern fixture swing back and forth. If I could just stick my foot inside as far as the light bulb.

"It would be glory."

"I'd like to live in a place where there was no death, where nobody got upset," she said, smiling as if she had just discovered such a place.

Now she is examining her wrinkled nails, invaded almost to their tips by cuticle so dry it splits and shreds at the corners. She blots her watery eyes on the handkerchief. She wants to be eternal. Little Sister Eternity.

"But a place like that *is* death."

"Breath?"

Let me laugh, ha ha. I think it was this sly creature who wrote the anonymous letter with thousands of denunciations. Lião a communist and manufacturer of bombs; Crazy Annie, a drug addict rapidly turning into a prostitute; I, an indolent amoral parasite living off my dissolute mother, a wicked old corrupter of young men. ("What can one expect from a girl who has a mother like that?") She has more bitterness toward Mama than toward me: "An unscrupulous woman who hospitalized her mentally incompetent husband and went to burn up his money with a lover who could be her grandson." Which isn't true, Mieux isn't that young, eeeh, if Mama ever found out. And that other letter denouncing Sister Clotilde as being Sister Priscilla's lover, very murky waters. Ana went in to talk to Madre Alix and saw the letter on the table. Provided she wasn't lying, the letter demanded drastic measures to put a stop to such a terrible abomination. And Mother Alix? Tranquil. She would never allow herself to be sucked into such a whirlwind.

"Isn't there a recipe for curing insomnia in your notebook?"

"Dozens, child. But they're bad for my liver."

Then keep on composing your marvelous letters, dearie. One for the manager of the supermarket, another for the amusing ladies in the two-story blue house, yet another for the breadman, the milkman, thousands of anonymous letters in the inspired hours of insomnia, her eyes dripping, the callus on her finger growing larger, though the finger itself is retracted out of

89

remorse or fear. Ceaselessly producing letter after letter, her handwriting disguised, her style disguised, begone, Satan! And Satan seated on his rolled-up tail, licking the stamps. There exists the principal Devil, king of all the rest. The others are lesser demons, collaborators in the secondary work involving two-bit sins. These are the ones which occupy themselves with me. "It is necessary to believe in the reality of the Devil!" said the Pope. But Your Holiness, I don't believe in anything else! In olden times they lived in the deserts, rolling about under the sun, rubbing the scalding sand over themselves, and riding on camels, but now the ideal dwelling place is the human body. Never before have so many demons sported in so many bodies, which like the desert are hot and have the advantage of being soft. Their favorite spot is the womb, or rather, all the southern zone with ramifications in the privates. I clasp my own. When M.N. enters they'll come bounding out. Exorcism through love.

"*That which we think is reflected in three mirrors of the absurd*—" I read in the poetry book which I open at random, I consult poetry the way Daddy used to consult the Old Testament, always at random. *Three mirrors of the absurd.* This one is mine. And the other two? If M.N. doesn't make love with me urgently—I'll turn into a book!

"You speak so softly, Lorena. What?"

Oh dear Jesus, why doesn't she use one of those marvelous contraptions. There's a little gray wire that comes out of the button in the ear and runs as far as the street like a plastic-coated antenna, it makes things so much easier. Mama described the crime in detail, she probably has an album of cut-out police articles just like Bulie here has an album of medicine labels: The old pederast who was strangled by his young boyfriend with the cord from his hearing aid, listening to Death approach over the battery-powered wire, croaking hoarsely, what are you doing, love? And his love pulling the knot tighter.

"After all, they're too old."

She puts her hand up to the small bump to which her ear is reduced beneath the veil.

"Crime!" I yell. "There's been a lot of crime lately!"

"Out of all proportion, dear. It's the bomb, it must be the bomb. In my time you didn't see even the slightest fraction of this violence. Even the medicine labels, you should see the frightful things they say these days. What a difference! Before, they were encouraging, delicate, it was a delight to read the instructions of medicines. But these days—! So full of threats, so harsh."

Boy Kills Brother at Play. Boy Kills Brother—that could be the headline in the scandal-sensation newspaper. For the feature, the testimony of the youngest sister, we print only the initials since those involved are minors. *L.V.L. said that they were playing. Romulo was running, chased by Remo who suddenly decided to get the shotgun. It was in the office where the rancher kept it, usually unloaded. Once in possession of the gun, he shouted at the brother: "Run, Romulo, I'm going to kill you!" and fired one shot, fatally on the mark, into the chest of the victim. Although there was a large number of employees working on the ranch, none of them witnessed the accident; only the younger sister saw the boy fall down bleeding. Stunned, she ran to call the mother who was in the back of the immense old colonial-style house. The rancher had gone to the capital that morning, only to return in the evening, when amid shock and despair he learned of the tragedy that had befallen his household.*

Was there a photo? No, but every paper has its artist and this one did a fine job with his vigorously sketched reconstruction of the scene: The mother sitting on the ground with Romulo on her lap, one of her hands holding up the trunk of his body, the other hiding the wound. She is disheveled and in tears but even as she suffers she somehow projects an inexorable calm, the calm of one to whom the worst has happened and who knows that nothing worse can ever occur. A recognized artist, it wasn't by accident that his sketch was compared to the Virgin succoring the Dead Son. Giovanni Bellini. Museum of Milan.

"In Milan there's a square for deaf-mutes, they meet there every afternoon. Their gestures create a rustling sound like foliage, I would close my eyes and hear them, sssss."

"The most famous was the crime of Dona Brunilda, a rancher's wife who was found without her head," says Sister Bula holding onto her own. "It was dreadful. For months and months they looked for the poor lady's head," the nun went on, turning her uneasy gaze toward the shelves.

"Did they find it?"

"Not at all. Neither the murderer nor the head. Everyone was saying it was the husband, apparently she liked her daughter's

91

music teacher, a very handsome young man who played the piano and wore a flower in his lapel."

A carnation. Shubert's *Serenade*. Spells and perfumes. Strains of violin music when nobody was playing the violin. A rustling of wings: the Seducer Angel in the shadow of the curtain.

"Somebody wrote an anonymous letter to her husband," I say. Why do I think of my father? Of Romulo? I lose the desire to joke. If only M.N. would say to me, "I love you." Or Fabrízio.

"Do you remember Fabrízio?"

"Fabrízio? That boy with the motorcycle?"

I run to the window, was that the phone? The empty windows. Empty garden. Her membranous eyes question me. Virgin eyes too, no, I don't want to be like that, not me! Ah, M.N., my love, my love. I pull the amber necklace tight around my neck and stick out my tongue.

"If he doesn't call or come see me, I'll kill myself. I'll be the first suicide case to be canonized."

She laughs her little gnome's laugh, hah, hah, hih, hih.

"Ah, child, marriage would cure you. Why don't you marry this Fabrízio?"

"I can't. He has a mechanical leg."

"He has what?"

I go to get a glass of liqueur.

"A mechanical leg."

She shakes all over, coughing and laughing. Her gums appear, rosy plastic with enormous sand-colored teeth in Indian file, why do dentists make false teeth so big? Prodigalities to make up for the lost teeth? The Prodigal Son came back toothless and in rags, the years topple heavily but teeth fall like the breadcrumbs that Hansel and Grefel scattered in the forest, the poor things wanted to mark the way back. And the birds came and ate up the crumbs, farewell warm hearth, farewell childhood. Why, my love, why so many children? And to mix himself up in this church group, what do you intend to do, save your marriage? Your marriage is rotting away, what is there to save? Naturally it was she who had the idea, the witch. A gorgeous man, imagine if a witch would give up easily. Five kids. She must be extremely fat. Thighs full of cellulite. Floppy breasts. In short, a cow.

"Sister, I'm getting awful, awful. Pray for me."

"Is this apricot? I like it better than that peppermint one. Pure nectar."

I dilate my nostrils, squeezing my solar plexus. The smell of Sister Bula is stronger than that of liqueurs and cigars: dry flowers, with a vague touch of disinfectant added, and something of the sea coming through pallid scales, ah, if I breathed in now I'd die. I suspend my life in the air and hide under the pillow: Death is here in yet another costume, staring at me with pickled eyes. I'm capable of killing myself but I don't want to die.

"Playing hide-and-seek? Child, child!"

She drains the last drop from her glass, she's wild about liqueur. I return her liqueurish smile. Sister, dear Sister, promise you won't send me a letter denouncing the Japanese who runs the lunch counter for making sandwich filling out of my cat. Oh Lord.

"Another glass, Sister?"

She rests her hands on the armchair cushion, ready to get up. Now I don't smell the scent of sea and flowers, Death has disappeared and in its place is only an old woman, deaf and virgin, who has lost Paradise because of some letters. To love my neighbor as myself. I reach out my hand toward her. But suddenly she becomes distrustful, she wants to leave, just my wanting to like her is enough to send her running away in panic, she's afraid of me as I was of her.

"I need to help Sister Priscilla grate coconut, she decided to make coconut candy but she cut her finger, I must go," she repeats.

"First try one of these biscuits, you haven't tried these yet," I say. When I come back with the can she's looking with great interest at her feet. Since she has short legs, her feet don't touch the floor and her legs hang in the air, like those of a child in the visitors' parlor.

"I must go, dear."

But she doesn't. Sister Priscilla is already grating her other finger, ah, how distant the word from the act! If I didn't talk so much about making love, if Ana Clara didn't talk so much about getting rich, if Lião didn't run on night and day about revolution.

"It's still early, Sister Bula. Here, this magazine came just yesterday," I say offering her the biscuits and the magazine.

93

She strokes the cover photo of a girl.

"But why do these girls always have to have their pictures taken with their legs apart that way? Why do their legs have to be so wide open?"

"I agree, my dear. Wide-angle sex. Women have lived so long with the angle narrowed that now they have an ax to grind, poor things."

"Speak up!"

"Lião must have written ten papers explaining this, liberation through sex, dearie. The easiest door, it's very extensive," I scream as I change the record.

Bach? I rest my cheek against the cover. M.N. my love, I want so much to go to bed with you while listening to this prelude. I won't ask for anything more, I'll go away forever but you *must* make love with me, it has to be you, do you hear? He doesn't. I pick up a fallen rose petal and put it in my mouth. I make it split apart with a kiss, and sticking it to my lips I thrust the tip of my tongue out through the hole, the way we used to play with flowers on the ranch. Want to see how well she can hear?

"Sister, oh Sister, I think I must be unbalanced, I think about sex so much."

"Do you really?"

"All the time."

If the Devil wanted to be agreeable, he would carry Bulie away on the breeze, and by return breeze bring me M.N. We'd lock ourselves in my charming bathroom and if Ana Clara or Lião turned up I'd call out, "Not now, dearest, I'm taking an immersion bath that has to last two hours." And turn on the tap.

"Ana Clara said she was going to be on the cover of a lot of magazines. I haven't seen anything yet. Have you, child?"

I carry my box of manicure instruments to the bed—I always keep this box close at hand. Whenever I sense the beginning of liquid and uncertain conversations, I get out my emery board and cuticle scissors so as not to waste time. Thus my nails are in beautiful shape. I even gave myself a complete pedicure the other night while Lião was rehashing Simone de Beauvoir. From Simone de Beauvoir to sex was only a step, why the first sex, why the third sex, why the second. As always fatally happens, we started talking about the act of sex itself. And the

94

spirit of Herr Karl hovered over everything. She grabbed my arm so hard I actually winced. "You're *not* going to tell me you're still a virgin!" I breathed in; Yes dear, I am. So she bit off the last fraction of fingernail that she had left on her favorite finger. Of course it was all M.N.'s fault, "Incompetent bourgeois!" she muttered cutting something out of a newspaper, she keeps folders and folders overflowing with newspaper cuttings about politics. There was only one subtle way out: "It's not every day one meets a Guevara," I said and her eyes softened. The Nazi eagle turned into a dove, coconut palms swayed, *coqueiro de Itapoã, coqueiro!* Dona Diu smiled from her hammock. "When everything seems to be lost, when even Miguel can't manage to cheer me up, I think about Ché and there comes to me the certainty that I *will* overcome. Sometimes, Lena, sometimes I think he had to die for me to be reborn." I agreed. But I would have gotten upset if she'd attributed the source of life to him, is it the Gospel according to Mark? "Marvel not when I say to you, ye must be born again." I kept my mouth shut and went running to get whiskey to toast the revolution. I felt light enough to fly; finally I had stopped thinking about M.N. And about this whole dramatic affair of my virginity. I confess, from time to time I need to talk about it, I bring the subject up and provoke people's reactions with an awful urge to be center-front stage. But then suddenly I feel so ashamed (though *shame* doesn't really describe it) that I can't stand the slightest reference, my problem, I state emphatically, DO NOT ENTER. Whiskey for her and guaraná for me, I adore guaraná. When Lião saw the two bottles together she looked thoughtful. "President brand, Lena? Our poor guaraná looks pretty insignificant beside that." I quickly explained that it was a present from Mama when *in reality* it was a present from M.N., these little lies that facilitate our mutual well-being weren't condemned by Pope John XXIII, a sainted Pope. Knowing I don't drink, M.N. offered me the bottle, "Wouldn't your friends like some?" Greater delicacy couldn't exist. "The only thing those fools know how to do," said Lião, serving herself a generous shot. "The movies they see have a lot of class too," I ventured but she didn't even hear me because she was already warming up for her principal lecture, in which the decadence of the establishment is proved through the illustration of drug abuse. "I can't explain it but it's a mistake to think that drugs
95

reflect an antiestablishment attitude, see. The last time I was in Salvador I almost went crazy, I felt so sorry for them, there's armies of junkies," she sighed and her eyes filled with tears. Mine did too, ah, it was too too sad. The Bahian so close to the Indian in his state of innocence. I mentioned this very idea to Lião but I must have been *gauche* because she stared at me half-sadly, shaking her head. "This tone of yours, Lorena. This tone," she repeated. Then, shrugging her shoulders, "I can't explain it, but . . . " and for hours she explained that the fastest way to kill the Brazilian Indian is to try to civilize him. For a while I followed her speech but then I began to tire of it. Yes, the Indian. I adore Indians. But can I help it if I always start thinking about the nineteenth-century poet Gonçalves Dias and his noble savages? Now she was talking about civilized vices. I got an opportunity to quote the verse, "Oh, Tupan, what wrong have I done you / That from your fury you pluck for me a poisoned arrow?" But Lião is not impressed with poetry. Unexpectedly she began a discourse on the fall of the dollar and this time she was right in saying that she couldn't explain because she didn't explain a single thing. If that was the kind of subject she wrote about in her little leftist newspaper, the readers would be in fine shape. But fortunately, her journalistic duties consisted of gathering material. I asked her what she was doing in her spare time now that Miguel was in jail. "There isn't any spare time, see. I distribute pamphlets, direct a study group and translate books. As long as some more important mission doesn't come up," she insinuated, tying her shoelaces. The dirt had incorporated itself so completely into the canvas that even the most ingenious chemical operation couldn't get it out. But the laces were clean, mysteriously clean. Wasn't it strange they should be so white? Thinking about the shoelaces I asked her if her friend was still incommunicado. "Which friend, Lena? So many of them are incommunicado, an infernal crisis. We need money, people, everything. I almost lose my mind with the tons of urgent things that need attention. But what can you do without yenom, what? Even so, I don't lose my faith. The structure for revolution is completely intact, all we have to do is connect the little motor—us—with the central motor." She stood up and with her air of a political rally paced to and fro, holding forth on the difficulties of organizing the workers, the great majority of whom were habituated to servitude, misery, the inheritance

96

transmitted through generations of conformity. "Their fear, Lena. Fear of assuming responsibility, it's shitty enough to make you cry. We have a good group ready for whatever happens, the problem is with the older ones and the intellectuals. Only about half a dozen are worth anything. The rest sign their little manifestos, hold their secret meetings, the secret smile of the Mona Lisa, glass in hand. Big deal." I looked at the glass she was clutching as energetically as an athlete carrying the baton in a relay race. When Ana Clara takes hold of a glass, she raises her little finger with the refinements of a truck driver at a wedding party but Lião closes her fist and digs in her nails, that is, the places where her nails should have been. Better to bite them all off, imagine her bothering to cut them. I returned to the shoelaces: but why were they alone clean? Lião stopped talking and stared at me like someone who has lost his way in the forest, made an enormous circle and suddenly discovered that he is back where he started. Sitting down on the floor, she took out a cigarette and rolled it between her fingers. "My friends are all in jail, I could be arrested when I walk out of here—" she began softly. "Manuela is in a mental hospital, crazy, and Jaguaribe is dead. And you worry about my shoelaces."

"I ascribe importance to things that have none," I begin and stop.

It isn't Lião who is here but Bulie reading with enormous interest—but what *is* she reading with such interest? She has put on her glasses with their telescopic lenses and raised the magazine up about half an inch from her nose. She doesn't notice in the slightest when I pull it up to see the title, *Erotic Love*! Oh Lord.

"What an exaggeration," she murmurs without taking her eyes off the page. Why is it that at times I hurt Lião when I want to see her happy? She looked so sad there on the floor that I went running to get the can of biscuits and the hairbrush. I knelt down and began brushing her hair. "You look like Angela Davis," I said and she smiled but I could tell that her thoughts were still far away, where Manuela went crazy. Where Jaguaribe was shot. Who was this Manuela? And Jaguaribe? You never mentioned him to me, I said and she stroked her tennis shoe, caressing the ink-scribbled rubber toe. A little black

97

flower, carefully drawn, stood out in the tangled design. "These were his," she said grabbing their tips with both hands. I poured more whiskey into her glass, courage, Lião, don't get depressed I have my saints who listen to me, you don't believe in them but leave it to me. "If you must pray, pray for Ché, see, he's the one I need," she answered. And her finger touched the black flower drawn on the rubber. I remembered that Romulo was dead too and started to cry, so moved that Lião was obliged to forget her own losses in order to console me. She told me there was no definitive death, not even for her, a materialist. That death and life are part of each other, complement each other as perfectly as a circle and so therefore my brother was still alive: Life needs death to live, "I can't explain it, see," she explained. All of a sudden she became happy again, humming along with the Vinicius record and asking after M.N. in her best humor. "How's the old man?" I grew happy too: I cry when others cry near me, but when their spirits soar, mine zoom upward too. I went off to make some hot tea because after drinking like a sponge, Lião adores hot tea with biscuits. We drank a whole pot, and if she hadn't gone to make pee-pee and I hadn't decided to take a bath, we would undoubtedly have gone on that way until five in the morning.

"Such nonsense," mutters Sister Bula closing the magazine. I blow on the cuticle of my thumb where the scissor point has left a half-moon of blood, and choose a blues record.

"Did you read it all?"

"I don't know why they waste so much paper on such nonsense," she adds putting away her glasses. She dries her eyes on the sheet-sized handkerchief which would absorb the mucus of a battalion. "These people act as if sex were the most important thing in the world."

And isn't it? Or one of the most important. In one night alone Crazy Annie had dozens of orgasms, which is a lie, naturally. But what about the others? The conversations I hear, people talk about their sex lives so much. Some of them are a bit mad, obviously they should talk to a doctor. It must be an exaggeration, not natural.

"Dear, do you suppose you could put on some Chopin music? One of those *Nocturnes*, perhaps? These singers of yours tire one a little, don't they. I used to think you girls were fighting, so much shouting. I'm used to it now. Sometimes I ask myself, do the words make sense?"

98

And how. The words are trivial, but in triviality is tragedy. How could it be otherwise: The grass in the garden is just grass, the soup in the soup bowl is not concealing any mystery, and the hummingbird is the very negation of mystery. But if we're in a state of grace, we can intuit all sorts of things spreading fanlike in a variety of directions: Dona Guiomar's cards. The jack of spades means marriage if it comes close by the seven of diamonds, which is bad news when coupled with the five of clubs, which in turn means a journey when linked to the king of hearts, which becomes a death sentence without appeal when it comes arm in arm with the queen of spades—oh! circumstances. Lião gets furious if I mention fortune-tellers, I'm wild about them. She says there's no such thing as destiny, there's nothing at all because we're free, completely free. "I can't explain it but if I go to jail one day, my being jailed will prove my freedom." I didn't see, it was suffocatingly hot, almost a hundred degrees in the shade and Lião in the mood to explain Sartrean doctrine to me. She kept talking to herself about the nausea she felt for nineteenth-century literature with all its characters destined either to Good or to Evil like trains running fatally down the rails they had been placed on, "There are no rails!" So fine, let me laugh. *That old black magic*, he sang when he was condemned to the gas chamber, an old condemnation, the day he was born he was already marked, if we escape the fire we can't escape our signs. I ventured to speak of signs and she accused me of being a half-assed Christian: "How can a Christian believe in that stuff?"

"I'm a Pisces."

The nun was looking at the ceiling.

"I read that young people need violence to channel their complexes. Did you see the other day where a fourteen-year-old boy dumped gasoline on his grandmother's wheelchair and set fire to it, she was fried like a piece of bacon. They say it's necessary. So we have to wait for these young people to get tired of so much violence, what else is there to do? When they get tired of it, they'll be old like we are."

"Smart," whispered Lorena rubbing the soles of her feet on the rug as she looked for the Chopin record. "One more glassful," she chuckled, "and I'll get an explanation for the generation gap!" Bringing the bottle she refilled the wineglass which the nun offered her amid weak protests, "I'll be tipsy!" The protest was transformed into an *ah!* of beatitude as the first chords of the *Nocturne* sounded.

"Do you prefer to read or write, Sister? Write diaries, for example. Letters . . . ?"

"Neither, dear. My eyes have gotten worse . . . " she answered turning toward Lorena with an expression of faded innocence. "And your brother, is he still in Italy?"

"North Africa. North Africa!"·

"I heard you, Lorena. Is that Romulo?"

"Romulo is dead, this is Remo."

If he comes back, he remembers, thought Lorena opening her hands palms-up in a gesture of oblation. He had analysis, took courses, made love to beautiful women, fathered beautiful children, traveled, more women, more children, more cars. If he comes back he remembers. All he has to do is look Mama in the face, she's transparent. The face engraved on Veronica's handkerchief.

"*Attendite et videte!*" she exclaimed stretching her arms frontward to exhibit her open-book hands. "Do you think I'm crazy, Sister?" she asked, bending toward the nun's ear.

"Do I think what?"

Lorena smiled. She folded her hands together and stared at her fingernails. Even Remo's fingers, too heavy for the piano, got slenderer and lighter, until they could have been Romulo's fingers if Romulo had lived. Yes, it was better for him to stay on in his exile, sending presents, cards, pictures. Immense houses surrounded by green lawns stretching into the distance. The children in their colored knits always running after some dog. The shining car parked nearby. Ana Clara chattered so much about a Jaguar, poor thing. The Jaguar was so outdated. She should take a refresher course in the showroom where Remo always bought the latest models, he had a passion for machines. "If he comes back, he remembers." Meetings with him should be in faraway places outside the country, like that time in Venice. The museums, the shops. Ruins and wine. "Mama will buy a gondola yet," he said as he helped take packages out of the trunk of the car. And kissed Lorena's only purchase, a small antique beaded purse she had discovered in the jumble of a bazaar. Daytimes and evenings bursting with commitments, yes, other countries were a necessity. Other people. Here, in the first available hour he would start to talk loud and fast. Mama would start to laugh stridently, both trying to cover up the murmuring sound rising from the grayish bottom. The river. In summertime, the water would grow so warm it would seem impossible it could turn into the icy flood of winter. Even then the two of them would swim in it, purple and panting. Remo, the daring one, would yell, "Wanna feel hotter? Go wash your butt in the waa-a-a-a-ter!" Under the surface, Remo's black hair was still black, but Romulo's blond curls turned grayish. The color of ashes.

"Was your brother handsome?" asked Lorena.

The nun blotted her overflowing eyes on her handkerchief and drank the last gulp of liqueur.

"Not really handsome. But he was a fine boy. He went on a picnic with his schoolmates, I've told you. He was drowned in the ocean. When they recovered his body I was there, dear Lord Jesus, what a frightful thing, all those shrimps on top of each other, moving around in his eyesockets."

Lorena closed her eyes and thought about Romulo, his pale teeth, how could that be? How could teeth grow pale? And on his red shirt, increasing, the stronger red of his blood. Mama's hand covering the hole which bubbled like a bottle of wine drenching a towel.

"I thought a cork might take care of it."

"Years and years I went and couldn't bear the sight of shrimp. Then I gradually forgot about it, one forgets. . . . Just the other night I ate shrimp casserole that Sister Clotilde made, I enjoyed it so much. Upon my word I didn't even remember."

With a slow, reflective gesture Lorena corked the bottle of liqueur. Wasn't it strange? Such a small, insignificant hole and all that blood. Her mother didn't understand either. "What's all this?" she kept repeating. We need to stop it up quick, put your finger over it, or better yet your hand, like this Mama, like this! Mothers fix everything, know everything, stop it up tight! And the blood kept running out. Underneath her hand, look there, the red shirt fading out, so much more powerful this other red, my God, so strong. I looked aside quickly because she was hiding the wound with the same shame as when she hid her breasts from us if we wandered into her room when she was getting dressed. "Don't look, I don't have my clothes on!" I allowed her time to dress her voice. And the wound. She was calmer than on that afternoon when he had cut his finger slicing the water-

101

melon. "But what happened, Lorena!" she asked, hoarse. Only hoarse. They were playing, I guess Remo was the bandit, I only know that he got the gun and pointed it at him, it wasn't his fault, Mama, really it wasn't. Imitating her hushed voice, I offered to call the doctor almost in a whisper. Or Lauro. Do you want me to call for Jandira? She shook her head no, it wasn't necessary. I stayed nailed to the spot, my mouth opening and closing, dry and soundless. Romulo's mouth was opening and closing too, silent like the mouth of a fish thrown onto the sand where the water cannot reach it. He gradually relaxed. If he could have, he would have asked us to excuse him for dying.

"Dreaming, dear?"

I close Romulo and the bottle of liqueur behind the glassed-in door of the bar. Pull the curtains shut. And M.N. hasn't phoned. And this *Nocturne* playing with that sun outside, ah! what I'd like to do is climb on the motorbike and zoom away, disembodied, free from thoughts, come get me, Fabrízio! Suppose I died in an explosion, M.N. would see the gory remains arriving, "Lorena!" Incinerated and deflowered.

"I'm carbonizing with passion, Sister. Marcus Nemesius!" I scream. I throw my arms around her and place my lips next to her ear: "His father was a Latin scholar, all the children have declinable names, his sister is *Rosa, Rosae* like *excreta, excretae.*"

She doesn't understand, but she smiles. I go with her to the door. Her bones crack. Will I get old this way someday? I'll kill myself first. I bow my head. She blesses me and prepares to go down the stairs. I turn off the record player. A sound of voices. *The isle is full of noises.* A few meows mixed in with the noises. How would you say *meow* in English? I open the dictionary.

Chapter 6

The small room was low-ceilinged and poorly lighted. In it were two very old desks, an ancient typewriter and a few straw chairs, two of which had holes in the seats. On the floor, a pile of folders and newspapers with a bundle of clothes on top. Tied together with a piece of twine, two pillows and a blanket. The blackish floor, full of cigarette burns, had been swept, as was indicated by the wastebasket overflowing with trash, a broom sticking up out of the middle. Over the broom handle had been thrust a roll of toilet paper.

Lia took her bag from her shoulder and hung it on the nearest chair. She surveyed the dust-covered table, the rolled-up calendar half-visible behind the typewriter, the glass with a heel of coffee in the bottom. She unrolled the calendar: Occupying more than half the page was the colored photo of a blonde in a bikini, her fleshy mouth half-open to drink from a bottle of Coca-Cola. When Lia dropped it, it rolled up again as if it had springs. Her gaze turned to the grayish ceiling, specked with squatting flies, most of them dead among the old spiderwebs. She smiled. "Lorena would have a fine time here," she thought. In the center of the globe-shaped light fixture was a thick spot created by accumulated insects which had entered and died imprisoned.

"Very weak," thought Lia examining her index finger with severity. She turned to face the young man who had just come in.

"We need a stronger light bulb. Where were you?"

He wiped his hands on the seat of his jeans and shook his head.

"The john is something else, Rosa, you should see it. It's down at the end of the hall. You have to close your eyes and remember the Queen."

"I'll get you a chamber pot. I have a friend who's got a china chamber pot with gilt edges and angels, see. If she'll take the fern out of it I'll borrow it for you."

He pulled up a chair and straddled it.

"I moved everything myself, everybody else gave the orders but it was only me who did any work. This place was a dump, I emptied three wastebaskets already and there's still that one. There are even mice, look there at the bugger's tunnel," he whispered, pointing at a mouse hole in the angle of wall and floor. "He's smart, too. Made me run after him like a damn fool and then quietly retired to his private quarters."

"Probably a cop disguised as a mouse."

"When I came out of the movies yesterday they asked me for my identification. I was so scared, Rosa. Don't you get scared?"

Lia ran her tongue over her gnawed fingernail. She did not answer at once.

"Fine. Tomorrow I'll bring a stronger bulb. And a calendar without a Coke ad. Where did this marvel come from?"

"Shit, I have no idea."

Going to the window, the young woman tried to open the venetian blinds but the cord was stuck. She peered through a crack between the worm-eaten slats.

"The inside court. Do you know what's across from us?"

"A tailor shop, I spoke to the old man when I got here. Neat, Rosa. You see the wire netting down there? In case of an emergency, it's perfectly possible to jump onto it and get away through the old man's window."

"And he's a super-squealer, if we stick our heads in the window he'll grab us by the neck, like this," she said pulling Pedro by the collar of his pullover sweater.

Locked together, they pulled and jerked in a short, fierce fight and separated laughing. He examined the bite on his wrist and she gathered her hair, which he had pulled loose, at the nape of her neck.

"Gee, you're strong! I think I would have gotten beat up if you'd kept on," he muttered examining his arm.

"Look, Pedro, I know a nun you can look at and say, wow, there couldn't be a nicer little grandma. You should read the anonymous letters she writes everybody. I just hope she doesn't discover the address of the Federal Security Police, she's almost blind."

"Anonymous letters? How super! Have you gotten one?"

She tapped her fingers against the cracked glass of the window.

"We'll cover this with newspaper. Got any glue?"

"None, not a drop. No Scotch tape, no paper, nothing."

"Tomorrow I'll bring some stuff. Did Bugre leave any money?"

"He said tomorrow. All I hear from everyone is tomorrow," he groaned scratching his head. "I don't have change for cigarettes, even."

After offering him her pack, Lia stared up at the glass globe with its timid aura of light.

"A trap. The bugs go in and can't get out again. And even if they do, there's the spiderwebs outside, an even worse death. Death without a battle, annihilation. Inside a spider's guts."

"They could get out the way they got in, couldn't they?"

"If they could, they wouldn't be in there dead."

"But the politicized ones got away."

Lia was cleaning the typewriter keyboard with the green cambric handkerchief. She wiped off the table, rubbing energetically at the more intransigent spots, and then, throwing the blackened square into her bag, looked about for an ashtray. Smiling, she flicked her ashes onto the floor.

"I have a friend who's so fanatic about cleanliness and order that I'm picking up her habits. Wherever I go she comes after me with a little ashtray in her hand," she added taking a newspaper cutting out of a book she had brought. "Do you read French?"

"I read a little English."

She scanned the clipping, and turned to Pedro.

"This is an interview with André Malraux about Guevara. Do you know who Malraux is?"

"A writer, isn't he? Who just died a while back?"

"The one who died is André Maurois, he's of no interest. This is Malraux, a very important guy, see. His novel was one of the most fabulous things I ever read, *Man's Fate*. It's available in translation."

We were drinking coffee with milk. Hot ham-and-cheese sandwiches. The happiness that rushed through me when he said, "Let's have some coffee, we're freezing." My knees against his, our sandwiches so close that I could bite the one he

105

was blowing on. Hot steam came out of his mouth. I can't explain it, I said, but if you get arrested I'll go and turn myself in too. He didn't answer. He took the book from his canvas bag and opened it on the tabletop. "This Malraux is very good, the problem is you've marked the whole book up with these crosses, why did you do that? You underlined everything, look there." But Miguel, isn't it my book? I asked and he spread jelly over his bread. "Don't talk like a Nazi, sweetheart. You have to think of the other people who are going to read it, you can't impose your taste on others. You interfered with my reading," he mumbled kissing me with his mouth smeared with jam. Orange marmalade. I stare at the cigarette that has fallen off the matchbox where I balanced it. It rolls, no longer burning, over the table.

"Bored, Rosa?"
"Let's get to work."
Inside the cluttered drawer there was everything but paper. Having succeeded in finding a pencil, Pedro took a red-handled toothbrush out of the bottom. He aimed at the wastebasket and threw the toothbrush but it hit the broom handle and glanced off, landing near the window.
"I never did understand the billiard-ball effect," he said and faced me. "I'd like to ask you something, Rosa, can I? It's something I want to know."
"Sure."
"Did you ever have an experience with a woman?"
"Yes."
"Really? How super! And ... ?"
"I don't understand what it is you want to know," I say laughing inwardly because I know exactly what it is he wants to know.
"Nothing extraordinary about it, Pedro. Very simple. It was in my hometown, I was still in high school. We were students together and since we both thought we were ugly, we invented boyfriends. When I remember! . . . how wonderful it felt to be loved by boys, even boys who didn't exist. We sent each other love notes, she pretended her name was Ophelia and I was Richard, with the green eyes and a certain mockery in his gaze, oh, how she suffered from that mockery. But a little suffering only added to the fun. I don't really know when Richard's name

started disappearing and mine stayed on. I guess it was one night when I put on a sentimental record and asked her to dance, may I have the pleasure? We started dancing all in giggles but while we were twirling around something was changing, we grew serious, so serious. We were so terribly ashamed, see. We held and kissed each other with such fear. We used to cry with fear."

"Were you happy, Rosa?"

I run my hand over his strong chin.

"It was a profound and sad love. We knew that if they suspected we'd suffer even more. So we had to hide our secret like a robbery, a crime. So many alarms. We started to talk alike. Laugh alike. So close it was as if I had fallen in love with myself. I can't explain it, but the first time I went to bed with a man I had the sensation of loving a *strange being*. The Other. The mouth, the body, no, I was no longer one, we were two, the man and me."

"Did you think that was good?"

"When we want something, it becomes good. And I wanted to know what it was like in order to be able to choose. I chose. But when I remember . . . Oh, why do people interfere so much? Nobody knows anything but they all talk, judge. There are too many judges. One night she called me up in tears, her family was about to make a scandal, I had to disappear, or in other words, appear in the form of a boyfriend. Reinvent with urgency a boyfriend, the boyfriend of the beginning of our game. I'd have to send her letters, keepsakes from a fellow who wouldn't be Richard any more, what name then? I bribed the kid from the bakery to talk over the phone, we needed a voice for Ricardo, we chose Ricardo for his name. We had to lie so much on account of other people that we got contaminated with lying. We weren't lovers but accomplices. We became formal. Suspicious. The fun had gone out of the game, it went sour. Then she left her ficticious charmer for a real one. As for me, I let myself be squired about by a cousin, there was talk of an engagement."

"And what about your family, Rosa?"

"My father was aware of everything but never said a word. My mother made a few guesses and panicked, she wanted to marry me off to the cousin as quickly as possible. The neighbor would have been OK too, an old man who played the cello. She did everything she could to tie me down, but I packed my *necessaire* and came here."

107

"What's that? *Necessaire*?"

I open the newspaper article on the table and glance at my watch.

"One of my friends is always talking about preparing your *necessaire*—foolishness. It means pack your bag, your toothbrush kit. Let's get to work?"

"I'm at your service, Rosa de Luxembourg."

I take two chocolate bars from my bag, one for him and another. And the other for him too, I decide. I throw him the second bar, I have to lose ten pounds, don't I? Then I grab my share back and now I can't answer because my mouth is full. Miguel in jail, no money, father and mother far away, all my friends disappearing around me and I'm going to deny myself sugar?

We chew, concentrating.

"Who mentioned her? Rosa Luxembourg," I ask.

"Jango."

"A fabulous woman. She was murdered by the German police right after the First World War."

There's a malicious glint in Pedro's eye.

"I heard your father used to be a Nazi. That true?"

I slap the table with far more irritation than I feel.

"He had a fling at it. But look, we're not playing, I want you to get that through your head. Here I'm Rosa and you're Pedro. Period."

"Just one more question, only one more, I promise!"

"You ask too many questions, see."

"This Rosa de Luxembourg, was she pretty?"

"There wasn't any *de*. No, extremely ugly. But come on. Malraux was an old-time revolutionary, he was in China when things started. He participated in the Spanish Civil War, the French Resistance etcetera, etcetera. As he got older, he started to get soft and ended up as one of de Gaulle's cabinet ministers. But before that he was pretty neat. Look how lucid this comment on Guevara is, he considers Ché the greatest man of our time, but with the wrong technique, and the proof of this is that he died in an ambush, a trap even stupider than that light fixture up there. He was mistaken to think he was dominating those villages around him, I can't explain it but they were really controlled by the Americans."

"Slower, let me jot that down."

108

He finds an old purple felt-tip pen and licks it with the tip of his tongue; his handwriting is clear but his lips have purple spots. I put the clipping away. I'd like to put him away too, somewhere safe, like the bottom of my bag, protected, Oh! I'm turning into a sentimental old lady.

"Look at this, Pedro! Also, in Malraux's opinion, the revolution in Latin America will be of a Trotskyite character, it won't be a revolution of the masses."

"Hell, I think that way too."

I light our last cigarette. He takes a drag and his hand trembles slightly.

"You could include the testimony of a Peruvian priest, Wenceslau Calderón de la Cruz, isn't that a lovely name?"

"Wenceslau who?"

"Calderón de la Cruz. He considers men like Guevara and Martin Luther King to be modern-day saints."

"I don't like King," he mutters.

"Leave it just Ché then, but think again about Martin Luther King. In olden times saints were those who did the most penance, exercised the most charity, you know, all that stuff. But everything's changed. Today a Christian can't gain salvation of his soul without serving society *objectively*. I can't explain it but anyone who fights with his entire consciousness in order to help those in misery and ignorance, anyone who through his office or instruments of work lends a hand to his neighbor, is saintly. The roads may be crooked, it makes no difference. They're still saintly."

"At that point I could put something in about our priests, right, Rosa? You should have seen Brother Christóvão, yesterday he came down with a bad cold but still he went out in the rain to visit the little hookers down at the Maison Rouge, we almost had to beat up the madam. Their ages vary between thirteen and sixteen, they're only recruited in that age span. He went from there to talk to that blonde who hustles down by the cemetery gates, he takes them one by one, such a slow job, he has to use up so much spit. And the things he hears in exchange!"

"Romanticism. But even so, a more logical romanticism than the request of all those priests pouring into the Vatican. Marriage! A priest has to marry the Church! Otherwise he won't be a priest, he'll want to do other things. A halfway priest is like a

109

halfway politician, garbage. A priest shouldn't even be allowed to marry his own mother, how can people respect them? I don't attend Mass, mind you, but if I ever decide to go back some day, I want to find a priest with a clean mind to give me communion."

He chuckled. "So sex is dirty?"

"I can't explain it, Pedro, but in the case in point it interferes tremendously. It fragments. And the priest has to be whole, we're the ones who are in pieces. Priests who want to screw have no calling, they're ambiguous, and ambiguities are abominable."

"I'd bring halfway leftists to your attention too, God, what a shitty bunch."

I'm cold and hungry. I pick up a piece of twine from the floor and use it to tie back my hair.

"Sometimes I get so fed up with this group. And now with this business of the ambassador, dammit. It's fear."

He gets up, goes to the window, and peeks out at the night through the hole in the sleazy venetian blinds. He buries his hands in his pockets and looks at me.

"I think I'm scareder of my folks than of the police. My oldest brother is gung-ho on family and tradition, you should have seen how hysterical he got. I'm frightened to death of him."

"And your father?"

"Separated from my mother. Oh, Rosa, I really suffered over that. I used to cry at night and bite the pillow, I cried like an idiot. I wanted them both to die but I didn't want them to split up. Isn't that weird? Why should it bother me so much? I didn't tell anyone, they never knew it, nobody did. You're the only person I've told. I was so broken up inside. Just like the glass in my window where a rock hit it, I'd look at the window and see myself exactly that way. I never said anything. I'm saying it now and I'm already crying again. Shit, why do I have to cry, goddammit. How imbecilic."

I rub a spot on my blouse with the handkerchief. I know it won't come out but I keep rubbing as if getting the spot out were the most important thing in the world. Lorena would be radiant if she could see me.

"And did she remarry? Your mother?"

"I've noticed a guy hanging around who's actually not so bad. I have nothing more to do with it. I read lots of science fiction,

110

act absentminded so they'll think I'm stupid and leave me in peace."

He mounted the chair again, leaning his arms on the back and resting his chin on his arms. His mouth and fingers are dirty with ink like those of children who are just learning to write. I feel like cradling his head in my lap, go to sleep, Pedro.

"Families really are a pain. Mine live a long way away, we get along beautifully."

And together, didn't we get along beautifully too? But it's better for me to console him. He wets the pencil point in his mouth again and starts to draw in the margin of the paper. He makes a bird flying, a house. He reinforces the plume of smoke coming out of the chimney.

"As soon as I start working, I'm going to transfer to night school and move in with two other guys. Are you prejudiced against queers?"

"My prejudice is against lack of character."

"I think one of them is gay. He hates girls, he says they're *doors of the Devil.*"

I take off my socks and wad them into a ball. I want to laugh but he's absolutely serious. I leave my socks in the drawer, the irritation those socks caused me with their worthless elastic! How could a simple pair of socks perturb me so? One day I put a pair of foot-warmers in this drawer, black woolen ones. Could they still . . . I curl my fingers around them. Dusty but warm. I look at Pedro and for some reason I am filled with hope.

"If you're not interested, tell them before you move in, explain yourself clearly, right? No pretenses or evasions, that's the important thing. Are you a virgin?"

"Not exactly. It's complicated."

I know, a virgin. He and Lorena would make a great pair. I take his felt pen and draw a radiant sun beside his plume of smoke.

"Isn't it warmer now? You've got to learn to smile again, Pedro. Learn to fight back. And clarity, don't leave anything foggy. Don't be either pious or sentimental because then you end up hurting people more. Believe me."

"But it's other people who are sentimental! You should have seen my friend when he had a breakdown, the guy almost died when he came to tell me how unhappy he was, how cruel his family had been. He asked if I was going to act the same way

111

everybody else did just because he was nothing but a wretch. He didn't go down on his knees because I stopped him."

"But why a wretch? I can't stand panic or declarations of principles. Resignation or provocation. My great-aunt was so burdened down by the fact of sex that she hid herself in a convent, became a nun. Another aunt who was fond of controversies created so many that she ended up a whore. Both acted out of the same fear, the same fear. If only we weren't so afraid." "Neither night nor day," Lorena sentenced once. "They're in twilight, and twilight will always be uncertain. Insecure." "Literature, bah. Women are finding their way. The men will come along in good time. I think," I say grinning, "that in the future there will be only hermaphrodites." "Poor little things," Lorena would add. But when she speaks in her poetic tone she doesn't use diminutives.

"Are you in love with someone, Rosa?"

"Yes. Now take off that pullover, I need it today. You can wear mine."

"A mission? With Bugre?"

I take his hand between mine. Dry and dirty. "I didn't hear that."

He remounts his chair, did he blush? He blushed.

"Crap, I'm really stupid. Oh Rosa, for God's sake, be my girl. I'll give you my stuffed rabbit, my tricycle, my dove's egg, I have a dove's egg," he murmured laughing softly. "You can have them all."

I pull his hair. "I already have a man. Period. Now I have to go."

"Wait, what are the characteristics of a Third-World country? Ours, for example. I'm thinking of writing an article. But where would I publish it?"

And where would I be able to publish it? I asked. Miguel looked at me the same way I'm looking at Pedro. He straightened the pages of my manuscript and gave me an ambiguous answer, he who isn't ambiguous. I should keep on writing without worrying about getting published. Someday, who knows? If I felt the text was still valid. One could sense it had been written with love. With honesty.

I squeeze Pedro's hand as if I were squeezing my own.

"Don't worry about publishing, just keep writing. You want to be a journalist, don't you? So you've got to practice, later

112

we'll see. And remember, to write about underdevelopment isn't just to write about the children, afterwards I'll get you the exact number who die per day. There's illiteracy, the mushrooming of the slums, the people who flee from the droughts, you should take a ride out along the country roads sometime and hear what these people have to say. Traveling salesmen with combs, pencils, razor blades. Trash multiplying in the streets, what do they call those openings that are always plugging up along the sidewalks? The dirt in the cafés and restaurants, toilets, the apotheosized filth of these toilets, starting with the ones in the Department, oh, Pedro, just take a little walk around outside and your article will practically write itself, 'from general to specific,' as my friend says in Latin, she likes Latin. Now I really must go."

He follows me to the door. I paw through the bottom of my bag.

"Here's some yenom, money spelled backwards brings luck, remember that: yenom. We'll settle up later."

"But it's a lot, Rosa."

I give him a good-bye kiss on the cheek and enter the darkness of the corridor as he asks about my novel. I don't want him to see me when I answer that I ripped it all up, destroyed it.

"I thought I had talent but I was wrong, like these priests who are getting married all over the place."

"But how do you know you were wrong?"

"One knows, Pedro. One knows."

He embraces me so hard that I am actually alarmed, I never imagined he was so strong. His mouth, quivering, searches for mine. I go to meet it, good grief, he doesn't even know how to kiss. I'll teach you stage by stage, wait, what's the big rush? Don't hurt me, we're not enemies, I try to tell him with my tongue that flattens against his and teaches him to kiss slowly and deeply. At first he's completely clumsy, never mind, pretty soon things will smooth out. I still have fifteen minutes, I murmur in his ear. We draw back inside the room, holding each other. He reaches out and turns off the light, he wants it to be in the dark. Fine, in the dark and with the door closed, I decide pushing the door shut with my foot. His teeth hurt my lip, he has big teeth, oh, don't make it such a battle, I'll show you the way. It's suffering, yes, but it's pleasure too, don't worry about me, see. Come on, don't be afraid, I'm on your side, not against you.

113

"Don't be like that, Pedro. Relax, take it easy. We have time."

He kisses me and sobs with affliction and anger, bewildered. I have to take the initiative, he may fail out of sheer emotion and become desperate. "Come on, Pedro. It's not a door of the Devil," I whisper in his ear and we laugh. "Not of God either, just a door like any other. Come inside." He explodes in a torrent of sperm and tears.

"I'm sorry, Rosa, I'm sorry!"

"If you say that again I'll kill you right now, on the spot."

"It was awful!"

"What do you mean, awful? Wasn't it good for you?"

I take the handkerchief from my bag and dry his face. I feel him smiling and smile too. "You'll orient Pedro," Bugre ordered. Right, a complete orientation. A good deed or a simple desire to make love? Oh, I don't know, I don't know. I know I love Miguel even more after the betrayal. If this is what you could call betrayal. I tousle Pedro's hair; he's coming out of his depression with alarming speed. He laughs at nothing, he's high as a kite. He kisses the palm of my hand and places it against his burning face.

"I love you Rosa, I love you."

"Great. Now go and find yourself a girl."

"Wait, Rosa!"

I gather up my belongings. He grabs me but I'm stronger. I leave him lying on the floor, completely tender and silly. He wants to know if we'll see each other tomorrow, if my boyfriend really is Miguel, he asks questions, questions.

"Good night, Pedro! Write a good article, you hear?"

The circular stairway is dark. Somebody is coughing, half-suffocated. Pedro will feel the cold in my light sweater but he can drink some coffee and tomorrow look his girl friend in the face, oh, Miguel, how I need you. How that boy needed me. Who knows, maybe someday I'll write well. It could happen. I've thought about a diary, that might be simpler, something plain. Lorena advises me to write in unadorned language, she finds me baroque. I *am* baroque, from head to toe, I admit it. Draperies and stars. Genialities without genius, is that it, Miguel? An honest diary. Dry, telling about my work without bragging, without any glory. Until I get arrested and die in obscurity, only with the name I chose: Rosa. I need some fresh air

114

at once, I'm getting so emotional. I open the door of the building and a burst of rain and wind hits me in the face, the rain comes in bursts, like gunfire. Gunfire isn't a good word but backwards ... erifnug? Rosa was hit in the chest by erifnug is less serious. I run to the corner, we arrive at the same time, Bugre and I. The car is the color of the night.

"Well, Bugre?"

"Everything was postponed, more important things are happening. And some good news for you. Is your watch working? I lost mine, can you lend me yours? Leave it there in the glove compartment."

She took off her wristwatch. "Good news for me? Tell me, Bugre."

"Wait a minute, I can't see, have you got a handkerchief?"

The windshield wiper, stuck, could not remove the heavy mist; it would travel halfway in its appointed semicircle across the glass and return tremblingly, like the antenna of a crippled insect, too weak to fulfill its function. The right-hand wiper only vibrated; it didn't move at all.

"Want me to drive?"

"It's better now. Light me a cigarette, OK? They're in the glove compartment. Oh, that cap, get it out, it's yours. You can wear it."

She unrolled a black rib-knit cap.

"Mine? But how gorgeous, Bugre! This hair has been driving me crazy."

He took the cigarette and looked at her in the mirror.

"You look like a sailor, Rosa. That'll be useful on your trip."

"What trip?"

He shifted gears and turned to look at her.

"Miguel is on the list of prisoners to be exchanged for the ambassador."

"On the list?" slowly she raised her head. "Miguel on the list?"

"Your man is about to embark. Algeria. One of the top guys on the list, I wish I was in his place. The news will be out tomorrow, you'd better get your passport in order."

"Algeria?" she thought. She stared at the water drizzling in broken spasms over the windshield, forming pools near the wiper rods. Algeria, Algeria. For a long moment she pressed the

115

handkerchief against her eyes, then sniffed and wiped her nose with the back of her hand.

"Miguel? In Algeria? We're going to be together? Too much, Bugre, too much! I can't explain it but I'm so stunned! We're going to be together, is that it? I'll have to get together the money, excuse me, yenom! Is it expensive, the ticket? Never mind, that's not important, I'll talk to my folks, the *gens lorenensis* will help too, obviously. Algeria!"

I stifle my tears and laughter.

"And get your passport ready right away, the operation has to be quick. Now I'm going to take you home, I have something else to do, tomorrow we'll talk. A good journey, sailor girl!"

She opened her mouth and breathed carefully, afraid of inhaling too deeply. With one finger she wrote the word "journey" on the white moisture-coated window, thinking of arriving in Algiers. As she started to wipe it off, the middle letters ran together into a smear, leaving only the *jo* and the *y. Joy* . . . Quickly she erased them with the handkerchief.

"Oh, Bugre. My head is whirling. I'd been having horrible thoughts, I don't know. But how did all this happen, what's going on?"

"It's a long story, Rosa. I'll tell you about it later. Just enjoy your good news for now. You're going to have a hard life."

"I know. I know."

"A lot of work. But you'll have good contacts. No problem with your family?"

"After crying for three days my mother will get busy raising money to send me, she'll want to protect me from dying of hunger in *foreign parts*. My father is a sentimental German, but he's contained, he understands. I may even send them a photo of me in a bridal gown to guarantee good family relations, I'll force Miguel to pose as the groom, ah! they'll be so proud showing off their picture in a silver frame on the parlor table."

She would strike a movie-star pose, what was the name of that actress her mother liked so much? Rita Hayworth. She pronounced it Hi-worch. Her father was absentminded and didn't remember actors' names, but there was one he had never forgotten: Claude Rains. "An unpleasant old man," her mother would complain under her breath. "Actors should be young, handsome."

"Later you have a word with Mineiro. About the passport. Is this your street? I can't read the sign."

116

"The next one, go on a little further. What about the Corcel?"

"Tomorrow morning it will be outside your door, with the compliments of the revolution."

"Bugre, Bugre, this cap and this news, see. But where are you going? It's here," she advised leaning over to kiss him good-bye. She thought about asking if Miguel had mentioned her but grabbed her bag and book and asked only if she could keep the pack of cigarettes.

"Take the matches too. And this green handkerchief, isn't this yours?"

She went in protecting her head with the bag; the rain had grown heavier.

"What weather," she said to herself shaking the rain off in the vestibule of the big old house.

"Lia? Is that you, Lia?" asked Mother Alix opening the door of her office. "Come in for a second, dear. Sit down here beside me. Would you like some coffee? It's fresh, see if it has enough sugar."

Lia left her bag and book on the floor. She smiled helplessly, wanting to be alone, to think and plan.

"Insomnia, Mother Alix?"

"No, lots of work. What a lovely cap."

"Yes, isn't it? A present from a friend."

"With your hair pulled back that way you look just like a sailor. And a German sailor at that, you have your father's eyes."

"That's what my friend said, a sailor girl," I answer drinking the coffee. Too hot. Too sweet. "Did you have a letter from my mother?"

"A long one. I like your mother very much."

I gaze at the clock in the form of an 8 hanging on the whitewashed wall. The sound it makes is antique too.

"In my house there's a clock just like that one."

"Do you miss home, Lia?"

"I can't explain it, but my home is kind of like this coffee, sweet and hot. My mother used to smother me with so much love, at times I used to wish she loved me less. My dad pretending to frown, aunts and uncles always coming and going, battalions of cousins. Coziness, little parties. I remember them all, I

117

love them all, but I don't want to go back. Is that missing home? My time there came to an end. Here another phase began and now a third period is about to start; so I'll have these two to look back on. Is that the same as missing them?"

"Perhaps. When I was a novice, I used to think about my people, I knew I wouldn't go back but I kept on thinking about them so much. Like when you take a dress out of a trunk, a dress you're not going to wear, just to look at it. To see what it was like. Afterwards one folds it up again and puts it away but one never considers throwing it away or giving it to anyone. I think that's what missing things is."

I crush my cigarette out in the ashtray decorated with roses, Sister Priscilla paints china. So many things I have to see about, oh, this news. Algeria. Crazy, wild, Algeria? Algeria. And here I am hearing about the dress. I meet Mother Alix's steel-gray eyes, isn't it the dress she's talking about? a poem Lorena recited to me once, I'll have to say good-bye to the rose-pink shell. But wherever I go, and no matter how much time passes, I know I'll never forget her incenses. Her recitations, her music. A thousand years from now I'll still be able to see her, pale and skinny in her black leotard, lying on her back, pedaling in the air.

"I'll have another cup," I say taking the thermos bottle.

She pulls her white headdress over her ears, isn't her head too small for her body? I try to imagine her as a young woman putting on the habit for the first time, a gray life behind the veil that shields her head like a helmet. But why *gray life?* Didn't she put more than half a century of the greatest possible love into her work? So there's nothing gray about it. A Christian Soldier, how does the hymn go? . . . *Onward, Christian soldiers* . . . Half a century thinking the same thoughts.

"And how are your studies, child? Did you cancel your registration?"

"Well, things have taken another direction, see. I'm going on a journey, Mother Alix. Outside the country. That's all I can say for now, soon I'll be hauling up my anchor, see, I've got my cap on already," I say and for some reason am moved. "I won't forget your patience toward me, I know I'm aggressive. Complicated. You must have wanted to throw me out in the street at times, but you opened the door to me instead."

She puts her glasses away in their leather case, and places one hand over the other. My eyes fix themselves on her silver ring.

118

"You girls seem so unmysterious to me, so open. Just when I think I've learned everything about each of you, I'm suddenly startled to discover I was wrong. I know very, very little. Almost nothing!" she exclaimed, spreading her hands wide in a gesture of amazement. "What, in the end, do I know? That you're a militant leftist and that you've failed the year because you missed so many classes? That you have a boyfriend in prison, are working on a novel and planning a trip to I don't know where? What do I know about Lorena? That she likes Latin, listens to music all day long and is forever waiting for a phone call from a man who never calls her. Ana Clara, there you are, Ana Clara. Since she seeks me out and confides in me, I should feel secure in the impression that I know all about her. But do I? How am I to separate reality from invention?"

When she stops speaking, I hear the ticking of the clock. The mahogany chairs with the crocheted antimacassars on their backs, they were almost threadbare, those antimacassars. But they had been crocheted by Grandma Diu . . .

"You're too modest, Mother Alix. In reality you know us better than you think."

"You're young girls, Lia. I wasn't counting on really knowing you well. But being at a distance as I am, how can I be useful? And I wanted to be useful," she repeated. The cloth of the mantle wrinkled, modeling the wrinkles that deepened on her forehead. "Ana Clara is the only one who really opened herself without reservation. But I feel just as useless before her as I do before you and Lorena, reduced as I am to a tape recorder, I accept the charge, I record what she tells me, but when I try to influence her, to change what needs changing, she slips through my hands like an eel! I plead, I demand. One day she is repentant to the bottom of her soul, she makes promises, plans. I begin to believe in her recuperation, you know I have unlimited faith in miracles."

She's waiting for me to contest this view but I'm not going to swallow the bait. Not today, oh, how I want to enjoy my happiness all alone in bed, in the dark.

"You've helped her so much, Mother Alix. Don't I know? You've been her confessor, her nurse."

"And now, her denouncer. I've been talking to my cousin who is the director of a sanatorium. She can't be hospitalized by force, she has to be in agreement. She's already said she agrees,

119

but then she changes her mind, thinks she's cured, more promises, ostentatious projects. I'd like to have a talk with this fiancé."

I go to the window and look out at the night sparkling with rain. I want to go back to writing, after all, who's to say? Whether or not I have talent. Lorena and Miguel weren't very enthusiastic. They weren't enthusiastic at all. But couldn't they be wrong? I shouldn't have ripped it up, a hasty move, hysterical. But that's no problem. I can always rewrite it if I want. Lorena's too sophisticated and Miguel is too cerebral, he scorns fiction.

"Do you know him, child?"

"Who?"

"The fiancé. It seems he's very wealthy, but she doesn't love him, she loves the other one, Max. She talks a great deal about this Max, he's an addict too. Complete chaos."

Seen from the back, with her veil and gray apron, she looks like a peasant woman, the very old-fashioned kind, too clean a model even for an academic painter. I take aim and flick my cigarette butt into the potted plant. Was that Lorena who peeked out the window?

"So she goes into the hospital and gets detoxified. Splendid. After a week or a month, she's released, she can't stay in a hospital for the rest of her life. And then she starts all over again, you know it as well as I do. I don't see any solution.

"She wanted psychiatric help, I promised to pay for the treatment, she was supposed to see about a doctor but when I ask her which doctor she chose or when she's going to start she gives me vague answers, postpones it, she's incapable of making a decision. Yesterday someone came to deliver clothes she bought. I sent them all back, she can't pay her roominghouse bill, I don't even expect her to. More debts, and an insolent bill collector demanding a down payment. Good heavens!"

This floor with its wide boards, so light-colored it's almost white. In my house I used to love to lie on the floor while the grown-ups talked on into the night. It was good, to fall asleep to that sound of conversation.

"At times I want to shake Annie, slap her, she makes me so mad. Oh, I know she's sick, of course, but the disease itself makes me furious. Do you think an analyst would do any good at this late stage? She's already had dozens of analysts, Mother
120

Alix. Dozens. Some she went to bed with, the others she didn't pay. Recuperable cases are recuperable. Period. The less crazy of the crazy, about like us. A neurosis that doesn't call too much attention to itself because it fits in. As long as a neurotic is able to work and love in this reasonable madness, there's no real problem. But when he goes beyond that very fine line, as fine as a strand of Lorena's hair, when he steps over, he falls straight into the yellow waters. *Kaput.*"

The steel-gray eyes are about to spill over, she likes poor Annie very much. And she's smart enough to realize there isn't much hope for her.

"She hasn't appeared since yesterday. She called to say she was at the fiancé's country house."

"Fiancé. Pardon me, Mother Alix, but Ana is the product of this wonderful society of ours, there are thousands of Anas out there, some surviving the life they live, others falling to pieces. The intentions for helping them, etcetera, are the best possible, it's not Hell that's overflowing with the well-intentioned, it's this city. I see you go out with other kind ladies, giving soup to the beggars. Good advice, blankets. They drink the soup, listen to the advice and go running to trade the blanket for a quart of rum because the next day it's warmer, who needs a blanket? Everything continues the same as before, with one more drunken night furnished by the benefactor. A priest who is a friend of ours went to teach catechism to a little nine-year-old girl whose father sold her to a brothel and almost died from the beating he got from the proprietress's hireling. He learned his lesson, oh, did he ever! Individual charity is romanticism, I came to that conclusion just recently. The priest is still working with us but within a different framework. 'We forget ourselves, we relax,' says Bela Akmadulina, 'and everything slides backward.' "

I go to the thermos bottle and pour myself more coffee but I wish I had a sandwich. Ham and cheese. A bee buzzes against the windowpane and suddenly its buzzing becomes more important than our conversation. Where could it have come from on a night like this? I wish I could write like bees make honey. And I almost break out laughing: The grasshopper of the fable was certainly silly with her singing but the little ant with the broom in hand wasn't much better.

"I have so many things I want to say to you, my child. And I don't know where to start. This political movement of yours, for example. I wonder if you're safe?"

121

"Safe? But who can be safe, Mother Alix? To all appearances you are very safe here beneath your bell jar, but you're intelligent enough to know *from what* this bell jar protects you. Certain priests have broken the glass, like that one I was telling you about. By chance are they safe? No. And they're not even worried about safety when they go to sleep on a bare mattress with no pillow or when they perform their Masses on an old crate turned into an altar."

She smiles. A sad smile which I am sorry to have provoked.

"But I'm not in a bell jar, Lia. You're wrong on that point just as you were wrong when you said I'd like to put you out in the street. God knows my greatest wish is to protect and keep you always, if that were possible. If I don't involve myself, if I don't come closer, it's because I don't want you to think I'm spying on you, interfering in what you do. The three of you would fly off all the faster."

There, she's hurt. It's this terrible habit I have of arguing. A Bahiana turned political subversive, what could anyone expect?

"I can't explain it, Mother Alix, but what I meant is that you, although apart from the world, fight in your own way, and I respect your fight. I even respect the fight of those who want to destroy us, yes ma'am I do, they're doing what they think is right. Just as we are, weakened, betrayed, divided, you can't imagine how divided we are. But we keep on. Those who are left have to run like dogs to pass the torch on to the next person, who takes it and runs to the one after who is continuing the race, see. From one to the other. It's slow, but we're not in such a hurry."

"Torch, Lia? You say torch, but what I see is one leading the other to violence, death. A trail of blood is what you leave wherever you pass. We have a Supreme Guide and violence has been eliminated from His transcendent scheme. Spirituality—"

There you are, the victory of spirituality. I jerk loose a shred of fingernail which brings a piece of skin with it. Blood seeps out; I suck on my finger. A bullet, bam-bam in the chest, would hurt less.

"The Golden Calf is installed in the public square and you talk to me about spirituality. Its worshippers are not spiritual because they are its worshippers, see. They have before them the unattainable example of pleasure, comfort. glittering luxury, and grow desperate. These crimes and accidents happen because of their desperation, the masses are without hope and don't even realize it. So they climb telephone poles, shoot each other at random, drink kerosine and gasoline, all out of sheer affliction. Fear. I used to be the same way, disoriented. Now I know what I want to do."

"Something violent too?"

I can't stay in my chair, I get up. I assume the risk.

"No, Mother Alix. I confess that I'm changing, violence doesn't work, what works is the union of all of us to create a dialogue. But since you speak of violence, let me show you something," I say and look for the press statement I took to show Pedro and forgot. "I want you to hear part of the statement of a botanist before the tribunal, he had the audacity to distribute pamphlets in a factory. He was arrested and taken to the police barracks, listen to what he says. I won't read the whole thing:

"'There they interrogated me for twenty-five hours, as they shouted, "Traitor to your country, traitor!" Nothing was given me to eat or drink during this time. Afterwards they carried me to the so-called chapel: the torture chamber. Then a ceremony was initiated. It was frequently repeated and took from three to six hours each session. First they asked me if I belonged to any political group. I denied it. So they wrapped wires around my fingers, beginning the electric torture: they administered shocks to me, weak at first and then becoming stronger and stronger. Next, they obliged me to strip off my clothes; I was nude and unprotected. First they beat me with their fists and then with clubs, principally on my hands. They threw water on me so that the shocks would have more effect. I thought I would die then. But I kept resisting and I also resisted their beatings which opened a deep wound in my upper arm and elbow. Sergeant Simões and Lieutenant Passos put a live wire into the wound. They forced me to apply the shocks on myself and on my friends. In order for me not to scream, they stuck a shoe into my mouth, or, at other times, fetid rags. After some hours, the ceremony reached its high point: They hung me on a perch, tied my hands in front of my knees, behind which they had placed a broom handle, the ends of which were supported by tables. I remained hanging in the air. They then inserted a wire into my rectum and fixed other wires in my mouth, ears, and hands. The following days, the process repeated itself with greater duration and violence. The blows they gave me were so strong that I imagined them to have broken my eardrums; I

123

could not hear well. My wrists were raw due to the handcuffs, my hands and genitals completely black due to the electric burns.' Etcetera, etcetera."

I fold up the piece of paper. Mother Alix faces me, an affable expression in her gray eyes.

"I know about this, my child. This boy is called Bernardo, I've been in close contact with his mother, we went together to speak to the Cardinal."

Now it's me who doesn't know what to think. *Very special,* as Lorena would say. Never has anyone suggested to me so strongly the union of fire and ice as she does. She had grown pale but now her color has returned, the little veins crisscrossing each other on the surface of her cheek in a fine net, as if made of hair, broken here and there, the almost-lost ends searching for each other and joining hands until they form one transcendent and indefinable Whole like the One being who unites the universe. A universe which is that of her infancy, humanity's own infancy.

"Good night, Mother Alix. I enjoy talking with you very much."

"Take care, Lia. I don't want you to suffer, be careful, I beg you."

"I'm very strong."

"No, Lia. You're all so fragile, child. You, Lorena. Almost as fragile as Ana Clara. Whatever happens, don't stop sending me news. You can count on me."

"I'll send you my diary, Mother Alix. Instead of letters a diary of my travels!"

She goes with me to the door.

"May I give you an epigraph? It's from Genesis, will you accept it?" she asks and I smile. " 'Go from thy country and from thy kindred, and from thy father's house, to the land that I will show thee.' . . . That's what you're doing," she added. She hesitated an instant. "It's what I did."

Chapter 7

Sister Clotilde came in triumphantly with the bouquet of daisies and the bag of fruit.

"I bought oranges, melons and apples. And bananas, too, look what a lovely bunch."

I interrupt my bicycle exercise but continue to lie on the floor. With my fingertips I blow her a kiss.

"You're a saint."

"Don't I wish."

With her arms hanging limply inside the sleeves of her habit, she bows her head and becomes pensive, looking inside herself. What she sees must not be encouraging.

"Would you really like to be one?"

She smiles her yellowish-green smile, her dentures are a vague vegetal shade. She sniffs the daisies, her face still uninspired.

"When I was an adolescent I wanted to be Saint Theresa, she was my model. I did everything she did, I even painted little oil pictures, do you believe it? I didn't manage to have the fever, my health was always excellent. Later I wanted to be Saint Theresa D'Ávila."

Harder really. I stare at the ceiling.

"*Las Moradas.*"

"Have you read it?" she asked clasping her hands in enthusiasm. "I used to know it almost by heart. '*No es pequeña lástima y confusión, que por nuestra culpa no entendamos a nosotros mismos, ni sepamos quién somos.*'"

Her lead-gray apron reaches down to her well-turned ankles. She has a slender waist. Naked she must look a lot better.

"Many nuns are no longer wearing habits, haven't you thought of doing that? Your legs are pretty, Sister."

"'*Teribles son las ardiles y mañas del Demónio para que las almas no se conozcan ni entiendan sus caminos.*'"

125

I stick my first two fingers against my forehead and make a face, which is lost because she's looking inside herself again, even deeper. *Confusión y lástima.* She opens her mouth and inhales, surfacing.

"Ah yes, I was telling you I wanted to imitate the two Theresas. I didn't have the candor of the first nor the intelligence of the second. I learned the lesson, it's foolishness to copy others. The state of grace of a soul resides more in a state of unconsciousness than in anything else. I very much like the primitive painter before he discovers he's primitive," she adds examining the small purse Annie left on the table. The clasp is open and from the top of it escapes a fine eyeliner pencil.

"This friend of yours, for example. Couldn't she be closer to God than we who live for that ideal?"

Oh Lord. If she keeps it up I'll kill myself.

"Isn't that the phone, Sister? I'm expecting a call." She listens. She hugs the tray she brought against her chest and fixes her almond-eyed gaze on me: neither sweet nor bitter. The sleeves of her habit end in points, like wings: a bird not of the earth nor of the sky. Battles of conscience, poor little thing. She knows it is less serious to make love with a woman but still she must burn with remorse.

"It's next door. There's a phone that's always ringing somewhere in the neighborhood and nobody answers."

I close my book and lean my head against it. More war than peace, Mr. Lev Nikolaevich Tolstoy. If one added up all the wars in the world, just imagine. Some day I'll defend that thesis in International Law: Peace Is an Abnormality.

"He was murdered."

"Who, Lorena?"

"This neighbor who doesn't answer the phone. Mama adores stories about crime, the other day she told me about a horrible crime that was committed in France. By a priest."

"Priest?"

"It was quite a while ago. He murdered his pregnant lover in the forest, cut her open and removed the fetus, baptized it very properly and then buried woman and child under an oak tree. He even fixed a cross of little sticks on top of the grave. What I wonder is, what did he name the child?" I say, catching an orange as it rolls to the floor, she's arranging the fruit on the tray.

"It wasn't a priest who commited the crime, it was a demon. A demon took possession of his soul."

126

"But not completely, Sister. He baptized the fetus and then put up a cross over the grave, remember. It must be on account of crimes of this kind that the church used to tolerate pederasty in olden times. If he'd had a lover . . ." I say and am already sorry.

It's getting late on the planet. The silence is so complete I can hear her gestures as she arranges the fruit in a pyramid. I am exhausted but I start pedaling again, it's necessary to do something. It would be marvelous to sing if I had a decent voice. Oh Lord.

"Is that all right, Lorena?"

She tries to balance the apple on the top of the pyramid. I want to stroke her big scuffed shoes, parked at right angles. She's all right angles, poor thing. Who invented the tale that she was a lesbian? And why did I believe it? Why do I always believe the worst? I cross my legs in Oriental fashion and sit up on the rug.

"And it isn't the worse, of course. This idea that just came to me," I quickly add. "You are a person in the pluperfect tense. What tense do you suppose mine is?"

"Don't you know, dear?"

"No."

"You're too young, you haven't found yourself yet."

Eeh, the classic bla-bla-bla, who am I? Where did I come from? Where am I going? Lião gets raving mad when somebody starts philosophizing over this. "Work, see. Be useful, participate, and then see if you still have time to sit around admiring your own nave-all." She says nave-all. I agree, Lia de Melo Schultz, I agree, but oh, the thousands of hours I've spent contemplating mine. What am I? Abundance Overflowing if only he would call me up and say "Hello." Hellolorena.

"Were you ever in love, Sister? Before taking your vows, of course."

She picks up some of the daisy leaves from the floor.

"Don't forget your carrots, they're in our refrigerator."

Carrots. I would like to eat pure beauty and she offers me carrots.

"I'd like so much to be pretty."

The silence. Every time I mention this there is a certain silence. And yet I keep mentioning it, ah, I need the charity of you all.

127

"Why, dear, your type is so . . ."

Special? I examine the palms of my hands.

"When Mama was a girl, she had a friend who was very pure; she woke up one day with the marks of the Crucifixion on her hands. Isn't that extraordinary?" I ask.

But I don't want an answer, I want to be alone. I like people but sometimes I have this voracious need to be free of all of them. Solitude enriches me: I become gracious, intelligent, not this ugly resentful girl who smirks out of the mirror at me. I listen to the same record two hundred and ninety-nine times; I remember poems; I do pirouettes, dream, invent; I open all the doors, and when I chance to look inside, happiness has installed itself in me.

"It's not the first case. Of the Crucifixion marks," says Sister Clotilde straightening her body and grabbing the flowers like a sheaf of lances in her fist. She starts toward the bathroom, "May I?"

She asks permission to go in as if she were running the risk of finding a man inside. I tell her by all means, there's no need to ask permission. I fall onto my back. *This fruit has fire inside it.* Oh how horrible-marvelous to live. I listen to the water running from the faucet, penetrating the copper mug. An act of love. Will it run over?

"This business of not eating meat, child. You're pallid."

"I'm a vegetarian, dear."

Fervently I inhale the newborn air of the morning. I spread open my hands stretched toward the ceiling and my solar plexus opens too and whirls around like a sunflower. "*What does the flower know of the root?*" I ask out loud. The poets have presentiments but they're not right.

Consolatrix afflictorum! I scream inside myself.

The root is locked in the gilded monstrance draped with a golden cloth. The key is Truth, I ask only for truth and give truth in exchange. Is it so high a price? From what I can see, extremely high indeed. Who's interested? They all look at me, pat me sympathetically on the head, and run off to buy their tickets for the Fantasy Train with its tunnels of painted cardboard and plastic passengers. It runs through landscapes made of artificial flowers and fake waterfalls, all a farce effected by a set of mirrors.

128

"Ana Clara, too, she's the color of yogurt," said Sister Clotilde reappearing in the doorway. She dried her hands.

"Even Lia, who used to look so ruddy, is losing her color. I don't know what's happening to you girls."

She knows very well, thought Lorena taking the tract on social legislation from the bookshelf. She shuffled it, making the long strips of paper that marked the pages rustle. She read the notations made on the end of one of them and, leaning out the window, looked into the garden. The Law blossomed spontaneously like those flowers sprouting in the middle of the brush. "But along came the caviling men and complicated everything with their faultfinding," she thought pulling out another bookmark. After reading it carefully she tore it into pieces as small as confetti, which she blew from the palm of her hand. Did Jesus ever cavil? Of course not. Those who came along later made sly faces and invented the *sed lex*. Which in the end wasn't that hard. Cavil, she had learned that word from Mother Alix. "That cat of yours is such a caviler," she said pointing to Astronaut who, at that exact moment, began to clean his privates. I went to the dictionary: to carp, quibble, resort to trivial faultfinding. The expression was common in the Northeast, everything fitting: Mother Alix was from the state of Ceará.

The baritone voice of Sister Clotilde dominated the buzzing noise of a low-flying helicopter.

"It looks like a bathroom in the movies. I never saw a girl as painstaking as you."

"Disorder depresses me, Sister. Ah, if only I could order myself on the inside, everything calmly arranged in the drawers. Too much woolgathering."

She stooped to pick up something from the floor and opened the clothes closet. Lorena accompanied her movements by the small noises that the objects emitted when violated. "She's curious, she wants to see if my clothes look like the clothes in movies too," she thought examining the piece of notebook paper folded inside a book. The rough draft of a letter to M.N. A letter in verse, which she hadn't sent, like so many other ones imagined and outlined. "My heart arrived bleeding, red sail on the crest of the wave . . ." she read and smiled at the little zebra holding a flower in its mouth she had drawn in one corner of the page.

"My poetry is small in quantity but bad."

"What?"

Oh Lord. This one must be going deaf too. Lia had said it, hadn't she? The smaller orifices end up closing, in keeping with the principal one. *Res accessoria sequitur rem principalem*, she murmured turning to the nun. Her face lit up.

"What if I keep repeating, I am marvelous-divine and he is hopelessly in love with me, I am marvelous-divine and he is hopelessly in love with me, I am marvelous-divine. And he."

"That's it, dear. Positive thinking."

Lorena opened her book at random, read a passage about accidents occuring at the place of work, and then closed her eyes: She could repeat word for word what she had just read. Excited, she smiled. What about the things she saw with her eyes closed? Couldn't they really exist? Why couldn't delirium correspond to a reality? She stared at the daisies in the copper mug which the nun had placed on the table. Now their heads were pointing downward, their long stems without strength to support the blossoms which hung down, crowns of white petals. "Like timid brides," she thought, moved. She took the mug to the shelf where the picture of her father was. "Help me, Daddy. I know he likes me. But enough? Wife, children, so many people. I hate make-believe and he'll want it to be that way, oh, Daddy, I can say I'll resist, renounce him. But if he calls me I'll go running without even touching the ground, I'll get there two hours early, 'my love'!"

"In my grandparents' house there was one just like this," said Sister Clotilde polishing the gilded bars of the bed with a corner of her apron.

I give her a dustcloth and she rejoices, she loves to work. I've already told her that Mama's maid is forever coming around with her iron shoes and the efficiency of those fairy godmothers who tidy everything up by magic. But did she pay any attention? She needs to be doing something with her hands, big bony hands, the square nails cut straight across. She's been here for hours and hours, what if she's in love with me? A priest's woman turns into a headless mule, what about a nun's woman? The straight-cut nails. Her trademark. They need to be cut with the utmost care, such extremely important instruments, oh, for shame! Why do only things of this kind go through my perverted mind? So innocent to look at. A child.

"Only one-third of us is visible, did you know that? The rest is unseen, the reverse side."

130

"Only one-third visible?"

I turn the page. Still about accidents, bla-bla-bla-bla. I already know it. The summary must be just ahead, what to bet? There, bla-bla-bla-bla. I face her. She has stopped in suspense, the flannel stretched between her hands, ready to resume her movements of a shoeshiner on the bars of the headboard which shine like gold.

"Only one-third, dear. I see your mantle, your face, your hands holding that cloth. Very little, isn't it? And the rest? Where is the rest that I can't see?"

She looks satisfied with her high percentage of mystery.

"The rest is everything, my girl. But it belongs to God."

Her heavy oxfords have taken on her physiognomy; the shoes of someone who knows her business. And does it well. Her toes point outward, feet open in the measured step of a stolid duck moving toward the water, plak, plak. Virgin? "Yes, in a way," answered Lião rather reticently, she hasn't done research in this area yet. The dash to Sister Priscilla's room has to be barefoot. The whispers. The sighs, nuns must pant doubly hard when making love. Short sentences. Short breath, in the style of the little eighteenth-century pornographic books where the Abbess with a French name recounts to the novices her most secret memories.

"When I get old I'm going to write my memoirs," I say. "The problem is that the delirious thoughts, so beautifully disheveled, end up meticulously combed. Triumph of the norms of conduct."

She's in the bathroom washing her hands, after each thing she does, she washes her hands.

"In my time all the young girls had their diaries. But you girls nowadays can tell everything to your boyfriends, your analysts. Why bother with diaries?"

She probably likes to wash her feet too. At night, before the midnight sprint, plak, plak, her toes spread wide, free of the oxfords, choosing the boards that creak less in the floor which is creaky by nature. Oh Lord. It's no wonder Sister Bula's eyes water all the time, with the things she must see or guess at through her keyhole. The parade: Lião with her tennis shoes carrying the weight of the world. What's in those packages, pamphlets? Bombs? Next, Crazy Ana with her golden shoes and drunken step, her heel catching on her long neckscarf à la

131

Isadora Duncan. Pretty soon, this one here appears with her cotton-and-lace nightgown, her feet too big for any subtlety whatever among the squeaking boards, ah, the inspiration of the ancient convents with their subterranean passages. Closing the sequence, Cat with her velvet paws, her swollen belly dragging on the floor, where would be a good nest to unload the kittens? The order of entrance on the scene subject to variations, with the effect unaltered. Bulie wiping her eyes on the hanky-bedsheet and leaning tremulous over the windowsill, she wants to see me chaste and tranquil, hope of salvation, "You're all right, my child?" And the child possessed by demons, wide-open in the night and begging for help in Morse code, tum-tum, tum—tumtum. Horrible, horrible. The solution is immediately to write another anonymous letter to Mother Alix, who will read it and tear it up, magnificently above and beyond everything. *Ostende nobis, Domine, misericordiam tuam.*

"Well, I must go now. Anything else?"

I want to ask her pardon.

"Take some fruit, Sister. Before long another fruit basket will arrive from Mama's house, I'll never eat it all. Throw me a banana, would you?"

She scrutinized the bunch, frowning.

"They'll only be at their best two days from now. Every fruit has its right day," she added and instead of looking at the bananas she looks at her own hands. "It shouldn't be eaten either before or after."

A light cloud settles on her posthumous face. Neither before nor after, poor thing. I quickly turn her attention to me.

"My loverboy thinks I'm too green."

"Green?" She hands me a fig which she is holding by the stem. "How old is he? Isn't it that boy, Fabrízio?"

"It's another one, Marcus Nemesius. His father was a Latin scholar, all the children have declinable names, isn't that neat? Rosa, Rosae. Servus, Servi."

Like excreta, excretae. I bite into the almost-obscene fig. The cloud is still there. She has hidden her hands in her pockets. When unoccupied, she becomes sad.

"We're lovers. I'm expecting his child."

"Silly girl!" she exclaimed laughing.

At least I managed to make her laugh. I run and fill her pockets with fruit.

"Do you know any medicine for the disease of love? I'm sick with love."

"Dr. Humphreys' Marvel Curative Liniment. It cures whatever's wrong with you, put some compresses on the chest, beside the heart. Good-bye!"

On the stairway she meets Lião.

"Can I come in?" she asked, already inside the room. She went to the cluster of bananas and pulled off two.

"They're green, dear," Lorena advised.

Lia shrugged her shoulders. "One of her recipes? I heard her mentioning compresses, see."

As if she had caught a butterfly by its wings, Lorena held up the stem of the fig. She looked around her. Where to put it? Not in the ashtray, it would mix with the ashes and create an odor. Getting a plate, she collected the banana peels which Lia had been holding cupped in her hand. She knelt in front of her friend and carefully rolled up the bedraggled hems of her blue jeans, then tied the laces of her canvas shoes. Inspecting the black turtleneck pullover, she thought, "That's one I haven't seen," and looked with interest at the cap.

"Where did you get that?"

"A present from a friend. Your mama's car is there in front, the hard part is finding the key."

"Everything go all right?"

"Perfectly," said Lia.

Methodically she piled up mimeographed sheets, loose cigarettes, a toothbrush, and half a sandwich wrapped in wax paper. She dumped out the rest of the odds and ends: a few coins, a black comb with shreds of tobacco accumulated between the teeth, a silver keychain and a little ball of dirty cloth. Lorena recognized her handkerchief as it rolled to a stop near her feet. She waited for the second handkerchief to appear, but from the bottom of the bag there came only breadcrumbs mixed with bits of paper. She sat down beside her friend and looked up at the ceiling.

"Lia de Melo Schultz, I'm sad but you are happy."

"Very," said Lia putting the keychain on top of the table. She knelt on the cushion, pulling off her cap, and her hair exploded enthusiastically into the air. "Something great has happened, see. The problem will be the yenom, but my father will help out and if you could, too—"

133

"How much?"

"I don't know yet, I'll tell you later. It's for a trip. A trip overseas, later I'll tell you all about it. Oh Lena, I'm boiling over inside."

Lorena came closer. Sitting on the rug, she folded her legs and gazed at her bare feet.

"Get your microphone and interview me."

Lia grasped the banana firmly and extended it toward Lorena's mouth. "Do you swear to tell the truth, the whole truth, and nothing but the truth?"

"I do."

"Your name, please?"

"Lorena Vaz Leme."

"A university student?"

"Yes. Law."

"Do you belong to any political group?"

"No."

"And by chance do you take part in the women's lib movement?"

"No, not that either. I am concerned only with *my own* condition."

"Am I speaking, then, with an alienated young woman?"

"Please don't judge me, just interview me. I can't lie, I would be lying if I told you that I worry about women in general, I only worry about myself. I'm in love. He's married, old, thousands of children. Completely head over heels in love."

"An indiscreet question, may I? Are you a virgin?"

"Yes."

Asking permission, Lia peeled half of the banana she was holding. She bit off a large piece and breathed vigorously, her mouth full: "You mean you aren't lovers. Would it be presumptuous of me to ask the reason?"

"He doesn't want me. He doesn't try to see me any more, it's been days and days since he called."

"But are we talking about an impotent man? A homosexual? If memory doesn't fail me, I heard something about children, didn't I?"

"He is a gentleman."

"Ah."

"But if he sent for me, like the last of the Mohicans, I swear I'd go running, did you call? I'd go live with him in a cellar, un-

134

der a bridge, on the road, in a brothel, Lião, Lião," she whimpered pushing the banana away, "I don't want to play any more, I'm so unhappy."

Lia frowned, knitting her heavy eyebrows. She chewed in concentration. She started to reach for the wadded-up handkerchief which lay between the ashtray and the comb, but changed her mind. Cleaning her hands on the rug, she lightly stroked her friend's hair.

"I can't explain it, but I bet it's your fault. Didn't you start talking about marriage? If you did, the guy got scared off, this mania you have about getting married. Virginity."

"Things got much worse after he started going to that church group."

"He's going to a church group? If that's the case he wants to save his marriage. You're not going to have lover or husband. End of story."

"But who wants to get married?"

"You. Oh yes you do, yes ma'am, that's all you think about! Well, so let's find a guy who's free, dammit! What about Fabrízio?"

"Who knows? He's disappeared. He saw me with M.N. and I was pretty frank, you know I don't like to deceive anyone."

Slowly Lia's thumb came closer to her mouth. She started to bite her thumbnail, and suddenly snorted.

"Pedro is too inexperienced, he'd never do. There's our priest who's probably inexperienced too, but with the advantage of his age, you're an Oedipal case. A priest like you always dreamed of, *marvelous*. Dying to get hitched."

Lorena giggled silently, her shoulders shaking.

"Is he really, Lião?"

"It's what he wants most in the world," said Lia taking an apple from the tray and shining it on her pullover sleeve before biting into it.

"Now that it's been proven that marriage doesn't work, all the priests are wild to get married, dozens of resignation petitions. It'll be the death-blow they deal the church, a mercy killing. *Kaput*."

With her fingertips, Lorena delicately brushed together into a pile the bits of debris scattered on the small area of rug where Lia had emptied her bag. She gathered the pile onto a mimeographed sheet but before emptying it she read: *"Never again*
135

have we re-encountered liberty, since the day it was placed upon the earth," wrote Marx in 1844. Sadly, reactionary rule and submission have been continually maintained in German history up to the present day.

"It doesn't make sense, Lião. If you're a leftist, you have to accept these renovations that are part of the picture. It's the New Church rising up from the ruins of the old one, let's have unrepressed priests, contented ones. Latin America needs to make more love than other Americas. The tropics!"

"I can't explain it, Lorena, but the Church has opened her legs too wide. What saves her are priests like those who battle out there, I almost cry from admiration, shit, how they fight. They're the only thing in the whole structure left alive."

She unwrapped the sandwich, took a vigorous bite and put the scattered objects back in her bag.

"To pack a machine gun is OK, but get married, *verboten*. Is that it?"

Lia recovered and ate the piece of ham from the front of her sweater where it had fallen and stuck. She can't talk, her mouth is too full. I reroll the faded hems of her pantlegs. And these dusty black socks, where in the world did she get them? Ah, Lia de Melo Schultz. Pure prejudice of Dona Diu mixed with the Nazism of Herr Schultz. A priest making love? To the gas chambers with him! As if we were in the dawn of time, when Jehovah separated the water from the land, the darkness from the Light, the Good on one side and the Evil on the other. And the twilight area?

"In the twilight remains love which transgressed, dear. The zone where it's neither night nor day but penumbra, halftones. Silence. The zone of those who prefer to stay quiet. Homosexuals belong there, adulterers, the incestuous, those of tenebrous love, isn't it a splendid classification? From my own little head. Priests who want women fit in there, too. Ambiguity, fear."

Slowly Lia wadded up the wax paper into a ball and placed it beside the overflowing ashtray. She hauled off her sweater. Lorena looked at her cotton undershirt which she had put on inside out.

"Boy, are you square," muttered Lia. "Square and romantic, which comes to the same thing."

"Your shirt's on inside out," Lorena advised.

And wished she hadn't. It was very probable that the right

136

side was even yellower. She waited, eyes lowered, while her friend undressed.

"But look, Lena, if they get tangled up with women they'll be even more fearful, that is, they'll have more problems. Why marry? If they don't want a political cause, there are thousands of other causes around needing full-time attention. I think priests have never been needed so much as now. People going crazy, dying, 'I want to confess, I want to take communion!'" she yelled shaking her arms and legs in convulsions. "And the bastards abandoning their career. Fantastic, see. Is that Chopin? Change it, I want something happy. I'm happy, Lena. But what are you doing?"

Bent over the other's neck, Lorena was trying to undo the knot in the string which held the little silver fish and the bell. "Just a minute, dear, wait, I have a silver chain I never wear, this string is ugly, wait, I'll change it. But these priests, eh?"

"Our Indians catching syphilis, kids dying of overdoses, slums and rats, multiplication of whores and scarcity of bread. And *now*, of all times, these guys worry about declaring a *nihil obstat* to screw."

Finally the knot came loose. Lorena went to get the chain and rang the little bell.

"It looks so pretty, Lião. Wait a minute, don't move, I want to put a little cologne on your neck, that horrible string left a mark, imagine. This is a delicious perfume, it makes you feel so fresh. Smell."

With a certain resignation, Lia bared her neck and scratched her nose, thinking, "I'm allergic to perfume." She scowled:

"You can't believe how enthused I am over these priests who are fighting the problems. Action, Lena, because we've had too much contemplation already. To go out, talk until your mouth is dry, walk until your bones poke through your skin, take the curses, the doors slammed in your face, the stones hurled at you, and still continue without fainting, keep on even in the midst of the misunderstanding and hostility, keep on till you die, didn't they choose to live that way? Are they soldiers of Christ or not? Did Christ stop to relax in a hammock? I picture Christ as a dry dusty man in broken sandals, plodding over the roads like a demented person, facing hunger, thirst, sarcasm and mud, even the disciples doubting, getting fed up. And Him? I can't explain it, Lena, but I turn into ground glass when I hear this business

137

about priests sitting down on the job. And stop that, will you, I'm allergic, I can't breathe with all that perfume. I have to go."

She took the chain, kissed it. She kissed Lorena and stuffed her sweater into her bag, then slung the bag over her shoulder.

"And our lunch, Lião? Weren't we going to have lunch together today? I'd love to offer you a marvelous lunch, strawberries with cream, remember? We haven't had lunch together for ages."

"Another day. Come to the gate with me."

"Wait, take some yenom, I'm loaded."

"But that's a lot," I say as she thrusts a wad of bills into my bag.

"Offer a reading lamp in my name to your group."

"A reading lamp?" I repeat and laugh. I feel almost ashamed to be so happy. "What I'll do is buy some stuff at the office-supply store, there's nothing in our office but trans-Amazonic poverty."

We go down the steps hand in hand. She stops halfway down and lets out a yell. I look at her bare feet, did she hurt herself?

"Lião! Later this afternoon how about a movie? There's a werewolf film on."

"No, today I can't, see. I've got so much work to do. And I have to see about—" I begin and stop in the middle of my sentence. Sister Clotilde is coming in our direction. "Well, things."

"Lorena! Barefoot on these rocks! Aren't they hurting the soles of your feet?" she cries in alarm.

Leaning harder on my arm, she turns to the nun and makes a martyred face.

"Horribly."

Giggles. Comments from both about the beauty of the day. Lorena confesses that she wants to *holler* on a day like this. I pick up a stone and squeeze it hard in the palm of my hand, oh, it resists, I can squeeze until the end of time and it will stay intact. The happiness I get from things that resist that way. I put it away in my bag, now it's me who has to holler at the sun, Miguel! World, we will save you. We will save you, I repeat and my eyes are swimming in tears.

"Do you know if the grades are out?" asks Lorena in a stage voice.

It's the signal. I bend my head to hear the secret she's going
138

to tell me. Sister Clotilde waves a discreet good-bye and moves away with her loaded shopping basket.

"Tell me."

"Ana Clara is pregnant again."

"The fiancé?"

"Better it were. But with the fiancé everything is platonic, she's pregnant by Max, the other one. She has to have an abortion urgently and then plastic surgery in the southern zone, can you imagine? She's in terrible shape, poor thing. On heroin, Lião. I've seen the marks."

"Last night she came in during the wee hours and got the rooms mixed up, she came into mine. She went straight to my bed and started shaking me, I almost died of shock, I thought it was the police."

Lorena holds me by the waist. Her feet are hurting but she needs to punish herself.

"We have to do something, Lião. It's madness, madness. She can't go on this way."

I look at the withered pitanga tree that never bore fruit. It looks dead. But there in the heart of the stem it's still alive. Lorena follows my gaze. She picks a leaf, crushing it between her fingers, and sniffs it. Suddenly, she turns her back to me and climbs up on my feet, "Carry me!" I hold her around the waist and, stuck together like Siamese twins, we make our way slowly down the driveway, she guiding me because with her head in front of mine I can't see where I'm going. She is as light as the scent of soap in her recently washed hair. It covers my face like a handkerchief flying in the breeze. I think of Carla, why do I think of Carla? I squeeze her harder. She laughs, she's ticklish. We love each other, yes, we do love each other, this is love. I can't explain it, but I love Pedro too, and Bugre and Crazy Ana, I love them all. I'm capable of caring for them all, principally Miguel. Her feet slip off mine, she loses her balance. I almost fall on top of her.

"Come on, get down."

She won't obey, she wants to play more. I lift her up by the waist; in the air she stiffens and strikes a ballerina's pose. I deposit her in front of the gate.

"When I was a kid I used to walk for miles like that with Romulo."

"Is that the diplomat?"

139

"Romulo died. The diplomat is Remo."

"I'm always getting them confused."

"Everybody does. You know that trunk I stored in the garage? Inside there's an album of old photographs, one day I'll show it to you. The house on the farm was beautiful, that very pure colonial style. It was a hundred and twenty-odd years old, can you believe it?"

I open the gate. But there's still something I have to do, what was it? I bow my head, oh, I know.

"I'm tied hand and foot, Lena, I can't do anything to help Ana Clara. If I get involved with drug addicts! Even if she were my own sister I couldn't, wherever there are pushers and addicts there are dozens of cops, they're doing all they can to make it look like we're mixed up with drugs. I can't take the chance. I know she's sick but it's a sickness that makes me want to strangle the patient. They go down with their astonished faces, they all sink one by one, you pull them by the arm, by the hair, yell, threaten, do everything and they go on sinking like cement blocks thrown into a swamp. Even animals, Lena, animals react, kick back. Not them. They sink with that empty expression, dead inside. What is there to do?" I ask and pull on the gate, oh, how hard it is to do what one wants. "I'm already late, Lena. My trip, millions of preparations."

Lorena leans on the bars of the gate and groans, whether from pain or discouragement I don't know.

"I feel so sorry for her. I feel like an accomplice because I help her, there's a word for it in Penal Code, *connivance*. But how can I refuse? Mama already deposited the check for my car, I can give her the yenom for the operations, there's no problem. But I know it isn't yenom that's going to help her, not now."

"I'm going to need some too, Lena, the trip is coming up soon. What a pain to get a passport, oh, how many papers. Requirements."

"The other night she told me she had seen God."

"There's not a junkie who hasn't. I think God is getting more popular, a good sign."

The red Corcel flashes in the sun. A boy on a bicycle crosses the street. From some yard a dog barks loudly. There's a man in a dark suit standing under the tree on the corner. Noticing he's being observed, he takes a newspaper out and begins to read.

140

"What's the matter, Lião? Why are you looking like that?"

"That man," I say.

His wife comes out of the garage. She opens the door of the car. He gets in. I breathe to the very center of the earth. Like a child, Lorena sticks her fingers through the iron grillwork of the gate and hangs from the rusty curlicues.

"What if it's true, Lião? That she saw God, like she said."

"Have you seen Him?"

She grows tired of the position and now regards the red marks on her hands.

"Mama had a friend at school who woke up one day with the marks of the Crucifixion on her hands. Romulo, my brother, heard about the story and the next morning shook me awake, I have the marks, I have the marks! He showed me the impressions on his hands. But my other brother Remo was smarter, it was Mercurochrome! Can you believe it? I used to make enormous soap bubbles, neither Romulo nor Remo could make bubbles as big as mine."

A little yellow-spotted beetle is climbing up the sleeve of her cambric shirt. Already I'm remembering her this way, barefoot with her little beetle and her virginity, puzzling over the bubbles she used to blow.

"Oh God, this trip."

"Bahia?"

"Farther, I told you, pay attention, Lena! Overseas. Later I'll tell you the details, now I can't answer any questions."

"We'll have a going-away party, eh, Lião? Guga can come with his guitar, drums, I have all kinds of liquor, shall we throw a party? You can invite all your friends."

"My friends? *Verboten*, oh, *die Zeit entrinnt*," I say and open the gate.

Crazy German. My father. Sometimes when he drank he would sing and then he seemed like a god to me, only strange, because he sang in a strange language. And then he became a stranger with all his prestige of war and exile. His strong soldier's voice, how did the song go?

"Wie einst Lilli Marleen! Wie einst Lilli Marleen!"

Lorena repeats the refrain, tapping out the rhythm enthusiastically. "Sing some more, Lião, sing some more!" She tries to detain me, was I sure I couldn't come to lunch? How about a ride in the Corcel? An ice cream at the club? I go out and slam

141

the gate. Behind the iron fence she looks like a prisoner trapped in her garden. I feel mildly sad but immediately I want to laugh. Points of view: Don't I look like a prisoner to her too?

"Ask Mama if she has any old clothes she wants to get rid of, we accept anything, shirts, underwear, sweaters, whatever."

She reaches through the gate and tucks in my shirttail.

"Of course she has. Maybe she'll even decide to give Romulo's clothes away. He was only thirteen but he was so well-developed, you know my sweater with the blue stripes? It was his. She put everything away, it's so morbid," she sighs pulling my chain with the little fish outside my shirt. "And Mieux's stuff? He buys shiploads of fabric and then changes his mind, you can even make uniforms."

"For revolutionaries without a revolution?" I ask.

Lorena leaned her head on the gate and followed her friend with her eyes. She pulled up her loose shirt and scratched her stomach vaguely, her fingers descending in circles to her navel. The tenuous triangular shadow which showed through her white panties claimed her interest briefly. She smiled at the little bird that flitted through the tip of the pine tree and perched on the wall of the house next door. With childish respect she dropped a curtsy: "Good morning, Mister Brown. Good morning, Mister Smith. How is your father? My father is very well, thank you. And your mother? Oh, my mother is a cat. A very little cat. So sorry."

In the silence of the sun-filled garden there echoed a woman's sunny laugh. Lorena made her way painfully over the sharp stones, her hands cupped over her breasts, ah! the breasts of statues. Especially those seminude mountains belonging to the four bronze ladies seated at the foot of the pedestal, the old man in a vampire's cape perched on top. In the Praça das Rosas. And the rosy full-blown udders swollen with milk at the due times. Milk from the ranch, so foamy and white. The moonlit nights, milky white too. But when the moon went behind the clouds, the old man's canine teeth grew long and sharp, and he would come down to caress the erect nipples of the exposed breasts, shouldn't I? You should, they reply silently, offering the bronze blood from their necks. She smiled the smile that the statues must smile. And caressed the retracted nipples of her own almost nonexistent breasts, sighing. She would like to be a cow. A

142

cow with a humid muzzle and rosy teats, washed clean like the cows on the farm. A big spotted cow. "Look at the hindquarters on this one," Daddy would say patting Snowdrop's rump lovingly. "Hindquarters," thought Lorena leaning against the pitanga tree. She cleaned the sand from the soles of her feet. How much more dignified *hindquarters* than *ass.* "Has this one been bred yet?" he would ask and the cow would answer with a tender moo, chewing a green cud, green spittle, green shit, *verde que te quiero verde!* She would moo mossily when M.N. rested his face against her green-dripping muzzle: "My beloved." The pastoral love of a cow surrounded by bulls on all sides. And virgin, a cowbell around her neck in case of emergency, clang, clang, clang! A novitiate heifer. Ana Clara's first man was a German who farted like a bull when he threw himself on top of her, like an SS falling on top of the enemy during a silent bayonet attack. But hadn't she later said that her first lover had been that philosophy professor, a black beard and a feather touch? "In short, with Crazy Ana everything's delirious anyway." She thought about Lia with her first lover, staring at the ceiling and smoking, horrible, horrible. "I can't explain it," she began, and explained in detail that she had chosen her partner coldly, the way one would choose a toothbrush, this one's fine, let's go to bed. "And then, Lia, what did he do?" Lia was sewing a zipper into some jeans that should have been washed long ago. "Well, we lay in bed smoking and looking at the ceiling. We talked about so many things, see." Unbelievable. "But it's unbelievable, Lião, the first time and everything so cold," she exclaimed. Lia regarded her with a tired expression and bit off the last available scrap of fingernail. "Why cold? I wanted to know what it was like and took the necessary measures. What's cold about that? One doesn't have to get hysterical. He's a nice guy. A medical student, one of our group. The other day we had a Coke together, he's going to get married." I watched Lia sewing in the zipper with her big aggressive stitches, she sewed in the same tone she spoke, with irritation. "Strange, though," I ventured and she gave me a sarcastic look. "As simple as drinking a glass of water. How would you expect it to be?"

I was washing my combs in hot water with a few drops of ammonia, I've already showed them countless times that combs should be washed this way but did they pay any attention? Ana Clara puts an ancient plastic comb, all yellowish, into her Dior

143

purse and Lião insists on black combs, always suspect because they don't show the dirt. The only solution is to go into their rooms, collect their sinister combs and wash them along with mine. I gave such a lovely one to Lião, it even had inlaid mother-of-pearl on the handle. I warned her that it had belonged to my great-aunt. She thanked me profusely, stuffed it into her bag of lost-and-found articles and I never laid eyes on it again. You'll see, it broke in half the minute she raked it through that hair, Bahians have very stiff hair. "But how would you expect it to be?" she asked and I answered that I expected it to be like in her novels, just imagine if any of the characters in that peach-scented city would go to bed with a man as a mere act of liberation. And for the first time, too. I see now that I lost a good opportunity to keep my mouth shut. She ended up destroying her manuscript, poor little thing. She knows now that it's not included in any law or article thereof that an intelligent woman *must* write books. I think I'm very intelligent—but did I keep on writing poetry?

I climb the stairs slowly so as to feel the warmth of the stones on my feet. A butterfly lands on the banister well within my reach. I take it by the wings but it trembles so hard I let it go. It flies off in confusion as though it has been imprisoned for a hundred years. On my fingers, the silvery powder. So brief, everything. I was holding happiness thus a minute ago but it struggled so hard I opened my fingers before it hurt itself, one can't force it. If I'd squeezed a little harder there wouldn't be powder left, but its soul. I go into my shell. Yes, M.N. I chose you because you won't ask me if it's the first time. Nor smoke looking at the ceiling, you know I'm super-complicated about sex, careful, careful! Neither will you say that you're grateful to have been chosen. Grateful. Abominable. Oh Lord. I'll kill myself if M.N. speaks of gratitude or so much as glances toward the ceiling. I want fervor, fervor, you know what that is? True, he hasn't manifested very much, but couldn't that be because he's self-controlled? Controlled, of course, a gentleman can't show his excitement. "My fiancé has a real hard-on for me," said Ana Clara one night when she went on one of her binges, her C-grade vocabulary comes out when she's really exuberant. I have a particular dislike for that expression but here it is appropriate: One could say that M.N. desires me, but doesn't have a hard-on for me—*that is the question.* If I had those breasts.

144

He must think I'm unhealthy, his hands protect me more than they caress. As if I were made of porcelain. "Be careful with those porcelain objects!" Mama warned the movers. And the rude, hurried men unexpectedly forgot their haste and began to cushion with straw and cotton the transparent ballerinas from the china closet where the bibelôts were kept. The watered-down blood of the end of a breed. If I ever had a child by a man as white as I am, it would disappear among the white of the sheets, look at my baby! I would say to the people who searched, where, where? It would have to be placed on a black sheet.

I stretch my hands to the sun which beats through the window. Fragile nails. Weak fingers. M.N.'s are energetic even in respose, the square nails very well-brushed, gynecologists wash their hands more than anyone else. The sensibility of the fingertips that are so familiar with our private parts. That understand our roots so perfectly. I am perturbed when I think of this but it's exactly this thought that gives me the sweet sensation of security: I'm in good hands.

Chapter 8

I sit on the bed and watch the room revolve. I'm motionless I'm the axle. "Sit here this is the axle of the world," Jorge used to say sticking up his middle finger. Bastard. Rotten with syphilis, now I know it was syphilis. He must be dead too. He used to wake me up screaming. "Coffee! I want coffee!" My mother in bed, vomiting into a towel. "I think you're going to have a little brother." Halfwit. Ah, very kind all halfwits are nothing but kindness. The prick would shake me awake and I had to get his breakfast before sunrise because his shitty job was way off at the other end of the world. I'm coming I'm coming you asshole. I could never sleep as long as I wanted because there was always somebody shaking me awake, get up, get up! I'd love to sleep for five days and wake up in that Turk's office, what's his name? That analyst. Shit I forget. Never mind. I'd like to talk about the swamp with my mother's face in the black water. I get away as fast as I can, swimming hard, I don't know how to swim but I keep on swimming, pulling plants and slime up from the bottom, they rub against me and clog up my mouth, let me go! I shake my hands and free myself of the gelatinous creatures, leaves, fish. I know that just ahead I'll see the swimming pool, it's right up there, see it? I dive head first into the clean water and wash my whole body, laughing with Lorena who's swimming alongside me. I know how to swim, I say and she shakes her head and makes faces, saying pool-blue, pool-blue. I want to laugh at her faces but I clap my hand over my mouth, I've lost my bridge. My bridge! I lost my bridge, Ma! I scream running my tongue over the place where it should be, there's only the gum slippery with slime. She saw, she saw. I start to struggle in the water because I can't manage to stay afloat any more, I sink with the plants tangling about my feet let go!

"Dr. Hachibe. His name is Dr. Hachibe," I say wiping my face which is dripping sweat. I dry my hands. "That analyst of mine."

Max leaps out of bed and hops on one foot, laughing and groaning. "My leg's asleep, Bunny! Completely asleep, completely!"

I drink from his glass. Dammit. Another dwarf dressed in red flashes by, chuckling. Or is it the same one? I chuckle too. It doesn't matter.

"Change that record, Max. All those Negroes howling."

With the tips of his fingers he lifts another record from the pile. Lorena's gesture. He likes Bach too. The Mademoiselle with the little watch must have worked in both their houses, teaching the same things. The tiny gold heart on a chain must have been removed at night so as not to strangle the little girl. They don't even need to talk and they recognize each other from a distance like the Christians from the catacombs passing each other in the public square. They can mix with others yet they don't mix. She can utter indecencies and not be indecent, become a whore without being a whore. A ring with a coat of arms. This one here has his ring too, God only knows where he put it. But he has one. The family life. I suffered so much because I didn't have one but now. Still, it's all over, the decline has been setting in for a long time, I could see that in the album.

"The nha-nha has a photo album in her trunk. Velvet cover, silver clasp. All the ancestors posing in sepia. She pretends to be indifferent but that's all she thinks about. She couldn't rest until she had showed me every single one."

But the woodworms came and attacked them so subtly, they went through the taffetas of the skirts, the English flannels of the trousers, and arrived at the respective asses. In sepia. Very slowly they began to gnaw the bottoms, Nha-nha says "bottoms" puckering up her lips. Fine. The bastards gnawed the bottoms and got down to the bones, shit, the appetite woodworms have! Time for the bones. If she put her little ear against the trunk she could hear the scratch-scratch of the woodworms burping, also in sepia. The color of the times.

"Gimme a light," he says collecting the matches from the box which has spilled over his chest.

"Her mother lives with a gigolo. Lorena's mother, that little skinny girl that talks nha-nha-nha. The widow robbing cradles in order to throw away her money. But even so."

"An old American hag wanted me to live with her and travel all over the world in a golden yacht but her face was enough to

148

stop a clock, her nose was on one side, look, like this! Her mouth was over here, everything crooked, look. Look, Bunny!"

"She's in love with a doctor. An old guy. He's married, lots of kids, really awful. But when he disappears she goes nuts. Her brother is a diplomat. 'Remo, my brother,' she says every two minutes. He sends her divine presents, the guy has taste. When he was a kid he killed his younger brother."

"He killed who?"

"His brother. He had a shotgun and he aimed, boom. Liquidated his brother."

"What a sinister story, Bunny."

"Never went to bed with anybody."

"The brother?"

I pound him on the chest. He defends himself by crossing his arms, rolling over with laughter.

"It's her, it's her who never went to bed with anybody," I repeat and for each *her* I give him a harder punch. "All excited with her little hummingbird voice, 'my loverboy.' Loverboy. Silly combination of lover with boyfriend. She says she's contemplative-passive."

"Does she prefer other women?"

"Don't be ignorant, love. Contemplative is one who contemplates, don't you know that? There's the active and the passive who is so passive the birds make nests in his hair. She recites nude in her room. She goes wild over poetry and Latin."

"Aren't you friends?"

I want to say *yes* but now I can't. Or can I? Isn't that what friends are for? To tell us everything. Unflinching honesty.

Ana Clara sat up on the bed, closed the cigarette in the palm of her hand and dragged on it, thinking. Didn't she like her? She did. She liked her a lot. So.

"She's a snob, she thinks she's really something. But she's my friend all right. Who else gets me out of trouble? Not you. Not that asshole either, it's her. My friend. She thinks I'm beautiful, she has the greatest admiration for me. She thinks my eyes are extremely special. Do you think my eyes are extremely special? Max, I'm talking to you, pay attention!"

He kissed her lengthily.

"Panther's eyes. I want this panther . . ."

"I can't," she said and rolled herself up in the sheet, crossing her arms, hands clenched. "Now I'm a mummy."

149

He bent toward the floor and looked vaguely around. He picked up the bottle but put it back.

"I'm hungry, Bunny. I want to eat something, come on, let's eat together," he called running toward the kitchen. He opened the refrigerator. "Great! Fabulous, I'm finding things, look how much cheese. Wine, there's wine, eeeh . . . I'm cold, Bunny, I want to get under the covers."

"What time is it? I need to leave right away. What am I saying, what am I saying. It doesn't matter. I'm depressed."

He put on his sweater and stretched it almost down to his knees, then went running back to the kitchen.

"Come here, Bunny! A fabulous sandwich."

He's already peeled a whole loaf of bread and now he's on the second one, scratch-scratch with those indecent fingernails. Sickening. What if I call? This is his fiancée. Please tell him that I'm late because I suffered a slight accident and had to file a police statement, millions of questions. Nothing happened to me but the poor priest. Why priest? To make it more unusual. It's not every day that a priest has his head mashed under a wheel. The black smock. The black suit with that white backwards collar, I love those little white collars. But that took you all this time? No. That wasn't it. The problem was that my friend Lia was shot. The guerrilla. Guerrillas are like that, they let their attention wander for one minute they get plugged. I'm here in the Emergency Clinic I have to hang up because there are millions of people. I don't know which Emergency Clinic it is, I don't know. How can I. The address? You want the address? He wants the address. Already suspecting it's a lie, the scaly one doesn't know anything didn't see anything but he's already suspicious.

"Come on, I found some more stuff," calls Max but his voice is lost in the middle of the sound of china breaking. "*Aiii*, I dropped everything."

I hide my head under the pillow. I'm scared Max. I'm scared. Lião said. Who cares, she's just jealous. Why doesn't she save her advice for the flea-bitten types in her group? All she's good for is to flap her big mouth about Guevara Guevara. Who cares. Next year. Mother Alix will be matron of honor, she loves me to pieces she does a lot for you all, but for me—! Lorena will be a bridesmaid too, she'll bring her mother who is a VIP. The mon-eyed rural class you know what that means. Lião can come

150

dressed however she likes, an intellectual leftist could go as a Gypsy and be interesting but Lorena and her mother. So. The nuns with their little party clothes. All the clergy doing me honor. I'll have to come in on the arm of somebody, who can I ask to give me away. Professor Langue, there. Professor Langue with his stamp of a lord, he could even wear a dark business suit, a decadent lord but classy. Shit what class. My dress very simple but rotten chic. Everybody thrilled the scaly one thrilled just look at the bride I came up with. She was on magazine covers she modeled in London last month. A university student. She dropped out but next year.

"Max, next year I'm going to re-enroll at the university, you hear?"

Everybody is dropping out, swarms of girls and they all tell me the same thing, "I dropped out."

A fiancé usually gives important presents. He could give me the leopard coat couldn't he? Why give me money? Does he think I only need enough to pay for a low-rent boardinghouse and buy pins? That's what he thinks, the bastard. I have debts I'm going to have my tonsils out.

I tip the bottle into my mouth my pores open my chest opens. Life. If only it weren't for this Negro howling I really don't like Negroes. Or whites either, I don't like anybody. They're all a bunch of bums who don't miss a chance to piss on my head. Now it's my turn to piss, I scream and laugh from happiness. Max I love you I love you I love you. I kiss his shoe which is on top of my bikini. His shoe. I love his shoe I love all of him but I have to go I have to go. When I get unblocked we'll wallow in pleasure together, I want to wallow in pleasure. I kiss my Agnus Dei which I pinned to my bikini I love my Agnus Dei I love Mother Alix my saint don't be sad because in January my saint my saint. Shit now where's my clothes. They all disappeared. I'd like to be invisible and go out like that guy in the funny papers what was his name? He goes in and out and nobody sees him.

"I have to go, Max."

The drawer falls out. It doesn't matter he doesn't ask questions. He's not like the other one who even suspects Nona. I got sick, why not? A feminine sickness I'm very feminine, so there. So come on Annie because my brother is a gynecologist he'll examine you let's go there immediately, let's go dear, open your

151

legs a little more please? Now relax, very good. There, wasn't that quick? You can put your panties on because you're the prettiest knocked-up fiancée my little brother could ever find. Lorena is sick. It's Lorena who has to have an abortion. "Abortion? What kind of crummy friends do you have, anyway?" Your sister's the crummy one. Lorena's from a rich and ancient family. When your Nona was eating rotten bananas in the hold of a ship, Lorena's family—. And even Lião. A guerrilla and all but her father was a very important Nazi officer. Her mother had a sugar plantation. My friends. So. So get dressed you bitch. What are you waiting for there in your birthday suit.

"I'm making some fabulous food!"

Ana Clara steadied herself against the bathtub and surveyed her reflection in the mirror. Wrinkling up her lips she examined her teeth, her tongue. She sat on the edge of the bathtub to urinate. Holding her head in her hands she twisted a curl of hair around her finger.

"Do you think I look older than twenty? I think I look so old."

"There's this guy I know," he said coming back into the room. He rubbed his hands over his wine-spotted sweater. "My friend. The greatest cook in the world. We could . . ." He lay down silently, carefully, as though he were afraid of waking someone who was sleeping on the other side of the bed.

"And if I got cramps all of a sudden? Wouldn't that be a solution?" she thought sponging her belly and genitals with a wet towel. "That's it. I'll tell him I got the cramps, took a very strong pain-killer, went to sleep and lost track of the time." She wiped her face with the towel. "It's not proper for a fiancée to mention such things but that's tough." In the mirror she studied her shiny face. And Lião with her theories about the superiority of women. "What an idea. Stupidity. One case of the cramps and everything's screwed up. If it isn't cramps it's a kid hanging onto her and that's that. Even a guerrilla can't escape it. Women have to be the way they are. Get dolled up. Wear beautiful things. The only advantage I see, the only one, is our being able to make love without getting all messy. I need to tell Lião that so she can repeat it during one of her little meetings," she reflected and laughed, pouring cologne over her breasts and thighs. She jumped on one foot, giggling and wincing, "Shit, it really stings!" In the red lacquer medicine cabinet, beside the talcum powder, was a silver cup, which Ana Clara took out.

With the point of one red fingernail she affectionately traced the name engraved in the middle of the wheat-and-flower design: *Maximiliano*. She filled the cup with water, added a few drops of lavender, and gargled. She spat into the sink, grabbing the shower curtain so as not to fall down. She brushed her hair with renewed energy, teasing it until it stood up in a crown of rings. With the moist point of her eyebrow pencil she accentuated the rust-colored line of her eyebrows. Her hand trembled as she put eyedrops in her eyes. With the other hand she secured her wrist as she began to apply eyeliner; the brush slipped, smearing her eyelid. Again she began the difficult cranelike movement, her left hand sustaining the right, arm glued to her body, mouth half-open. She shut her eyes. "Am I drunk?" Taking a packet of aspirin from the cabinet she chewed one between her teeth and drank from the faucet. She sat down on the floor to put on her stockings and black silk jersey blouse. Around her neck she wrapped the silver chains that were spread over the rug.

"Give me your mouth," Max began, making an effort to open his eyes. His dilated pupils rolled upward and disappeared in the back of his eyesockets.

She put on her black velvet coat that almost reached her patent-leather shoes with their antique-style buckles of hammered silver. Her head throbbed between her hands. This pain. Discovering Max's pants beside the armchair, she explored the pockets and with an automatic gesture removed a roll of money and put it in her coat pocket without counting it. Under the chair was a pack of American cigarettes. She thrust two fingers inside and searched the bottom. In her tweezerlike grasp she drew out a fine strip of carefully folded tissue paper from between the cigarettes. She pinched it gently and closed her hand over it, then turned euphorically to the bed. Max slept tranquilly in his blue pullover. She covered his legs, adjusted the pillow under his head.

"Sleep, love. I won't be long, go to sleep."

Picking up the cigarette that burned in the ashtray, she buttoned the collar of her coat and went softly out, walking zigzag but upright, with her back straight and her head high. In the street, she moved faster beneath the drizzle which was thickening into rain and squinted up at the tumultuous sky. "Shitty night. Shitty town," she muttered signaling toward the cars that passed at high speed, all going in the same direction with head-lights beaming high and horns complaining at those who lagged. Ana Clara motioned at a taxi which didn't stop. She waved harder at the second one, protecting her eyes from the glare with her purse.

"Imbecile! Bastard!" she screamed at the fleeing driver.

The bald man in the lustrous black car drew up beside her. He made a sweeping north-to-south gesture:

"I'm going that way, want a ride?"

She summed up the man and car in a rapid calculation. Panting, she leaned toward the door which opened. As she got in, she lost her balance and fell against the steering wheel. Violently she jerked loose the hem of her coat which had caught in the door.

"I've been on this corner since eight-thirty. Would you have the time?"

"Since eight-thirty?" the man replied in amazement. He pointed a gloved finger to the dashboard clock: "But it's almost eleven o'clock, miss. Any trouble?"

Ana Clara clenched her head between her hands.

"What a headache. Do you have any aspirin? Give me a cigarette."

He slowed the car and turned down the volume of the radio, which was commenting on a soccer game. He examined her in the rear-view mirror, from which hung a little velvet teddy bear.

"You're upset, have you had some trouble? There's everything you asked for in the glove compartment, you're welcome to it. What I don't have is water. Or whiskey either," he added with a smile.

She ripped open the envelope of aspirin with her teeth, choking in a sudden attack of coughing.

"I was at a party when they told me. I'm afraid it may be too late, I don't even know if he's still alive."

"Who?"

Painfully she swallowed the aspirin tablets. She rested her head against the back of the seat, rolling her hair around her finger.

"My father. He had a stroke in his office. Could you drop me off in the São Luiz neighborhood? Please, take me there. But let's go faster, could we? Sorry."

154

The man accelerated the Mercedes and turned off the radio.

"But when was this?"

"I've lost all notion of time, I have the impression I've been on that corner for hours. I was at a party when—oh, my poor father! My poor father! He was coming out of his office, he's a lawyer."

"Is this the first?"

"What?"

"Stroke. Is this the first one he's had?"

"I think it's the second. The first was when my brother was arrested, my brother is a terrorist. To this day nobody knows whether he's alive or dead. He disappeared."

The man chewed the ends of his long moustache.

"I'm an industrial executive, not a doctor. But if I can help you, I'd be glad to."

You can. By closing your factory, you bastard. Murderer. You throw the debris on all our heads and then. Next year I'm going to throw mine too. A house on the beach and another in the country. The rabble can go screw themselves.

"This air would give anybody a heart attack. Do you live downtown?"

"Well, lately I've been practically living in my country house, I have a delightful estate outside town. And now with the helicopter it's like going from here to the corner. Have you ever ridden in a helicopter?"

It's all I do, thought Ana putting away the pack of cigarettes she had taken out of the glove compartment. Furtively she inspected the chrome-plated lighter.

"What kind is it? Your industry?"

"Meat-packing," he muttered and slammed on the brakes as the light changed. "See that? It's too much, the green light turned red without any warning. Where's the yellow caution light? On vacation?"

She looked for the lighted cigarette that had fallen from her hand into her lap. Imbecile. Mongoloid. He ought to learn to drive.

"It was nothing. You drive marvelously."

"You have to be suspicious of even the traffic lights, let alone other drivers."

"Really. I have a Corcel but I avoid driving."

The man examined her, disturbed.

155

"His office is in the Rua São Luiz? Your father's office."

"Yes, one whole floor. He's a big-time lawyer, my father. Fransisco de Paulo Vaz Leme."

"But do you think he's still there? He couldn't be, what would he be doing there? Naturally they will have taken him to the hospital."

She rolled down the window to throw away her cigarette. Bending over frontwards, she clenched her hands into fists against her body. This crumb-bum wanted to know everything.

"My uncle, the cardiologist, has a clinic on the same floor, the other time my father stayed right there in the clinic," said Ana Clara resting her head on her knees. She laced her arms around her legs. "Oh, I feel so depressed. Do you have a handkerchief?"

He took one from his suit pocket.

"Here, I haven't used it. But what's this? Don't cry, calm down, don't cry! Your father's being taken care of, isn't he? What's your uncle's name? The doctor?"

"Loreno. Loreno Vaz Leme. I'm named Lorena after him, he's my godfather."

The man stroked Ana Clara's hair lightly.

"I know several doctors on that street, but not that one. Vaz Leme? . . . No, I don't know him."

"In reality he spent most of his professional life in the United States."

I'll say I went with Lorena to a conference, it's settled. The guy talked for two hours without stopping and that was due to good luck because he knocked over his pitcher of water. And where was this conference? At the university dear. A lawyer who is a relative of Lorena's all the important lawyers are her relatives. We sat in the front row and couldn't get up and walk out because during conferences and during a fuck you don't get up and walk out, it's not polite. And I'm polite. Don't you want to marry a polite girl? So.

"You've been drinking, girl. Do you hear me, Lorena? Lorena!"

I lift my head. I fell asleep. Didn't I tell you? Always somebody poking me. Now it's this man with his little hands, look there at his little hand. Is he going to ask more questions? He is indeed. He gives one a ride but he charges. He reminds me of the scaly one.

156

It doesn't matter. I'm Lorena now.

"You've been drinking, haven't you? And quite a bit."

"I mixed champagne and whiskey at the party. I'm not really used to drinking but I'm feeling better now, I'm fine, Mr.—?"

"Would you like a cup of coffee? Let's stop at a café ahead, you'll feel like a new girl. And don't call me *Mr.*, I'm not so very old, am I? Shall we go to a café?"

"No, no, please, they're waiting for me, I'm worried. I'm sorry but."

"What do you do, Lorena? You're a charming girl, do you know that?"

"I'm in my senior year of Psychology at the University of São Paulo."

His hand again, this time on my knee. Not even with my father dying does this pig show any respect.

"Beg your pardon!" he screamed. "These idiots! Did you have a scare? Beg your pardon."

We almost ran into a truck and he begs my pardon. He's the one who had a scare. Is he going to hold the wheel with both his little hands now? He is. Or I could say that I had an auto accident. I was a witness, a three-car collision and I was in the third. The drivers caught in the wreckage. Oh I need to. Quick quick.

"Can we go faster?"

"But you're not feeling very well, Lorena. How . . .?"

"I'm fine, really. It was just a shock, I thought you'd forgotten about it."

"Call me Valdomiro."

"In reality I've never felt better, if it wasn't for this business of my father. Here, you can leave me here on the corner, quick, that's a great help. You're a saint."

"But what if he's not there any more? I can wait, Lorena, don't panic, is it in that building there? But the door's already locked, isn't it?"

"No, it isn't there, it's farther ahead. Stop here, I want to walk. The fresh air will do me good."

"But it's raining, girl! Here, keep my card. It has my office phone. Will you call me?"

"Of course. First thing in the morning. Tomorrow."

He kisses my hand. I open the door and fall to my knees on the sidewalk. And he's still talking I think he's coming up behind me. I run away. I wish I had skates. I always wanted skates. To go skating off down the road, all by myself. The rain has passed but I'm freezing cold. I could have asked him for a loan. Would he have given it to me? What about the card? Who knows, I threw it away. Valdomiro. Mercedes-Benz. He wouldn't give me a thing.

"Cognac," I order the bartender.

He just stares at me. Why does he look at me that way? I raise my head and get my money out, do you suppose he's thinking.

"Domestic?"

"No, imported, the best you have."

I stick my hand in my pocket and tear open the tissue paper. I drink slowly. My eyes and mouth fill with water. How hidden we are. And how free. Hell, why does that fool Lião talk so much about liberty. We're free, look here nobody knows what I have in my pocket. Nobody knows what I'm swallowing. Thousands of people all around me and nobody. Only me. Right this minute swarms of people are murdering and being murdered and who takes any notice. Right in this building up above. Thousands. That's neat. Do things right in front of others.

"Good evening."

There's an old man in front of me saying *Good evening.* Now what does he want this old man. He looks like a beggar in that raincoat people are getting overconfident. He wants my company, the bum. He's unaccompanied. Me too. The night of the unaccompanied. I drain my glass. I'm serene as a queen it's glorious to feel like a queen. To feel like somebody else. Enough of Ana Clara. I'm Lorena.

"I'm waiting for my husband."

He wants to say something and doesn't. He leaves, scraping the dirty soles of his shoes on the dirty tiles of the floor. And what if he's my father. What if all of a sudden he should be my father. I run after him and tap him on the shoulder. I look for myself in his face.

"Do you know what time it is, sir?"

He shows me his wrist with its gray hairs, the man who could be my father doesn't have a watch. I need to control myself so as not to burst into tears. What joy. I'm happy happy. Maybe he is. Maybe he isn't. It doesn't matter he doesn't know that he's two people, the one who stays in the bar and the one who goes

158

off arm and arm with me. I have forgiven him everything. I was certain we'd meet some day. The men in the doorway multiply as though reflected in mirrors. I walk proudly between the clusters, passing among them with my secret, like a ship. I'm a ship sailing by in the distance, all lighted up. I see myself passing far away and it's spectacular to see myself parting the sea. I raise my coat collar and become a muffled ship. The voice the voice calling me. I turn around and there he is arm and arm with me. My father and I in the sea-filled night. He doesn't know anything. I'm a little girl and he doesn't even know.

"You are beautiful. Beautiful!"

"Thank you," I say and smile. He'll never know why I thank him.

He puts his arm around me. I can feel his desire like a heavy weight, his desire is an anchor but the night is so light, could there be a more weightless night? The father and the daughter. They meet in the night. I rise up weightless like the night and everything is silent where I am. The stars pass, pass and illuminate me I can grab that one by the tail. Taxi?

"Taxi?" I cry and the headlights blind me.

"We don't need a taxi, Gorgeous. The apartment is close by, a lovely little place, come on. Lean on me and I'll help you. What's my pretty girl been drinking? Naughty little thing! Aren't you going to tell me? Huh?"

"Rain."

He laughs. Teeth. He has good teeth. He doesn't have a watch but he has teeth. The watch doesn't matter, but the teeth. Shit, he's handsome. He had to be a handsome man, I knew it. My father is with me. I'm protected. Protected.

"My whiskey is first-class, we can have a drink and listen to a little music, do you like tango? I have a collection of Gardel records, I'm crazy about Gardel. But my God, you really are beautiful, you look like a goddess," he says squeezing me harder. "I dress sloppy this way because I don't care about appearances, I'm the Bohemian type. But if I'd guessed I was to meet a goddess like you, I would have worn a tie and tails!"

I've become transparent. Transparent. I can see myself because I'm transparent, my rose-colored tissues my intertwined veins, my organs organized in their compartments I'm completely in order inside like that plastic man in the store window there was a man turned inside out standing in a store window.

159

All order and light. So much light that I need to close my coat so nobody can see, the Heart of Jesus is in my breast. The shock makes me so dizzy that I trip and cry out. It's Him.

"It's Him!"

The man is startled too and grabs me. We fall down together. "What happened, what's the matter with you? What was it? We could break a leg, Gorgeous. Did you get hurt?"

If I tell you will you believe me? Mother Alix, listen. He is here hanging inside my chest with the crown of thorns I don't pray or anything and He chose me, do you see? He came to reside in me, of all people! I want to shout because it's damned glorious for Him to have chosen me but I'll only tell you only you. I have to be serious and dignified with my Resplendent Heart. If He chose me it's because I deserve it He saw all that humiliation so much suffering He remembers what I suffered with all those bastards who. I was a child and those bastards I couldn't defend myself or anything I was a child.

"I couldn't, shit."

"Crying, Gorgeous? Do you hurt somewhere? Tell your *hermano*," he murmured, humming as he picked up her purse which she had dropped, "*Si precisas una ayuda, si te hace falta un consejo . . .*"

"My name is Lorena, Lorena Vaz Leme."

"For me you're Gorgeous, I'll just call you Gorgeous. You'd win any beauty contest easily, when I see the hags that enter them nowadays. You have an exceptional face, I can't see what's underneath your coat but I can guess, I'm an expert on the subject. But don't cry that way, can't you walk a little farther? Lazybones. We're almost there, I live very close, a Bohemian has to live in the Bohemian zone, right?" he exclaimed, laughing. "You'll like my little old-fashioned place, there's even a Victrola that winds up, you know how they work? What a stupid question, you were only born yesterday. Gorgeous, gorgeous. That's it, I want you laughing, I like happy people. And I'm a sad man. I adore tango music, we'll hear some tangos."

"But I'm not alone."

"Of course you're not, what amazing news. Careful, Gorgeous, hold onto me, did you twist you foot? Later I'll give it a massage, I used to be a masseur. Masseur, sportswriter, radio announcer, real estate dealer, oh, the paper I sold. I've been many things, everything but rich. When I was young I even had a body-building school, to this day I do my exercises, put your hand here. See? Forty-six years old and not a sign of a tummy. A bullfighter!"

I was late because. My father and Jesus I know I know it's hard nobody understands. So simple. He crushes up the bread and the rat it's a rat he has in his hand. I meet his gaze full of anger and fear. I'll never be afraid again. I'm made of light and he's nothing but scales. Scales and darkness. It doesn't matter.

"I couldn't care less. So."

"Look here at all my old stuff, I surround myself with antiques."

The wide bed, covered with a crocheted bedspread, occupied almost the whole room, which was made cozy by silk pillows and family photographs pinned to the walls, among them snapshots of seminude men in athletic poses. The family pictures were old, yellowed and conventional with their groups of men and women in black, surrounded by children in sausage curls and boots. On the bedside table was a lamp with a shade fringed in colored beads and a little Victrola protected by a lace doily.

"My family," she said opening her arms. "My family."

He took off her coat, folded it over the chair with the satin cushions and knelt in front of her. She swayed. Lightly he ran his fingers over her black stockings.

"What a physique. Your physique, Gorgeous! Those legs. I don't want you to take off your shoes or stockings, I adore black stockings, very long like these, do these go all the way up? They sure do," he murmured kissing the buckle of each shoe. "Gorgeous, gorgeous."

"The pictures," said Ana Clara pointing in wonder at the walls. "The boy with the cat. My brother, shit, my brother."

"Yes, Gorgeous, we're all brothers, let the world go by outside and here in our little corner . . . but come rest a little, lie down here, put your head on the pillow, pure kapok, isn't it soft? Are you comfortable? Gorgeous. Let's have a little whiskey to warm us up, what about a drink? Scotch. My friend keeps me supplied, he works for the customs, I have friends everywhere! But let me look at you. . . . Gorgeous."

"My cat disappeared."

"Don't worry, I'll find you another one, come on, drink. Can you hold the glass? I'll put on a tango to complete the atmosphere, a real tango, hum? I was a singer for a while but my

161

voice started to crack, I smoke too much. Cigarettes are poison."

"I have to go," she moaned, twitching. She threatened to get up: "What time is it?"

"What's this, what silly talk is this? The night is young, Gorgeous, come on, drink. Careful, don't spill it on your blouse . . . oh, you already did. Never mind, it'll dry. Gorgeous."

"Next year. Next year. January. I already said."

He adjusted the handle of the Victrola and wound it up. The violins surged nasal and vehement. At each turn of the disc the needle hurdled the deep scratch and lost control in its descent, then re-encountered the groove. He drew close to her.

"I want you to stay very quiet, just like you are, completely dressed," he murmured with a heavy voice. "I want you to stay nice and quiet while I read something to you, are you comfortable? Give me your glass, I'll give you some more later, now stay just as you are. Isn't it lovely, this tango? *'Bien sabes que no hay envidia en mi pecho! Que soy un hombre derecho!'* . . . wait a second, I'll be right back."

Slowly she rolled her head back and forth on the pillow and crossed her clenched hands over her breasts.

"I have to go. My father. It doesn't matter because my father."

With controlled gestures he undressed. He folded his clothes, methodically piling them up piece by piece, until he was naked. Then he inhaled and exhaled, expanding his chest, contracting his abdomen. Gravely he walked to the drawer of the larger table covered with an old Spanish shawl. From it he took a tattered magazine, with the picture of an old movie actress on the cover patched together with pieces of adhesive tape. He lay down beside Ana Clara without touching her, his entire body trembling. From beneath a red satin cushion embellished with tea-colored lace he brought out a pair of glasses and put them on. His hoarse voice stumbled over the words.

" 'When on that dismal afternoon at Waterloo, a desperate Napoleon ordered all batteries of his near-defeated troops to pour out their ammunition in a concentrated volley, a deluge broke from the floodgates of the firmament, engulfing the battlefield. At that moment, hearing the artillery drumming half-buried in the mud and the celestial thunder rolling amid the drenching torrents of rain, the phenomenal man whose Caesar-

ean glory glimmered in the final twilight of the Hundred Days must have exclaimed with his eyes turned to the heavens, We concede!'"

He paused. He breathed with effort, wheezing through dilated nostrils, his teeth whitened with saliva. He turned over on his stomach and straightened out the magazine which was open on the pillow. His stringy muscles continued rigid, left foot tensing spasmodically in a cramp. He bit the cushion and raised his head, pulling his lips back into a grimace as he read under his breath:

" 'Other famous conquerors, upon releasing the final expirations from their heroic breasts, perhaps have heard the cosmic elements of Nature resound with fury in the awesome solidarity of thunderbolt, lightning-streak and flood. Great leaders do not succumb without tempest, tumult and storm, in order that their fearful glory might further magnify the terrifying splendor of the loyal and choleric heavens. No one will deny that Rudolph Valentino was the greatest conqueror of our remarkable times.'"

Moaning, he pulled himself so close to the sleeping Ana Clara that he could almost press his foaming mouth against her cheek. He relished the scent of her perfume, teeth grinding between clenched jaws. Placing the open magazine on her belly, he drove his elbows into the mattress. With painful breath he adjusted his foggy glasses and lowered his haggard eyes to the text:

" 'Of course he did not make Andromache a widow, nor accept the duel with Achilles. He did not conquer Gaul, destroy Carthage, nor take Constantinople. He did not fight in the battles of the Crusades nor was he at Trafalgar. He did not cross the Berezina River nor pierce López of Paraguay with his lance. However, he did more, infinitely more . . .'" he croaked ripping off his glasses. The bedspread wrinkled under his twitching hands, as his sweat-soaked body jerked in contortions. His voice was a thick wheeze.

" 'He conquered the hearts of all the women who saw him on the screen, and they barely saw him . . . yet having only glimpsed him, they experienced the swoon of Platonic love . . . which, according to the physiologists . . . is the most dreadful and subtle form of passion . . . that finds no end that finds no end in infinite insatiability!'"

He sank into the pillow, arms open, and grew still. The pasty sound from the wound-down Victrola gradually faded.

163

Chapter 9

Ana Clara making love. Lião making speeches. Mama making progress with her analyst. The nuns making dessert, I can smell from here the warm aroma of pumpkin cooking. I make philosophy. To be or to exist. No, it's not *to be or not to be*, that's already been thought of, let us not confuse it with the philosophy I just invented. Absolutely original. If I *exist*, then I am not *being* (something or somewhere) because for me to exist it is necessary that I *not be* something or somewhere. Now where can I do that? A very good question: Where can I exist without being something or somewhere? Only inside myself, of course. In order for me to exist entire (essential and attributes) it is necessary that I not be anywhere except inside myself. I do not disintegrate in Nature because Nature takes me and gives me back wholly; there is not competition but identification of elements. Only that. When I am in the city, I disintegrate because in the city I don't *exist*, I *am* (somewhere); I compete and within the rules of the game (there are thousands of rules) I must compete well; consequently I have to *be* something—competent—in order to compete as well as possible. Thus to compete as well as possible I end up sacrificing existence, mine or somebody else's, it all comes to the same thing. And if I sacrifice existence for mere being, I'll end up disintegrating (essential and attributes) until I'm totally pulverized. Vanity of vanities, all is vanity. We come to a Biblical conclusion but it answers all the questions of this confused and disintegrating world. The madmen ruling over the living and the dead. Those few who manage to hang onto the reins of madness will prevail, who will they be? Polluted lungs and minds. An important role is reserved for the psychiatrists. And for the prophets, I have even more faith in them. I think I'd be more useful if I'd studied medicine, what good will laws do us in the future if they're already in the state we know so well? A marvelous psychiatrist.

The unfortunate thing is that when I read a book about mental illnesses, I discover symptoms of almost every one of them in myself; I'd be a psychiatrist too well acquainted with madness. Saved through love. Oh Lord. Why doesn't M.N. call if only just to say . . . I'm not pretty, an undisputable point. But isn't my IQ much higher than normal? And I do have a certain charm. Somewhat obscure, it's true, but "*if you search you shall discover the gold buried in the earth.*" *L'or caché.*

I close my tract, it's already very tractable. I wish the exams would start, oh, this strike. There was a time (a good while back, right?) when we used to study together, Lião and I. Ana Clara wasn't yet so ambulatory-delirious, poor thing. She used to study one or two problems with us, muse over her plans, and then try on my clothes, but she didn't bother us much. It was the period of research, Lião wasn't committed to the revolution yet, she was studying normally. Statistics. Formulas. She even wrote a paper about what causes drivers to hang trinkets from the rearview mirrors of their cars. There were two clear-cut groups: those who did hang up knickknacks and those who didn't. The latter revealing an obvious intellectual superiority over the others, in the Lianine view. For me, a simple matter of good taste, you hear, M.N.? Would Plato have hung his little boy's bootie on the mirror of his Porsche if he had driven a Porsche? Naturally it was his wife or daughter who hung that miniature hat up. A little Mexican sombrero, *ay, yay, yay yay!* Didn't Mieux hang up a little erotic baby in Mama's Corcel? If Lião had seen the sombrero hanging in M.N.'s car she'd have turned her thumb down, *kaput.* And Lião knows. She knows everything, even the number of prostitutes who derive pleasure from their work and those who don't, she's researched that as well. She wandered about the red-light zone for an entire month, bag and briefcase in hand, asking the most original questions. When she started working with doped adolescents she joined her famous group. If she'd stayed on a little longer she'd have been wearing a white apron by now, working in her child-psychiatry clinic, they all start out very humbly and pretty soon they're booked solid until November. The adults have already dived into that whirlpool up to their ears, now it's the children's turn. One less psychologist, which is la-men-ta-ble. Her thesis would have been: The Importance of Black Embroidery Silk in the Pre-natal Individual.

166

Consolatrix Afflictorum. I go into my bathroom. If I close my eyes I can imagine myself entering a forest of eucalyptus trees, Sebastiana was very free with the air scent. But the real perfume is different. I sit on the edge of the bathtub and join my thumb and forefinger together forming a ring so that the water from the faucet runs through the middle. With his thumb and index finger, two extremely important digits, M.N. will undo my brassiere, which I never wear since I simply don't need one, but which is indispensable at this point. Ana Clara told that the German ripped off her blouse, the fabulous German, the first man, first love, first everything. M.N.'s breathing will alter: It will be as if he had been climbing up a rather long staircase, one of those winding ones, let's say. I interrupt him because I'm terribly thirsty, I want a drink of water. Which is nothing new; I've been that way ever since I was a child: Before leaving the house Mama, the nurse, everyone would ask me if I needed to make pee-pee, etc. No, I didn't. We'd get in the car, the farm was about fifteen minutes out of town, and before long I'd start squirming. Or we'd be coming out the door of the church. At the exact moment the procession was starting, with the line of angels right in front, I'd run back because I was thirsty or needing to go to the bathroom, which was more complicated because of the wings tied onto my shoulders underneath the satin gown. To this day I don't know why getting my panties down involved dislocating my wings. "A little whiskey in the water?" he asks, so far he has only taken off his coat and loosened his tie a bit, very good. In spite of the slight heat, my blood pressure must be down in the basement, a drink is indispensable. I ask emphatically for a strong one, I don't normally drink but at times like these only a drink loosens one up. I drain the glass, glug-glug-glug. The dizziness that begins in the back of my neck ends up in my mouth, in the midst of a slow juicy kiss. In slow motion—everything unhurried—he begins to take off his clothes with the air of someone who wants *only* to move more freely, "It's a bit hot, isn't it?" In spite of the unhurriedness the moment has come for the undershorts, Oh Lord. The horror I have of men's undershorts, beginning with the word. No matter how modern and fancy they are. I become completely constrained when I see an actor in his undershorts in the movies. "I can't imagine why he has to wear those white undershorts during the whole movie," I complained to Lião, the camera would whirl around pre-

167

tending to focus on something else, and then go straight back to the undershorts, with their telltale bulges. "I want to see his face, too," I complained. Over a sandwich, Lião gave her own explanation: "I can't explain it, but it seems that all the film directors are queers these days, and queers have more of an obsession for the prick than women, see?" I told her about my complex regarding undershorts, but she had already branched into politics and by the time we got back to the boardinghouse everything could be blamed on North American imperialism. The dream republic would be a beach, with the two of us in bathing suits, a beach is so much more poetic. Well, it's no good now, because we're in an apartment where he has to take off his undershorts with an ease so easy that before I realize it, he's naked.

I dive into the bathtub. Delicious, delicious. I open the cold-water tap. Calm down, Lorena Vaz Leme, take it easy. Better to start with the elevator, you just got into the elevator. Alone? Of course, alone. But why doesn't he get in with me? "Don't forget I'm married, dear. We can't take the risk." I open the bottle of bath salts and pour some into the water. Eucalyptus perfume, still the artificial forest. Foam. Isn't it depressing, this fear he has of getting caught? It suggests a mask, and I have a horror of masks. I'd like only to be truthful. Honest. "The world of the bourgeoisie is the world of appearances," Lião is always saying. M.N. and I belong to the bourgeoisie, therefore we are condemned to this world. But are we really? I'd like to *exist* but I'm going to *be* tangled in the web of make-believe. "I like it so much when you call me M.N.," he said. I blow the foam which comes up to my chin. Like it or find it prudent? Only initials. When, just before the rainstorm, he asked the office worker if he needed a ride (he'd gone to the Department to see about his son's transfer) and the fellow said no, he had a car, and then when he turned to me and repeated the question—when we went quickly out of the half-light of the halls into the dark night, I retained only the impression of a dark-haired man with a pipe. Nothing more. In the car, I became aware of his well-groomed scent, a light touch of lavender mixed with tobacco, I've always loved the smell of tobacco. During the ride I noticed that he had strong, tranquil hands. A discreet wedding ring. I inhaled his essence of a man of medium age and medium happiness, which is worse than complete unhappiness, according to

168

Aunt Luci who has been married various times. I felt at ease there with him. His style of driving impressed me too, I never felt so secure in a car. The storm broke in the middle of a story I was telling him about our ranch. When I got out at the gate, he got out too and before I could stop him, he took off his coat and covered me. We ran together through the garden blue with the lightning flashes that electrified our path, his right arm around my shoulder while with the other arm he held up the raincoat opened above our heads, a canopy in a procession protecting the sacrament.

Pallium. Incredible how in an instant of disorder a small detail stands out with such force: thunder, lightning and my fingers discovering his initials. I took him by the waist to conduct him and then I felt the letters embroidered on his shirt. "What letters are these?" I cried when I drew away from him to go up the steps. "M.N.!" he answered and his voice became stronger than the storm, M.N.! I stopped on the steps and looked at him. He continued in the same place, protecting himself with the raincoat. "Return, M.N.!" I yelled. He confessed to me the next day with his lopsided smile that he had been in doubt: Was I ordering him to return to the car, or return to see me again?

The foam of the bath salts begins to crystallize on the surface of the tub. I hug my legs and visualize myself running crazily like the woman in the Canticles, fainting with passion as I search for my beloved with the legs like columns, he plays golf, he must have muscular legs. At the right moment (he will intuit that moment) I see him extend his knowledgeable hands. Refinement and cultivation in his fingertips polished to the utmost, like those of a safecracker perfecting his tactile sense. *Tactile* with a *c* to impede precipitant haste; certain words should have their doorsteps as a measure against uncontrolled people, watch your step! He is careful, oh indeed he is. So much so that he already has both hands on my breasts without my even perceiving how they got there. A first touch, the light twirling of the buttons to the left and to the right. A pause. One more almost-imperceptible movement and I'll spring wide open, every secret revealed.

"The treasure of a young girl is her virginity," I heard Mama say more than once to the young girls that worked in our house on the ranch. Since she never again gave that warning, I calculate that the treasure was only valid for that time. And for that

169

type of young girl, daughters of peasants or orphans. But what if I should come up to her and say, I have a lover. Pale with alarm, she would stare wide-eyed for several hours, it always takes her a while to adjust to new situations. "A *lover*?" I quickly look for a decisive argument, You don't want me to remain a virgin the rest of my life, do you? Of course not, she wouldn't want that under any circumstances, she's made thousands of ironic allusions to girls who die virgins and turn into stars. You wouldn't want me to become a lesbian, if I don't go to bed with a man, I'll have to go with a woman, won't I? She shakes her head, terrified, no, no! Although catastrophic, at this point she's not thinking about *the worst* that could happen to me but rather a normal and healthy hypothesis: Why a *lover* and not a *fiancé*? I concentrate in order to exposit all of Lião's theories against marriage. But my arguments are terribly weak, I think marriage is the best thing in the world, I'd marry M.N. in a thousand churches and courts. Oh Lord. In the end I give the lecture with that so-sincere sincerity that seizes us when the grapes are sour. She starts smoking one cigarette after another, a sign of insecurity. To show how up-to-date she is, she rejoices in unrestrained youth, she's super-liberal but she can't help mentioning a few of her perplexities: "For example, I can't understand this gulf between my generation and yours. Have centuries gone by, or only a few years? The scandal it caused when my cousin had a baby four months after she was married, you'd have thought the world was coming to an end. And how old do you think she is today? Forty-two! Imagine if *now* anybody would so much as comment if one of your friends by chance—" she leaves the sentence dangling, she's just remembered that she's said all this before, there's not a card-partner of her acquaintance who hasn't thrilled to the differences between her own times and those of her daughters. Granddaughters. Or nieces, in cases where there isn't a direct descendant. She grows quiet, thinking. Her expression starts to wax dramatic when she visualizes me in bed with a man, the faces contorted in pleasure, the moans WITHOUT MATRIMONIAL INTENT. Which is a bit like spying, isn't it? She squeezes her eyes shut. The sponge of bitter aloes begins to drip from her slow smile. Still a child (she thinks of me as being about twelve) and with a *lover*, an old faun drooling his filthy spittle over her baby. Disappointment slowly is transformed into rage, she paces back and forth with her arms

170

crossed because she can't bear to sit still any longer nor to look at me. *Mea culpa, mea culpa.* "I'm an insensate woman, a frivolous creature. To leave my little girl in the midst of people whom I don't even know and go off to live with a man who ridicules and betrays me as often as he can. If I didn't drink my tea black, he would have killed me long ago with a dose of arsenic in the sugar. A mother can't separate herself that way from an almost-adolescent girl, you've actually shown a lot of judgment, another girl in the same circumstances . . . " the self-punishment grows less severe when she announces that the romance with Mieux is truly liquidated. She wants now to live a retired life, without worldliness, "completely centered around my little girl. God forbid that I should ever marry again," she'll say, without recalling that she said the very same thing and with equal emphasis right after Daddy was hospitalized. She allows that my friends are partly responsible: "I find them very odd, those two girls who live there. The pudgy one who looks like a lesbian and that other who is so vulgar. Could they possibly be the right company for a young lady?" She squeezes the young lady's hand to signify her appreciation for my being truthful and not telling lies (she can put her fears to rest on that point) and under the pretext of consoling me (because he's married) she consoles herself, nostalgic. "But if you're happy, then so am I," she says and smiles that wan, melancholy smile to show her contentment. Every time the present becomes distasteful to her (which is happening more and more frequently) she takes refuge in the past. The memories collected without temporal order are always the same ones. "Do you remember, dear?" I am playing at the fountain on the ranch and I have a red flannel scarf tied around my neck because I have a sore throat. Daddy snapped the shutter when I lost my balance and fell down on my bottom in the water. Somebody (Ifigênia?) yells from inside the house, "That child will catch pneumonia!" Now I'm riding on the back of Remo's bicycle, my face so clear you can see the gap left by the canine tooth that was pulled out the night before. The tooth swings on the end of a string in a pendulum motion, "Where's the tooth that was here? The cat got it! . . . Where's the cat?" My first bath in a silver basin, with gold chains and bracelets in the bottom, through the water I see the gold destined to transmit its shine to me. I told her I remembered this bath and she laughed, "Impossible, dear, you were only eight days old!" But I do remember it. I see the water and the tangle of gold shining in the bottom, I would recognize that jewelry if it hadn't all been melted down, the thing that lasted the longest was the enormous chain that looped around and around and around and one time around Mieux made off with it. My first day of school, when I threw my lunch pail away and wouldn't let go of the legs of the bed. She was wearing a white linen dress and had pinned a little bouquet of jasmine to the neckline. "I used to like that dress so much," she repeats, reconstructing the dress and the rest. She keeps on staring at me. "I should never have sold the ranch, I should have stayed on there. I could have arranged for a male nurse, he wouldn't have gotten worse the way he did if he'd lived in the midst of the things he loved so much, his plants, his animals. To die alone in that cold sanatorium, without anybody to hold his hand. Romulo dead. Remo so far away he might as well be dead too. My little girl the lover of a married man. And I in the company of a cynic who betrays and exploits me, oh, what punishment, what punishment!"

I slide deeper into the bathtub. My eyes are swimming, I've become emotional, why did I complicate the picture this way? I'm very much moved and I wasn't supposed to be moved at all. Better not to mention the fact that he's married, if he isn't married she might have hope, and to deprive Mama of hope is the last thing in the world I'd want to do. I'll just say that I don't have the *slightest* interest in marriage. She takes heart: "You don't right now, but you will, all young girls say that but when they start wanting children, then they want to marry too. It always happens. So much more practical, Lorena. On trips, at hotels. And in your life together! You have financial interests, dear. Who could be better than a husband to administer one's financial interests?" She remembers her own unadministered ones (What, trust that irresponsible scoundrel? That futile turncoat?) and takes my hands between hers, that's the gesture she uses when she wants to speak to me *woman to woman.* "You are *established*, dear," she says solemnly, she has incorporated the word *established* into her vocabulary but she doesn't know exactly what it means in this context. "It's your decision. Do what your heart desires." What my heart desires. What does my heart desire? Eeeeeeh, Mama. My heart desires to stay with him even without being married, without anything. She blinks stiffly because of her false eyelashes, my doll used to blink exactly the same way. "But if he doesn't want to separate from his wife it's because he's *in love with her*, not with you!"

End of story, Lião would say. I wash the corners and curves of my ears where the Seducer Angel has again distilled the dew of lasciviousness and envy. As if laziness weren't enough. I open the tap and watch the foam revive under the hot stream of water. *Anyone who through action, voluntary omission, negligence or imprudence causes detriment to another, is obliged to repair the detriment. Not fulfilling his obligation, the debtor is held responsible for loss and damage.*

"Loss and damage," repeated Lorena searching for her reflection in the mirror. Through the dense steam she could only see the dark spot which was her hair and a pinkish section of knee emerging from the foam like a vague spongy plant. "This is a norm, my love. A judicial standard. Through your negligence, I lost my happiness," she thought as she wrapped the towel around herself. She rubbed her feet on the bathmat and made some faces, without much conviction, at the mirror. "I'm sad." She powdered her body with talc, spread the towel over the back of a chair, and put on her red bathrobe. Suddenly she felt fascinating, ah, if M.N. could see her *now*. Running to fetch a book from the shelf, she took a letter from inside it and sat down on the big cushion. The typewriter ribbon must have been nearly worn out; the letters seemed to dissolve into the bluish onionskin paper.

"Loreninha."

She smiled at the young man who had silently opened the door and was smiling at her through the crack.

"Hi, Guga! Come in. I just finished my bath."

"So I see."

"Want to take one? If you do, help yourself."

"Not now," he said untangling himself from his canvas backpack. He sat down on the rug beside her. "Are you going to hear the rock band play today? Down at The Shed?"

"I'm not in the mood, Guga. Are you going?"

"I don't know yet. My brother's the sax player, I'd only go on account of him. But I'm not sure," he answered crossing his legs and grasping his sandals by the toes.

She was looking at the little yellow sun embroidered on the front of his cotton T-shirt.

173

"Did you do that?"

"Yeah. Did it come out all right?"

"It's wobbly," she said leaning over to kiss his cheek. With her fingertips she smoothed his beard. "I know how to embroider a beautiful duck, bring me a shirt and I'll decorate it for you."

"This is my only one."

"Your only one? Oh Lord. What poverty, poor Guga."

"Want to adopt me? I'm looking for someone who wants to take me in. And love me."

"Wait, I'll go get some whiskey," she said running to the record player. "Have you heard Chico's latest album?"

"I don't think so, I'm really kind of out of touch, Loreninha. Or, to put it better, in touch."

She brought a bottle and a glass, and placed an ashtray near his hand which held a lighted match. They fell silent, sitting side by side listening to the music.

"In touch, how?"

He smiled. "In touch. I stopped running around like a madman. I was acting insane, studying without any desire, doing things without wanting to, everything forced, just to prove myself. Now I don't want to prove anything. I'm at peace with myself. That's what's important, isn't it?"

"Is that why you disappeared from school?"

"I stopped studying, Loreninha. I left home and quit school. We rented a basement, me and some guys, each one gives so much per month. We're living in a commune."

"Eeeeeeh."

"Why eeeeeh?"

"It never works out, dear. You'll end up fighting, there's always one that's more confused than the others and messes everything up. Even Jesus couldn't stand the community He set up, remember? *'Oh faithless and perverse generation, how long shall I suffer you?'* He exploded one day, He said that or something very like it. And He was Jesus, imagine!"

"So let's form a community of two, can I live with you?"

She took his hand and kissed it.

"You're a sweetheart but I'm in love already. And hopelessly, too," she sighed making a face. "How's the theater?"

"I left that too. Was that theater? Everything so poorly done, so meaningless. I want to live profoundly."

174

She turned her eyes away from his feet, dusty and thin inside his loose sandals.

"But what do you call living profoundly? This protest? This marginalization?

Tranquilly he served himself another drink. His gestures were soft, his voice gentle. He faced her:

"But who said I was protesting? I'm not protesting against anything, Loreninha. Not even that. To protest is to take a stand, do something. Who wants to take a stand? My little flower, all I want to do is things that give me satisfaction. I read, I talk to others, I listen to music, I make music. I make love. Everything so simple. I learned to think, that was an important discovery. To think."

She jumped up and got a nail scissors.

"I'm enjoying this conversation very much, but while we're talking just let me cut your nails? Please, Guga, I'm asking *please*," she implored as she saw him draw back, hiding his hand inside his shirt. "It'll only take a second!"

Resting his head in her lap, he relaxed and gave her his hand. He laughed softly.

"Very well, Delilah, if it gives you so much pleasure. You remind me of my mother, as soon as she sees me she runs for the scissors. You say I want to attack, to protest. Bah! What I really want is something very different."

After cutting his fingernails, she cleaned them with an orange stick. "I think you fit into the doctrine I invented, it's neat, listen to this: To be or to exist. Either you *exist* or you *are* something or somewhere. You prefer to exist, *ergo*, you *are not* in the university nor are you on the stage nor are you in the little political-action groups or art groups or whatever. You're existing within yourself, right? But Guga, you can exist freely. And at the same time fulfill your destiny, you have a destiny, dear."

"Oh, Loreninha, read less and live more. You're a book. Come live with us and forget theories for a while."

"You guys make pee-pee on the floor, I'd spend the whole day cleaning the bathrooms, perfuming the thrones."

"Thrones?" he laughed and pulled her close to him by her hand. He kissed her neck but when he tried to kiss her mouth she turned quickly away from him.

"No, Guga, don't."

"Don't, why?"

175

"Because I'm in love."

"Fabrízio?"

"I wish it were. It's a married man, old, etc. I'm consumed with passion for him."

"Oh, look how literary she is! Finished?" he asked examining his fingernails. "I'll have natural rose polish, please, I was going to buy some for my mother, natural rose."

Lorena swept the nail cuttings into a tiny pile.

"I'd like to read you the letter he wrote me, may I?" She picked up the sheets she had left on the big cushion and returned walking on her knees. Bending her body backward she balanced on her heels. "I won't read it all, just a part, listen: *'I have lived on two planes, that of the day-to-day, real with its humdrum duties, its ties that bind me to fond persons whom I love and for whom I am a determined individual having a certain identity, a past, present and future which tie me to a quiet path of consciously accepted responsibilities. From this world, L., you are absent and when this great emotion, which I at times must deny, is absent too, I feel that this is the real world, the true one, and that we should not, cannot . . . that it is necessary to stop at once and flee, keeping only the friendly remembrance of an enchantment which could have been—' "*

"That's enough, Loreninha. I don't want to hear any more."

"Wait, dear, there's an important part coming up, wait!"

"That's enough, I said. I'm not interested in this guy, I'm interested in you. I don't even understand what he's saying there."

"Just this one little part more, it's important, please: *'Yet when your fragile and so lovely world, L., unexpectedly breaks forth and installs itself in me—like now, as I am engulfed by this emotion—then I believe above all in this disturbing joy at having received a gift so miraculous and high. I believe above all in these times, times made up of your image and built from small facts and details: a telephone call today, a quick meeting tomorrow, a hope for God knows when. Such uncertain facts, so scarce—and yet they constitute all our visible history. I feel I could let go of even this small portion if you so desired.' "*

I stop because my mouth is completely dry. I run to the water jar and drink a gulp, then return. Guga is looking at me with his mouth half-open, as if he hasn't understood a single word.

"But why does he write that way?"

"What way?"

176

"So complicated, Loreninha."

"I told you he was a lot older, married, didn't I? It's his style, dear. Just listen to this last sentence, listen, just the final one: *'This pure and deep affection, secret and proud, which I keep like a precious possession. Which even you couldn't reach again if everything were to end tomorrow. This affection which gives you back to me, re-creates for me your image, now so much mine for always, so friendly and so much a part of me. M.N.'"*

I fold up the letter. Guga stares intently at me.

"What does this M.N. mean?"

"His initials. They stand for Marcus Nemesius."

"He's too complicated, Loreninha, he gives me the jitters."

I blow off the excess talc accumulated on my feet. One more lesson: Why read the letter to him? Is it to discourage myself that I throw my poor love before the lions? Lião, exactly, Lião. *I can't explain it* and she explained that it was the letter of an old man in love but full of fear. More fear than love. But why do I expose him that way? Incredible. Only Annie was marvelous, when I would have imagined that she'd be exactly the opposite. She'd been drinking and had come to return the stole I loaned her. She yanked off her shoes and sat down to have a whiskey. I wouldn't have showed her the letter if I didn't trust the subterranean instinct of crazy people and drunks, Daddy taught me that . . . and then afterwards, poor man. So she crossed her beautiful legs, told her little lies about how she was going to be photographed for magazine covers in Rome, the Count Cigonga had invited her to dinner, etc. Once she quieted down, secure in her power and glory, I showed her the letter. Halfway through it, she stopped. Her eyes were full of tears. "Shit, I'd like to be loved by a man like this." I was enormously happy, "Yes, don't you think so, Annie? And Lião saying—." She adjusted her cigarette in its holder, for a while she went around with a cigarette holder that has since disappeared. "A pragmatist like her couldn't understand a love that is fully spiritual. I'd fall in love with him too." When she left, I gave her the stole, it was very pretty but the fringe would drag on the floor when I wore it, why does Aunt Luci think I'm so tall? A dwarf dragging the fringe of her stole over the rug. Oh Lord.

"Sad, Loreninha?"

"No, dear, of course not."

177

"You wilted up like a little flower."

"Fainting Magnolia. Did you know that's my nickname in the Department?" I ask hiding my face in my robe.

"Loreninha, don't cry, don't cry!"

But I'm not crying, I try to say. He doesn't give me time, he has gotten up and is holding me by the shoulders, kissing my forehead, my hair. My robe comes open. I fight to close it but how? His arm is wrapped around me while his tongue penetrates my mouth which for a moment (a century) responds to his. I jump to one side and he jumps with me, I pull his beard, his hair, No Guga No! I bite the hand which is flattened over my breast. He releases me. We measure each other, panting. I attribute my red face to anger but actually I'm not so certain. He picks up his bag.

"Guga dear, I'm in love with somebody else," I croak tying my bathrobe belt.

"You already told me. No problem."

He's smiling again. I give him the bottle of whiskey and now he laughs looking at me and smoothing his beard with his fingertips; he has beautiful hands. He kisses me very lightly.

"This boyfriend of yours has a facility for complicating things, he reminds me of my father. My father talks for hours to me and I don't know what he's trying to say."

I caress the sun embroidered on his chest, why don't I want him to leave any more? I brush the ashes from his jeans with their three spots faded almost to white: one at each knee and the third at his crotch-bulge. I turn my gaze to the sun.

"I know how to embroider, come and get a shirt with a duck embroidered on the sleeve, next week I'll have it ready, it'll look lovely," I say and go around behind him, speaking into his ear: "You aren't taking garbage, are you, Guga?"

"Not necessarily."

"What do you mean by that, not necessarily?"

He arched his eyebrows calmly.

"Just what I said, Loreninha. Not necessarily."

My heart throbs.

"Guga, let me take care of you."

"What do you mean by taking care of me? Cutting my nails?"

I hug him from behind. As I do so I discover he has very wide shoulders.

"Number one, I'm going to keep your registration open, you dummy. What if you decide to go back, eh?"

"Ah, she wants to see me with my little diploma. Didn't I tell you you're just like my mother?"

Before disappearing around the curve of the drive, he turns around and throws me kisses. I return them and feel my eyes moisten, whether from emotion or from the sun that spreads its rays wide like the sun on his shirt I don't know. I thrust my toes through the curlicues of the banister and look at the big old house. Isn't that the phone? From the window, Sister Bula waves at me, opening and closing her hands like a little child. I pause to listen to the motor of an airplane going through a cloud, no. It isn't the phone. And even if it were, it could only be Mama calling to tell me how perverse Mieux has been, I like her so much better when she's gling-glong. But she's only gling-glong when she's happy, when she's depressed her voice grows more sullen than that of a black beetle which has fallen on its back, *vuuuurrrrr* . . . And Fabrízio? Tangled up with that sinister poetess, was that the way he loved me? What kind of love was it, if all I had to do was turn slightly to one side. I squeeze the banister until my fingers grow white, Guga, Guga, take care of yourself! He didn't forget me. The fun we used to have, eh, Guga? One afternoon he pretended to be crippled and went walking through the streets all doubled up, drooling, with me beside him, very serious. We walked for miles like that. Everybody staring, feeling sorry for us. "This way, Guga, this way," I would say and he'd turn the opposite way, tripping over people. Another day he put on dark glasses but nobody reacted, there are tons of blind people in the city. So I had to grab his arm and say horrible things to him at the top of my lungs, I didn't care who saw that I was furious because I wanted to go to the movies and I couldn't, "Why do I have to be the guide? I'm tired of being a seeing-eye dog!" I yelled when two indignant old ladies came up. The one with the umbrella almost hit me, "You brutal girl! Don't you have a heart?" The other one, chewing and chewing: "Such savage youth! You savage!" When they went away, he took off his glasses and roared with laughter but in the midst of his merriment I noticed something painful. In the line for the movies he complained with the greatest bitterness, "I was blind and you mocked me." Oh, Guga. How long ago that all seems, isn't it strange? After I met M.N., he and Fabrízio became children as if they had been a part of my childhood, like Remo and Romulo. Daddy would take me by the hand to go to the barn and see the new baby calf that had been born the night before. Now I hold out my hand and nobody comes to take it, I could hold it out until the end of time. *Ad seculum et seculorum.* Nobody. Remo's hands were banal but Romulo's were golden, the golden down of his arms extending to his knuckles, which became gold in turn. Daddy's were dark with waves of hair swirling across the backs of them, he would swing me from them. Daddy has monkey's hands, Daddy's a monkey!

"Dreaming?"

I almost fall down the stairs from fright. Lião is behind me but how did she get up here without a sound?

"Don't do that, Lião, I almost died, look how I'm trembling!"

She laughs.

"I came on tiptoe, see. You were so quiet there, thinking about the day the calf died . . ."

I grab her.

"*Calf*? Did you say *calf*, Lião? Extraordinary."

"What's extraordinary about that?"

"It's because I was just thinking about calves, I was remembering that my father would take me by the hand to see the new baby calf, there was always a calf being born in the night. Incredible."

"So let's have some tea, I have important things to tell you, are you alone?"

"Guga just left," I say and lower my voice. "Lião, Lião, he kissed me on the mouth, I got all unstrung."

"And then?"

"Well, that was all, I closed my bathrobe quick and sent him away, but isn't it strange? He's all hairy, beard and nails grown out, half-creepy, you know? And I, who dream of a superbly groomed man, got so excited he actually noticed it, I felt like rolling over the floor with him, all dusty and sweaty! But I remembered M.N. and the magic moment was broken."

Lião flops onto the rug and giggles, embracing the big cushion.

"Lorena, Lorena, how stupid you are!"

I start laughing too. Isn't it the truth?

"Madness, Lião, total madness."

180

She unloads her bag, surrounding herself with little piles of things. I fill the teakettle.

"It's a shame I have to leave, because if not I'd prove as easy as ABC that you're in love with a fantasy, see."

"What fantasy?" I ask.

"Hell, this M.N. Haven't you realized yet that he's taking the place of your father?"

I take out the teacups. I'll kill myself if she resorts to her marvelous analysts in order to repeat what's in any teenage magazine. And even in the comic strips, eeeeh, the story of the young secretary identifying her gray-haired boss with her progenitor, in those stories *father* is "progenitor." On second thought, it was better for Lião to get into minority politics than keep on explaining autoidentification and transference. Bla-bla-bla.

"What was the name of that psychiatrist, Lião? You used to quote him all the time, the Frenchman."

"Lacan?"

Ah. That's the one. There was this Lacan and another American woman doctor, I used to know her name too, but never mind. Now she's turned anti-Oedipal, we're all more or less crazy, it's nonsense to lock up some, *see*. Mental illness comes as a result of the system. Finish the system in order to put an end to mental illness.

"Speaking of mental illness, *she* continues flitting about. She called yesterday, she's at the country estate of some rich friend. Glitter and glamor."

"I warned you I wanted to talk about serious things and you bring up Crazy Annie. I'm getting my passport," I say but Lorena has already ducked into the bathroom.

The collection of bells is on the shelf within reach of my hand. I ring the biggest one. The sound of goats. I pull my chain out from inside my collar and ring the little bell she gave me.

"I'm coming, Lia de Melo Schultz, I'm coming!"

She reappears wearing her black ballet leotard and bringing the copper mug of daisies in her hand. She approaches as if she were on stage carrying an amphora, when she wears this leotard she walks like a ballerina. Or does she always walk that way?

"I adore daisies," she says putting the mug on the shelf beside her father's picture. "There used to be so many of them on the farm. They were the flowers that covered the casket of Romulo, my brother."

181

"I need to go and pick up the clothes your Mama promised and I haven't even had time yet, I've been so busy. I'll take the woolen things for myself, I'll need them, Lena. Algeria. The African winter is more wintery."

"She's asked me a thousand times if you were lesbian."

I laugh, I'm so happy. Everything is funny.

"The situation becomes even blacker because at the moment I can't exhibit Miguel, oh, how people worry about the sex of their neighbors. When they should be worrying about other things. Even you."

She takes a daisy by the stem and kneels in front of me, extending it toward my mouth.

"Lia de Melo Schultz, would you grant me an interview? If you please, come closer to the microphone. I would like your distinguished opinion on masculine and feminine homosexuality."

"First give me some tea. Isn't the water boiling? You said that tea is no good with water that has boiled, run!"

Perfect. And now, the money. Yenom, right, Lorena?

"It was almost boiling," she says dropping the tea leaves into the pot.

I notice the talcum-powder footprints that her feet leave on the rug, she must have just finished her bath. How many baths does she take per day?

"I talked to my father yesterday, he answered the phone, my mother had gone out. He's fabulous, see. 'Dad, don't ask me any questions, I'll explain everything later but now I just want to tell you that I'm leaving the country, I'm going overseas.' He didn't say anything. I asked him, 'Did you hear me, Dad?' and he answered 'Yes, go on.' 'I'm going to need some money for the airplane ticket,' I continued. 'And it's expensive, as you know. Can you give me the money?' He was so quiet for an instant, so quiet, see. The connection was so close it was as if we were just around the corner from each other, I could almost hear his heart beating. 'Answer me, Dad, can you give me the money?' " I look for the handkerchief in my bag, what ever happened to that damn handkerchief? I dry my eyes on my shirttail. "Then he said, 'You can count on us, daughter. I'll see about one or two things and get the money for you, don't worry. Can you wait until the end of the month? I'll send not just the money for the ticket but also a reasonable margin. I don't know where you're going but I know it's expensive.' "

Lorena is already bringing the tea tray and from her face I perceive she hasn't heard a single thing I've said. She balances her tray on the big cushion.

"I have a presentiment that M.N. isn't ever going to call me again."

"Then I hung up and kissed my hand, because I wanted to kiss his hand and couldn't."

"Do you agree, Lião?"

"What?"

"That M.N. isn't going to look me up any more. Do you think so too?"

I pour tea into my cup. She waits, her eyes pinned on me. I take a deep breath, clear down to my heels.

"You start talking about marriage! He's afraid of his wife, see."

She wraps her hands around the teapot, she always has cold hands. Cold feet.

"But I don't want him to *marry* me, just *call* me!"

"It comes to the same thing, Lena. After the phone call you'll want the wedding, that's all you think about. With Mama offering the reception."

She pushes the plate closer to me because I'm eating cookies, and there are crumbs. But is that all she ever thinks about, the ashes or crumbs that might fall on her rug? Is that all that ever passes through her head? And this M.N. who must be a big turd, oh! Now I feel like howling because she has started rolling up my pant legs, every time I wear these jeans she comes running and starts to roll up the ever-loving hems. I have to laugh.

"You really are crazy, Lena. But pay attention, I've said it a whole batch of times and you didn't even hear me, my passport is almost ready, I'm going to be traveling very soon. I-am-leaving, you hear? I'm off."

"But Lião, so suddenly? I know you've been talking about it but I thought it was something more remote, you said that you've already got your passport! Overseas?"

"The place is secret, very secret. I haven't even told my father yet, I'll send a letter from Algeria. I'll be meeting him there."

"Him, who?"

"Miguel! Miguel is going to be released, we're going to meet in Algeria, I get off the plane in Casablanca. And don't ask for more details, I'll give them to you later, that's enough for now, I'm going to Algeria."

183

"Algeria? But how marvelous, Liāo! Why didn't you tell me sooner? Algeria, imagine! Lia de Melo Schultz going to Algeria! And she says it so nonchalantly, with such tranquility . . . how fantastic! We'll take a look at the map immediately. My brother Remo knows that part of the world pretty well, he lives in Carthage, in Tunisia. I've been hearing you talk about a trip sort of bla-bla bla but I never imagined . . ."

She jumps up to get the map and opens it on the rug. A drop from my cup falls on Asia but in her excitement she doesn't see it.

"Here's Algiers," she points out and pushes aside her hair which has uncoiled softly like a ribbon over the map. "Bordering on Tunis, see? And Morocco on the other side. Look at the Sahara. Sand, sand. If I were to meet M.N., I'd go running on the tips of my toes, I'd cross the desert and knock on this little door here, tap, tap!"

She folds up the world map. I stuff my mouth full of cookies, oh, these sentimentalisms.

"The problem is this. Dad can't send me the money until the end of the month—"

"Yenom, yenom!"

"The yenom, see. I said that was fine but I'm hoping to go sooner, things have speeded up. Could you loan it to me? The minute my father sends it, see. It would be, like, an advance."

"But of course, Liāo! Mama deposited a fortune in my name, the famous sports car. I don't want a car, at least for the moment I haven't the slightest interest, imagine. Aren't I going to loan Ana Clara some money for whatever it is she needs? How much is the ticket?"

"I'm going to find out today."

"Take a signed check and fill in the quantity you need but with a wide margin, Liāo, for goodness' sake! A good wide margin for you to get started. I'd never forgive myself if I found out you were going hungry. Oh Lord, it's wild, this trip of yours! I'm electric!"

"What about me. I haven't slept for days, I lie down and start thinking."

I open my checkbook as I listen to Liāo munching cookies. I'm going to lose her. She'll never come back, I'm going to lose her. Like I lost Astronaut. My eyes swim and my handwriting

184

submerges, the *Leme* last, so shaky. Who will interview me now, your name? Lorena Vaz Leme. University student? Yes. Virgin? I turn the page and sign another check. The tears return to their obscure source.

"I want you to wear a cross there on your chain, promise you will? Come on, promise, if you don't . . ."

I grab her by the wrists, she's almost ripping up the check.

"What kind of blackmail is this, Lorena? I'll wear it, I'll wear a dozen of them if you insist, no problem!"

"Promise you'll leave it there on the chain."

"I promise."

She kisses me, radiant. With her geisha gestures she goes to get me more tea and fills my cup.

"One day, all of a sudden, you'll squeeze this cross in your hand."

"Will I?"

"I'm certain of it, Lião, certain. Your head is completely turned with politics, etcetera, you're in a whirlpool, dear. My diagnosis: a sleeping faith. Latent."

I put the check in the bottom of my bag where the links in the chain of my journey are gradually coming together. Where is this bank? I find one more fingernail to bite. Down near the booking agent's office. Fine. When I open my eyes, I meet Lorena's; she's watching me. I pat her on the head. Oh yes, God.

"I was an angel in church programs too, an altar attendant, everything. I used to believe fervently, with that beautiful childish certainty. For that very reason, I was reconciled to things, see? I can't explain it, Lena, but as soon as I started reading the papers, becoming conscious of what was happening in my city, in the world, I got so angry. Furious. Of course He exists, I thought, but He's all cruelty. From that stage I went on to that of irony, I became ironic, He's a *bricoleur*, do you know what a *bricoleur* is? In my street there lived a Bahian image-maker who would get scrap objects, haphazard fragments with no plan. He would put the pieces together with talent, he was talented, and would create little machines out of those pieces. I started to think that God was simply that, a *bricoleur* of people. He picks up one leftover bit here, another there, and makes his contraptions. Using what's available, see? According to caprice. When one *bricolage* starts to work, when it begins to function

185

for good or ill, he loses interest and picks up another one, millions of undestined little human machines bashing their heads here and there like crazy. *Kaput*."

Now Lorena is lying on her back, arms open, pedaling. I gather the crumbs from the rug onto the tray. One has only to mention machines and she's already mounted on her imaginary bicycle, shifting gears.

"Little human machines, Lião?"

"Little machines that pedal, eat, shit, fuck."

She fell on one side, laughing. "How dreadful, my ears almost exploded, dear!"

"So I'll use more subtle words. *Chier, baiser,* doesn't that sound refined?"

"I want to know if this idea is your own."

"What idea?"

"The one about the little machines."

"I read. French philosophy."

She goes "Ho, ho, ho!" and curls herself up, clutching her feet and rolling over in somersaults like a little black ball. One can count her ribs through the clinging leotard. The music on the record player recommences, it is part of all this just like the walls and floor. A cat meows close by, it sounds as if it were under the rug. She frowns expectantly, she must be thinking of Astronaut. Or God. Her perplexed little face is lifted. Although she has pedaled and rolled, she doesn't show a drop of sweat.

· "And the little machines that dream? Explain that one to me, Lião, what about the machines that dream? I'm a dream machine, can you believe it? Mama, my brother Remo, my aunts, gobs of people, they could be machines. But my brother Romulo and I were always different. Especially him, he was so extraordinary, my brother."

Everything's behind schedule, lists of things to get done yet today, and here I am partaking in metaphysical digressions, watching Lorena show off in her black leotard. But isn't this almost good-bye? How many more times will I come up to this room? I take one last biscuit. I know that I'll remember her as she is now, without dust or sweat, looking inside her vague world.

"See you later," I say.

"But at least you believe in Him. As a *bricoleur,* but it doesn't matter, you believe."

186

"We'll discuss the subject another time, I really have to go. What I think is that you'll never be like me and I'll never be like you. Isn't it simple? And complicated?"

Lorena went to the door with her, tucking in Lia's shirttail.

"You yourself once said that there isn't such a thing as *never again*, remember? Aren't we alive? What if some day I'm executed *a las cinco en punto de la tarde* in Palestine? And what if you enter a convent in Spain?"

Lia went down the stairs laughing. When she looked back, Lorena was making faces at her.

Chapter 10

Cat sleeps between two daisy-planters, her bursting belly turned to the sun. Will I be here to see these kittens? Mimosa always liked to whelp in the hammock, remember? The blind furless kittens would tumble from between the fringe tassels and she would gather them one by one in her velvet mouth. Miguel doesn't want to even consider having children, at least for the time being. Of course I agree with him, but at times I feel such a desire to lie down like that tabby cat, full to satiety, filled and fulfilled with my pregnant body, which is so crowded there isn't room to fit in even a wisp of straw. I'd call him Ernest.

"Good morning, Cat!"

She lifts her head, asking to be stroked, and goes back to sleep. Two more calico cats cross the garden which has turned into a cat kingdom, they know that here they won't be murdered. Even so, Lorena's cat Astronaut packed his *necessaire* and took off. Independent Left with Anarchist shadings. I kick the gravel. The idea that I'll never see this garden again makes me a touch sad. *Never again?* There isn't any *never again* in the present, present meaning unforeseen, everything I can see now. Or in a little while when it's *now* again. Algeria! I want to yell. A pretty name for a little girl. Has Algeria come home? Is Algeria calling? It's a pity that in Bahia they'd immediately transform it into Gegê, the mania for nicknames. If I didn't have the ticket, I'd swim there, walk. Rivers, hills, valleys, mountains, and an oasis. A month, a year. I'd arrive covered with dust and blood, I gave my shoes to the man with the jeep who picked me up on the road, I gave my shirt to the man at the bar who offered me something to drink, there was another one who wanted me nude and I took off my clothes and afterward he divided his rice with me, is it still a long way? Yes. There's a desert and after the desert a river. Which saint was it who gave herself to the boatman in exchange for her passage? My mother used to tell

189

the story of this saint who met up with a nasty boatman demanding that she strip and give herself to him. So she removed her mantle, took off her sandals and let him have his way in order to be able to get across the river. She crossed the river and entered Paradise. "If you believe in Man, then you believe in God," said Mother Alix. I can't explain it, what I mean is that believing in Man doesn't make me as happy as believing in the absurd stories that men tell. The simpler and more innocent they are, the more they fascinate me, telling the exploits of saints and heroes, come, Mother, come and fill me with superstitions which don't enter into my scheme but which nevertheless I don't forget, come at night to scratch my back and then look through my hair, that pig Ivanilda passed her lice to the whole class. Her apron, the color of coffee with milk, had a songbird embroidered on the pocket.

I open the gate. Mama's red Corcel is parked in front, with the chauffeur inside. He's reading a newspaper.

"Waiting for Lorena?" I ask.

"For over half an hour. She asked for the car but then went out and hasn't come back, she must have forgotten, she lives in outer space. I think I might as well go."

"Are you going to her mother's? Can I have a ride? I have to pick up some clothes there."

I get in beside him. A gray-haired mulatto man with the air of someone who has been waiting not half an hour but half a century. Outer space. My grandmother used to talk a lot about people who lived in another world. The lunatics. Lorena didn't see just one flying saucer in the sky, but a whole squadron of them in formation.

"Have you worked for the Vaz Leme family a long time?"

"Oh, so long I've lost track. I used to carry Loreninha on my lap. Before being a chauffeur I used to drive the tractor on their farm."

This man, for example. Would he be interested in joining the group? Obviously he's become complacent. His armchair is far more modest than that of his employers, but it's still an armchair. He'd want nothing to do with us. And his son?

"Do you have any children?"

"A girl about your age, miss, and a boy a little older."

"What does he do?"

"He works at the Mercedes-Benz office. He's doing real well,

190

too. My late employer had a cousin who worked there, he helped my boy get started. Yes, I'm very happy with my son. At the end of the year he'll be promoted and then he plans to get married, he's engaged."

My eyes are fixed on the little plastic baby hanging from the rearview mirror. Its face leers so mockingly that I can't stop staring at it.

"And are you happy with your daughter too?"

He takes a minute to answer. I see his mouth harden.

"This fad you young girls have, this liberation business. She's gotten entirely too free for my taste. Just lately she's decided to study again, she's taking one of those short-term courses to get her high-school degree."

"And isn't that good?"

"I only know that before I'm laid to rest I want to see my girl married, that's all I ask God for. To see her married."

"Guaranteed, you mean. But she could study, learn a profession and get married besides, couldn't she? Wouldn't she be even more guaranteed that way? If her marriage doesn't work out, she'll be alone and unemployed. Older, with children, see."

The leering baby shakes with laughter as the car hits a bump. I discover that it's not his masturbating that nauseates me but his shiny, satisfied little face.

"Miss Lorena talks that way too, but you're from rich families, you can afford such 'luxuries. My daughter is a poor girl, and the place for a poor girl is at home with her husband and children. Studying will just make her worry her head while she's doing her laundry at the washboard."

The living-room chairs covered in plastic. The television. The soap opera about rich people and the soap opera about poor people, the poor ones more sincere but with more problems. Partially solved in the final episodes when virtue is rewarded. Although two of the cynical characters go unpunished, there were too many people. The conformity to the status quo only darkened by the ambition to own a new car and a bigger TV, a colored one—oh, but wasn't it a scheme of that sort that I was yearning for a little while ago when I was looking at Cat? My face grows red as I imagine myself dragging Miguel to look at store windows during the spring clearance sales. Closing him in, using up his strength and patience with the junk of everyday life, refusing him an encouraging word on the day he is disenchanted, a negative presence, no! If I am to fail as so many have failed, let the winds blow my airplane with all the force in their cheeks onto the sharpest peak of the cliffs, all the passengers saved except for a young Bahian coed who was plunged into the abyss. End of story.

"And what if she marries some no-good and later starts walking the streets because she doesn't know how to do anything else? Have you thought of that? I'm sorry to speak so harshly but you'll be responsible before God if you start telling her 'get married right away honey or your Daddy won't die happy.' If you believe in her, I'm sure she'll want to show you she deserves your confidence, she'll be responsible. If not, it's because she hasn't any character, she wouldn't amount to anything either married or single."

There, I've made my speech. I get out and slam the car door. He's a bit confused.

"But I never thought . . ."

"So think!" I say sticking my face through the window. "And something else—if you don't want to get ground to bits in an accident, yank that baby off the rearview mirror. Who put it there? I can't explain it, but that thing has terrible vibrations. I knew two people that had trinkets just like it in their cars. One drove off a bridge into the river and the other was sandwiched between two trucks. Both they and their cars got pulverized, fire, shipwreck, everything. Only the plastic babies were found, laughing. Intact."

I'm laughing too as I go into the apartment building.

"Yes?" said the butler opening the door a crack.

Lia straightened the pile of books under her arm.

"I'm a friend of Lorena's. I came to pick up a suitcase of clothes."

"Isn't she coming?"

"I have no idea, see. Her mother's expecting me."

With an evasive gesture he pointed to a chair in the shadowy vestibule. His gaze once again floated indifferently on the stagnant surface of his eyes. He closed the door and studied Lia slowly, hesitating.

"I don't know if she'll be able to receive you today."

"But I called yesterday morning, she said for me to come."

"Your name?"

"Lia. Lia de Melo Schultz. Schultz, my father is German, I can speak German."

He turned his back on her and walked away without a sound over the rug-strewn marble floor. Why do the king's servants end up bigger turds than the king himself? thought Lia tucking in her shirttail. Her fingers explored the empty belt loops—who might be wearing her belt? She smoothed back her hair. Examining her inflamed thumb, she moistened it with her tongue where the nail was bitten down to the quick. On the wall, the tall mirrors reflected her from all angles. How to get sick and tired of yourself. Quickly she bent forward until she was below the level of their frames, settling herself on the rug. How could Narcissus get free, enslaved by his own reflection? She grinned. Lorena was fond of mirrors too, just like her mother. How did the lorenense philosophy go? Being was the stagnation of existence. "If I want to *exist* I can't even *be* in the mirror," she added to herself, interested in the pale-brown and blue pattern of the rug. Once accustomed to the gloom, she could see the twisting design more clearly: A tiger pursued a gazelle until pouncing on it in the next two sections, digging claw and tooth into its flank, from which flowed a filament of bright-blue blood. Other pursued and wounded gazelles multiplied over the wool and silk of the miniature Oriental tapestry. No matter how fast they ran—and run they did!—they were all condemned. She stroked the terrified head of one that was jumping out of a thicket and searched among the leafy intricacies and arabesques for a different route the gazelle might take to escape the imminent tiger: It would have to jump off the rug. The enthusiasm with which men created or destroyed the element of fatality in all they touched! And then attributed responsibility to the gods. "You are free," she whispered into the panicked ear of the gazelle. *Now* it was free. It was *still* free. She covered the attacking tiger with her book and lay down on her back. The chandelier with its crystal prisms was another fatality hanging there from the ceiling. And the wall clock inside its long black-and-gold case. The pendulum was in the shape of a lyre but the hands were aggressive arrows. "Only our numbers count," they advised sternly, pinning down their target. The energetic beat of the mechanical heart inside the case. What a magic thing time was. Time of Algeria, suddenly it had become the time of Algeria. What would it be like? Improvisation. Adventure. Certain only the desire to fight, to survive. Certain, the diary. "I want everyone to know that nobody in the world ever loved his country or his people more," she would write in the introduction. Words already bled dry by the politicians in their campaigns. But she would use them to express a new sentiment. A live one. She'd talk to Miguel at length about that: If the New Left didn't unite with the other groups they would all end up so divergent and weakened that when a common language was attempted, nobody would understand anybody else. "The Church is already living out its Tower of Babel," she remembered tapping her cigarette ash into the tiger's eyes. "Are we going to follow in its footsteps? I ask for a brick and they throw me a rafter. Fractionalized, divided. How to organize the masses in such a confused state?"

Lia blew on the little roll of ash, which came apart and gradually disappeared into the rug. She smashed the cigarette out against the sole of her blue tennis shoe. They were fated just like those gazelles, after every two, the third would be caught by the neck, skip two more and the blood would gush out in a blue stream. "No!" she exclaimed turning over on her stomach. The diary would be in a simple style like that of the notes and memoranda in her notebook. She opened it at random. She had difficulty in deciphering her own large sprawling handwriting. "Today, the twelfth, Lorena said was bath day. I went into her shower and was almost boiled alive beçause the cold-water faucet had something wrong with it. Next she offered me lunch, which means raw carrots, a boiled egg and a glass of milk. If I hadn't attacked the bananas, (I must have eaten half a dozen) I could never have accomplished the thousands of things I did. On the way out I met Depressing Ana who was coming in extremely depressed, she had had a conversation with Mother Alix who must be losing her patience. She spoke in a whisper to Lorena, she wanted to borrow some money. Then she asked to borrow a sweater. And told me that she was in anguish, which is nothing new, either she's riding high or down in the dumps. Why does her slightly cross-eyed expression make me dizzy? After picking up my passport—Algeria, Algeria!—I went to the office and there found Pedro and Elizabeth at work. They are in love, or rather, Pedro is ardently impassioned but she seems very cerebral to me. And people like that fall in love in a different way from the passionate ones like Pedro and me. She leads a femin-

194

ist movement and was composing an article about women's jobs in our market. Why am I moved by the thought that Pedro is going to suffer? Shit, he has to suffer. Drink kerosene and gasoline because that's how one builds personality structure, I believe. But in my heart of hearts I get sentimental, I almost say, as Lorena would, 'poor little thing!' From there I went on to Bugre's apartment. Dil, Ivone, and Eliezer were already there listening to music. Chico Buarque and Caetano. Bugre arrived and we started to work. Four solid hours of extremely fruitful study. From economic theory to philosophic idealism, from philosophic idealism to the crisis of physics in the beginning of the century, from there to Hegel, all passing through the tortuous paths of folly, ignorance and love for Brazil."

Miguel is cerebral, thought Lia closing her notebook. But wasn't that a good thing? He averaged out with her, who was the excessive type, in the explosive moments at least one head needed to be able to reason. Or not? I'm the stupid one if they catch me with these notes. Why am I walking around with them?

"She's just finishing her bath, she'll see you right away," announced a pink-aproned maid entering the foyer. She collected Lia's already-dead cigarette in an ashtray.

"Come into the living room. Isn't Loreninha coming?"

Is that all anybody can ask around here? thought Lia as she followed the maid. She piled her books on the floor of the living room, which was brighter and more spacious.

"I haven't seen Lorena today. I can come back some other time, no problem."

"But she wants to see you, wait just a little. It's that today this house is in confusion. The poor thing has hardly stopped crying, her eyes are all swollen up . . ."

"But what happened?"

"Dr. Francis died!"

"Who's Dr. Francis?"

"Why, the doctor who treats her nerves! The funeral was yesterday, she didn't know a thing about it. Would you care for some fruit juice? Or do you prefer whiskey?"

"A little whiskey, straight. But listen, I only came to get a suitcase full of clothes, can't you take care of it?"

"Wait, miss. You talk to her a little, it'll do her good."

Without much enthusiasm Lia took the glass. In the first

stage, the dim foyer and the butler with his stagnant face. Now, the more important waiting room with the relaxed little maid offering things to drink. Feeling herself a visitor in ascension, Lia drew closer to the oil portrait dominating all one side of the wall. Mama rejuvenated and revivified by a recent transfusion of fresh blood. Lorena adored vampire films; well, there was her mother in a gauzy dressing gown, her face very white, her eyes sepulchral. Even her hair was dense, like two black clots hardening against her high forehead. The Countess Dracula.

"Do you like it?" the maid wanted to know, simpering with her hands in her apron pockets. "It cost a fortune, that portrait."

"It's unsettling."

"And it's been two days since he showed up. Why, just today three women called asking, 'Is the doctor in?' " the maid mimicked in a flutelike voice. "Well, after all, he could be her son."

I egg her on. "But is he a doctor?"

The woman giggled hiding her mouth in her pink apron. Her face bore a resemblance to that of the plastic baby.

"He has a doctor's degree in pleasure, that's what!"

I fill my mouth with almonds. At the Banquet of Inconveniences this faithful servant will sit at the head of the table. With my fingertip I test the blue canine tooth of the Chinese porcelain dragon bristling on the marble table. On the smaller table, the little silver tree with four enamel-framed photos hanging from its branches like oval fruit: the small snapshot of a pale dark-haired man wearing the expression Lorena wears in her mystical moods. On the parallel branch, Mama in a wide straw hat, holding a pair of garden shears, a bouquet of jasmine at her breast. Just below, on a smaller branch, a picture of Lorena as a little girl, laughing her tinkly laugh, hee-hee-hee. On the neighboring branch, a sulky little boy with a crew cut, Romulo or Remo? Only the four on the tree. And the other brother?

"Come on, she's calling," advises the maid. She grows formal once more as a remote bell sounds the second time. "Not that way, that door leads into the office. Haven't you been here before?"

"Everything looks different."

Corridors and salons as the tunnel narrows and darkens, becoming more secret. An entrance leads into a shadowy bedroom. Bedroom? For the first time I am entering a veritable

196

alcove, where I can see no windows but only curtains, and the languid draperies of a canopy sustained by four slender bedposts. I come closer. The draperies descend in soft gathers composing a sort of vaporous cocoon enveloping the gilt-backed bed. Stuffiness and perfumes. Half hidden among the sheets and embroideries, she rests upon the piled-up pillows, two cotton pads covering her eyes. The lamp on the bedside table is lighted; outside the sun explodes but in here it's night.

Her voice is humid, cottony. "Sit down, dear. Where's Lorena?"

"She's probably on her way."

"Today I need her very much. Today I need all of you, you know what happened, don't you? He was my friend, my brother. Half of me died with him. Oh God."

"I can come back some other time, Mama. No problem."

Delicately she removes the cotton pads from her eyes and puts them into a silver dish beside the bottle of rose water. With effort she raises her eyelids.

"I like so much the way you call me Mama. You see, I'm losing everything, people dying and disappearing. And you come to me and say *Mama.* I always liked you, Lia. I often tell Loreninha, 'It's such a relief to know you have a friend like her nearby.' "

I laugh to myself. Relief? I sniffle and sneeze because I can't blow my nose on the handkerchief I didn't bring, oh, I'm allergic to this perfume.

"I've caught a miserable cold."

"How painful to think that he's dead, that that smile, that gaze so strong and at the same time so sweet . . . 'Well then?' he'd ask me. And I'd answer in the same tone, 'Well then, Dr. Francis?' Oh God, my dear friend, above all else my friend. I'm alone again. Completely alone."

She is crying and I search for but cannot find anything to say as she cries in silence. She was wearing a white suit when we met, a flannel suit that Lorena would call *impeccable.* It was on a Sunday, she had come to bring half of a roast turkey with walnut stuffing, which Ana and I devoured while Lorena nibbled on a wing. She had just had a facelift and was euphoric. But can this be that attractive lady? She has melted like a chocolate ice-cream sundae, more cream than chocolate. I draw back on the little bench; she is trying to see the maid who was behind me but isn't any longer.

197

"Do you want something?"

"Oh, Bila's disappeared. Just push that button there, four servants and none of them to attend when I call, all four sit around talking in the kitchen, push again, they don't hear. Oh God. He seemed so steadfast, do you understand? Everything could fall apart, go to ruin. But not him. As though he were immortal. So refined and at the same time authoritarian, powerful. Rough and yet genteel. I've only known of one other man like him and that was in a novel. A novel by Cronin. The character was like him, but people like that don't really exist. Dr. Francis. I didn't even see him dead, nobody told me. He had played tennis that afternoon, he played tennis marvelously, even participated in tournaments. I can imagine him with the racquet in his hand, his movements so energetic, elastic, all of him had such energy and elasticity. Oh God, Oh God. My dear friend. 'Well then?' he would ask me. 'Well then, Dr. Francis?' "

The tears run, dripping down her stretched face which hasn't the slightest wrinkle. But her hands are gnarled like exposed roots of a plant pulled up from the ground, oh! the desire I have to be anywhere but here. I'll think about Miguel, Miguel rhymes with farewell, a poor rhyme but so rich, I'm coming! The Mediterranean Sea. Democratic and Popular Republic of Algeria. The ocean, what color will this ocean be?

"You can find another analyst, that's no problem. All it takes is money, you can be treated by the best psychiatrist in the world."

"Seven years. Seven years. I'm back to zero, everything I've said and done, everything's been lost as if in a shipwreck. With his death, I'm reduced to nothing as if—oh God, how can I accept it? How can I accept it?"

He's the one who probably hasn't accepted it yet, I think and take advantage of the opportunity to blow my nose on my shirt-tail, she's closed her eyes. There won't be time, the office will have to wait until tomorrow. I'll phone Bugre and explain, if he can leave the message with Mineiro. Okay, a call will take care of that. A screwed-up day. Loreninha might have come to hold up her end of things, mightn't she?

"I gave myself to him entire, on a tray—past, present, he took it all. With his death he gives it all back to me again. Those rocks. I had taken them all off one by one, so many rocks piled up on top of me, here on my chest. I took them slowly off, he would encourage me, 'Come on, girl. Take a deep breath!' at times he'd call me that, '*girl.*' 'What's the trouble, girl?' *Girl,*" she repeated covering her mouth into which tears are running. "Now the rocks have fallen back in place, heavier than before, there are even more of them. How can I go to someone strange, who doesn't know about anything, and repeat it all again? . . . seven years. He could tell how I was feeling just from the way I walked, at times I would decide, today I'll bluff, I want to pretend I'm cured, 'I'm fine, Dr. Francis, today I'm just fine!' He would just look at me, that penetrating stare that could pass right through one. And then I'd burst into tears because that was exactly the thing I needed to do, to cry. I'm back to zero."

I'd sure like to know who picked up my *Writing Degree Zero* which I haven't even read yet. Mayakovsky and Lorca I'll give to Bugre. Malraux, the Beauvoir and Sartre go to Pedro, he'll be thrilled. Eliezer can keep the Brazilian authors, analyze Indianism down to the last feather, it's necessary, it's necessary. The history of philosophy and the dictionaries can go to Loreninha. Psychology books for Ana Clara, who knows, she might still get unkinked and finish her courses. Crazy Annie. Even Mother Alix, who's been the faithful keeper in person, is beginning to get a bit neurotic; neurosis is contagious. Like a spark in dry straw. The whole thing burns up.

"God knows that if it wasn't for him, I would already have thrown myself out that window."

I look in the direction she points, only now can I manage to visualize a window behind the draperies. Lorena is the type who withdraws into her shell too, but she likes fresh air.

"How can a Christian lady talk like that? Aren't you a Christian?"

The tears have started again, more slowly, running from the corners of her eyes and infiltrating her hair.

"He was my father, my brother, my lover. In the spiritual sense, you do understand me, I hope?"

"Perfectly."

"Everything I had and lost. I was thinking, the terrible thing about life is that things end. Everything ends. On my ranch we used to have a sugarcane grinder, the children loved to drink the juice we'd squeeze. Roberto, my husband, used to like to choose the sugarcane himself. It would go into the grinder so green and

199

fresh, it would go in alive and come out the other side a dry pulp, all smashed to bits. Not a drop of juice, only pulp. Life does the same thing to us, my dear. Just the same. And people do their part in grinding us up. I ask myself how she could possibly have been so cruel."

"Who? Who was cruel?"

"Those viper's eyes. The nurse. A snake-in-the-grass!"

"Who, Mama?"

She took a handkerchief from under the pillow and let it hang suspended from her fingers. A handkerchief as soft and transparent as the canopy hangings.

"You're from Bahia, aren't you, Lia? I think that's why you're so polite, Bahians are especially polite. Do you study Law too, dear?"

"Social Sciences."

"Ah yes, Social Sciences. I'm so happy to think you're Lorena's friend. My dear little girl. So pure, so honest and sensitive. So refined. It's not just that she's my daughter, but I know it's hard to find a girl like her. When I committed this madness of marrying again, when I fell in love with this man who has made me cry tears of blood, I asked her opinion, 'What do you think about it, daughter?' And she took my hands between hers and answered with that sweetness you've already seen, 'Whatever Mama does will be the right thing.' She doesn't even know the half of what's happened to me, I don't want her to be hurt, to suffer. This boyfriend of hers, the latest one, do you know him?"

"Only slightly."

"I somehow got the idea he might be married, a reference Loreninha made, but I don't quite know . . . when I was a young girl I read a charming book, nobody reads it any more but my mother's generation delighted in it, *The Exemplary Girls*, by the Countess of Segur. Have you ever heard of it? When I see Loreninha with her delicate old-fashioned air I remember that book." She sighs, covering her eyes with her handkerchief. "I don't care too much for that other friend of yours, the redhead, she was at a nightclub the other day with a very strange group of people. Undoubtedly very pretty, but so vulgar. What's her name?"

"Ana Clara."

"That's it, Ana Clara."

"She's a nice girl," I say and flex my leg which has fallen asleep. I get up, I sit down again. But why was the nurse cruel?

"You were telling me about the nurse, remember?"

She pushes back the sheet. One lace strap of the nightgown slides down, exposing her breast. A dark wilted orchid, oh, can it still be daytime outside?

"The nurse who worked for him, Estella. A real snake-in-the-grass. I got there so cheerful in my turquoise-blue dress, he loves that color, I arrived early thinking that it would be a lighter session, without complaints or tears. I wanted to make him laugh a little with me, say funny things. Have you ever had analysis? Before going in one always thinks about the accumulation of things one's going to say and then one doesn't say them but others instead, everything changes. But this time it was going to be as I'd planned, enough lamenting! There's the little anteroom where one arranges oneself before and after the session, particularly after. The countless tissues I've taken out of that box to dry my eyes! I always take a handkerchief in my purse but sometimes I forget. Or lose them."

I wait for her to tell me the story of the nurse, but it appears that the story will be as Dona Lã, the retired fortune-teller, used to prophesy: Far in the future a distant happiness . . . My mother was godmother to her child. On the dressing table is a picture of *him* wearing sideburns and smoking a pipe. The pose of a movie actor blowing his discreet puff of smoke. How absurd for a woman her age to fall for a type like that. What good did all that analysis do? Seven years. And on top of everything else she falls in love with the doctor who fades away without solving the problem, it remains present and entire.

"I'd like to die. If I could just die without leaving the slightest trace, I hate the idea of funerals, of people taking us by surprise. Only young people's coffins should stay open."

"Young people's and vampires'," I say wanting to lighten the atmosphere.

No good. The low front does not offer the slightest visibility. "Due to technical difficulties," begins the stewardess in a cheerful voice just as the airplane loses half its left wing. Everybody tightens their seat belts, fear, fear. I'm a land animal and I'm going to have to go up in one of those. I'll get drunk, if the damn thing explodes I don't want to be aware of it. Hell, fasten your seat belt.

201

"I have a horror of people who come in without knocking, or come up from behind to surprise one—a horror of being unprepared, and that's exactly what death does, it doesn't give us time. I consider it a betrayal!"

There's something sinister about that lineless face, doesn't it resemble one of those shrunken heads, speared on a post? A mummy, see. And the nurse? Wasn't there a nurse? Now I have to find out what happened with this nurse, Lorena has the same habit of leaving stories half-finished.

"Why was the nurse cruel?"

"She always hated me, always. A horrid woman, she doesn't know how to dress or do her hair, a viper who decided to get old. Is it my fault if I look younger? If I like to take care of myself? She was green with envy of me, she was in love with Dr. Francis, now I'm sure of it, she was passionately in love with Dr. Francis. I think she was radiant over his death, *Neither mine nor anyone else's!* Isn't that a form of victory?"

Among the pillows of the divan I spy a gold-wrapped box, bonbons? I am almost drooling as I stretch my hand toward it, "May I?"

"I arrived dressed in turquoise-blue, so lighthearted, almost happy. I looked in the mirror and felt that I was exactly as old as my face appeared; I had a facelift but I know that the important thing is to have inside us the age that is on the outside. I rehearsed what I was going to say. 'Dr. Francis, today I woke up feeling so well!' As if during the night a fairy godmother had come to me, one of those good fairy godmothers from the old tales, with a magic wand. Don't suffer any longer, dear, she said touching my head with the wand, don't suffer any longer, don't suffer any longer, she kept repeating and just then I woke up and felt different. I *am* different, Dr. Francis, different! No resentment toward Mieux, let him have his deceits, his pettiness, isn't it better simply to say good-bye like two well-bred people whose life together has become insupportable? That's all. No rancor, no bitterness, isn't it better that way? He is younger, let him find someone his own age, as he did before we lived together. Let him go away and leave me alone, I'm preparing myself for solitude. Look in my eyes, Dr. Francis, I swear I'm not bluffing, I woke up breathing deeply, my chest open and my head high, the fairy godmother touched my head, remember? Don't suffer any longer . . . I don't want to promise anything,

Dr. Francis, but I think that today a new phase is beginning for me, I'm feeling splendid. Or almost so. Or almost so,' I repeated to myself as I brushed my hair, smiling at the mirror, making the face I would make as I went in: 'Well then, Dr. Francis?' I heard her footsteps coming from behind me, she always manages to come up from behind. Her rubber-soled footsteps, she wears those nurses' shoes. I started when I heard her voice at my shoulder: 'What are you doing here?' I just stared at her. What? Has she gone crazy? How can she ask me something like that, what am I doing here. 'Have you forgotten? Don't I have an appointment today?' I panicked slightly, I'm absentminded, have I gotten my days mixed up? Isn't this Tuesday? So then she gazed at me a long time and smiled, I swear she smiled as she put her hand on my shoulder, 'But Dr. Francis is dead, hadn't you heard? He died. He was buried yesterday, they say he had a cardiac arrest, how could they not have notified you? The funeral was late yesterday afternoon.' I grabbed my purse and ran out, I didn't even wait for the elevator, I ran down the steps with her voice accompanying me, the funeral was late yesterday afternoon. Late yesterday afternoon, oh God. I wonder how such cruelty is possible."

I unwrap the third bonbon which is also a chocolate-covered cherry. Besides the invention of Scotch tape, I consider them one of the most important inventions of the century, these liqueur-filled bonbons with a cherry in the middle.

"I can't explain it, Mama, but I don't see how that was cruel. Didn't he die? If so, then she had to tell you. It wasn't too skillful, obviously, but I don't see why *cruel*."

"An excellent occasion to humiliate me with his lovers, the time was hand-picked. Just today the maid answered two telephone calls, the more daring one gave her name, Karin. 'Do you want to leave a message?' the maid asked and the little prostitute giggled, ha, ha, ha, no, it was better to give it *in person*. I'd like him to turn up right now so I could tell him to pack his bags, Pack your bags up immediately and get out of my house! Get out of my life, you wretch! In the beginning, little presents, flowers, how deluded I was by his politeness, there couldn't have been a more attentive man. He wanted to open an interior-decorating store, so I gave him the money. Then after that he invented an advertising agency, more money, I spent what I had and what I didn't. Cynic. Scoundrel."

203

This one instead of a cherry has a grape stuck fast in its rose-colored cream. And I don't really know why there comes to me the phrase of a genial politician: *To govern is to grasp.* Very refined, as Mama there would say. I wad the bonbon wrappings up into a little ball. Courageously I take a deep breath. Here we go:

"But are your problems real? If it's a toothache, what can a psychiatrist do? I want to study structuralism and don't understand it because I'm too stupid, what good will a doctor do me?"

I almost say, if your problem is old age, and if old age has no cure, see. She doesn't see. She stares at me from deep in the pillows but she'll never see that she is old and that no psychiatrist in the world is going to make her young again. Was the role of this Dr. Francis to help her accept old age? Or to keep the famous flame burning, even letting himself be loved like the character in the novel? Spiritualities. I don't know, I'm getting exhausted. Another route:

"Don't you have faith in God? If so, then He's more important than Dr. Francis, He's above all else. I can't explain it, but what good is it to have God, if in a difficult moment you can't draw sustenance from Him?"

She smiles.

"I'd like to go into a convent. I think I'd be happy in a convent. I would stay there so quietly, watching the world from far away, growing old in peace, without witnesses, I'm terrified of witnesses. I've discovered that what frightens me most about life and death alike are the witnesses. I'm always meeting someone who remembers me on this or that date, the witnesses are so attentive, their memory! Why do people have such memories? I was at a dinner having a lovely time and someone came up and stared at me. He stared hard and then started one of those conversations that make my flesh crawl: 'I don't think you remember me . . . ' Oh God, when I hear this beginning I go cold all over, it starts like that, I'll bet you don't remember me! I look vague and disguise my reactions but it doesn't help, the witness is a voracious beak pulling the meat off my bones, peck, peck, it won't turn its prey loose, what voracity! 'Wasn't it on . . . ' the date. Before anything else they recite the entire blessed date. Even the hour. This one wanted me to remember him from my début dance, which coincided with my birthday, remember? I quickly say I remember, 'Oh, how could I ever forget? I remember everything, I certainly do!' But he was insatiable, he started reproducing the entire party as if it had been yesterday, we danced to *Stormy Weather* cheek to cheek, at the time that song was obligatory, just as it was obligatory to dance with one's faces together, right?' Mieux was laughing with sheer joy, he was across the room but when he intuited the subject he came running. 'There was an enormous cake on the table, all white, do you remember?' I had forgotten the cake entirely but not he, 'A cake with little doves made of spun sugar, fluttering over a satin bow whose ends reached to the floor. You offered each guest a dove, there were fifteen because you were fifteen years old that day, remember?' I swear I could hear the wheels turning in people's heads as they made their rapid calculations, if she was fifteen on that date, then today she must be . . . Oh God oh God. I had to drink almost half a bottle of whiskey in order to stay at the party until the end, laughing and talking, even smiling at that monstrous imbecile who came up looking like the cat who ate the cream and asked me if perhaps he had committed an indiscretion, 'You aren't mad, are you?' 'Of course not, I adore you, let's dance cheek to cheek like on that night,' I said, wanting to shove his face into the fireplace, let him be cheek to cheek with the fire. Oh God, how awful, how awful."

I get up. I want to make pee-pee, walk, get a drink of water, eat something salty. Oh, the session with me was a double one. I begin to see why they charge so much. *Kötig.*

"Is the bathroom here? Excuse me just a moment."

The night of the bedroom extends into the lilac bath, which sparkles with starlike reflections. I have to leave the door open because she continues to talk as I fight with the zipper which pinches my skin. From the toilet (pardon me, Lorena) from the throne I see the objects glittering on the marble console; they remind me of the ones in the rose-pink shell. Colored bath salts in crystal bottles, ermine powder puffs, pots of cream, gold rings from which hang towels with a large M embroidered in purple, Lena's L is in pink. Her voice flows heavier and faster:

"He made me go out with him almost every night, parties, parties, 'Don't you want to go? Then I'll go alone.' I didn't want to go but I would, more clothes, more hairdressers, every morning early I'd be at the beauty salon, my scalp was burning from so much hair spray and dye. I got a little relief when I bought five wigs. I'd change my wig, put on my makeup and go running after him, nightclubs, dinners, cocktails, *vernissages*, he took to investing in paintings, he never had the slightest culture but he thought he was an art connoisseur, he was on the point of opening a gallery. In the intervals, the absolute multitudes of his friends, he'd meet a couple today and tomorrow the couple would be installed here, little drinks, little outings. My eyes closing, my face falling, 'But do we need to entertain so much, Mieux?' 'Of course we do, isn't it part of my profession as a decorator?' Later, the profession of advertising also demanded contacts, contacts, and naturally the profession which was to come afterward, that of *marchand*. Oh God, oh God. 'But what's the matter with you?' he would ask. 'Are you tired?' 'No, of course not, I'm fine!' I would answer wanting to lie down on the table from exhaustion, I started taking stimulants to withstand the late nights and keep my eyes open, 'It was wonderful, wonderful!' He'd laugh that little laugh, how well I know that little laugh. 'It was fun wasn't it? Didn't you enjoy it?' All on purpose. Pure mental cruelty, my dear. Do you know what mental cruelty is?"

I open the jar with the powder puff. I unscrew the bottle of perfume covered in mirrors, she collects perfumes like her daughter collects little boxes, bells. Mental cruelty? I was still a child when I heard Grandma telling about the husband who insisted that his wife, who wore false teeth, should try some carmelized guava, it wasn't sticky at all. Today I'm going to write a long letter home, the more I see of other people's parents the more I love those two, my German and my Bahiana. Your kind of letter, Mom, full of good judgment and asking your blessing. They're eaten up with worry over my militancy, I don't want any more of that, I'll say this trip is part of my odyssey, Dad read the *Odyssey* and finds a certain heroism in the gypsy wanderings of youth because of their lack of calculation and altruism. Oh, Dad, I love you but I can't stand morbid love, mine is wholesome. A Nazi, just as he could have been a Communist, he's the passionate type too, capable of being moved by a uniform, a hymn. A really crazy German. When he discovered it wasn't the way he thought, he ran so far he ended up in Salvador, *saravá* brother!

She is still talking about mental cruelty, illustrating it with a story that has a caterpillar in it.

"I have to go, see. What about the suitcase?"

"Wait, dear, have some tea first, press that button again, what do they do there in the back? Four servants," she sighs, taking up the mirror from among the sheets. She looks at herself, puckering up her lips as if to kiss her own reflection.

"And what about Loreninha? We had planned to go and visit Dona Guiomar but it seems she's in jail, I don't know why the police persecute these poor people. She has never failed, she predicted that Remo, my son, would go to North Africa, she foresaw the death of Dr. Francis, 'You are going to lose a very dear person,' she warned me. She predicted Mieux's betrayal, she prophesied everything. If Lucretia were still alive she could give me her blessing, I think she was once a slave."

"So I can take the suitcase today?"

"Certainly, dear, Bila packed everything, there are lots of winter clothes, Mieux is worthless but his clothes are very good. You know how to drive, don't you? Take the car and leave it there with Loreninha, maybe she'll decide to come. My dear little girl. She was such a well-mannered child, so sweet. She would collect pebbles, leaves. She was always saving some little animal that had fallen in the river. Is she still a virgin?"

"Yes, still."

"I'm so happy to know that she continues to be pure," she murmurs with an expression of beatitude. But at once she frowns. Her voice becomes fogged over: "Don't you think she shows too little interest in sex? At times I'm so afraid, do you understand what I mean? Lately there seem to be so many of them, these girls . . . "

I chew on a bonbon.

"I don't want to be rude, Mama, but I think it's completely absurd to worry about that. You speak of mental cruelty. Now there's the worst form of it, a mother worrying whether her son or daughter is a homosexual or not. I understand parents who worry about drugs and so on, but worry about other people's sex? Taking care of one's own is hard enough. Excuse me, but I get upset over any interference in the southern zone of others, Lorena calls it the southern zone. The northern zone is already so overrun, so bombarded, why can't people free themselves and let others be free too? A prejudice as hateful as racial or religious prejudices. We have to love our neighbor as he is and not as we would like him to be."

207

As I say this I think immediately of Ana Clara. I have to love her. Hard, yes. I get irritated and impatient. But then, am I trying to be a Christian?

"A woman without a man ends up so unhappy, so full of complexes."

With a man too, I want to tell her and hand her the mirror.

"Full of complexes because everybody keeps nagging at her. That isn't Lorena's case, I'm no longer thinking of her, I'm only saying that it's already so difficult to grow, to be loved by the person one loves. And for someone else to come along and determine the sex of that person—!"

"And you, Lia? Are you in love with someone? You needn't reply if you don't want to."

I'm laughing as I answer, it took her a long time to ask.

"No problem with me, see. I have a lover, he needs me and I need him, he's traveling just now but we'll be together again soon."

She gazes at me as though from a distance, shaking her handkerchief lightly as if to shoo away flies. She sprinkles cologne over her forehead and neck.

"I think I'd die of distaste if my son Remo or Loreninha . . . I want my funeral to be unadorned, simple. She even knows the dress I want to wear. The makeup, we've planned every detail. The coffin will stay open only if I'm looking extremely well; if not, nobody will have the *pleasure* of seeing me dead. Before I used to panic at the idea of him poking through my papers, those old yellow papers that I hate so, a death certificate records your age, it records everything. Just imagine the radiant face he'd make upon discovering my true age, he's always wanted to discover it but I didn't let him. I never let him. Dead, I'd be defenseless, do you understand what I mean? But now I can die in peace, my dear little girl will take care of everything, that perverse cynic will never humiliate me again!"

The maid comes in on a gust of air. I breathe like a condemned man inside a gas chamber.

"I've been calling for hours! All right, all right, I know. Bring some tea at once," she orders waving the hanky in the girl's direction. Turning back to me: "This new flirtation of Lorena's, isn't he married, by chance?"

"I haven't any idea."

"That's strange, you're such close friends," she murmurs cov-

208

ering her eyes with her hands. "Everything's so strange, isn't it? Why is it that in front of Dr. Francis I wasn't ashamed of being old? I didn't have the slightest shame, I wanted to look pretty, yes, elegant, but I wasn't ashamed the way I was in front of other people. With certain people I sometimes want to hide myself as if I'd committed a crime, hide my age like a criminal hides the victim, a terrible panic that they'd discover it, spread it around. Isn't that odd? Certain people make me even more ashamed, as if I were naked in a display window. Now with you I'm completely at ease, with you, with Loreninha. My dear little girl. I've lost so many things but I still have my daughter, now we can live together again."

"But will she live with you? Come back under your wing? I know you're the perfect mother, mine is too, but just for that very reason one has to cut the umbilical cord, see. Otherwise it gets rolled around one's neck and ends up strangling one. Castrating. Forgive me, but I think this is the most mistaken idea in the world. If one's child is mature, he has to fly away from the nest as quickly as he can so as not to become what we know so well . . . oh, I think I'm talking too much."

I roll down my shirtsleeves. She'll vampirize her daughter whose blood is already as watered-down as that of the gazelles on the rug.

"This apartment is enormous, dear. She'll have an entire section all to herself. Why don't you come and live here too? I'd have the greatest pleasure."

I don't even answer. Oh Lord, as Lorena says in moments of affliction. I look with more sympathy at the man with the movie-actor pose, pipe and cloud of smoke.

"That little tree with the photos, is the boy Remo or Romulo?"

"Remo. Romulo couldn't be there."

"No?"

"He died when he was a baby, dear."

"A baby?"

"He wasn't even a month old, he didn't even live that long. The doctors said that he had no viability. A heart murmur."

I jump up with a wild desire to pull down these drapes, rip everything open and let in the light of day. But is it still daytime?

"Wait a minute: Remo shot him when they were playing,

209

wasn't that it? A shot in the chest, he would have been about twelve, wasn't that what happened? Thousands of times Lorena told me the story in detail, he was blond. He was wearing a red shirt, you lived on the ranch."

She is smiling a sad smile, looking at the ceiling.

"My poor little girl. She never knew her brother, she's the youngest. She was still a little girl when she started to invent this, first only to the servants who would come and ask me, I didn't even deny it, I covered up, where was the harm? She continued to talk, at school, at parties, the problem began to get more serious. Oh God, the discomfort I would feel when they wanted to know if . . . I didn't want them to think she was lying, she was always such a truthful child. The doctors calmed us, it wasn't so grave, it would pass with time, an overactive childish imagination, probably when she became an adolescent . . . It didn't pass. Roberto was always so confident, so secure, he would reassure me, it's nothing. I spoke to Dr. Francis, he had a talk with Loreninha, found her intelligent, sensitive. Do you understand what I mean, dear? He didn't give it the slightest importance."

I feel slightly nauseated, the chocolate? I hold my stomach and stare at the rug, this one is solid color. Honey-beige. But what is this? That whole story she told me so painfully, oh, Lorena. Oh, Lorena. What a meaningless thing, why? Why? I keep thinking and come closer to the cocoon where she sleeps wide-awake, her eyelids hardly concealing her burning eyes. What if she's lying? What if the real version is Lorena's? Didn't she say it? Neither the doctors nor her husband, nobody gave Lorena's story the slightest importance. Why not? Because she was the sick one, the sick one was the mother altering the tragedy in self-defense, much easier to imagine that the son died as a baby and return him to limbo, he had no viability. The young boy in the red shirt, chest pierced by his brother's shot, is subtracted from death and reduced to a baby with a heart murmur. Hm? I look for a fingernail, aren't they ever going to grow out? I bite on a remnant that comes loose with a pain as sharp as a stabbing thorn. At the same time, Lorena with that fixation on the truth, complicating even the smallest matters. "And the dream machines?" she asked, her little face growing as secret as this alcove. The striped pullover was his, wasn't it? He must have existed. I know so much about him, it's as if he had been my

210

own brother. And now. I need to see her photo album urgently, the *gens lorenensis* must all be there from beginning to end. Either way, how sad. "Who knows but what Mama might give you his clothes?"

"Back to zero, my dear. I had a facelift but crying the way I have been it must have gotten ruined. My sister Luci discovered a Scandinavian cream made with turtle oil, it must be excellent, turtles live for centuries," she adds raising herself up on her elbows. "Oh God, that's the terrible part, that things come to an end. Everything comes to an end."

Chapter 11

With a soft gesture Ana Clara pushed back the ringlets of hair plastered to her forehead. She buttoned her coat collar high at the neck and, clutching her purse tightly against her chest, started up the steps. She tripped and fell to her knees. As she put out her hands to catch herself, she screamed: The ground was boiling with cockroaches. The biggest of them stood up on its hind feet, its chest stiff in a fencing tunic, foil in hand: *En garde!* She bent over, laughing because the roach was laughing too behind its wire mask, was it a joke? She peered at it more closely, then tried to hide her chest but it was too late: The foil pierced her from one side to the other. Blood spurted from the heart crowned with thorns, squirting into her mouth so violently that she choked on it. When she tried to breathe she doubled up, coughing.

"No more, no more," she groaned.

"Take it easy, dear. Lean on me," Lorena ordered, taking her by the arm.

The horse. The roach was left behind making a spiral dive into the collard greens. She picked up its foil that it had dropped on the ground, pinned her collar shut with it, and mounted the white horse. She laughed as they galloped through the starry countryside; there were so many stars she could see the crystals sparkling on the shelves. She patted the horse's neck. It smiled. Lorena? It was Lorena. Her body relaxed.

"It's so good here."

"Didn't I say you'd like it? I'm going to turn on the hot water," advised Lorena. "Come on, lift up your head."

She obeyed. Giggling weakly, she curled up in the bottom of the bathtub. "Shit, if you only knew."

With one arm Lorena supported the trunk of Ana Clara's body, using the other to lather her breasts with the soapy bath sponge.

"Where did you ever get so dirty, Annie? Incredible. You were dirty as an armadillo, dear. There was even mud in your ear, can you believe it?"

Ana Clara spoke with difficulty, voice thick and jaws clenched. She opened her eyes and began to laugh again.

"A bath? Are you giving me a bath?"

"Come on, wash the southern zone now. Here," ordered Lorena guiding her hand. "Come on, rub hard right here. No, don't let go of the sponge! Oh Lord."

"I have to go. What time is it?"

"Be quiet, Annie! Don't splash me, hold still, it's still early, dear. Come on, rub."

"Give me some whiskey."

"All right but first rub the sponge here. That's it."

"Sober. Scratch scratch, I'm completely sober. I get mad as a bitch because my head. Scratch scratch."

"Eucalyptus perfume, smell it? Isn't that a delicious smell, it's eucalyptus."

"Eucalyptus."

Now Lorena was soaping her hair.

"Close your eyes and don't open them until I say."

"I want my purse."

"I'll give it to you but now close your eyes, come on, do as I say. What I'd like to know is where you've been. Where were you?"

"At a party."

"What party? Wait, let me rinse off the soap," said Lorena circling the other's waist. "Be careful, Annie!"

She rolled her up in a towel and guided her into the bedroom. Ana Clara shuddered, pointing at the window.

"Who's that peering in there?"

"Where? That's just the curtain, dear. Calm down, there's no one there, the two of us are alone. The nuns have all gone to bed, calm down."

"Mother Alix! Mother Alix!"

"She's coming. Lie down, wasn't that a lovely bath?"

Lorena rubbed the towel over Ana's hair, staring at the purple bruises on her breasts and arms. She opened a box of talcum powder.

"Annie, Annie. Where can you have been?"

"He got arrested," mumbled Ana Clara opening her eyes.

214

She clenched her fists and folded her arms across her chest. "He got arrested."

"Who? Who got arrested?"

Dry, tearless sobs racked her. Her speech became more painful.

"Scratch-scratch. It's all right, I'll say—" She raised herself up and then fell back again on the bed. "God came and lighted on my chest, right here, right here. He flew away, the little bird was God. He came and then."

I wrap my red bathrobe around her and brush out her hair, which shines like live coals, cut short this way it'll dry fast. But what madness! Madness. Imagine if Mother Alix. From the floor I collect her filthy clothes, they look like she's been wallowing in a swamp. And those purple spots? And the frightful odor of vomit mixed with day-old perfume, oh Lord, Lord, Lord. Country estate, indeed. I take the bundle of clothes to the hamper, a good thing tomorrow is Sebastiana's day. The coat I'll send to the dry cleaner's. I place her shoes side by side, isn't that curious? They're hardly dirty. As if she'd been walking upside down, poor little thing.

"Ana, who got arrested? You said somebody got arrested."

Her head rolls back and forth on the pillow as she clutches her hair, pulling it. Her words come out stonily:

"Max disappeared, disappeared! Loreninha, help me,— Max."

"Ana, talk softer, do you want the nuns to wake up? Do you want Mother Alix to see you in this state? Is that what you want?"

"Max disappeared. He's not there, I waited."

"Well, he probably went on a trip. Doesn't he travel a lot?"

"Yeah."

"So he's probably traveling, silly."

"I waited."

"You went on a binge, is what you did. Where have you been, anyway?"

Now she is giggling, cheeks pink, slightly crossed eyes shining.

"If you only knew."

"Knew what? I don't know but I can guess. You're going to quit these binges, do you hear? You're going to have to develop some sense."

215

"I don't want sense."

"It'll have to be pounded into you this time, dear, whether you want it or not. Mother Alix is getting tired, everybody's tired."

"The big ant was laughing the bastard. Then the cockroach got there and the championship race started. Max was first the Japanese. That guy. What's his name that Japanese? That guy. That Japanese guy!"

"I don't know dearie. I only know that I was reading about the stars when Miss Depressed and Depressing Ana tumbled into my arms."

"I was with God, He was here. It doesn't matter any more the things that then I said no no and He came and there was a sort of light everything lighted up in my head and He let me fly so high, with His hand holding mine. Very chic. Enough Max! Max is it you?"

"It's Lorena, dear. Your feet are like two ice cubes, let me rub them. Be still, Ana! Now your name is Ana Bacchante. Bacchante and Dilettante. Do you know what a bacchante is? Those nymphs who danced in the cortège of Bacchus. I'm going to crown you with grape leaves. Rotten chic, eh?"

"Give me a whiskey, I want a whiskey."

Lorena massaged her feet and covered her with a quilt.

"Lorena. Lorena Vaz Leme. Nha-nha-nha."

"Ana, be quiet or I'll call Mother Alix! Stop laughing, nothing's funny."

"I want a whiskey, Leninha. Just one, gimme. I promise I promise."

"I'll pour some into your tea, I'm going to make some nice hot tea," said Lorena covering her with the quilt which she had thrown to the floor. "If I ever have to work for a living I'm going to be a *femme de chambre*. I think it's the one thing I do perfectly. In another life I must have worked in a castle for a courtesan very much like Ana Clara Conceição."

"I want my purse. My purse."

I give her the purse and go to fill the teakettle. Why do things always have to happen at the same time? The strike ending, exams starting tomorrow, Mama going berserk, Dr. Francis dying just now when Mieux decides to take off, isn't it really a dose for an *iguanodon*? How would you translate *iguanodon*? Lião howling with impatience, discourses and other sentiments and

216

here I am with Ana Clara. I should be studying, shouldn't I? Yes I should. The abyss between *existence* and *being*. I *am* with Annie and to be with Annie is to be with the winds, the rocks and the tempest, ah, M.N., why don't you give me a job as a nurse in your hospital? Did you get my note? And aren't you going to answer it?

"It's on the ceiling."

"What's on the ceiling?" I ask.

I sense my expression to be so sad that I'm moved by it. I'm feeling sorry for myself and that's not healthy.

"The time! I need to know right away!" she cries still staring at the same point near the light fixture. "Never mind. Next year without fail. Next year."

She must be promising God the same bla-bla-bla she promises Mother Alix. Neither of them believe her and yet, because she's the blackest sheep in the flock . . . "*Miserere Nobis*," I say and spread my hands wide above the lid of the teakettle. It retributes my gesture with a hot puff of steam. Ana Clara lets out a groan and says something so mixed-up, what, Aninha? I make her lie down again, a pain somewhere? It must have passed because now she's cackling with laughter. Her curly hair grows shinier as it dries; her pleasure-crossed eyes have darkened maliciously. The collar of the bathrobe is open and her neck thickens as she laughs, tense and corded. The bruises on her breasts. The spot on her arm, pressing like a finger against the principal vein. "*Res accessoria*," I say vaguely. I watch her, fascinated. Her tongue rolls up, obscene. A possessed Dionysian figure contorted in the red robe. I pull the quilt up to her neck and hold her still. She grows calm. Her crazed eyes soften.

"It's cold, Lena. I'm so cold."

I adjust the pillows closer around her body.

"You're going to drink some nice hot tea."

"I'll say that—"

Her eyes close. Hands folded, asleep, she has turned into an angel. I pick up the red bath towel from the floor and roll up her blood-stained blouse, I didn't see the blood but I could feel its moisture on my hand and I folded it fast because I thought Mama wouldn't like people looking at the stained shirt, since the blood was being washed off his chest in the bathtub. She locked herself in with Romulo and didn't let anyone help her: "I'll bathe my son." Romulo, Romulo. At times I feel that you

217

continued to live in me, your gestures in mine. Your speech. Later, I'm left by myself, you tell me that I need to be alone, that I'll be happy that way, ah, Romulo. How you've grown!

"Give me your hand," she pleads.

I give her my hand, which she squeezes and then lets go. What is she dreaming about? I tuck her hand under the cover and run to the boiling water. I turn off the stove. The scent of the tea tranquilizes me just as incense does, I must burn a little. Drive away the evil spirits, Annie came in loaded with them as if she had descended into Hell, are you all right, Annie? I asked in alarm when she tripped on the stairway. She smiled, cross-eyed: "The horse." I fold my hands around the cup and sip the tea. When I undressed her, her expression was that of the Seducer Angel, a brilliance in her eyes which drifted in and out of focus. "You, Lena? What are you doing to me?"

I open the window. How could nobody in the house have heard her scream? She was screaming when she arrived. And not a single nun appeared, not even Bulie. It's lucky all these TV serials are on in the neighborhood, there's always wailing and gnashing of teeth in the background. The cats catting at the top of their lungs as they run through the flower beds. If we were a calm society Ana would draw attention from all and sundry, but in this erotic society all and sundry are occupied with eroticism. Few, very few, are praying. Or thinking. Me, reading about the stars, imagine. They are born and die just like us, the cosmic vision is the same as that of the world, did you know that, M.N.? I survey the Milky Way. The larger stars are the younger ones, my generation. The others, old ones, get smaller and smaller just like Bulie. Until they dissolve, cease to be, isn't it lovely? "I'd like so much to grow old in peace, to quit this sleight-of-hand game," Mama said so sincerely. "I'm exhausted, daughter. I'm ready for the wrinkles, the white hair, the freckles, the grandchildren. I'm sick and tired of sex!" The sickness is short-lived. When the body starts to get lonely, she reacts with energy, what energy! All it takes is an intriguing invitation which doesn't even need to be from a man, even a girlfriend of the stimulating type makes her raise her head and go running off on the tips of her toes. "Now we'll live together, dear. Like in the good old times," she recalls. But during those good old times she used to complain so much, were they really that good? Abandon my shell, my delicate world which I love so much . . . If it were

218

at least to go live with M.N., why doesn't he ask me to come with him on these trips of his? These high international congresses in which he's forever participating. I'd fit into his *necessaire*. And you, Fabrízio. A neurotic little poetess, ask me what it's like to live with a neurotic and I'll tell you. If at least Guga would come to get the shirt which I haven't bought yet. I'll embroider the duck on it but I'm not thinking about the duck, I'm thinking about his beard, his mouth. The smell of tobacco, sweat, and dust. And his satin dagger of a tongue that I had to expel, but why expel? Oh Lord, I never imagined that those goatlike feet, ill-concealed in his sandals and those jeans with the faded white island at the crotch—I turned my eyes away but I kept on seeing that faded spot where I had such a desire to ... M.N., M.N., so you're the only one who hasn't the courage? Because I'm a virgin, is that it? Does it make that much difference? We could live in the country, I adore the country. A natural-brick house. A lawn. Books, music. I want to read you all the poets I admire, my voice isn't pretty but at least I've learned to make it sound serious; when I try I can correct this nasal squeak I was born with. They'll say: alienation, flight. We'll say: integration, return. To ourselves, to the sun. To God. My note is decisive: Answer, I wrote a decisive note. The decisive notes. Everything summed up in this: I love you. It isn't a simple friendship between a man and a woman, but a sort of unification, an absolutely harmonic unit in this chaotic world. The profound feeling. Profound, I repeat and look at Ana Clara. Asleep. Lião is forever preaching that society expels that which it cannot assimilate. Ana was driven out with a flaming sword, she said she'd been run through with a fencing foil, but it wasn't a foil, it was a sword. Which comes to the same thing. Peaceful coexistence, the teachers teach. And in practice.

"Lia de Melo Schultz!" I say.

She has arrived. The window of her room has just lit up, ah, Lião, I think your presence has never been so welcome. If it weren't so late, and if Annie weren't in her present state, I'd shout with all my strength, "Lia de Melo Schultz!" And you'd shout back, "Present!" I put on my sandals, change my shirt, and cover up Ana Clara's feet which have come uncovered. Then I go out the way I learned from Astronaut, leaving the solid mass of my body behind and taking only its rarefied equivalent. I can't see the moon, only a sky scorching with stars. The brighter ones are wearing low necklines, palpitating. Virgins? let me laugh. Even the daisies are agitated, their exposed crowns shaking in the wind. I scratch at the window blind. She opens it and as I jump in my heart contracts. This will be the last time I jump through her window into this room. I almost trip over the yellow leather suitcase. I pick it up. Very heavy.

"Packed? Already?"

Lião closes her notebook on the table, she's been writing. The diary? Oh Lord.

"Don't you recognize Mama's suitcase? I was with her for hours. The death of the analyst who was very refined, the break with the lover who was very gross, so much drama," says Lião and suddenly stares closely at me.

"Why are you looking at me like that?"

"Nothing, see. It was a session that would finish even a professional," she mutters grinning. "I like her. Very refined, very refined."

I take the peppermint out of my mouth in order to talk.

"If you only knew, Lião. Imagine: I was reading about the stars, feeling very poetic, when I heard this uproar on the steps and a scream so blood-curdling my book jumped up to the ceiling, guess who it was. She was hanging over the banister, shouting that somebody had stabbed her in the chest with a fencing foil. In short, high as a kite. Complete madness. And talk about filthy! Her clothes had mud on them, charcoal, some very suspicious stains. And the smell. I gave her an immersion bath, even her hair was foul."

Lião is laughing so hard I can't finish. I wait. Going to her bag, she takes out a ball of twine and starts tying together the small piles of books lined up on the floor. She lights a cigarette and uses it to burn the twine loose after tying each knot.

"And then what?"

"I put her to sleep in my bed. Oh, and purple bruises on her breasts and arm. Horrible breath, poor little thing, she must have vomited beforehand."

"But wasn't she at the country home of some VIP?"

"Good grief, country home! When I asked her she gave me one of those delirious answers you already know, mixing me up with her boyfriend; she cried, laughed. And tomorrow morning at eight o'clock sharp I have a final exam, the strike is over, an exam in Social Legislation. I know it pretty well, but I should at least have taken a look at one or two points, and did I? The problems fell on me in clusters today. One can go smoothly along for ages and ages and then all of a sudden."

Lião ties another stack of books together and begins her caged-in pacing back and forth.

"I came back in Mama's car, a fabulous idea because I got my list of things almost finished, I did all sorts of errands, told friends good-bye—" she says and stops in front of me. "Everything's speeded up so much, Miguel has already left."

"Left?"

"He should be there by now. That means that I'll be going sooner than I expected, I want to get the earliest reservation possible, I've got everything ready, I'm tingling. All I needed was a suitcase and Mama gives me this one, I'll travel with a millionaire's bag, oh, Lena! Two more days and I disembark in Casablanca. Then Algiers."

"Lião, Lião, you're kidding! And what about our farewell party? We were going to have a farewell party!"

"There's no time. One day we'll throw a party because the time for celebration is coming, but now I've got to pack up and take off for the airport, oh, am I scared. I'm no bird," she mutters picking up the suitcase. She places it on the table. "When I came down from Salvador, the stewardess, a very refined girl as Mama would say, advised over the microphone that due to technical difficulties something-or-other was going to happen and therefore we should all put out our cigarettes and tighten our seat belts. I didn't understand what was going to happen but after the *due to technical difficulties* the airplane parted soul from body. I had the worst case of diarrhea the world has yet known."

Lorena makes a panicked face, laughs and sits down on the newspapers piled up on the floor. She sighs as she takes a peppermint lozenge from her pocket.

"So you're really going. I know you've been talking about it, the trip the trip, but I thought it was more vague, almost a joke. Ah, Lião," she sighs. Then, taking heart: "I'll go to see you off at the airport, naturally."

"Better not, Lorena, no good-byes," I say and look at her snow-white sandals, so white they could have come from the store this instant. "I'm going to leave with the greatest discre-

221

tion, even my coat is black, Mama gave me a fabulous coat, she says she went all over Europe in it, a *cache-misère*, she explained. Isn't that neat? Except that in my case it really will be hiding a misery much bigger than all the philosophic mothers dream of, oh, Lena. If I don't go crazy first, I'll send you letters from over there, postcards, diaries."

"I don't think you'll write. Or come back either."

"No, don't talk like Mama, shit, if you'd heard her. In spite of her suffering and whatnot she wanted to know if I had *anyone*. I spoke of a man and that magic word resolved everything, thank goodness, I wouldn't pollute you after all. She asked if you were still a virgin. 'Unfortunately,' I almost said. She was happy to learn this but unhappy at the same time, it's more complicated than it seems, why is it that to this day, you being the marvel that you are, nobody . . ."

Now Lorena giggles, covering her mouth and I laugh with her, the same conspiratorial laugh. Two infidels enjoying their unfaithfulness.

"Tell me some more. Did she mention Ana Clara?"

"Naturally. She believes in bad company, she doubts everyone, even the nuns could exercise their influence, see. Then, turning the page: The man you've been hanging around with, *by chance* isn't he married? *By chance* I answered that I didn't know and she was most alarmed, how could I not know? More tears etcetera, and after tea and presents I said good-bye with the greatest gratitude. End of story."

"Federico García Lorca," Lorena murmurs looking at the black-and-white poster thumbtacked to the door of my wardrobe. She crushes the peppermint between her teeth, breathing through her mouth. "How marvelous-looking he was."

"It's yours. You're going to inherit books, too, I'm leaving them all behind, I'll only take three or four. Say, is your alarm clock working? I loaned mine to somebody who didn't bring it back and I have to get up at the crack of dawn," I say approaching the bookshelf. "But tell me, why didn't you go to visit Mama? I did the best I could to hold things together, I was very refined, but the dear little girl was very much missed."

Lorena bent over to examine the mounds of books that spilled over the shelves onto the rug, forming a sinuous trail to the bed. She peered under the bed and pulled out a green knit blouse and two more large stray books.

222

"I could say that Annie ruined my plans but that's not true, I had the whole evening free to go and didn't because I was waiting for a phone call from M.N. I left a decisive note for him at the hospital."

"Did he phone?"

"No. Only Mama, she talked with me for five hours right after you left. She wants me to move in this week, can you imagine?"

"And are you going to?"

Prudently Lorena sniffed the blouse, spreading it out on the floor. She rolled it up with the socks that were among the newspapers.

"I have to, Lião. The psychiatrist, Mieux, and of course the drama of getting old. It's sinister, this drama, all of a sudden she seems a hundred. She needs me."

"Fine. But get out as soon as you can, see. Say you're in need of your shell, a vacation in your shell, and take off. Is she likely to marry again?"

"It depends, dear. I know exactly how it'll be, it was the same way with my grandmother. Granny would get dolled up and so on, but every time something really unpleasant would happen, she would assume her old age until the displeasure passed and she would gradually resolve to get in shape again. This happened several times, she'd fall and get up again, fall and get up again. During one of these falls . . ." Lorena sighed. "Oh, now I remember, there was a nursery rhyme my nanny used to sing, listen, listen:"

She straightened herself, cleared her throat and, after taking the lozenge out of her mouth, sang in her weak, polite voice.

> "Theresa fell upon the floor,
> There came three gentlemen
> All gallantly with hat in hand
> To help her up again."

I squat down and sing with her in the most serious tone I can manage:

> "The first her noble father was,
> The second was her brother,
> But to the third she gave her heart,
> For she would have no other."

223

We laugh softly, hunched together.

"My aunts thought that rhyme was a sacrilege, on account of the third gentleman," I say and have a happy surprise, my cap! I thought I'd lost it. I yank it down over my ears. "But look, about Mama. I'd love it if tomorrow she'd bathe herself in those perfumes and go running out—"

"On the tips of her toes!"

"That's it, on the tips of her toes."

Lorena goes back to sucking her peppermint. She starts piling up the papers.

"I've seen Mama go to pieces and recuperate three times, poor little thing. The first, when Romulo, my brother, died. The second, when Daddy was hospitalized, she suffered more on the day he was hospitalized than on the day he actually died. The third time was when she had to sell the ranch. She recovered all three times, of course. This is the fourth, dear."

"Well, then she'll recover again," I decide as I kneel in front of Lena. I shake her by the shoulders, she seems to have become a child again, oh, if she goes back to live with her mother she'll be even more of a child. "You've got to live your life in your own way and not the way other people decide, oh Lena, Lena, I can't explain it, but that story of Time devouring his children, wasn't it the god Cronus? He would give birth to them himself and then devour them all. But the truth is, it's not Time that swallows people but a mother like yours. A little like mine, too. Pay attention: Get out and she'll dedicate herself to another cause, to charity, God, who knows, maybe she'll even adopt a child. My mother adopted one, she's radiant back home with a little girl whom she kisses and punishes as much as she wants. But at any rate, yesterday I took some measures, I can embark in peace."

"Measures? What measures, Lião?"

She's extremely excited, she must be thinking about M.N. I grab her as though I were taking hold of an insect, by the ears.

"Oh, forget that guy, forget him! All you two ever do is exchange little notes, letters, as if one lived on Venus and the other on Mars, ridiculous. It's fright, he's quaking with fright. This very minute I'm trembling just to think about getting into an airplane, but it's healthy to be afraid of airplanes, we're land animals, perfectly all right. But fear of *loving*?"

"He can't stand the idea of other people suffering, dear. His wife, gobs of kids. The problem of remorse."

224

"But what remorse?"

Softly Lorena rolls onto her side, her head pillowed on the clothes she has collected.

"In one of his letters—" she begins. She implores patience as a I lift my arms: "Wait, dear, let me tell you, in one of his letters he described how when he was a boy he found a periwinkle on the beach one day, one of those mother-of-pearl kind, the underside rolling up in spirals and ending in a ruffled crown, you know how they are? He took a piece of wire and poked the snail out through the bottom, it came out in pieces. Then he washed the shell, poured alcohol, ammonia and perfume into the opening, and left it in the sun to dry. Two days later it began to smell frightful, as if the dead snail were still inside. He poked at it again, more water, more soap, nail-polish remover, gasoline, he tried everything. The next day the smell was still there. Through the acetone, gasoline, alcohol, there was still that horrible stench. He ended up throwing the periwinkle back into the sea; he knew he'd never find another one like it, but he threw it back into the ocean."

Now Lorena has discovered some cigarette butts; she gathers them up and looks underneath the newspapers as though searching for something. An empty matchbox turns up. Continuing her housecleaning ritual, she sticks the butts into the box. I wait. And the metaphor of the periwinkle? Isn't it a metaphor?

"Then what, Lena? The periwinkle?"

"Well, the smell of the periwinkle is like the smell of memory. The rest of his life he would smell that odor, can you imagine? His wife's suffering, his children's. His own suffering too, wasn't it Tolstoy who said it? Man experiences only two kinds of suffering: physical pain and the pain of remorse."

"Perfect. If I understand it right, you're the periwinkle, which isn't much of a compliment, a very trashy metaphor. But if this periwinkle was such a rarity, with a crown and so on, he could have tried a little harder, couldn't he? If he weren't so selfish and comfort-loving. Much easier to throw the periwinkle into the ocean, by this time you're in the middle of the Atlantic. *Kaput.* So don't talk about this man any more, enough. You're going to love Guga, we talked a great deal, he knows all the facets of the drama and is disposed to save you. Super-divine."

"But where did you see Guga?"

225

"I stopped by the theater, he was experimenting with the guitar, he composed a fabulous song. He's enthusiastic about the idea, enthusiastic."

"He is?"

"Of course. If Mama presses too hard, he'll even get married in a frock coat, he'll go through anything. As able as you are, in six months' time he'll be taking two baths a day."

"Lião, are you crazy? You mean you gave him encouragement?"

"Obviously. At times he smokes a little pot, but with a more or less balanced girl like you he won't even take aspirin any more."

"More or less? Did you say *more or less* balanced, Lião?" repeats Lorena rolling over the newspapers.

Slowly Lia took the clothes out of the open suitcase on the table. She smiled. They smelled just like Lorena's closets. Very refined, very special, she thought unfolding a gray cashmere pullover, oh, wouldn't that just fit Miguel? She rubbed it against her face, laughing. A little more contact with the *gens lorenensis* and she'd be branded on ears, nose, and throat. She turned to look at Lorena who had become still, dreaming among the newspapers. Had he really existed? This Romulo.

A jet engine's roar pierced the night and died away. The meowing of nearby cats grew fainter until it blended with the howling of a dog. Someone threw a rock at it and the dog ran away whining. The cats remained.

"For the next twenty years I'll be elegant in the wintertime," said Lia trying on the red cashmere. She hugged herself. "I feel like a kitten, oh Mama, my very best wishes, may you rise up and sally forth again!"

"Amen. Oh, I almost forgot," said Lorena rolling up two pairs of jeans that she found under a chair. "Sister Bula was very happy to tell me that the new boarder is about to arrive, the medical student. Apparently she's something of a genius. She comes from Pará, how about that?"

"Pará?"

"Santarém. I already told them she could have my shell," she sighed, a light shadow passing across her face. She shook herself: "My maid can wash these tomorrow, you have to travel with everything in order."

"But those jeans are clean, Lena."

226

"No, dear, they're not. Leave it to me, she launders divinely."

"Look at the *cache-misère*! Isn't it sumptuous?" asked Lia putting on the coat which was in the bottom of the bag. "And the scent, Lorena. The scent of riches."

"Softer, Lião, they'll wake up. We're shouting."

"Let them wake up! I'm too excited, I can't talk any softer," she retorted, coming nearer Lorena. "I visited Mother Alix today. She's quite a strange woman."

"Strange, how?"

"Quite strange," repeated Lia looking at the garden. She brought her hand to her mouth and ran her tongue over her fingernails. "She reminds me of the ocean at Amaralina Beach back home in Bahia. I know that ocean better than my own hand, the color of the water at any given time of day, all the fish, the shells, the rocks, no surprises, see. But one afternoon while I was diving, a plant rolled itself around my foot. I brought it back to the beach. It was sort of blue, I'd never seen one like it, with smooth little leaves like tiny blue fish and meat-colored roots, so there must be other things like this plant under the water? I began to view the ocean with greater respect."

"What did you talk about?"

"Assorted biscuits. At times she pretends to be innocent, but she's as much aware of everything as we are. Or more so, the woman is really something. The main topic was Ana Clara."

"Oh Lord. I have to go immediately, I actually forgot about her. And my exam tomorrow morning at eight. But what's the matter, Lião? Why are you staring at me like that?"

The family photograph albums are in the trunk in the garage, Ana said she saw the oldest one with the velvet cover. On top of the trunk, covering it, are old chairs, rolls of carpet, boxes, frames. The octopi guard the mystery of the sunken ship.

"There's no more time, see."

"For what?"

"Research," I say and watch Lorena jump out the window with the elasticity of a ballerina. She grasps the bundle of jeans and balances it on her head, glancing toward the window of her room.

"What are we going to do, Lião! About her. If only this famous fiancé would show up."

"I bet this famous fiancé doesn't exist."

"No?" she fixes terrified eyes on me. I turn my own away.

227

"Who knows. She's so confused. Can I borrow Mama's car tomorrow early? I'm going to take my suitcase to a friend's house near the airport. And do one or two other things."

"Of course dear. Mama must have taken kilos of tranquilizers, she won't wake up until late."

I watch her cross the garden, carefully choosing where she will step like a cat wearing gloves. She pauses in the middle of the driveway and listens, then proceeds. Only a silhouette cut out of the fog, a fog as white as her sandals has gathered. I lean over the windowsill. Just a few more hours. I should tell Lorena that I won't even be here long enough for those clothes she's washing to dry. I remember the broken hourglass, once I went into Dad's office to get a red pencil and bumped into a glassful of time. I panicked, seeing time arrested on the floor, two handfuls of sand and .the broken glass. Past and future. And me? What became of me now that the *was* and the *will be* had been smashed to pieces? Only the narrow funnel of the hourglass had survived the fall, and in it was a grain of sand in transit, it hadn't yet committed itself to either side. Free. *I am*, I say and feel like running to Lorena and advising her that if we keep on woolgathering at the present rate, we can participate in the next philosophical convention wearing little silver owls on our shirt collars, oh! I take a deep breath and look outside. In the lighted window Lorena is making frenetic signals to me, she's beckoning me with her hands, her head. When she sees me start toward her she disappears. I trip over two cats who flee in the direction of the wall, trample the daisies, and get halfway up the steps. I'm out of breath. My legs buckle as she bends down, leaning out of the open window. Our faces are so close that I don't even need to go up another step to hear her.

"She's dead."

I extend my hand wanting to grasp her voice through the fog.

"What, Lorena. What are you saying?"

The whisper is as icy as her minty breath.

"Ana Clara is dead."

228

Chapter 12

"Did she faint?" asked Lia. "Was that it?"

She waited for an answer, still immobile on the stairstep. "It's impossible, it can't be. Can't be can't be," she whispered to the garden below, which seemed to be a garden from another time, seen under the same circumstances, with a voice from beyond the window telling her in a whisper that someone was dead. The same fog. The same hollow feeling in her chest. But now the night smelled like peppermint lozenges. She turned to the window: empty.

"It's impossible," she said, entering the room.

Lorena was mounted on Ana Clara, massaging her heart. There was still the cool odor of mint. Or was it camphor?

"I gave her an alcohol rub but it didn't help. Let's try this, oh Lord."

Crossing her arms against her body, Lia tried to control the tremor which was causing her to shake from head to foot. She clenched her jaws in order to speak.

"You don't know what you're doing Lena, let's call a doctor. The emergency clinic, call the emergency clinic. Mother Alix has the number. You don't know how to do this!"

"But I do. I'm doing exactly what should be done," said Lorena, massaging with determination. She turned her face to Lia without interrupting her movements and lowered her voice as if afraid that Ana Clara would overhear. "She's dead. I'm only trying, can't you see? Oh Lord, Lord, Lord."

But didn't it seem like a joke? "It can't be," thought Lia letting her bewildered gaze wander about the room. The silver-buckled shoes placed side by side at the bathroom door. The patent-leather purse on the floor, next to the head of the bed. The red-and-green plaid blanket covering only Ana Clara's feet, a good thing because she didn't want to see her feet. She stared at Lorena astride her waist without the slightest weight, knees

229

dug into the mattress, features hardened in the effort of concentration. A cup with a little leftover tea in the bottom. The box of talcum powder with the yellow puff, Lorena hadn't had time to clean off the talc that had fallen on the table. She glanced again at the purse; it was half-open. Again the cup and her stare fell unresisting on the dead girl's face. "Dead? But she isn't dead!" Lia wanted to scream. She came closer. Ana Clara watched them through the green crack of her eyes. "You're kidding us, right, Annie?" The half-moon of cross-eyed glass was almost ready to open, the half-smile of the mouth was ready to say something, rehearsing something funny to say, why didn't she say it? As if suddenly she found it funnier not to say anything. Lia took her hand, opened it. In the palm, a little talc ingrained in the cracks. And the memory of warmth like an electric iron unplugged—how long ago?—preserving the heat in its metal plate.

"She was sleeping in the same position as when I left her," said Lorena jerkily, out of breath. "I was happy because I was afraid she might wake up and try to go out, she must have had a date with somebody. I put her dirty clothes in the hamper and laid my hand on her forehead, a strange chill. Then I called her, shook her, pounded her on the chest, that works sometimes . . . nothing. Nothing. I even did that test with the mirror, I got my little hand mirror from my purse. Oh, Lião."

"But was it before you went out? Do you think it was before?"

"How should I know? She came in shouting that she had a fencing foil stuck into her chest, it must have been a pain in her heart, I don't know, I don't know, Lião, for the love of God, dear, don't talk to me just now."

Lia drew nearer. She pressed Ana's static pulse with such intense searching that she only transferred to the dead girl the throbbing of her own inflamed fingers. Had she said the *dead girl?* She surveyed the half-naked body beneath the red bathrobe, how thin she was! Only now did she realize how much weight Ana Clara had lost, she paid so little attention to her. The purple bruises on her breasts and arms. What had been done to her? What had she done? Wait, wasn't she breathing? Didn't that gasp come from inside her?

"Go on, Lena, don't stop, I think she's breathing!"

Lorena's voice was the murmur of a mother who, already tired out, calls to her daughter hiding in some dark corner:

230

"Ana, Aninha, can you hear me? Ana, come on. Come back, Ana. Do as I say, I know you're there, I know you are. Come on, come back."

She steadied herself on her knees, squeezing Ana's flanks between her feet, pointed toes turned inward. Her hands pressed strongly against the other's kidneys; she galloped lightly without touching the saddle, only her hands moving up and down to the rhythm of artificial respiration.

"Thousands of times she came in drugged, see. Thousands of times! What was it she took this time?"

Beneath the blind curtain of hair, Lorena's voice rose and fell with the movement of her hands, at times reduced to a whisper:

"'*Come, then, Advocate: turn your merciful eyes upon us.*' Upon us!" she exclaimed throwing her hair back over her shoulders.

Are they crazy, these two? What kind of a sinister joke is this? thought Lia. She wanted to say something but couldn't; she was accompanying the variations of the massage. Lorena was creative, she was inventing movements like this caterpillar one, her wrists glued to Ana Clara's chest, only the fingers opening and closing like caterpillars burrowing in the ground, slowly outlining the obstinate heart.

"Lena, what if we called them? The nuns have experience!"

"They wouldn't do any better than I'm doing. Close the window."

Why bother with the window and not the record player playing that saxophone music over and over? She ripped her cap off and her hair sprang outward, electric. She pulled the cap on again, jerking it furiously down to her neck, and whirled around on her heels. The tremor was back; she hugged herself hard. Oh, the absurdity of that saxophone howling like a damned dog. Yet at the same time. She couldn't explain it, but wasn't it the music that somehow created an atmosphere of expectancy? As long as there was the saxophone and as long as Lorena continued to perch on top of her, battling. Silence would be the worst possible thing. She splashed some whiskey into a glass and gulped it down with her eyes shut, if she could only scream the way people do on the mountaintops. Or in the ocean, scream until her voice gave out, drain herself screaming and, beaten, go on screaming though only the voice of the opponent could be heard. "Shit!" she said between her teeth, almost crushing the glass in her hand.

231

"I should have done something to help her and what did I do? Made speeches. This bitch of a habit of making speeches."

"There was nothing anybody could have done, dear. Nothing."

And Lorena dominating the situation, tense but contained. Oh, Lena, go ahead, make her work like that miserable clock that would stop out of caprice even when it had been wound, if you had quick fingers you could hold the pendulum and swing it back and forth, once, twice, go on by yourself now, go on! She pounded the wall with her fist. Seen from behind, gasping over the body, Lorena appeared to be trying not to make her breathe but to take part in some desperate erotic game. Lia needed to bite her lip not to scream, "Enough!" She drew closer. A drop of sweat ran down Lorena's forehead and fell on Ana Clara's breast. It rode sweetly, softly, in an abandon which contrasted with the tension of the rider galloping firm and fast above.

"Nothing, Lena? Let me see."

With difficulty Lorena straightened her body and raised her hands so Lia could put her ear against the exposed breast. The cold smell of camphor, and beneath, the talc almost as intimate as sleep.

"I thought she was reacting. Hm, Ana Clara? You really aren't coming back?" moaned Lorena wringing her hands. "Mother Alix will be sad, or my Lord, give me inspiration, for the love of God, inspire me," she pleaded and jumped to the floor: "Let's check with the little mirror."

"Enough, it's no good," thought Lia covering her face with her hands, oh, the dreadful scene of the little mirror luminously reflecting the doll's mouth, she had learned this from her uncle, he had done the same thing with Grandma Diu, did Grandma go on a long journey? There was no answer, he couldn't look her in the eyes. She doubled up her sob-racked body.

"It's so senseless!"

"Be careful, Lião, you're going to wake up the nuns!"

"So what? Can't I cry out loud? She'd dead, Lena, she's dead! Why are you whispering? Why all this mystery?"

"I have an idea, I'll tell you later, but for now don't yell, for the love of God be calm."

"Calm? But aren't we going to call Mother Alix? Wake her up, wake everybody up immediately? Isn't that what we're going to do?"

232

"Wait, Lião, we're not going to wake up anybody yet, I already told you, I have an idea. Take it easy, okay?"

I rub my face against the cushion and before my eyes overflow again I see Lorena take up her missal, she has discarded the mirror and opened the black missal. During the massage she was pinkish, but now she's pallid again, hair thrust behind her ears, lips pursed. Ana Clara too is now in a formal position, the robe closed, her arms folded across her chest. Simply taking a rest after the bath and the talcum powder. Lorena must be satisfied, she managed to give her a complete bath before she died.

"You mean we're going to hang around waiting for the nuns? And the police? Is that what you want? Celebrate her death with whiskey and biscuits? We have to wake up Mother Alix, Lena! To explain that there wasn't any miracle, she was hoping for a miracle, isn't that sweet? A small miracle," I say and stuff the cushion into my mouth, oh! if I could only howl from pain and anger.

Just a minute, please, motions Lorena with that gesture I know so well. She is standing straight, praying from the missal, her lips moving almost silently, eyes transparent. Total beatitude. I wait, desperately eating cookies from the tin, I would explode right now if I didn't have something to chew on. In the midst of her imperturbable reading, she places her hand on Ana Clara's forehead.

"'Agnus Dei, qui tollis peccata mundi, dona ei requiem sempiternam.'"

I feel like hurling the cushion at her head, now she's playing Mass. I pour more whiskey down my gullet and almost come apart from coughing. My voice feels like a flame coming out my throat:

"Lorena, use some sense and stop these theatrics, see. You're going to call Mother Alix and I'm going to disappear, give me time to close my suitcase and get out, I can't be anywhere in the neighborhood when this death explodes and the police install themselves in this place! The papers will say she died of an overdose of barbiturates, you know what that means, don't you? I've got to get out of here," I say drying my eyes on my shirtsleeve, I don't want to cry but my eyes continue to flow like waterfalls. "You're perfect, the nuns are saints, but what about me? We'll leave the body in her room, we won't call anyone, or better yet, we'll carry the body . . ."

233

I can't go on. I pull off the cap and wipe my face: Ana Clara has become *the body*. Names, nicknames, they've all disappeared and only *the body* remains. I said *the body;* I accepted her death. And Lorena taking charge of things with hardly any affliction, if she cried at all it was only a few sparse tears I didn't see, Loreninha completely composed, lighting her incense and telling me to be calm.

"Of course you have to disappear, dear. Leave the rest to me."

"The rest?"

She blows on the lighted stick of incense. The smoke begins to escape in tenuous threads through the holes in the gold incense-burner.

"I have an idea, I tell you. Leave it to me."

"But dammit, I want to help you! It's best she be in her own room, we can take her now, afterwards you come back and lock yourself in here, tomorrow you go take your exam, you don't know anything. I left yesterday, you didn't see me, I want to Bahia, to Alto do Xingu, I wasn't in town when she died. End of story. Isn't that what we're going to do?"

I kick the cushion. No, it isn't. The idea is something else.

"Go on, Lião, don't worry about me, you can go."

"But first I want to know what you're planning, I'm not going to run out on you like a rat, I want to help! What marvelous idea is this you have?"

She has opened the closet and is choosing a dress. So the wonderful idea is to dress Ana? Of course not, she must have more things up her sleeve, she looks at me with the air of a priestess. A stained-glass tone of voice. I squeeze Ana Clara's hand. Is it colder or is it only my impression? Her hair uncurls as a I stroke it between my fingers. The smell of soap is very much alive. I pull her by the ear and her head slides obediently in the direction I pull, oh, Annie, what confusion, girl. The night before I leave.

"But what happened, Lena? Didn't you say she was better after the bath? That she talked, laughed? Wasn't she better?"

Over the chair Lorena spreads a long black dress with silver embroidery starting at the high collar and following the line of buttons down to the hem.

"She talked, laughed, cried, the same old delirium with some-

234

thing lucid in the middle, oh, how could I have known? She saw God, last time she saw Him too . . . She called for Mother Alix, for the boyfriend, she thought he'd been arrested, I calmed her down. She asked for whiskey, I promised I'd pour it into her tea. She wanted her purse, I gave her her purse. Then she asked to hold my hand, the last thing she asked for was my hand, she wanted to hold it."

She bends over to look for something in the drawer, her shoulders shaken by silent sobs, the same slow crying as Mama. Whiskey, she had wanted whiskey. And the purse. I whip my head around as if there on the floor it were a snake instead of a handbag. Half-open, exactly, half-open. While Lorena was making tea, changing the record. It was inside her purse, she thrust her hand down to the bottom and got it, see. My head throbs. Lorena dries her eyes with one of those handkerchiefs of hers, she gave me two, what ever became of them? She doesn't want me to see her crying, she has to give me a good example, she hides her tears by pretending she's still looking for things in the drawer but she already separated the smoke-colored pantyhose and the lace lingerie. I grab her by the shoulders from behind:

"Lena, I was horribly rude, forgive me. Will you forgive me? I lost my head, this trip, her dying, the best and the worst all at the same time. I feel like I'd taken a beating."

"I had an intuition that something like this was going to happen. And what's more—" she murmurs touching the dress. She's livid. "My brother Remo sent me this kaftan from Morocco. I swear I thought, Annie can wear this, I'll never use it because it isn't right for me, imagine. It'll be Annie who wears it. For always, I intuited. I actually trembled when I shut the closet door, it was as if I were closing her coffin."

There, the illuminations are starting. I turn my eyes away from Lorena.

"Rotten chic, eh, Annie? Morocco."

"It matches her shoes, poor thing. It's a shame I don't have any silver earrings."

Did she say *earrings?* Earrings. She's going to pretend that Ana is alive. Better yet, we should dress her in a *chache-mort* of the same genre as the *cache-misère* Mama gave me, it's more important to hide death than to dress it up. But young people don't need to close their coffin lids.

235

"I don't have any cigarettes," I say, dumping out the contents of the purse that waits for me, open.

Quickly I spread out the thousands of little items and search. What are these envelopes? Aspirin. There's everything in Ana's purse, from wads of dirty cotton to a spool of black thread with a needle stuck in it. There's even a man's watch. And a small silver cup with a name engraved on it: *Maximiliano*. That's the lover. Isn't it strange he doesn't know yet? At this very minute he must be waiting for her in some bar, some nightclub. Or at the apartment where they usually met. I look at the watch: It stopped at midnight. Or at noon, there's no more time, no more death, he's just wondering why she's late, but then she's often late. I open the zipper of the little plastic makeup kit stuffed with lipsticks, various colored pencils, powder puffs, brushes. A little bottle of green eyeliner pops up like the pit of a peach. Nothing, nothing else. The handbag has returned to its state of innocence, futile, merely futile. Her student card is out-of-date, from the time she did her entrance exam. A little photo of her with long hair, denser eyebrows. The signature in a defiant hand: *Ana Clara Conceição*. Between the student card and its plastic cover, a photograph of a laughing boy, blond and radiant in a black sweater. Max, the Max of the silver cup, etc. I tear up the picture into little pieces and advise Lorena:

"Before the police come, get that little address book, that black one, remember? And rip up pictures of any gentlemen you find. I thought I wanted to see that SOB behind bars but now I don't know."

"I won't leave any clues, dear. I spent my childhood reading detective novels, I know what I'm doing," she says as she fastens the silver buttons of the dress. "What are you looking for, Lião?"

"Nothing," I say grabbing a cigarette. I stare at the comb which more than once I saw Lorena washing in her ammonia-smelling solutions. I cover it with a handkerchief when she approaches:

"There's a watch here, and this cup, put them away."

"I'll give the cup to Mother Alix, poor thing. The watch you keep, didn't you lose yours? Keep it, dear. It'll be very useful on the trip," she decides adjusting it on my arm. "It's a good-quality watch, the police would have gotten it, can you imagine? But isn't it really strange? Ana Clara doesn't have a single relative, nobody in this world, nobody! I was thinking about this a while ago, there's not a single person to notify, not even a friend, she mentioned some names but they were all very vague. Only the nuns. And us. I'm not even going to tell Max, it's more prudent for him not to show up, poor thing. What about the fiancé?"

"The fiancé," I repeat and don't have the strength to look at Lorena. I prefer to look at Ana Clara in her evening gown, is it a party? I cover the watch with my hand. Out of all this I am gaining a watch.

"Incredible. That she has nobody in the world."

"There are things more incredible still," I say and look closer as I see her open the plastic case that was in the purse.

"What are you going to do?"

But it isn't necessary to ask; her gestures are clear. Orderly. She takes out the pinkish base cream and begins to put makeup on Ana Clara's face. She uses only her first and middle fingers for the operation, or to be exact, only the tips of them, spreading the makeup in circular movements as she squeezes it out of the tube. Her hands move quickly, models of efficiency.

"Many a time I helped Annie when her hand shook too hard. And lately she was so unsteady, she'd turn up here completely out of kilter, sometimes she couldn't even put the brush back into the eyeliner bottle! Oh Lord. What madness."

She says *what madness* so superficially, the words don't correspond to the order that reigns in this room. In this death. The importance of appearances, Mama underlined. Nausea rises in a gush to my mouth. I go into the bathroom. If I ran my fingers down my throat . . . but Lorena already warned me, no noise. Music yes, the record is there turning around and around, a little more and the needle will wear through the plastic, but cries and vomiting, no. Why? Who knows, she's the one who's taking charge of the evening, she has her reasons. Ideas. She's been doctor and priest; now she's the perfect undertaker inspired after the American pattern. Tirelessly, unflinchingly, she prepares the customer as if she had spent her whole life doing nothing else. Her nickname in the Department is Fainting Magnolia.

"I'd like to get drunk, see. And I can't."

"Come here, Lião, come see how pretty she looks!"

I wash out my mouth and go to see how pretty she looks.

237

Kneeling at the head of the bed, Lorena is brushing green eye-shadow over Ana Clara's eyelids. From time to time she moves back a touch to see the effect. She looks satisfied, the brush in her left hand and the eyeshadow box in her right, she's left-handed. Luminous under the pink makeup, the face now seems more distant to me. Disinterested. Is it only my impression or did the half-moons of her eyes diminish? They're slightly cloudy, as if the mist of the night had invaded them. I don't remember ever having seen her so well dressed or so well made-up as she is right now. On the armchair are the silver chains.

"What about the necklaces?" I ask.

"The dress already has embroidery, it'll look better without them," she breathes, getting the hairbrush. "It's dry."

Her hair. Special attention to her hair. I go to get the bottle of perfume, I insist on bringing the perfume myself.

"This kind, Lena?" I ask and can't contain myself any longer. I take a deep breath before I speak: "You're exaggerating, see. You know you're exaggerating, don't you? We're here like two complete lunatics, pay attention, Lena, they're going to put her on a stretcher or something and from here she'll go straight to the autopsy, do you know what an autopsy is? The doctor comes and cuts everything up and then sews it together again. End of story. All this stuff you're doing will be undone on the marble slab. It's meaningless, Lena, meaningless!"

"No, it isn't. Let go of me, dear, we're late."

"But she isn't going to any party!"

She takes the silver-buckled shoes from the floor and delicately slips them onto the dead girl's feet. The nylon stocking formed a wrinkle at the ankle. Smoothing it, she smiles through her tears:

"That's where you're wrong. No, dear, I'm not crazy, not at all. It's that idea of mine. While I was praying, remember? I asked God to give me an inspiration and He did. The car keys are in your pocket, aren't they? I saw them. Excellent. Wait a minute, let me put on my sandals."

In two large leaps, Lia went to the window. She threw it open and inhaled through her mouth, smoothing her hair down with her hands. She fumbled for her cap in her pocket, slowly pulling it down over her ears, and regarded the big house. Not a single star. Not a single cat. The fog was so dense that when she

238

stretched out her hand she almost expected to encounter resistance. She shut the window. Lorena had already put on her sandals and was folding up the red bathrobe. Lia touched her shoulder.

"Lena, pretty soon it will be morning, I have to get out before morning comes, right? But I don't want to leave you alone, tell me quick what this idea of yours is and I'll help you, but hurry, hurry because your watch says it's after three!"

"Yes, let's go immediately," she says entering the bathroom, the red robe tight against her chest.

She must be remembering her brother with his red shirt, oh, what a night! What a night! thought Lia closing her eyes. She heard Lorena open and close the dirty-clothes hamper.

"Just think, I had almost forgotten the *Agnus Dei* on her blouse, it was pinned on the inside, poor thing. Mother Alix gave it to her, let me pin it on, it will go with her. Please, dear, get the purse. Is the card inside? The student card?"

"Everything's here. She's so thin, I think I could carry her alone but it's confusing, better for you to get one arm and I'll take the other. Shall we go?" she said and stopped. Why had Lorena asked her if the car keys were in her pocket? She patted it.

"Let's go, Lena, this purse is in the way, you can take it later."

"But the purse has to go with her, dear."

"To bed?"

"But she's not going to bed," said Lorena. She faced her friend: "Ana Clara is not going to bed."

"No?"

"Of course not. She's not going to be found in her room, she didn't die here in her room, she died somewhere else."

"Where?"

"In a little park. Why do you think I went through all these preparations? She'll be found in a little park, I've passed by it thousands of times, there's a bench under a tree, it's the prettiest park that ever existed. She sat down on the park bench after the party, she went to a party and on the way back, sat down there. Or was left there, it doesn't matter. They'll find her, call the police, advise Mother Alix, the whole business. Now do you understand why the purse has to go with the student card in it? God made Mama send the car," murmured Lorena pinning the medallion on the underside of the collar of the dress. "Look how everything is fitting into place: the car, the fog. I've never seen a more providential fog, the night was absolutely clear, remember?"

Lia sat down on the floor, closing her perplexed mouth. She shook her head back and forth repeatedly and sniffed, hands over her face. Then, laughing:

"Lorena, you're joking, aren't you? Do you mean we're going to take Ana Clara out in the street, or better, leave her sitting in a charming little park and come back? Is that your marvelous idea, Lena? Is it? Is that why you asked me about the keys? About Mama's car? Huh?"

"Please, Lião, don't start getting sarcastic, think a little, Ana Clara *cannot* die of overdose in Our Lady of Fatima Rooming-house. She cannot. Do you know what that might mean for the nuns? For Mother Alix? She loved Mother Alix so much, she wouldn't want to involve her in a scandal like that! I'm doing everything as Annie would want it done, God inspired me, I prayed for inspiration and He sent it, after I got this idea I felt a certain peace. I can alter things, dear. Even if death has no remedy, at least I can remedy the circumstances."

"What you mean is the *appearances*."

"Lião dear, I understand perfectly that it's a big risk for you, I'm not asking you to help me, of course. But I'm going to do exactly what I planned, there's no point in discussing it further," she said and glanced at her watch again. "I have half an hour to go and come back, can you imagine? Just help me down the stairs and then I'll do the rest by myself. Give me the key. I'll leave it on your windowsill when I get back."

With decisive steps Lia went over to the dead girl. She secured the strap of the handbag over her wrist and rubbed her eyes and nose hard.

"I've got a goddamn allergy, when I get nervous this itching starts."

"I have a decongestant pill, do you want one?"

"No, what I want is to carry this girl. Let's go. Have we forgotten anything?"

Lorena ran to turn off the record player.

"The light stays on, let them think I spent the night studying with a classmate, they must have heard us moving about. Especially Sister Bula."

That's why the saxophone's been wailing all night long? She thinks of everything, thought Lia wiping her nose on her sleeve. She grinned, taking Ana Clara in her arms.

"Never mind," she said as Lorena went to her aid. "On the steps you help me."

Light, yes. I knew she'd be light, I knew it. I open the window so that its light brightens the stairway a little. We divide the weight; Lião goes in front holding her by the legs and I come behind, supporting the trunk of her body. It curves sweetly back like a hammock. I smell her perfume. Good to have given her that bath. Good that this fog gathered.

"Don't let her shoes fall," I say as Ana Clara's foot brushes against the grillwork.

I had calculated this too, that the stairway would be the most difficult part, it's very narrow and we can't even breathe loudly, Annie is light when transported over a level surface. But down these long cramped steps . . . I knew too that Lião would be clumsy, she's strong but she panics, almost falls, if I'm not careful we'll all three roll down to the bottom. She's puffing, and to compensate I breathe as silently as possible, oh Lord, help us now, help us because it's terribly hard. No, Ana, don't slide, dear, why are you resisting all of a sudden? Help us, don't throw yourself around that way, the park is beautiful, you're going to like sitting there on the bench, the tree has birds, isn't that nice? Later Mother Alix will talk to Max, who knows but what your death will help him. The miracle that didn't happen with you, right? Help me oh Lord, help me.

"Careful, Lião! Slower, dear. Shall we stop for a second?"

We stop. I support Annie's head on my knees and thrust my hands inside her sleeves to hold her arms better. I feel her underarms beneath my fingers; just the other day I loaned her my razor, it's still in her room. A brand-new blade. And I remember the afternoon (when was it?) when the three of us were in my room: I was shaving my legs, Annie was tweezing her eyebrows with my tweezers and Lião was cutting something out of a newspaper. When she raised her arm (she was wearing a sleeveless T-shirt) I got up and gave her the razor, for the love of God, Lião, shave those underarms! She obeyed, making her distinctions: "Underarms is when they're shaved, see. Armpits is when they aren't." Now here I am recalling a nonsensical thing like that. With the same desire to laugh as I laughed then.

241

"Let's go, Lena. Are you rested?"

"Yes, let's go. Let's go."

Why have I never before noticed how long this stairway is? It's enormous.

"Didn't somebody turn on a light?" asked Lião. "Isn't that a light?"

"It doesn't matter, they can't see us," I whisper, more into Ana Clara's ear than into Lião's. "We're almost at the bottom, just a little farther."

We almost run when we reach the driveway. A cat begins to meow furiously, excellent, let its meowing cover our steps that seem to grind up the gravel, another thing I'd never noticed, how indiscreet these stones are.

"The noise they make! Don't kick them that way, dear."

"But who's kicking? Close your mouth, Lena!"

I don't close it, I want to talk, talk without stopping now that we're almost to the gate, the first part is over, hallelujah! We look up and down. The street is deserted, at least as far as we can see; beyond is only a wall of fog. The Corcel is opaque, without contours. I hold Ana Clara's body up against the gate as Lião opens the car door, ah, God bless Mama and her generosity, blessed be the night and the houses with their sleeping eyes.

"Now you go," I say. "From here on I can manage by myself, the most complicated part is over."

She helps me arrange Ana Clara on the front seat. Then she gets in. She sits on the other side, puts her arm around Ana and slams the car door.

"I'll hold her, you drive," she says without looking at me. "Let's get going."

I dry my eyes and turn on the headlights.

"Oh, Lião."

She's smiling with her teeth gritted.

"You're demented but I'm not going to leave you alone in this. It'll be lots of fun if they catch us transporting a cadaver, oh, what fun," she said shaking her head, laughing out loud. "Transporting a cadaver in the middle of the night, me with my passport in hand. Isn't it original?"

I begin to giggle too when I look in the mirror and see her black cap stuck over her eyebrows. Leaning against the seatback, Ana Clara's head seems to recline so naturally (I can't see Lião's arm locking her body against the seat) that we look ex-

242

actly as I had planned, two friends driving home a third who drank too much and passed out.

"They're not going to catch us, dear."

"A cadaver whose cause of death is extremely suspect," she continues opening the window a crack. "Don't you study law? You must know we're slightly illegal, don't you? You think of everything, think of an answer to give the policeman."

I drive slowly, with my face almost plastered to the glass, oh Lord, the friendly-enemy fog is even thicker, I have the impression that I'm driving through a nebula, the headlights are so powerless. Don't let a car come now, not now! I plead and continue talking, Lião is in a good mood, we need to maintain our good humor.

"I'll say that Ana got home in terrible shape, we decided to take her to an emergency clinic and got lost in the fog, who wouldn't get lost on a night like this?"

"You're imaginative, Lena. A very privileged little head, yours. But there's a thing called autopsy, the lawyer will say she was dead longer than you affirmed. Or not?"

I had almost forgotten that word: autopsy. The end as sharp as a stiletto. The marble. The rigor of the professional hand cutting so professionally, still the scent of perfumed soap, still the talc. But in any case, she's so pretty, isn't she, Doctor? So well made-up, so clean. I know you execute your duty dispassionately but this time you're going to do your work with a different spirit, beauty still arouses the emotions.

"Do you think I'm crazy, Lião?"

"Crazy enough. But I am too, see. And this one here beside us. I dunno, don't worry. Is it far? This park, we've been driving for hours! Quick, Lena, step on the gas pedal, we're slow as turtles!"

I don't want to tell her that I can't go any faster than this because I can't see a thing.

"We're almost there, take it easy. You get out first, I'll push the body from the seat and you pull her and lift her out, hold your arm around her to keep her upright. Then we'll walk, me on one side and you on the other, got it?"

"Perfect. Then the guard from the park can come and help us, right?"

"There's no guard. Look, here it is. Oh Lord, we made it, we made it, see the tree? Let's talk very naturally as we get out."

243

I turn off the motor. The headlights. I kiss the feet of God, *Hallowed be thy name!*

"Look on your side first. Nobody?"

She opens the door.

"Nobody. Quick!"

I kneel on the car seat and push Ana Clara toward Lião's extended hands. The head rolls and bumps against my lip, cutting it. "Be careful, Annie!" I almost say. When I get out, Lião is holding her as if the two of them were about to dance, arm stretched forward trying to take Ana's hand. They connect, palm against palm. She bends the arm and brings it around her shoulder with such a graceful motion that for an instant I have the sensation that Crazy Annie, touched by our efforts, has resolved to collaborate by encircling Lião with her arm. Lião has the harder job; I realize her strength when from the other side I secure Ana's dangling arm around my neck almost without effort. The little park is as round as the top of the blue-gray tree; it seems more intimate, more secret, closed in by the fog. I want to remember a verse of García Lorca's and can't but I quote at random, we need to keep talking, talking in low voices like two delirious friends helping a third, the unsteadiest one is also the prettiest, where was the party?

"As intimate as a little park, the idea is that but I can't remember, a poem of Lorca's do you know it?"

"I don't remember anything, I think I've forgotten everything and I'll never remember it again, see, I'll never again remember anything, anything," Lião keeps repeating as she looks from side to side.

The tips of Ana Clara's shoes drag through the fog-white sand. Lião tries to lift her higher and can't; I guess at the grooves the shoe-tips leave in the sand and remind myself to erase the marks on the way back. I hear a heavy motor (a truck?) pass close by and move away.

"Look at the bench. We can rest there a little, right, Lião? Maybe I'll remember the poem, it's about a park just like this one . . ."

"Deserted, isn't it? What's that up ahead of us?"

"There? It's only a little pine tree. Deserted. But that poem, do you remember it?"

"Perfectly. I remember, I remember. Quick, Lena."

"Don't you want to sit down a minute?"

244

She sits down, pulling Annie, who almost falls off her lap. The stone of the park bench is icy. But her face is exactly like it. Once seated against the tree trunk, she falls sideways in the direction she prefers and stays balanced there, her cheek on the stone, her hands folded against her breast. I pillow her head on the handbag, taking care not to mark her chin with the clasp. I pull the dress over her ankles, straighten the shoe buckle which was twisted on the way, and dust off the shoes.

"Lena, come on! Let's go!"

I clasp her icy hands, thinking of opening them. But she prefers them closed.

"We love you very much. God take care of you."

Lião encircles me and drags me off.

"It's by Lorca, you're right, it's about a park. Did you say intimate?"

I can't talk, I'm crying and undoing the shoemarks with the soles of my sandals.

We are in the car. I hear Lião's teeth chattering. Or are they mine? I drive around the park but I can't see either the bench or the visitor, only the top of the tree through the mist.

"And the night began with stars. Such big ones . . ." I say.

I look for the flannel cloth and clean off the windshield. Ana Clara's perfume is still with us. Lião must have had the same thought; she has opened the window slightly.

"The baby, Lorena! The erotic baby!"

"What baby?"

"The one that was hanging from the mirror! I gave him an indoctrination and it stuck, your chauffeur took it off! Perfect, perfect. Things like this give me hope," she murmurs relaxing her body. "I think it's been a month since I slept. Oh Lena, Lena, it'll be all right, won't it it?"

I don't know if she's talking about Ana Clara or the trip. The trip, of course. Of course.

"It's going to be marvelous, dear. I have an intuition, it'll be wonderful."

And I feel a brutal stab of joy. A desire to laugh, talk to people, say nonsense, write nonsense. Oh Lord, the exam. It's time to go in, jump into the shower, drink a glass of milk (I'm in the mood for milk), erase the clues in Annie's room and run to the Department. I'll need to go out before they—Before.

"But isn't it really marvelous, Lião? When we're on God's side," I say and brake the car.

245

"But is God on *this* side?"

I kiss her lightly, dry the last few tears (I'm not going to cry any more) and put my handkerchief inside my purse.

"We have thousands of things to do, Lião, thousands!"

"Right. We could stay here talking until the end of time, come on, get out. Hurry, Lena."

We get out. We're shivering with cold. I hear the little bell tinkling on her chain but it has rung other times during this night. I look at the hems of her pant legs. And her hair escaping from under the cap, raveled in the wind. It's good-bye but we're not to say it's good-bye.

"Come on, Lena, go in, quick. You go in front. Don't stand there looking at me, it's almost getting light!"

"The cross!" I remember. "I'll put it on your windowsill, on the outside, don't forget to get it! You won't forget?"

"Fine, perfect, I won't forget, now get going!"

I open the gate. When I turn around, she's in the same place, laughing. She raises her arm, first closed in the revolutionary salute. I blow her my most diaphanous kisses on my fingertips. I ascend the stairway in three jumps (it shrank), get the cross from inside my jewelry box, come down again, go across the garden and leave it on her windowsill. Lião is already inside and I know she saw me but she pretended not to. When I close the door of my room I have to stop and breathe deeply. Deeply. I turn on the record player and choose a record at random, without looking. When I hear the one I've chosen I grin. I go straight to the bed, make a tight bundle of the bedclothes, open the clothes hamper and push the bundle inside. The lid resists, grumbles, pops back twice but the third time gives up and stays closed. The bathtub with the bathwater still in it. A tenuous spiral of soapsuds floats on the cold surface. I turn my face away, stick my hand in the water and pull out the plug. While I wait I regard the bath salts in their glass jar, I never saw gold nuggets but they must look just like that. I open the hot-water faucet and while I lean over the tub, the residue I knew was there is carried away. I open the closet and choose some clean sheets, green? The bath towel can be white. I turn on the shower and feel its warm steam in my mouth. The mist outside is already dissipating and here another one is gathering, ah, I mustn't forget to advise the girl from Santarém that if a striped kitten answering to the name of Astronaut appears. Kitten? But hasn't he grown up? In short, a striped cat. Advise me and you will be generously rewarded. And if a rather obscure voice should call me on the telephone, the voice of a man who prefers not to leave his name. I view my profile in the misted-over mirror.

LYGIA FAGUNDES TELLES was born in Sao Paulo, Brazil in 1923, and is one of the most respected authors in Brazilian literature. In 2005 she won the Camões Prize, the greatest literary award in the Portuguese speaking world, and she is one of only three female members of the Brazilian Academy of Letters.

MARGARET A. NEVES has translated work by Jorge Amado, Antonio Torres, Moacyr Scliar, and Edgard T. Ribeiro.

PETROS ABATZOGLOU, *What Does Mrs. Freeman Want?*
MICHAL AJVAZ, *The Golden Age.*
The Other City.
PIERRE ALBERT-BIROT, *Grabinoulor.*
YUZ ALESHKOVSKY, *Kangaroo.*
FELIPE ALFAU, *Chromos.*
Locos.
JOÃO ALMINO, *The Book of Emotions.*
IVAN ÂNGELO, *The Celebration.*
The Tower of Glass.
DAVID ANTIN, *Talking.*
ANTÓNIO LOBO ANTUNES, *Knowledge of Hell.*
The Splendor of Portugal.
ALAIN ARIAS-MISSON, *Theatre of Incest.*
IFTIKHAR ARIF AND WAQAS KHWAJA, EDS., *Modern Poetry of Pakistan.*
JOHN ASHBERY AND JAMES SCHUYLER, *A Nest of Ninnies.*
ROBERT ASHLEY, *Perfect Lives.*
GABRIELA AVIGUR-ROTEM, *Heatwave and Crazy Birds.*
HEIMRAD BÄCKER, *transcript.*
DJUNA BARNES, *Ladies Almanack.*
Ryder.
JOHN BARTH, *LETTERS.*
Sabbatical.
DONALD BARTHELME, *The King.*
Paradise.
SVETISLAV BASARA, *Chinese Letter.*
MIQUEL BAUÇÀ, *The Siege in the Room.*
RENÉ BELLETTO, *Dying.*
MAREK BIEŃCZYK, *Transparency.*
MARK BINELLI, *Sacco and Vanzetti Must Die!*
ANDREI BITOV, *Pushkin House.*
ANDREJ BLATNIK, *You Do Understand.*
LOUIS PAUL BOON, *Chapel Road.*
My Little War.
Summer in Termuren.
ROGER BOYLAN, *Killoyle.*
IGNÁCIO DE LOYOLA BRANDÃO, *Anonymous Celebrity.*
The Good-Bye Angel.
Teeth under the Sun.
Zero.
BONNIE BREMSER, *Troia: Mexican Memoirs.*
CHRISTINE BROOKE-ROSE, *Amalgamemnon.*
BRIGID BROPHY, *In Transit.*
MEREDITH BROSNAN, *Mr. Dynamite.*
GERALD L. BRUNS, *Modern Poetry and the Idea of Language.*
EVGENY BUNIMOVICH AND J. KATES, EDS., *Contemporary Russian Poetry: An Anthology.*
GABRIELLE BURTON, *Heartbreak Hotel.*
MICHEL BUTOR, *Degrees.*
Mobile.
Portrait of the Artist as a Young Ape.
G. CABRERA INFANTE, *Infante's Inferno.*
Three Trapped Tigers.
JULIETA CAMPOS, *The Fear of Losing Eurydice.*
ANNE CARSON, *Eros the Bittersweet.*
ORLY CASTEL-BLOOM, *Dolly City.*
CAMILO JOSÉ CELA, *Christ versus Arizona.*
The Family of Pascual Duarte.
The Hive.
LOUIS-FERDINAND CÉLINE, *Castle to Castle.*
Conversations with Professor Y.
London Bridge.

Normance.
North.
Rigadoon.
MARIE CHAIX, *The Laurels of Lake Constance.*
HUGO CHARTERIS, *The Tide Is Right.*
JEROME CHARYN, *The Tar Baby.*
ERIC CHEVILLARD, *Demolishing Nisard.*
LUIS CHITARRONI, *The No Variations.*
MARC CHOLODENKO, *Mordechai Schamz.*
JOSHUA COHEN, *Witz.*
EMILY HOLMES COLEMAN, *The Shutter of Snow.*
ROBERT COOVER, *A Night at the Movies.*
STANLEY CRAWFORD, *Log of the S.S. The Mrs Unguentine.*
Some Instructions to My Wife.
ROBERT CREELEY, *Collected Prose.*
RENÉ CREVEL, *Putting My Foot in It.*
RALPH CUSACK, *Cadenza.*
SUSAN DAITCH, *L.C.*
Storytown.
NICHOLAS DELBANCO, *The Count of Concord.*
Sherbrookes.
NIGEL DENNIS, *Cards of Identity.*
PETER DIMOCK, *A Short Rhetoric for Leaving the Family.*
ARIEL DORFMAN, *Konfidenz.*
COLEMAN DOWELL, *The Houses of Children.*
Island People.
Too Much Flesh and Jabez.
ARKADII DRAGOMOSHCHENKO, *Dust.*
RIKKI DUCORNET, *The Complete Butcher's Tales.*
The Fountains of Neptune.
The Jade Cabinet.
The One Marvelous Thing.
Phosphor in Dreamland.
The Stain.
The Word "Desire."
WILLIAM EASTLAKE, *The Bamboo Bed.*
Castle Keep.
Lyric of the Circle Heart.
JEAN ECHENOZ, *Chopin's Move.*
STANLEY ELKIN, *A Bad Man.*
Boswell: A Modern Comedy.
Criers and Kibitzers, Kibitzers and Criers.
The Dick Gibson Show.
The Franchiser.
George Mills.
The Living End.
The MacGuffin.
The Magic Kingdom.
Mrs. Ted Bliss.
The Rabbi of Lud.
Van Gogh's Room at Arles.
FRANÇOIS EMMANUEL, *Invitation to a Voyage.*
ANNIE ERNAUX, *Cleaned Out.*
SALVADOR ESPRIU, *Ariadne in the Grotesque Labyrinth.*
LAUREN FAIRBANKS, *Muzzle Thyself.*
Sister Carrie.
LESLIE A. FIEDLER, *Love and Death in the American Novel.*
JUAN FILLOY, *Faction.*
Op Oloop.
ANDY FITCH, *Pop Poetics.*
GUSTAVE FLAUBERT, *Bouvard and Pécuchet.*
KASS FLEISHER, *Talking out of School.*

FORD MADOX FORD,
   The March of Literature.
JON FOSSE, *Aliss at the Fire.*
   Melancholy.
MAX FRISCH, *I'm Not Stiller.*
   Man in the Holocene.
CARLOS FUENTES, *Christopher Unborn.*
   Distant Relations.
   Terra Nostra.
   Vlad.
   Where the Air Is Clear.
TAKEHIKO FUKUNAGA, *Flowers of Grass.*
WILLIAM GADDIS, *J R.*
   The Recognitions.
JANICE GALLOWAY, *Foreign Parts.*
   The Trick Is to Keep Breathing.
WILLIAM H. GASS, *Cartesian Sonata*
   and Other Novellas.
   Finding a Form.
   A Temple of Texts.
   The Tunnel.
   Willie Masters' Lonesome Wife.
GÉRARD GAVARRY, *Hoppla! 1 2 3.*
   Making a Novel.
ETIENNE GILSON,
   The Arts of the Beautiful.
   Forms and Substances in the Arts.
C. S. GISCOMBE, *Giscome Road.*
   Here.
   Prairie Style.
DOUGLAS GLOVER, *Bad News of the Heart.*
   The Enamoured Knight.
WITOLD GOMBROWICZ,
   A Kind of Testament.
PAULO EMÍLIO SALES GOMES, *P's Three*
   Women.
KAREN ELIZABETH GORDON, *The Red Shoes.*
GEORGI GOSPODINOV, *Natural Novel.*
JUAN GOYTISOLO, *Count Julian.*
   Exiled from Almost Everywhere.
   Juan the Landless.
   Makbara.
   Marks of Identity.
PATRICK GRAINVILLE, *The Cave of Heaven.*
HENRY GREEN, *Back.*
   Blindness.
   Concluding.
   Doting.
   Nothing.
JACK GREEN, *Fire the Bastards!*
JIŘÍ GRUŠA, *The Questionnaire.*
GABRIEL GUDDING,
   Rhode Island Notebook.
MELA HARTWIG, *Am I a Redundant*
   Human Being?
JOHN HAWKES, *The Passion Artist.*
   Whistlejacket.
ELIZABETH HEIGHWAY, ED., *Contemporary*
   Georgian Fiction.
ALEKSANDAR HEMON, ED.,
   Best European Fiction.
AIDAN HIGGINS, *Balcony of Europe.*
   A Bestiary.
   Blind Man's Bluff
   Bornholm Night-Ferry.
   Darkling Plain: Texts for the Air.
   Flotsam and Jetsam.
   Langrishe, Go Down.
   Scenes from a Receding Past.
   Windy Arbours.
KEIZO HINO, *Isle of Dreams.*
KAZUSHI HOSAKA, *Plainsong.*

ALDOUS HUXLEY, *Antic Hay.*
   Crome Yellow.
   Point Counter Point.
   Those Barren Leaves.
   Time Must Have a Stop.
NAOYUKI II, *The Shadow of a Blue Cat.*
MIKHAIL IOSSEL AND JEFF PARKER, EDS.,
   Amerika: Russian Writers View the
   United States.
DRAGO JANČAR, *The Galley Slave.*
GERT JONKE, *The Distant Sound.*
   Geometric Regional Novel.
   Homage to Czerny.
   The System of Vienna.
JACQUES JOUET, *Mountain R.*
   Savage.
   Upstaged.
CHARLES JULIET, *Conversations with*
   Samuel Beckett and Bram van
   Velde.
MIEKO KANAI, *The Word Book.*
YORAM KANIUK, *Life on Sandpaper.*
HUGH KENNER, *The Counterfeiters.*
   Flaubert, Joyce and Beckett:
   The Stoic Comedians.
   Joyce's Voices.
DANILO KIŠ, *The Attic.*
   Garden, Ashes.
   The Lute and the Scars
   Psalm 44.
   A Tomb for Boris Davidovich.
ANITA KONKKA, *A Fool's Paradise.*
GEORGE KONRÁD, *The City Builder.*
TADEUSZ KONWICKI, *A Minor Apocalypse.*
   The Polish Complex.
MENIS KOUMANDAREAS, *Koula.*
ELAINE KRAF, *The Princess of 72nd Street.*
JIM KRUSOE, *Iceland.*
AYŞE KULIN, *Farewell: A Mansion in*
   Occupied Istanbul.
EWA KURYLUK, *Century 21.*
EMILIO LASCANO TEGUI, *On Elegance*
   While Sleeping.
ERIC LAURRENT, *Do Not Touch.*
HERVÉ LE TELLIER, *The Sextine Chapel.*
   A Thousand Pearls (for a Thousand
   Pennies)
VIOLETTE LEDUC, *La Bâtarde.*
EDOUARD LEVÉ, *Autoportrait.*
   Suicide.
MARIO LEVI, *Istanbul Was a Fairy Tale.*
SUZANNE JILL LEVINE, *The Subversive*
   Scribe: Translating Latin
   American Fiction.
DEBORAH LEVY, *Billy and Girl.*
   Pillow Talk in Europe and Other
   Places.
JOSÉ LEZAMA LIMA, *Paradiso.*
ROSA LIKSOM, *Dark Paradise.*
OSMAN LINS, *Avalovara.*
   The Queen of the Prisons of Greece.
ALF MAC LOCHLAINN,
   The Corpus in the Library.
   Out of Focus.
RON LOEWINSOHN, *Magnetic Field(s).*
MINA LOY, *Stories and Essays of Mina Loy.*
BRIAN LYNCH, *The Winner of Sorrow.*
D. KEITH MANO, *Take Five.*
MICHELINE AHARONIAN MARCOM,
   The Mirror in the Well.
BEN MARCUS,
   The Age of Wire and String.

SELECTED DALKEY ARCHIVE TITLES

The Princess Hoppy.
Some Thing Black.
LEON S. ROUDIEZ, *French Fiction Revisited.*
RAYMOND ROUSSEL, *Impressions of Africa.*
VEDRANA RUDAN, *Night.*
STIG SÆTERBAKKEN, *Siamese.*
LYDIE SALVAYRE, *The Company of Ghosts.*
Everyday Life.
The Lecture.
Portrait of the Writer as a
Domesticated Animal.
The Power of Flies.
LUIS RAFAEL SÁNCHEZ,
Macho Camacho's Beat.
SEVERO SARDUY, *Cobra & Maitreya.*
NATHALIE SARRAUTE,
Do You Hear Them?
Martereau.
The Planetarium.
ARNO SCHMIDT, *Collected Novellas.*
Collected Stories.
Nobodaddy's Children.
Two Novels.
ASAF SCHURR, *Motti.*
CHRISTINE SCHUTT, *Nightwork.*
GAIL SCOTT, *My Paris.*
DAMION SEARLS, *What We Were Doing*
and Where We Were Going.
JUNE AKERS SEESE,
Is This What Other Women Feel Too?
What Waiting Really Means.
BERNARD SHARE, *Inish.*
Transit.
AURELIE SHEEHAN, *Jack Kerouac Is Pregnant.*
VIKTOR SHKLOVSKY, *Bowstring.*
Knight's Move.
A Sentimental Journey:
Memoirs 1917–1922.
Energy of Delusion: A Book on Plot.
Literature and Cinematography.
Theory of Prose.
Third Factory.
Zoo, or Letters Not about Love.
CLAUDE SIMON, *The Invitation.*
PIERRE SINIAC, *The Collaborators.*
KJERSTI A. SKOMSVOLD, *The Faster I Walk,*
the Smaller I Am.
JOSEF ŠKVORECKÝ, *The Engineer of*
Human Souls.
GILBERT SORRENTINO,
Aberration of Starlight.
Blue Pastoral.
Crystal Vision.
Imaginative Qualities of Actual
Things.
Mulligan Stew.
Pack of Lies.
Red the Fiend.
The Sky Changes.
Something Said.
Splendide-Hôtel.
Steelwork.
Under the Shadow.
W. M. SPACKMAN, *The Complete Fiction.*
ANDRZEJ STASIUK, *Dukla.*
Fado.
GERTRUDE STEIN, *Lucy Church Amiably.*
The Making of Americans.
A Novel of Thank You.
LARS SVENDSEN, *A Philosophy of Evil.*
PIOTR SZEWC, *Annihilation.*
GONÇALO M. TAVARES, *Jerusalem.*

Joseph Walser's Machine.
Learning to Pray in the Age of
Technique.
LUCIAN DAN TEODOROVICI,
Our Circus Presents . . .
NIKANOR TERATOLOGEN, *Assisted Living.*
STEFAN THEMERSON, *Hobson's Island.*
The Mystery of the Sardine.
Tom Harris.
TAEKO TOMIOKA, *Building Waves.*
JOHN TOOMEY, *Sleepwalker.*
JEAN-PHILIPPE TOUSSAINT, *The Bathroom.*
Camera.
Monsieur.
Reticence.
Running Away.
Self-Portrait Abroad.
Television.
The Truth about Marie.
DUMITRU TSEPENEAG, *Hotel Europa.*
The Necessary Marriage.
Pigeon Post.
Vain Art of the Fugue.
ESTHER TUSQUETS, *Stranded.*
DUBRAVKA UGRESIC, *Lend Me Your Character.*
Thank You for Not Reading.
TOR ULVEN, *Replacement.*
MATI UNT, *Brecht at Night.*
Diary of a Blood Donor.
Things in the Night.
ÁLVARO URIBE AND OLIVIA SEARS, EDS.,
Best of Contemporary Mexican Fiction.
ELOY URROZ, *Friction.*
The Obstacles.
LUISA VALENZUELA, *Dark Desires and*
the Others.
He Who Searches.
MARJA-LIISA VARTIO, *The Parson's Widow.*
PAUL VERHAEGHEN, *Omega Minor.*
AGLAJA VETERANYI, *Why the Child Is*
Cooking in the Polenta.
BORIS VIAN, *Heartsnatcher.*
LLORENÇ VILLALONGA, *The Dolls' Room.*
TOOMAS VINT, *An Unending Landscape.*
ORNELA VORPSI, *The Country Where No*
One Ever Dies.
AUSTRYN WAINHOUSE, *Hedyphagetica.*
PAUL WEST, *Words for a Deaf Daughter*
& Gala.
CURTIS WHITE, *America's Magic Mountain.*
The Idea of Home.
Memories of My Father Watching TV.
Monstrous Possibility: An Invitation
to Literary Politics.
Requiem.
DIANE WILLIAMS, *Excitability:*
Selected Stories.
Romancer Erector.
DOUGLAS WOOLF, *Wall to Wall.*
Ya! & John-Juan.
JAY WRIGHT, *Polynomials and Pollen.*
The Presentable Art of Reading
Absence.
PHILIP WYLIE, *Generation of Vipers.*
MARGUERITE YOUNG, *Angel in the Forest.*
Miss MacIntosh, My Darling.
REYOUNG, *Unbabbling.*
VLADO ŽABOT, *The Succubus.*
ZORAN ŽIVKOVIĆ, *Hidden Camera.*
LOUIS ZUKOFSKY, *Collected Fiction.*
VITOMIL ZUPAN, *Minuet for Guitar.*
SCOTT ZWIREN, *God Head.*